JULIANA STONE

Cover design by John Kicksee
Cover photography by Jon Zychowski
Cover model: Dylan Solon/Agency Galatea

Published by Sourcebooks Casablanca, an imprint of Sourcebooks, Inc.
P.O. Box 4410, Naperville, Illinois 60567-4410
(630) 961-3900
Fax: (630) 961-2168
www.sourcebooks.com

Printed and bound in Canada.
WC 10 9 8 7 6 5 4 3 2 1

This book is dedicated with love to my mom, Miss Millie. Everything starts with you.

Chapter 1

Cain Black hadn't been home in ten years.

At the age of twenty he'd packed his guitar—a beat-up Gibson Les Paul—said his good-byes, and left. Always a rebel, he'd had no trouble disappointing half the town, and as for the other half? Hell, they'd expected it of him.

Cain Black—the star quarterback who'd had the arrogance to turn his nose up at a full ride to Michigan State University. The nerve, some said, after everything the town had done to support him and his mother. He'd left for Los Angeles one hot summer night in July and hadn't looked back until now, and—truthfully—he'd rather be anyplace other than Crystal Lake.

He ran fingers through the thick waves atop his head and cracked his neck in an effort to relieve the tension that stretched across his shoulders. Damn, but his muscles were tight, his legs stiff. He placed a booted foot on the top step of the Edwardses' porch and paused. He'd been traveling for hours and would just about kill for a bottle of Jack Daniel's, except he was fairly certain it would knock him on his ass. He was dead tired and knew he'd either crash hard or catch his second wind.

He smoothed his hair, trying to tame the waves a bit. It wasn't as long as it used to be, barely touched his shoulders these days. With the earrings and the nose ring long gone, he was almost respectable.

Or, at the very least, as close to some kind of respectability as he was ever going to get.

He glanced at his forearm. The edge of an elaborate tattoo peeked out from under the hem of his sleeve. It was the only thing left over from his hell-raising days, and that was way before *LA Ink* and Kat Von D had brought tattoos into the mainstream.

Now everyone and their mother had one.

Cain blew out hot air, tugged his shirtsleeve down a bit more, and glanced around. It was surreal, standing here after all this time. How many nights had he and the boys hung out, shooting the shit and dreaming of a future that would rock their reality?

He shook his head, a bittersweet smile tugging at the corner of his mouth. Too many nights to count.

His thoughts darkened, and he clenched his teeth tightly as the reason for his return hit him in the gut. Not everyone's future had turned out as planned. The unimaginable had happened, and it was a sobering reality check.

One that had brought him full circle. Back to Crystal Lake.

Back to this porch.

He glanced up at a pristine blue sky and a plane caught his attention—its drone a melancholy sound that echoed into the stillness. A warm breeze caressed his cheek, bringing with it the smell of summer—of freshly mowed lawn, flowering bushes, and warm lake water. He closed his eyes and the scent took him back. Memories rushed through him: Fourth of July celebrations that lasted the week. The annual boating regatta that filled the lake with hundreds of revelers. Christmas out at Murphy's sugar shack. Tailgate parties and football. Beach nights with the boys, a guitar, a couple of girls, and a case of beer.

He saw the kid he'd been—the teen who'd dreamed large and let nothing stand in his way. Hell, none of them had. The twins, Jake and Jesse, had realized their dream to serve their country, while Mackenzie had fought his way out from beneath his father's fists to make a life in the Big Apple.

Ten years gone and it seemed like yesterday. Like nothing had changed.

The Edwards family abode was a large, redbrick Georgian with a long rambling driveway lined with petunias in varying shades of violet. At the moment, every available space of blacktop was occupied. There were at least thirty cars parked in the driveway, and several had pulled onto the grass near the road.

He'd left his rental on the street, because if memory served, Mr. Edwards was pretty anal when it came to his lush green lawn.

Cain reached for the door, but something held him still. His fingers grazed the cool burnished-steel handle and he faltered. He hated hypocrisy, and at the moment it felt like his throat was clogged with its bitter taste. He was so far off the grid, he felt like he didn't belong anymore.

He took a step back instead. Christ, could he do this?

Less than twenty-four hours ago he'd been on stage in Glasgow. BlackRock—the band he fronted—had snagged the opening slot on the Grind's latest tour and had performed in venues all over Canada, the United States, and Europe. It had been the chance of a lifetime—one he'd been waiting years for—and the exposure had been more than a gift, it had been a godsend.

The tour had been a grueling, eye-opening experience with more than its fair share of drama, yet every drop of blood had been worth it. The record label was happy, and the buzz was incredible. BlackRock was a band on the rise, and after years of sacrifice, his dream was within reach.

It was a dream that had taken him from this town ten years ago, and sadly, it had taken a funeral to bring him back.

The door opened suddenly, and a small boy ran out, yanking it closed behind him. He skidded to a halt, barely missing Cain, his shiny shoes sliding across the well-worn wooden planks. He looked to be about six or seven and had a mess of russet curls, and large blue eyes that dominated his face. The child was dressed for church—black dress pants, white button-down shirt—and he clutched a bright piece of fabric in his hand that was a shade darker than emerald green. The boy's eyes widened as his gaze traveled the tall length of Cain.

"Who are you?" His young voice wasn't so much surly as defiant.

Cain cracked a smile. The kid had spunk. "I'm Cain."

"Oh." The boy's brow furled. "I don't know you."

"No, I suppose you don't."

The kid angled his head, peered around him, and frowned. "Why are you standing out here by yourself?"

Good question. "I just got in a few minutes ago." He nodded to the boy's hand. "What's that?"

The little guy's mouth tightened as he unclenched his fist. His face screwed up in disgust. "It's a tie. My mom made me wear it, but I hate 'em." He glanced at the long settee off to the side. "Thought I'd hide it so I didn't have to wear it the rest of the day."

Cain laughed out loud. "Good call. I'm not really a tie man myself."

"You won't tell her?" The kid grinned and ran to the settee, where he promptly stuffed the offending piece under the seat. He carefully placed the cushion in the exact way he'd found it and stepped back. "Do you think she'll know?"

"I'm pretty sure she won't."

Cain walked over to the boy and paused. They stood in front of a large bay window, and he heard voices—muffled of course, but he knew there was a good-sized crowd in the house.

"Did you know him?"

The child's question hit a nerve, and Cain clenched his jaw tight, fighting the emotion that beat at him. *Know him? He was like a brother.*

"What did you say your name was?" he asked the boy instead.

His reflection in the window didn't look promising. He'd been on a plane for hours, and then there'd been the long drive from Detroit. He hadn't showered since before the show in Glasgow. His jaw was shadowed, his clothes rumpled—the black shirt, faded jeans, and heavy boots were not exactly appropriate either.

He looked like shit and knew he'd hear it from his mother, but until now none of that had mattered. His only thought had been to get home in time for the funeral, which he'd failed to do. As it turned out, he'd been damn lucky to make the reception.

"My name's Michael." The boy's eyes were huge as he looked up at Cain. He shoved his small hands into the pockets of his pants and scuffed his shoes along the worn wooden floorboards. "Mom says he was a hero. I never met a hero before." He squared his shoulders. "*Did* you know him?"

Christ, but the kid looked earnest. His pale skin was dusted with light freckles, his round cheeks rosy.

"Because I didn't."

Cain looked inside but couldn't see shit. The reflection of the sun didn't allow it.

"Yeah, I did." A wistful smile crossed his face, and he glanced down at the kid. "Your mom's a smart lady. He was a bona fide hero." He nodded. "I was about your age the first time I met the Edwards twins."

The young boy smiled, but it faded as he glanced toward the door. "I should go. My mom is gonna wonder where I am."

They both turned when the front door opened and a slender woman stepped onto the porch. She wore a simple black skirt cut to just above her knee, a fitted blouse in a muted moss green, and low-heeled shoes. Her hair was held back in a ponytail—one that emphasized the delicate bone structure of her face—and was dark, a shade between crimson and brown, more like burnished amber shot through with bits of sun. Her skin was the color of cream, and when she turned toward them, Cain felt a jolt as their eyes connected.

Hers were blue—like liquid navy—feathered by long, dark lashes and delicately arched eyebrows. She was, without a doubt, one hell of a looker. A little on the thin side for his tastes, but Cain's interest was piqued.

Her eyes widened for the briefest of moments, and then she turned to the boy, eyes narrowed and lips pursed. "Michael John O'Rourke! What are you doing out here"—her voice lowered—"and *where* is your tie?"

She had a slight Southern drawl that rolled beneath her words. It was melodic and soft.

"It was tight and, uh, I took it off and I, um…" He tapped his foot nervously and shrugged. "Well, I'm not sure where I left it."

The boy shot a quick look his way, and it took some effort for Cain to keep a straight face.

The woman sighed. "Michael, this is a serious occasion." She walked over to them, ignored Cain, and bent forward to fix a stray curl that rested upon the boy's forehead before fastening the top button of his shirt.

Her scent was subtle, fresh with a hint of exotic. Cain liked it.

"I know, Mom. But, like, can't I be serious without a tie?"

A ghost of a smile tugged the corner of her mouth and Cain smiled. "He's got a point." Cain motioned toward his tieless shirt

She straightened, though her hand never left her son as her eyes traveled the length of him. Gone was the smile. The lady was all business. "And you are?"

Cain opened his mouth and then closed it. What to say? Obviously she wasn't a townie, because he'd sure as hell have remembered someone like her. For the moment he didn't feel like sharing his relationship with Jesse, didn't feel like owning up to his hell-raising days.

"A friend of the family," he answered instead.

She grabbed her son and pushed him toward the door. The boy opened it and a soft swell of voices spilled outside. He ran inside, but the woman paused. She looked at Cain as if he had two heads.

"Aren't you coming inside, then?"

Her abrupt tone kick-started him into action. Cain exhaled and followed in their footsteps.

The Edwards home boasted a grand foyer—the focal point, a massive centered staircase that led to the upper level. He took a second and glanced around.

The walls were no longer taupe and had been done over in pale, cool greens. The wood accents—the railing and trim—once oak, were now dark ebony, and the ceramic floors had been replaced with a funky hardwood. It was similar to what was in the house he'd shared with his ex-wife, but damned if he remembered what it was called.

Music wafted from the back of the house, and he assumed a good many people were gathered outside on the deck. It was the first week in June, so the weather was warm and the Edwardses' yard was renowned for its landscaping, pool, tennis courts, and prime lake frontage.

It was the sweetest spot on Crystal Lake and one not many could afford.

There were quite a few folks talking quietly. He felt their interest. It was in the understated whispers and covert glances directed his way. Cain ran his hand over the day-old stubble that graced his chin and winced. Shit, he should have at least shaved.

The woman and little boy disappeared among the crowd, and he took a step forward, suddenly unsure of himself. He was surrounded by faces he recognized, yet he felt like an outsider. Again he fought the sliver of doubt.

Maybe he should have stayed away. Sent a card or a flower arrangement.

"Cain, you came."

The whispered words melted his heart. Years fell away as he turned and gazed down into Marnie Edwards's face. She was older, of course, her face fuller, with time etched into the lines around her eyes and mouth. Her dark hair was elegant, hitting the curve of her jaw in a blunt cut. She wore a smart black suit, with a dash of red in the scarf draped loosely about her neck.

Marnie opened her arms, and he grasped her small frame close to his. She trembled against him. "I knew you would."

Grief welled inside him. Hard, like a fist turning in his chest. He couldn't speak; his throat felt like it was clogged with sawdust. So he just held her, took her warmth and strength into his body, and closed his eyes.

"Cain, thank you for coming. It means a lot."

Cain looked up, kept Marnie secure in his arms, and nodded to Steven Edwards. Pain shadowed the older man's eyes, and Cain swallowed hard. "Sir, I tried to get here for the funeral, but..."

Steven Edwards nodded. "I know, son."

"Jesse would be so happy to know you're all together." Marnie wiped her face and slipped from his embrace. "Mackenzie and Jacob are out back somewhere." She crossed to her husband's side. "You should go see them."

"Is my mother..." His voice trailed off as he struggled to gain control over the emotions inside. "I tried to get hold of her earlier, but she didn't pick up."

Marnie smiled warmly. "She's here somewhere, helping with the food, I think." She glanced up at her husband. "It's good now. We're all home." Marnie motioned toward the back of the house. "Go, the boys are waiting."

Cain nodded and slipped through the small groups of people gathered in the hall. Muted voices and snatches of conversations followed him as he entered the kitchen and headed toward the patio doors. He recognized a lot of the faces, smiled, said hello, but didn't stop to talk.

The deck was crowded, and conversation halted as he stepped outside. Hot sunlight filtered through the vine-heavy pergola overhead, and the scent of lilac filled the air. The bushes alongside the pool house had grown a lot. They were in fact twice the size he remembered and were full of fragrant white and soft purple-colored blooms.

His gaze wandered past the deck. There was no one here he wanted to talk to. Bradley Hayes, a classmate from back in the day, nodded and headed in his direction. They'd never been friends, and he sure as hell wasn't in the mood to pretend.

Cain turned abruptly and took the stairs two at a time to the patio below.

He cleared the bottom step, grabbed a cold beer from the nearest waiter, and took a long, refreshing draw. He glanced out over the backyard as his hand absently wiped the corner of his mouth. The tight feeling in his gut pressed harder, and his skin was clammy.

Cain was used to being the focus of attention but this was different. These weren't fans. They were old neighbors, teachers, acquaintances, and some he'd considered friends a long time ago.

Were they judging him? Was he the prodigal black sheep, returned?

He squared his shoulders. None of them were the reason he'd come back.

Two men caught his eye, and he moved methodically

through the crowd of mourners, nodding to those who called greetings, yet his gaze never left the duo several feet away from everyone.

The man on the left was dressed in a suit, his tall frame draped in expensive Armani. Cain knew this. His closet was filled with the crap. His newly minted ex-wife, Natasha, had insisted he wear nothing but the Italian designer whenever he accompanied her to one of her damn premieres. She'd spent wads of cash dressing him up like one of her West Coast buddies. After she had left, he'd considered getting rid of the lot, but hell, it had cost a fortune and he didn't see the benefit in throwing money away.

The man on the right was decked out in full military dress.

Cain stopped a few feet away, and they both turned at the same time to face him.

Silence fell between the three, their eyes locked on each other as a world of pain united them.

Armani raised his beer, a tight smile settling on his face, though his eyes remained shadowed as he spoke. "You look like shit."

The soldier stepped forward.

"I'm sorry...I..." Cain struggled to form a coherent sentence but faltered. Two arms enveloped him in a bear hug that was crushing and welcoming and hard, in the way it was among men.

The pain he'd felt for days, ever since he got the news, grabbed him, twisting his insides until he nearly choked from the intensity. Mackenzie stepped back, gave them some room, and Cain fed off the strength and energy that was Jake Edwards.

After a few moments Jake let go, grabbed another cold beer from the bucket at his feet, and tossed it to Cain—who nearly dropped the one he already had. Mac scooped one for himself, and they wandered down to the beach.

There were no words spoken. The easy silence of their youth enveloped them as if the passage of time meant nothing.

They'd buried one of their own today.

There was nothing else to say.

Chapter 2

DUSK FELL, BRINGING WITH IT THE SHARP DAMPNESS OF a Michigan June night. Cain was drunk. Hell, the three of them were a sorry-ass bunch. They'd sat on the beach for hours, drinking beer until there was none left. Then they'd moved on to the hard stuff, sharing a bottle of vodka as they talked crap, caught up, and reminisced about every detail of Jesse's life.

The men had kept in touch after they went their separate ways, but as was the way of it, time expanded and filled with other things. Phone calls and emails became less frequent, and Cain couldn't remember the last time he'd had an actual conversation with his friends.

Mac had moved to New York after graduating from Michigan State and was now an architect on the fast track to partner at a prestigious firm. The twins had joined the armed forces straight out of college and were never in the United States for long—military leave didn't allow it. When they had the good fortune to come home, they'd spent their time in Crystal Lake. Jesse of course had had a wife waiting for him, and Jake had never been far from either one of them.

Cain glanced at his friend and frowned. Jake was in a place of transition. The loss of his brother had hit him in a way that left scars beneath his skin. There was a darkness inside him that didn't belong. He'd always been the easy-going twin—the light to Jesse's intense, moody personality.

It was all wrong.

"So, Mr. Guitar God of the Year," Jake slurred.

"Yeah." Cain grinned. He couldn't help it. "Pretty damn cool." The latest issue of *Guitar World* had featured Cain and a host of up-and-comers, though he'd snagged the all-important cover and had been humbled when Springsteen sent him a note. Apparently the man liked his playing and songwriting skills.

"I want my copy autographed," Mac joked. "You should send one to your ex. Let her know what she's missing."

Cain's lip curled. "Natasha only cares about herself. Trust me, she's moved on."

Jake punched him in the arm. "Natasha fucking Simmons. How in the hell did a redneck from Michigan end up with a Hollywood hottie like that?"

"Don't ask." Cain was tight-lipped. His ex-wife was not someone he cared to discuss. He took a second to gain his balance and grimaced. "Boys, we need food."

"I second that. Liquid lunch is fine, but it only goes so far." Mac nodded toward the house. "Let's go."

There were a few lingering guests, his mother among them. Lauren Black was a tall, attractive woman who took great pride in her appearance. Her hair hung past her shoulders, a silken sheet of gold. Her figure, enviable by women half her age, was shown to perfection in the classic cut of the simple black dress she wore. At her ears were small pearls, and at her neck, the matching pendant.

She'd come a long way, his mother, and pride rolled through him as he studied her. She'd grown up with nothing and hailed from the wrong side of the tracks. But she was made of good stuff—her roots were humble and strong. They were the kind of roots that went deep, and she'd kept the both of them anchored. He might have been poor for most of his youth, but he'd never known it.

She was chatting with Raine Edwards—Jesse's young widow. The petite woman looked gaunt, her features pinched and her skin much too pale against the ebony hair that fell past her shoulders.

Cain glanced at Jake. The soldier's gaze was locked on to the widow with an intensity that was heartbreaking. Everything had changed, and yet so much remained the same. The hunger, the *want*, was hard for the soldier to hide, and Cain looked away, uncomfortable.

Marnie and Steven Edwards were in the family room, a large open space just off the kitchen. It boasted an entire wall of glass that brought the outdoors inside, and in the distance the stars reflected on the lake like diamonds on black velvet. They sat together on a leather sofa, an open book of photos displayed on the coffee table. A small group was gathered around them, their voices low in that polite, mournful way.

"Here."

Cain turned and accepted a plate of sandwiches from Mac. There was tuna, salmon, and, no surprise, the always-crowd-pleasing ham. It didn't last long. He hadn't eaten since the plane.

"Oh shit, here she comes."

Cain turned at Mac's harsh whisper. "Who?"

"Rebecca Stringer."

"Stringer?"

Mac guffawed drunkenly. "Seriously? You don't remember? 'Stringer-dinger, she'll ring your bell'?"

It came back quickly. Blond. Plastic. Head

cheerleader, homecoming diva, and queen of the backseat. They'd each dated her at one point or another—*dated* being a loose term.

He stifled a groan and glanced at Jake. He'd changed out of his military dress, but the plain white T-shirt and jeans did nothing to detract from the powerful energy that surrounded him. His short dark hair and even darker eyes only emphasized this. Afghanistan had changed the man in more ways than one.

The soldier was quiet, stuffing sandwiches into his mouth, his eyes still on his brother's widow.

"Well, well, well...the Bad Boys of Crystal Lake all together again." Rebecca's candy-red lips were glossy, as if they'd been coated in syrup. They were porn-star perfect and somehow out of place in northern Michigan.

"In case you hadn't noticed, we're missing one." Jake glared at Rebecca, his eyebrows knit into a frown, his mouth tight.

Rebecca's face flushed deep red, and for a moment she was speechless. "I'm sorry. Of course...I didn't mean..." Her voice trailed into silence as Jake shoved past them.

"Whatever," he muttered. "I need another drink."

Cain took a step, intending to go after Jake. The man was hurting.

Rebecca's hand on his chest stopped him. Her fingers grazed the fabric of his shirt a little longer than was necessary.

"Cain." The way she purred his name reminded him of his mother's old cat—all soft and fuzzy, with claws waiting in the wings. "Shame on you for not coming home sooner." Her shiny lips loosened into a pout.

She smiled so wide, Cain was afraid her makeup was going to crack. "Tell me," she said, and sidled up as close as she could. Cain glanced at Mac, but his buddy raised a bottle of water in a mock toast and moved away.

He was caught in the corner with Rebecca Stringer. Shit.

"You ever write a song about me?"

He nearly choked on the tuna in his mouth. "Uh—"

"I mean, that one they played on the radio a few months back." She paused and sang in a girlish voice, "'She had my heart, she stole my soul, I'll keep her close till I grow old.'" Her eyes glittered. "I think that could have been about me."

What the hell could he say to that?

She hummed it over again and grinned at him crazily. "We had some good times, right? Back in the day?"

Someone rescue me.

His pulse quickened when he spied the woman from the porch. She was tidying up the table in the kitchen, gathering empty plates and cutlery. From where he stood, Cain didn't see her little boy.

"Who's that?" he asked instead.

Rebecca glanced toward the table, her eyebrow arched. "The cleaning lady?" She lowered her voice, as if she were sharing a dirty secret. "Well, she moved to town about a year ago. Came from the South, Savannah or New Orleans." She shrugged. "I think her name is Sally, maybe? Dunno, she cleans my house too." Her eyes narrowed as she focused back on him. "Why?"

Cain's eyes hardened. He didn't like her tone or her attitude. Some things never changed. Money bought a lot of things, but class and humility sure as hell weren't on that list. "The woman scrubs your floors, and you have no idea what her name is?"

"She cleans my toilets too. *Should* I be on a first-name basis with her?" Gone was the sly smile.

Cain leaned in close. "You forget, Rebecca, there was a time when *my* mother cleaned your toilets and half the town's elite's, for that matter."

"But," she sputtered, "that's different. Lauren's one of us now, and technically they weren't my toilets, they were my mom's." Nervous laughter fell from her lips as she swept her tongue over what Cain now decided were collagen blunders.

The remainder of his sandwich was tossed into the garbage. He was tired as hell, and the beer and vodka hadn't helped. The day had been an emotional roller coaster, and he didn't have the time or patience for someone like Rebecca Stringer.

It wasn't as if he was looking to get into her pants. Hell, that boat had sailed, crashed, and burned.

"And what is it you do these days?" he asked.

"Do?" Rebecca looked surprised. "You mean, like a job?"

He nodded. What did someone like Rebecca Stringer do with her time?

"Well, I—I'm married." She shrugged. "I don't have to work."

"Figures." He glanced at her hands. The fingers were tipped scarlet, their perfection and length obviously fake. A large diamond sparkled on her finger. "Who'd you marry?"

Rebecca's eyes were now dark slits of anger, her pouty lips pursed so tight, she resembled a goddamn blowfish. She raised her chin and took a step back.

"Bradley Hayes. He's just been named junior partner in his father's law firm."

"Good luck with that." He'd spied Hayes chatting up a leggy brunette outside. The bastard was no different than his father. Cain's mother had stopped working for the family after the elder Hayes had been inappropriate one time too many.

He walked past her without another word. Rebecca was much like the bored, rich housewives who were a dime a dozen in LA—always looking over the horizon, loving no one but themselves and the size of their husband's wallet.

"Hey, need some help?"

The redhead jumped, her eyes wide as she glanced up at him. He'd startled her, and for one second she reminded him of a deer caught in the headlights of a car.

She regained her composure and looked away, her voice soft, the drawl he'd noticed earlier a little more pronounced. "No, thank you. I'm tidying up for Marnie. It's the least I can do."

"I don't mind." Cain grabbed the stack of plates she'd gathered into a pile and moved them to the counter near the dishwasher. He stared down at the machine for several seconds. He had one at home, a supersized monster, in fact. He'd just never used it before.

"Don't worry about dishes. The caterers will be here within the hour to do the real cleanup. Everything belongs to them."

She was there, beside him, placing several wineglasses in a neat row next to the dishes. Her fingers were long and delicate, the nails short and free of color. She was smaller than he'd thought. The top of her head barely reached his shoulder. Her scent lingered in the air, and Cain wondered what it would feel like to hold her. Would she lean into him, soft and pliant, with those big blue eyes looking up at him? Or would she be aggressive and hard, pushing and reaching for something more?

He took a step back, ran his hand along his forehead, and then rolled his shoulders. He really shouldn't be thinking about her like that. Hell, he shouldn't be thinking about anything right now except sleep.

"I see you've met our Maggie."

Lauren Black slipped her arm through his, and Cain gave his mother a hug.

Maggie. It suited her. His dark gaze swept back to the redhead, but her eyes were lowered. Her hands clutched a rag so tightly, her knuckles were white.

"We met earlier on the porch," he answered. "Though I don't think we were officially introduced. I'm Cain."

She looked up. Her eyes were darker than before, the deep blue now two shades past navy. A thin layer of freckles sprinkled the bridge of her nose, and an image of his tongue sweeping across her creamy skin flashed before him. Cain's groin tightened; his lips thinned.

What the hell was wrong with him? He was at a funeral reception for Christ sakes.

Jesse's funeral.

It was the booze. The lack of sleep. It had to be.

He nodded toward the far end of the kitchen.

"How's Raine?" When in doubt, divert attention.

Lauren shook her head. "Not good." Jake was at Raine's side, his hand on her shoulder, his eyes intense as he leaned in close to listen to whatever she was saying. "They loved each other so much. She didn't deserve this." Lauren paused. "I thought they'd live the dream, you know. I really did."

"Dreams sometimes turn into nightmares."

Cain and his mother turned back to Maggie. She looked pensive, surprised maybe that she'd spoken out loud.

"I, uh..." Her small tongue darted out and moistened her lips. They were full, kissable, free of gloss, and sexy as hell. She had the kind of mouth men fantasized about, lips meant for sinning, for gliding and nibbling. Cain's chest tightened as he stared down at her, an unfamiliar feeling warming his body.

She was really...kind of perfect.

"I didn't mean anything." She paused and nervously tucked a strand of hair behind her ear. "I just...when you love like that, you take a chance."

"On what?" Cain was curious. He'd never been hooked. Hell, the Natasha fiasco had been a whirlwind of hot sex and fantasy. In the end it had been nothing more than a train wreck, and when it finally derailed, he'd been left wondering what the hell he'd ever seen in his ex. There'd been nothing of substance, no glue to hold them together.

"On losing yourself." Maggie glanced at her watch. "I have to call a cab and get Michael home. He fell asleep over an hour ago."

His mother's grip tightened and she yanked on his arm. "Don't be silly. We'll give you a ride." She glanced up at her son. "Cain will drive you."

"No." Her answer was abrupt. "He's been drinking."

She was right. Cain couldn't drive.

"You have your driver's license?" Lauren asked.

At Maggie's nod, she continued. "Perfect. You take Cain's rental and drop him off at my house on the way."

His mother planted a quick kiss on his cheek. "I'm going to grab my purse and say good-bye to Steven and Marnie. Don't wait up. I have a prior engagement I can't get out of." She paused. "You *do* know where the house is, right?"

Her sarcasm was noted and he shrugged sheepishly.

His mother had married a wealthy financier from Chicago a few years after he left town. Cain had met the man a few times—they'd jelled over football and not much else. He'd been a proper sort of man and had doted on Lauren. Sadly, he'd died nearly five years ago, leaving the bulk of his wealth to his wife.

Her eyes narrowed onto his. She'd bought a new place a few years back and knew damn well he had no clue where it was located on the lake.

"No matter," she continued, "Maggie knows." She turned to the young woman. "If you could help us out, that would be great."

"Of course." Maggie turned abruptly. "I'll get Michael."

Cain's eyes followed her slight form as she disappeared down the hall, his eyes resting on the curve of her ass.

"Forget it, Cain. She's not for you." His mother pursed her mouth, and a frown creased her forehead. At his look of surprise, she did everything except shake her finger at him. "I mean it. She's not some groupie or model or anything like the women you've been with. The last thing she needs is someone like you filling her head with nonsense."

"What the hell is that supposed to mean? Someone like me?"

His mother's frown softened, and she pinched his cheeks just as she had when he was younger. He'd hated it then, and *that* was something that hadn't changed.

"Sweetie, you know I love you, I do. And God knows I'm ecstatic you came to your senses and kicked that Hollywood harlot to the curb, but seriously, you're not meant for someone like Maggie."

What the hell?

Cain gazed at his mother, a surly look in place that forced his eyebrows together. He'd moved from plain annoyance to a truly insulted state. "Not that I'm interested in"—he gestured toward the hall—"your friend Maggie, but would you care to explain what you mean?"

"Don't take it personally, honey." Her lips graced his cheek, and then she moved away. "But Maggie needs someone…solid, stable. A man who'll be there for her and be a father to her son."

Cain couldn't help but feel pissed. This *was* personal. "Okay, I get that for whatever reason, you're protective of this woman. And let me reiterate, I'm not interested. The last thing I need is a complication. I just got rid of one. But I sure as hell would like to know why you think I'm not good enough for her."

Lauren Black stared at her son for several long moments. Her eyes glittered like blue diamonds, their brilliant depths colored with pain. "It's not a question about being good enough, Cain. It's just that in some ways you're a lot like your father. I know you don't like to hear that, but it's true."

He bit his lip to keep quiet and glared at her. Sure as hell, he didn't like to hear that. His father was a bastard.

Being compared to him was a low blow, and it left a shitty taste in his mouth.

"You're here now, but tomorrow or next week or maybe even the week after that…you'll leave. It's what you do." She couldn't quite keep the bitterness from her words as she turned from him. "How many years will go by before you come back to us?"

Chapter 3

MAGGIE-GRACE O'ROURKE DRAINED THE LAST OF HER coffee and rinsed her cup in the sink before quickly drying it and putting it away. Her counter space was limited, and she liked to keep it free of clutter. She was a great believer in the saying Less Is More, though truthfully, when you didn't have a whole lot, it sure was easy to live by.

Besides, a dishwasher wasn't in the budget, and the one that had come with the house had never worked. She looked at it in disgust. It was there for looks only.

She glanced out the window above the sink and felt her spirits lift as sunlight crept inside. Honeysuckle climbed the trellis along the fence in her small backyard, and a tiny hummingbird flitted about, its wings a blur of speed as it sipped the precious nectar.

Maggie slid the window open and inhaled the subtle scent that the yellow blooms emitted. It was still early, barely past eight in the morning, and the forecast called for a warmer than average day. She'd have loved nothing more than to kick back in the small garden and work on her children's book, but time was her enemy these days. Her need to be creative, to draw and write, would have to wait.

There was always something. Like the need to earn a living and put food on the table.

It was Friday, and she had two clients slated. Luckily she had help. School was done for the summer, and

Michael's extra hands would knock off at least an hour of her time.

She slid the window back into place and locked it. The house wasn't air-conditioned, and if she didn't make sure they were closed and blinds drawn, it would heat up like an oven in no time.

"Michael, let's go. If we get done early, I'll take you for ice cream." She smiled to herself when the pounding started. Michael flew at her from down the hall, his feet hitting the worn wood floors like a herd of buffalo had been let loose.

"Ice cream! Sweet!"

"Did you comb your hair?" Her eyebrow arched as she studied her son. He was dressed in shorts and a wrinkled T-shirt. His feet were bare, though he had one sandal in his hand. Lord knows where the other one had gone to.

"Uh…" He shook his head. "Yep."

Maggie crossed over to him. "Really?" She fingered a stray curl, the one that always hung down his forehead. The one that she loved.

"I did." He was indignant. "It's not my fault my head looks like I stuck my finger in a socket." He squared his shoulders. "Can't we cut it? Brett Lawson got a buzz cut the last day of school, and it's awesome. He doesn't have to comb his hair for the whole entire summer."

Maggie shook her head. Michael's hair was the bane of his existence and one of her greatest pleasures. A compromise might be in the works. She rumpled the mess of it. "Teeth?"

"Yep." A smile tugged the corners of his mouth. "Anything else, Captain?"

"Did you brush *and* floss?"

He hesitated and bit his lip, his eyes sliding to just beyond her. "I brushed and made sure I got my back teeth really good, but...um..."

She gave him a quick hug and smiled wryly. "We don't have time now. You'll have to floss before bed." Maggie tousled his hair. "Your other sandal would be a good idea though."

Michael whirled around. "I think I left it in the bathroom."

"Hurry up."

She watched him disappear into the bathroom, and a familiar tug of emotion unraveled inside her. He was everything to her. *Everything*. She would clean ten houses a day if that's what it took to keep him fed, warm, and safe. When her life was at its darkest, he was the miracle that had gotten her through.

Maggie quickly packed a small cooler with sandwiches, drinks, and snacks for the two of them. She didn't own a vehicle—couldn't afford one and hadn't had one since leaving Savannah—so she kept things compact and easy to carry.

She and Michael either walked or took the bus everywhere they needed to go and were lucky that in a town as small as Crystal Lake, there was public transportation other than expensive cabs.

However, today was a treat. She had a ride—the large SUV parked in her small driveway needed to be returned.

She grabbed the cooler. "Come on, Michael. We've got Mrs. Landon today, and then Mrs. Black's." Ellie Landon was a widow, and her house wasn't much bigger than Maggie's. Lauren's, however, was much larger and took a lot longer to clean.

She grabbed the keys off the counter and studied them for a second. The fob was as impressive as the vehicle—a sterling-silver-and-sleek-black design. It had been a while since she slid behind the wheel of such a powerful machine.

"Do you think Cain will be there?" Michael hopped on one leg as he tried to snap his sandal strap closed.

"I hope not," she murmured to herself.

The last thing I need is a complication. I just got rid of one.

She turned the fob over in the palm of her hand and glanced toward her son. She'd overheard Cain talking to his mother the night before. *Complication*. Her cheeks burned at the thought, righteous indignation pulsing through her.

She shouldn't care. She wasn't in the market for a man. Especially one like Cain Black. He was enigmatic, charming, and way too easy on the eyes, with his dark good looks and perfect smile. She knew too well how deceptive those things could be. He represented everything she'd run away from.

"Miss Lauren told me her son plays guitar and that he sings too! Isn't that cool? She says one day he'll be a big rock star!"

"I'm sure he will be." She tried to keep the sarcasm from her words, but Michael frowned. Somehow she wasn't surprised the tall, good-looking man was an entertainer. She'd watched him the night before. He had a certain *something* that pulled people in, and in a crowded house like Steven and Marnie's, he'd easily stood out.

"Don't you believe her?" He bit his lip. "You don't think she would lie about something like that, do you?"

Maggie shooed her son toward the door. "I think all mothers want their sons to be rock stars at whatever it is they do." She watched his curls bob as he ran down the cement steps and jumped onto the grass, and her heart swelled all over again.

"So a police officer or a fireman can be a rock star too?"

Maggie locked the door behind them, checked twice just to make sure, and turned. She shook her head and laughed softly. "If they're the best in their field, then yes."

She unlocked the SUV and climbed in. Michael ran around to the other side and opened the passenger-side door.

"Uh, no, young man. You're too little to sit in the front. You know the rules."

"Tommy's mom lets him ride up front all the time." He pouted, but when she gave him "the look," he closed the door and climbed into the back.

Maggie turned the key, and the powerful engine sprang to life. She put the truck into gear, backed out of her driveway, and headed toward Main Street.

"Mom?"

She glanced in her rearview mirror. "Yes?"

Michael's brow furled. He chewed on his bottom lip and looked up. "So, when is a regular rock guy just a plain old rock star?"

Maggie's gaze returned to the street. "Jon Bon Jovi is a rock star. Maybe we should ask him."

"Who's Jon Bob Jodi?"

Maggie turned into Mrs. Landon's driveway and giggled. "Never mind, sweetie."

Three hours later, they'd finished Ellie Landon's bungalow and were on their way to Lauren Black's palatial home on the water. It was gorgeous—modern, but with an old-world flair, a wonderful combination of brick, stone, and wood. Maggie maneuvered the SUV up the drive and parked to the side, near the garage.

"Do you think there'll be time for a swim?"

"Nope." Maggie hopped from the truck and made sure no mess was left behind. "And before you ask, I didn't pack your suit."

"Miss Lauren has an extra suit. She keeps one just for me."

Maggie sighed and stared at her son. She didn't want to linger, because there was no way in hell she wanted to run into Cain Black. She didn't like him. Didn't want her son to like him either.

She clutched her cooler and walked toward the house as Michael ran to catch up. She doubted Cain was home anyway. He'd mumbled something the night before about returning the truck at her convenience, since his buddy Mackenzie was picking him up for lunch.

She ran her fingers across the top of Michael's head. "If you want a cone from The Pit, we need to head out as soon as we're done. The five o'clock bus won't wait. You know how busy it gets on a Friday night."

"I guess you're right."

She let them in with her key and poked her head around the door. The house was silent.

"Hello?" she inquired cautiously. No answer.

Maggie took a few more steps inside and shouted a greeting once more, this time with a little more oomph. Still no answer. In fact, the house was as silent as a grave. *Good*. It seemed that Cain had left with his friend Mackenzie after all.

Her shoulders relaxed as she dropped her cooler and turned to her son. "You know the drill, buddy." She nodded toward the back of the house, where the kitchen was located. "Grab an empty bag and collect the garbage."

Michael scampered off, his sandals squeaking along the ceramic tiles.

Maggie cleaned Lauren's house every Friday. It was too large to do the entire place in one visit, so the job was broken down into parts. The main floor and kitchen were done every week, but she alternated the bedrooms upstairs with the finished basement on each visit.

She headed to the laundry room. It was located on the main floor, just off the garage entrance. She peeked into the garage first—Lauren's black Mercedes was gone—before proceeding down the hall.

Today there were no linens; however, a pile of freshly laundered towels was folded on the dryer. Maggie scooped them into her arms, left the set of blue ones near the stairs leading to the basement—they belonged to the small guest bath down there—and carried the rest to the upper level. There were three bedrooms up here: the master, located straight ahead, and a guest room on either side of the stairs.

Maggie put away Lauren's towels and spent the next half hour cleaning her bathroom. When she was done she moved to the guest rooms. One of them would need cleaning for sure. Her son had smelled like a damn brewery.

The room to her right hadn't been used. The bed was undisturbed and the connected bathroom spotless. She gave it a quick dusting and moved on, shouting down to Michael to bring up the vacuum.

She stepped inside the second guest room and looked around in surprise. It too was spotless. A quick check of the adjoining bathroom told her the same thing. Neither one had been used. She shrugged. Maggie had no time to ponder the mystery of where Cain Black had laid his head the night before. For all she knew, he'd left or had gotten a more interesting offer.

From what she'd observed, the man had garnered the lion's share of attention at the Edwardses', even though he'd spent most of the evening outside with his friends. The women had been gaga over him. She'd heard the comments about his looks, his somewhat racy past, and his newly single status.

Who's to say someone hadn't dropped by after she let him off?

Maggie was willing to bet that a man as good-looking and charismatic as Cain Black didn't sleep alone too often.

She grabbed the vacuum from Michael and instructed him to dust the blinds on the main level while she finished up.

"Are you sure you don't mind being here with me today?" she asked suddenly, before he'd cleared the stairs. "What did Tommy have planned?"

Michael smiled, a dimple puncturing his right cheek. "It's all right, Mom." He shrugged. "They all left for sleepover camp anyway."

He ran down the stairs, and Maggie stared after him, a twinge of sadness tightening inside her heart. She wished that Michael could go to sleepover camp and play hockey or have the latest Xbox game or whatever it was the kids were into these days. But her reality was such that it wasn't happening anytime soon.

It was a good thing that her lack of funds bothered her much more than it did her son.

After she vacuumed, Maggie headed downstairs and attacked the kitchen with vigor. Michael settled in to watch TV in the family room, and they chatted during the commercial breaks.

It was nearly three thirty when she finished, and Maggie was hoping they'd be able to catch the four o'clock bus. They had a good fifteen-minute walk to the bus stop, since it didn't come as far as Lauren's house, so they'd have to get cracking. She pocketed the envelope left for her and hung the damp rag over the gooseneck faucet to dry.

She turned and spied the blue towels sitting near the basement steps. "Michael, I'll be right back. I'm just going to run something downstairs."

Maggie scooped up the towels and headed down. It was dark and cool. She shivered as the air rushed along her damp skin. The basement was a huge open space with a pool table and bar located at the far end and a sitting area to her left that featured the largest flat-screen television she'd ever seen.

Lauren had once confessed she never watched the damn thing and only kept it because it had belonged to her deceased husband.

Maggie smiled wryly. Typical. What was it with men and the size of their toys?

She hurried ahead toward the last door on the right, which led to a small office with an adjoining bath. The handle turned beneath her fingers, and she stepped inside. There were no windows in this particular room, so it was pitch-dark. She bit her lip and squinted. Usually a night-light illuminated the room.

Crap. Where was the light switch?

Her fingers crept along the wall to the right but came away empty. Maggie didn't clean the room often, because it didn't get used unless Lauren was entertaining, but she knew the bathroom was to her left.

She stepped forward, and her foot landed among a tangle of something on the floor. Shoes, maybe? She tried to balance, but her other foot got caught as well. A curse slid from her lips as she fell, and her hands reached blindly for anything to grab hold of. But there was nothing, and she cried out, twirled crazily, and went down hard, a loud crack echoing inside her head as her skull glanced off something sharp and unyielding.

She rolled to the side and took a second to get her bearings. Her eyes blinked rapidly, and her lungs grabbed for the air that had been knocked from her chest as she hit the floor. Maggie groaned. Pain splintered along her head, and her fingers touched the tender spot near her temple. She felt something wet and knew it was blood.

Dammit. She'd smacked her head against the desk. She pushed herself up and winced, her head swimming dizzily. Blood flowed freely now—she felt it trickle down her cheek—and a stab of fear shot through her gut. What if it was a serious injury? She was here, alone.

Michael.

Light cut through the dark suddenly, and she squeezed her eyes shut at the brightness, her hand cradling her head. "Oh God," she groaned, exhaling in an effort to focus.

"What the hell?" The voice was male, deep, and raspy.

Once the world stopped spinning, Maggie's eyes opened. She saw legs—masculine legs. They were spread slightly, and her eyes moved up to muscular thighs, a pair of plain black boxers that left nothing to the imagination, and abs that would make an athlete envious. She winced once more as pain shot along her skull and she angled her head to stare up into Cain Black's dark eyes.

His hair was mussed as if he'd just woken, and his jaw was shadowed with more than a day's worth of stubble.

"What the hell are you doing in here?" He was angry.

Unease uncoiled inside her, and she broke out in a sweat when he kneeled down. Shit, she didn't know anything about the man. Didn't know what he was capable of, other than the fact he looked damn good half-naked.

Oh God, she must have hit her head hard to be thinking such thoughts.

"Christ, you're bleeding."

She wanted him to move away, to give her some space and room to breathe. He was too close. Her thoughts were fuzzy, and she needed to think.

Michael. Suddenly her anxiety surfaced and her stomach churned crazily. Where was her child?

His hand reached for her and she flinched. "Don't touch me." Her words were hoarse, and she hated that she couldn't hide her fear.

Cain was silent for a few seconds, then rose. "You're hurt and need to see a doctor." His voice was softer now.

"No!" She was now on her knees. "I'm fine, I just..." Her voice trailed away and she clenched her teeth in an effort to combat the dizziness. There was blood everywhere, it seemed. On her T-shirt, her fingers…the carpet. Oh God, what would Lauren say?

"Mom?" Michael's voice cut through the haze inside her head. "Mom! Are you all right?"

"She's okay, buddy. It looks a lot worse than it is. Head wounds always bleed like a son of a…like crazy. But we're going to take her to the hospital just to make sure, all right? You think you can help?"

"Sure."

"Do you know where your mom left the keys to my truck?"

The boy nodded. "I think she left them on the counter in the kitchen."

"Good. Grab them and unlock it. Leave the passenger door open, okay?"

"Okay." Michael ran from the room.

Maggie heard the sound of a zipper. When she chanced a look, she was happy to see him dressed in jeans and a T-shirt. He knelt in front of her. In his hand was a towel, which she accepted and held against her head.

"Let me help you up."

She couldn't go to the hospital. She had no insurance. Panic set in at the thought, and she tried to clamp down on it, but it was no use. How could she? A trip to the emergency room would wipe out her savings, because she sure as hell wouldn't apply for Medicaid. That meant paperwork, and *that* left a trail.

"I'm fine, Mr. Black. Please give me some room."

"You're not fine. Ten to one, you have a concussion. At the very least, you'll probably need stitches."

He was right. Maggie gritted her teeth.

"And the name's Cain. Mr. Black really isn't me."

He offered his hand and reluctantly she used it. Once she was on her feet, the world tumbled again and her stomach rolled over. A groan escaped, and helpless tears threatened.

"Just give me a second."

His arms slid along her shoulders and under her arms, and he lifted her before she could protest. Cain filled the space around her—his hard, muscled body, the chocolate eyes that stared at her intently, and the solemn tilt of his mouth.

He held her close. Every inch of her was pressed intimately against his flesh as he lifted her into his arms.

"Please, I'd rather go home."

Cain ignored her, took the stairs two at a time as if she weighed no more than a child, and headed outside to his truck. His voice rumbled in his chest as he spoke, tickling her cheek. "Lady, I'm not giving you a choice."

The sun was still hot, bright, and it hurt her eyes. Maggie closed them and finally relaxed her limbs when he placed her in the passenger side of the SUV.

She rested her head against the soft leather and held the towel he'd given her against her head.

Cain slid in beside her, and the truck roared to life. "Seat belt on, buddy?"

"Yup," Michael answered from the backseat.

Maggie gritted her teeth as a wave of dizziness rolled through her head.

Guess the ice cream cone was going to have to wait.

Chapter 4

CAIN KEPT UP A LIGHT CHATTER WITH THE BOY IN THE back even as he drove like a maniac through the streets of Crystal Lake. The hospital was at the north end, and he thanked all that was holy the town hadn't changed much over the past ten years.

New construction was evident around the lake, and a small subdivision had sprung up near the one mall on the outskirts of town, but for the most part, it was old-school. The town had been founded in the 1800s, during the lumber boom, and was full of stately century-old homes, American pride, and a population that was tight-knit.

He knew exactly where he was going. Lord knows, as teens, he and the boys had visited the emergency room on numerous occasions. Mackenzie Draper had held the record for hardest head. Hell, he'd taken more hits to his cranium and had had more concussions than anyone else on the football team. It was a miracle the man had escaped brain damage.

And that didn't include any of the injuries his father had inflicted.

He glanced at Maggie. Her eyes were closed, her skin pale except for the blood smudged along her cheek. It was already congealing. At least he could be thankful for that.

Guilt washed through him. Christ, if he'd just

crashed in one of the guest rooms upstairs instead of hiding in the basement like a hermit, none of this would have happened.

Except he'd gone nearly forty-eight hours without sleep, had been half-drunk and jet-lagged, and had wanted nothing but complete silence and darkness.

His fingers gripped the steering wheel as he turned off Main Street onto Oak. They were nearly there, maybe two minutes out.

He glanced at Maggie once more. It bothered him… the look in her eyes when he'd knelt down to help her. She'd looked scared, and that made him feel even more like an asshole. He wasn't used to getting looks like that from women.

They barreled toward the emergency doors, and the SUV skidded to a stop in the no parking zone. Cain hopped out and yanked the passenger door open.

"Let's go." He reached for Maggie, but she hunched her shoulders and shook her head, her features pinched.

"I'll be fine. Thanks for the ride." Maggie slid from the truck, and Cain stood back as she took a couple of steps.

His temper flared, but he kept quiet and stood to the side.

"I got ya, Mom." Michael smiled up at his mother.

Cain watched the way they moved together—their steps in sync like a perfect harmony. There was no doubt the two of them belonged to each other. Michael tucked his hand into hers, and Maggie tousled his hair and kissed the top of his head as they walked away.

He didn't have that connection.

Family wasn't something he'd considered before—at least not one of his own. Natasha had brought up the subject once, but he'd shot her down cold. Even then he'd known she wasn't the one he'd raise kids with. Hell, he wasn't sure he wanted a family at all. It took a special sort to be a parent. His mother was an ace, but his father? Major fail. The man had left two days before his fifth birthday, and neither he nor his mother had seen him again.

Gerald Black was a sperm donor—nothing more—and truthfully, for all he knew, the man was dead.

His eyes remained glued to Maggie's slight form.

As far as he could tell, she was on her own, but the love of her son seemed to be enough. He thought of what his mother had said the night before and scowled. Who the hell did he have? Christ, he didn't even own a dog.

He thought of Jesse and his widow, Raine. If Cain died tomorrow, who besides his mother would mourn his passing? *Really* mourn him?

Hell, his record label wouldn't bat an eye. If his ass ended up on a slab in the morgue, he'd make them a fortune. Dead rockers sold millions.

"Son of a bitch! I heard you were back in town."

Cain turned toward a tall paramedic who'd just walked out of the emergency room entrance. The man had some paunch around his midsection, his light brown hair was thinning, and for a second, Cain couldn't place him. The paramedic smiled a wide toothy grin, and it came back in a flash.

He shook the hand that Luke Jansen offered. They'd played football together, and he'd been a member of the team Cain led to a state championship their last year of high school.

"Hey, sorry to hear about Jesse Edwards. I know

you guys were tight." Luke paused and looked around. "What are you doing here? Is your mom all right?"

Cain nodded toward the doors. "She's good. I brought a woman in who does some work for my mother, Maggie…possible concussion." She'd disappeared inside, and Cain took a step forward. "I really should go and check on her."

Luke's eyes widened. "Maggie…Maggie O'Rourke?"

At Cain's nod, Luke held up his hand. "Hold on." Luke shouted to the other paramedic who stood several feet away, near their ambulance. "I'll be back in a few minutes, Dave."

Cain was silent for a moment. There was interest in the other man's eyes, and for some reason he didn't like it. "She was at my mother's place and had an accident." He paused. "How do you know her?"

Luke walked alongside him, and they entered the emergency room together. "She rents the bungalow beside my house. Moved in about a year ago. I try to look out for her, you know…cut her grass and stuff when I can."

"She got family close by?" Cain was curious.

Luke shrugged. "Not that I'm aware of. I've never seen anyone visit other than your mom a few times, and Raine Edwards. I've asked her out, but she shot me down cold. I don't think she's interested in anything other than her kid."

"His name's Michael."

"What?" Luke looked confused.

"The kid. His name is Michael."

"Yeah, that's it…Mike." They stopped just in front of reception. "There she is." Luke pointed to the waiting area. Both men crossed over, and when Maggie looked up, Cain noticed her hand was trembling. She was flushed, her cheeks rosy, and sweat beaded along the top of her lip.

"Hey, Maggie, I'm going to make sure you get in to see the doctor right away, okay?" Luke turned. "I'll be right back."

She held a clipboard, a pen between her fingers. Blood was smeared near her temple where she'd wiped it. Michael's face was pale and he looked worried.

Cain winked at the boy and sat beside her. "Do you want some help with that?" He pointed to the forms she held.

"I…no, I can do it. I just…my eyes hurt. The lights are bright in here."

Cain reached for the clipboard and gently tugged it from her grip. "Let me help. I feel like a total ass as it is. If I hadn't left my crap on the floor, you never would have fallen." He knew that Maggie most likely had no insurance. The least he could do was pay for her visit.

Luke approached, a nurse in tow. "This is Tracy. She'll take you back to see the doctor."

"Oh my goodness," the nurse blurted. Cain glanced up.

"I heard you were back in town." She tucked a loose strand of hair behind her ear and giggled. "My older sister went to school with you. Patti Jones? Do you remember her? Our parents own the bakery in town?" Maggie was totally forgotten. "I think your band is awesome, especially that British guy." She paused, eyes wide. "Oh my God, I have your CD in my car. It would be so cool if you could sign it for me. Maybe get a picture with you too?"

Cain stood. "Sure. But let's look after my friend first."

His voice was firm, though he winked and smiled. "And I promise I'll let you take as many pictures as you want."

"Oh." Her flush deepened. "Sorry, of course." She laughed—a weird, strangled sound—and motioned to Maggie. "Follow me, hon. Dr. Karkoff will be back in a minute."

Maggie stood and grabbed hold of Michael's hand. She looked up at him, and Cain felt something shift inside as their eyes met. His muscles tightened and his mouth went dry.

She looked so damn vulnerable that it tore at him. This woman he barely knew had managed to tie him up in all sorts of ways he couldn't explain. He took a step forward, but stopped when her eyes darkened, a shadow of confusion reflected in their depths.

"Thanks for giving me a lift." Her hand went to her temple, and the guilt inside him tripled as she rubbed the tender spot. "I'm sure everything is fine." She looked at her son. "Right?"

"Yep." Michael grinned at him. "Thanks, Cain."

They turned to follow the nurse.

"I'll be waiting to drive you home…it's the least I can do." He spoke in a rush, nervous as all hell and not liking the feeling one bit. What was it about this woman that turned him into a blubbering moron?

She paused, turned her head to the side. "You don't have to. I might be here a while."

"I'll wait as long as it takes."

She disappeared with the nurse, and Cain finally relaxed. Luke stared at him, his face screwed up into a frown.

"Something wrong?"

Luke shrugged. "Not my place to say anything really.

I mean, Maggie barely knows I exist, but hell, she's not the kind of girl to play with, and you…"

Cain's tempered flared. Who the hell did this guy think he was? He cleared his throat. "And I…what?" Gone was the charm from moments earlier. He was pissed and had no qualms about letting Luke Jansen know it.

The paramedic glared at him, puffed up his chest, and stepped up to the plate. "It's no secret you played the field big-time back in the day, and from what I've heard, you're still that guy."

Cain's eyes narrowed dangerously as a muscle worked its way along his jaw. *Here we go*. Everyone assumed he lived the stereotype.

"But she's not like that. Maggie's special."

"First off, Jansen…" Cain clenched his hands together and felt the interest of those gathered in the waiting room, but he didn't care. He was used to attention—which didn't mean he liked it—and the paramedic was not. Luke's face was now mottled red, his cheeks ruddy patches of skin. "Don't make assumptions about my life and how I live it. You don't know me. You caught the pigskin I threw at you in high school. That's the extent of our relationship, and it ended over ten years ago."

Luke held his hands up as if to say *okay, back off*, and his mouth widened into a smile, though his eyes remained frosty. "Hey, I'm not saying anything that's not already out there. Come on, until recently you were known more for the women you've dated than your music."

Cain figured one shot and he could take the son of a bitch down.

"Shit, you dated that English chick, the one related to the queen, *and* you married Natasha Simmons."

Cain's jaw clenched painfully. He was dying to smash his fist into Jansen's nose, but what could he say? There was some truth there. He was no fucking choirboy, that's for sure, but he sure as hell owed nothing to Jansen.

"Jesus, Luke. You seem to know more about my life than my fucking publicist."

Luke's mouth tightened. "I'm not judging. Christ, you're living most guys' fantasy. I'm just saying that Maggie O'Rourke isn't one of those women, and I'd hate to see her hurt by some slick rocker who's come home for a few days, looking for a distraction."

Luke's mobile crackled to life as his partner's voice slid between them. There was a call, and the paramedic needed to go. "No offense, but it's not like you're going to stick around Crystal Lake. I'm just looking out for her."

He left without another word.

Cain's jaw ached as he ground his teeth in anger. His fist tightened with the need to inflict pain or pulverize something. *Anything*. He glanced at the back of Jansen's head. That would do just fine, except his ass would land in jail and his mother would kick it but good.

His cell phone vibrated and he grabbed it from his pocket. A quick glance told him there were a lot of missed calls, a couple from his buddy Mac and the rest from his manager. There were also more emails than he cared to count. Publicity. Marketing. Managers.

He sighed and stared at the information displayed on the screen. They were probably freaking out because he'd left right after the Glasgow show without telling anyone where he was going.

He scrolled down and clenched his mouth, pausing

as a familiar name stared back at him. Taunting him. Filling him with anger. Blake Hartley, the drummer in BlackRock. He'd emailed over a dozen times.

Cain looked away. Let the bastard stew. What the hell did he expect? An apology?

Tracy the nurse ran from the examination area, a copy of his CD in hand. He signed it as promised and posed for a few pictures with some of the other staff, several of them people he knew.

One question was asked over and over: "How long are you staying in Crystal Lake?"

Cain fingered his cell. It continued to vibrate every few minutes. Just listening to the device was tiring and made him edgy.

He thought of Jake and Mac. Of Raine and his mother. And of Maggie and her son. What did he have waiting in LA, except an empty house and a full bar? Before the phone vibrated again, he powered it down and shoved it into his pocket. Tension lay in wait, fingering out along his shoulders.

He needed a break. The last six months had been the most difficult of his life, both professionally and personally. He was, in effect, done for now—tapped out. The slow pace of Crystal Lake was exactly what he needed.

He glanced toward the exam room just as Maggie and Michael appeared. Her arm was around her son's shoulders, and she bent low, a smile on her mouth as her son said something. Something passed between the two of them. Something solid. And real.

He wanted that. He wanted her to look at him with the same easy grace that she gave her son. The thought was sobering and surprising, considering he barely knew her.

Michael pointed to him, and she straightened, her smile fading as their eyes met. A wary look crept into them and she stilled, like that deer caught in the headlights again. The woman was cloaked in invisible walls, and for whatever reason, he wanted to smash through them.

His decision was made before he stepped forward. How long was he going to stay in Crystal Lake?

His gaze locked onto Maggie and a slow smile curved his mouth. Cain thought that at the very least, he was going to stay a good long while.

Chapter 5

Maggie stared across the room at Cain and felt a jolt of *something* rush through her as their eyes met. It left her hot and flustered, and she hoped like hell she wasn't blushing like a complete idiot, but by the feel of her cheeks, she was probably three shades past pink. Not very attractive, with her red hair.

The man was compelling; there was no denying the charisma that rolled off every inch of him, like water across silk. It wasn't just his strong, masculine jaw; sensual mouth; or dark eyes. It wasn't even the thick coffee-colored hair that framed his Hollywood-handsome face or his tall muscular frame.

It was the sum of all those things, and yet it was so much more. He had that extra bit of magic that placed him above the crowd, and it was that extra bit that made her nervous.

She'd heard all about him while in the emergency exam room. The nurse assisting Dr. Karkoff had been more than happy to fill her in. Apparently Cain, his buddy Mackenzie, and Jake and Jesse Edwards had been quite the hell-raisers back in the day. According to Nurse Tracy, everyone knew he'd eventually make it in music. He was way too *hot* not to.

Of course, Maggie could have pointed out the fact that it usually took a lot more than hotness to sustain a career in music, but she had to admit her curiosity was piqued. Tracy explained how Cain and one of the band members, a guy named Blake, were like Lennon and McCartney, or Jon Bon Jovi and Richie Sambora. That they'd written loads of songs for other artists, but now their own band was finally making it. Maggie had never heard of BlackRock, though Tracy had happily informed her they were the next big thing, in spite of what had happened in Barcelona.

Maggie would have asked for more information, but the doctor had frostily asked for quiet so he could finish his examination. He'd narrowed his eyes at the nurse. "BlackRock, is it? Sounds like a bunch of nonsense to me." He'd nodded as he probed Maggie's neck gently. "Now, Hank Williams, he was a legend taken before his time."

Nurse Tracy had looked annoyed with the doctor, and as soon as she could, she'd fled, eager for a chance to talk to Cain and get her picture taken with him.

"I told you so, Mom," Michael had said with the greatest of pleasure. He'd held up his hands, with only his pinky and forefinger showing—like the points on a devil's head—stuck out his tongue, and shouted, "Rock star."

Uh, not quite, but she wasn't about to burst her son's bubble. He'd taken a weird kind of interest in the man, which made Maggie frown, because one thing was certain. Cain Black was someone she wanted to steer clear of.

Except that he was walking toward her, his eyes intense and focused. He moved like a predator, with the easy grace of a cat, and instantly her back was up.

"So, everything check out?" Was he asking out of concern or guilt?

"She has a confession," Michael answered.

Cain's mouth quirked in a quick smile. "You mean concussion?"

Michael nodded. "Yep, that's what I meant. The doctor said she can't go to sleep for too long, and if she pukes or her head still hurts in the morning, she needs to come back and see him."

"It's not as bad as it sounds." Maggie gripped her son's hands. "Thanks for bringing me to the hospital, Mr. Black."

"Come on, Maggie…it's Cain." He stepped closer, and though she didn't move, everything inside Maggie screamed retreat. He was too big, too male…and she was very much aware of the fact. "Mr. Black is cold, makes it sound like we're not friends."

"We're not friends. I barely know you."

Cain smiled down at her, and in that moment she caught the full, devastating effect of his charm. It curled inside her belly and flushed her skin there with a heat she'd never felt before.

"Well, I'm thinking I'd like to be your friend…" He paused, his voice low, caressing the air between them. "Maggie."

He said her name as if they were sharing a secret. As if she was the only one in the room with him, when in fact they were the object of over a dozen pairs of eyes and whispers shared behind hands.

Was he flirting with her? His gaze lingered just a little too long and then dropped to her mouth.

He's flirting with me.

This was all kinds of wrong. She changed the subject quick as she could, flustered and hoping it didn't show.

She didn't do flirting. Especially not with a man like Cain Black.

"I need to see about my bill." Maggie winced as pain shot through her head, and she licked her dry lips. "You don't have to wait. Michael and I will call a cab."

"The bill's been looked after. It's the least I could do, considering this whole mess was my fault."

Instantly her hackles were up. "I can look after my own affairs. I don't need your charity." She was annoyed, and though a part of her was secretly relieved, she sure as heck didn't want to owe him. She would not owe anyone anymore.

"I'll pay you back."

"If you're ready"—he ignored her comment and nodded toward the exit—"I'll take you home."

A heavy feeling pressed on her chest, everything tightened, and Maggie exhaled a ragged breath. She was being pushed into a corner and didn't like it at all. It seemed as if the ghosts of her past were circling hard. "I...Michael and I will get home on our own. Really, you've done enough."

Cain glanced at Michael. "What do you think, buddy? A ride in some smelly old cab or a quick trip in my truck?"

"Mom, if we call a cab, we'll have to wait *forever*, and I'm really hungry."

Okay, that was cheap. Using a child. She glared at Cain before turning to her son.

"Michael—"

"Please, Mom? Why pay for a cab when we can get a free ride? You always say we need to be smart about money 'cause we don't have a lot, right?"

"Michael," she tried again, hating that her cheeks burned as Cain studied her in silence. She was embarrassed, flustered, and tired. And her head throbbed like a son of a…

"Listen, I get that you think you're somehow putting me out, or you want your independence, or—"

"Maybe I just don't like you."

Surprise flickered across his face. His chocolate-colored eyes narrowed, but the easy smile that lay upon his lips never wavered. "Okay, I suppose that could be a valid argument, but you *need* to let me take you home. Trust me, I'm not pulling a Tarzan on you. It's more of a self-preservation thing."

"*Really.*" She sounded petulant but didn't care.

"My mother may look harmless, but she'd kick my ass all over Crystal Lake and back if I left you here."

"Come on, Mom." Michael tugged on her arm. "I don't see what the big deal is."

Traitor.

"Please?" Her son smiled, his dimples pronounced as he looked up at her.

Two against one wasn't fair. Maggie bit her lip and glanced around the emergency room. The covert glances and quick whispers had more than doubled. Nurse Tracy pointed toward her and said something to the woman at her side. Both of them stared at her as if she had two heads.

Crystal Lake was a small town, and she knew by nightfall most everyone would know she'd been to the hospital with Cain Black.

She wanted to be home, locked inside the safe confines of her house away from all the prying eyes and speculation. Like a balloon that had been punctured, her resolve faded. It slipped away and left her weak. "All right," she mumbled.

"Sweet!" Michael led her toward the exit. Cain was a few paces behind. She knew this because all the women huddled in adoring little groups were focused behind her, their shy smiles and quick little waves nauseatingly coy. Ugh. The man sang and played guitar. He wasn't curing cancer or saving lives. He was not a god.

Even if he looked like one.

She followed Michael outside and waited for Cain to grab his truck. It was now early evening and the promised humidity had moved in, coating everything with a fine mist of warm, damp air. It settled in Maggie's lungs and slithered across her skin. She looked up at the sky where dark clouds had gathered, blocking the sun and leaving a dull gray instead of the bright blue of a few hours ago.

They were definitely rain clouds.

She quickened her steps, even though she still felt a little fuzzy, and would have slid into the backseat, except there was a large guitar case in the way. Michael climbed in on the other side, and she carefully slid into the front. It wasn't as if she had a choice.

Cain pulled away from the curb. "What street do you live on?"

"Linden…the last house on the right."

"Old Man McCleary's place."

"So I'm told. His daughter collects my rent checks."

"He still alive?"

Why do you care?

"His wife died a few years ago. He's in the retirement home."

"Sorry to hear that. She was a nice lady."

"I wouldn't know."

"How long have—"

"Can we not do this?" Maggie interrupted.

He arched an eyebrow, and she didn't like the grin that claimed his mouth. "This?"

"This *thing*...whatever it is." She exhaled slowly and winced. She knew she sounded like an ungrateful bitch, but she couldn't help it. At the moment she did feel bitchy. "Look, thanks for the lift home, but seriously, we don't need to do the small-talk thing. It's all right.

"Besides..." She turned away from him, closed her eyes, and rested against the soft headrest. "I don't feel like talking."

Cain navigated his way around the hospital parking lot and back onto the street. He turned up the radio, and she settled into blessed peace, her eyes half-open as she gazed out the window.

It was nearly seven in the evening, and traffic was heavy. Friday nights were always busy, with folks spilling into the small town from the surrounding larger cities, some driving from as far away as Detroit. The town of Crystal Lake supported a flourishing cottage-rental industry, with boating, fishing, and relaxation being key selling points to prospective vacationers.

Maggie was toying with the idea of picking up a few seasonal clients, but it meant she'd have to clean Saturday mornings. She was undecided if the time away from Michael was worth the extra cash.

She closed her eyes. Michael and Cain chatted, but their words melted together into a soft whirl of masculine sounds. She couldn't be bothered to listen to their conversation. Her head ached, and damn, but she was tired.

"We're here."

Maggie's eyes flew open at Cain's words. She must have dozed off, which was surprising, considering the ride from the hospital to her home didn't take more than ten minutes.

He stood beside the truck with the door open, his eyes intense as he stared down at her. The skies had opened up and rain fell steadily, coating his hair with beads of moisture that glistened against the dark waves.

How long had he been standing there? His T-shirt was wet. It clung to his chest, emphasizing powerful muscles and broad shoulders.

Long enough.

If she took the time, she was sure she'd be able to count each and every ab. His jeans were low-slung, held up by a wide leather belt and intricate buckle that drew her attention.

"See something you like?"

Maggie's cheeks burned as she glanced up at him. "I..." she stammered, embarrassed.

"Hey, I was just teasing." His eyes glittered, their dark depths awash with a dangerous light.

Her mouth was dry. She tried to swallow but choked instead. She'd never felt so out of sorts before.

"I...where's Michael?"

His hand reached for her. "He's inside already. Let me help you."

"No," she answered quickly. "I can manage."

"God, you're stubborn."

His hand lingered in the air for a few seconds, and then Cain moved aside. She slid from the truck, took a few steps, and stopped. Why was he following her?

Maggie turned and pasted a smile she didn't feel onto her face. "Thanks again for bringing me home. Tell your mother I'll do my best to get the blood-stains out of the carpet. There's a new product that I'm certain—"

"Cain!"

What now?

Maggie glanced toward her small porch. Michael was jumping up and down, a huge grin spread across his face.

"There's *tons* of eggs."

"Eggs?" She looked at Cain.

"Mom, Cain said he makes the best breakfast for supper you could ever even imagine."

"Breakfast?" Okay, did she sound as confused as she felt?

"I told Michael I'd make him something to eat."

She shook her head—it was still fuzzy—ignored the pain of it, and pursed her lips. *No way*.

Cain was inches from her now and nodded toward the porch. "He said he was fond of omelets, and I just happen to be the king of eggs."

"No thanks," she whispered. "But, I'll…" She hissed as a jolt of pain ripped through her head. She massaged her temple and winced.

"You won't, and I will." His hands were at her back, gently nudging her forward, and the tone of his voice told her he wasn't taking no for an answer. "I'm not leaving until I'm positive you're all right. Concussions are nasty, and I know the drill. You need supervision for the next little while, and you'll need to be woken up every few hours tonight."

"You are *not* staying here tonight." Her belly rolled over at the thought.

They were on the porch now.

Michael had disappeared back inside the house, and she chanced a glance at Cain. *Wrong thing to do*. Something shifted between them, a subtle change in the air. He was inches from her, and yet the heat from his body slid across her skin like a caress of fire. She felt it. Everywhere. And it scared the crap out of her.

She'd stored those kinds of feelings away years ago, and damned if someone like Cain was going to rip them from the box.

"Fine," he said silkily.

Maggie swallowed, surprised he'd given up so easily. "Okay," she answered.

"I'll make supper while you relax, and when I'm satisfied you're all right, I'll go."

She started to protest, but his finger was on her mouth before she had a chance to react. He was much too close. So close that the spicy scent of him hung in the air and fell into her lungs as she inhaled a shaky breath. It was earthy and basic and male…and way too damn good.

"I'm not negotiating."

He walked past her, and just like that, Cain Black invaded the one space she'd managed to call her own for the last year.

Maggie swore under her breath and followed him inside. She closed the door and took a second to calm her nerves. *Breathe*. She could do this.

Michael assaulted Cain immediately, and the two of them were already in the kitchen. Pots and pans banged and the fridge door slammed shut. Her son babbled excitedly, and Maggie slid onto the sofa, a bittersweet feeling heavy in her throat.

She couldn't lie. It bothered her that Michael seemed so keen on having Cain around. Was he that starved for a male figure in his life? That thought alone made her feel awful, but she pushed it aside. Her head hurt too much to think about that kind of stuff.

Her bungalow was open concept, so she had a clear view of the kitchen area. Michael balanced on a step stool, and still his head barely reached Cain's shoulders. His curls bobbed as he listened to Cain explain his fabulous omelet recipe, and his giggles filled the silence.

"Mom, these are gonna be awesome!" He looked back and grinned before grabbing a bowl off the counter to hand to Cain.

Her heart constricted as she watched her son. He looked so small, so incredibly vulnerable, next to Cain. As always, she was humbled at the miracle that he was. Her little man.

Cain turned around. "Can I get you anything? Something to drink?"

"No," she whispered.

His eyes lingered a little too long, a smile tugging the corners of his mouth.

Maggie leaned back and closed her eyes.

Cain Black was all kinds of wrong for so many reasons. She didn't know what kind of game he was playing, but she knew she couldn't play along. Not that she was interested, and even if she was, he was way out of her league.

It wouldn't end well.

And Maggie didn't know if she could survive another loss.

Chapter 6

"Where the hell have you been?"

Cain closed the door behind him and stared across the foyer at his mother. The lighting was muted, small beams filtering in from outside through the floor-to-ceiling windows. The evening shadows on her face made her appear almost ethereal. She was dressed in an old pair of denim shorts and a plain white T-shirt, with her long blond hair tied back in a ponytail.

She stepped forward, and as always, his heart softened at the sight of her. The woman was free of makeup and she looked much younger than her fifty-two years. He smiled. How many times had he warned his bass player, Dax, that his mother was off-limits?

At the moment, however, anger marred her classic features into a dark frown. "I've been calling your cell for the last three hours."

Shit. He opened his mouth to respond, but she cut him off.

"I realize you're a grown man and not used to answering to anyone, but you could at least let me know where you are and when you'll be home." Lauren's hands were on her hips, and her arched brow still managed to make him uncomfortable. "When you're with Mackenzie and Jake, things tend to go off, and I just..." She shrugged. "I'd like a little warning is all."

"Sorry, I turned my phone off at the hospital—"

"Hospital?" Her anger vanished as she crossed the room. "Are you all right?"

Cain nodded. "I'm fine. Maggie tripped over my crap downstairs, and her head met the wrong end of the desk. She's okay."

"What about Michael?"

"They're both good. I took them home."

The look in Lauren's eyes changed. It was subtle, but he could see the wheels turning behind them, spinning until they narrowed thoughtfully. He shifted beneath her direct stare.

"When did this happen?"

He shrugged and walked past her toward the kitchen. "Fourish...maybe?"

"Cain."

Here we go.

"What are you doing?"

A candle burned at the center of the dark granite island. She slipped onto a stool, leaning her elbows on the counter as she continued to study him with her all-knowing eyes.

He crossed to the fridge and opened the door, keeping it propped open with his hip as he perused the contents. He wasn't hungry. Hell, he'd eaten more than his share at Maggie's, but it was habit to come home to his mother's and head straight for the fridge.

The door closed behind him as he turned, definitely not interested in anything inside. It looked like his mother's health kick and vegan status was still intact.

He met his mother's stare and folded his arms across his chest. "I took her to the hospital because there was no one else, and afterward I helped out a bit."

"Helped out," was her dry response.

His mother cocked her head but remained silent as she waited for him to explain himself. A sliver of resentment riffled through him, and he rubbed his scruffy jaw. How the hell did she do it? After all this time?

No longer was he a mature man of thirty. Hell no, he was once more a shadow of his teenaged self—the one who'd never become immune to the eyebrow and the pursed lips.

She's not for you. Her words echoed in his head, and he squared his shoulders.

"I fed Michael and made sure Maggie was okay before I left. She had a nasty head injury, and you can't be too careful with something like that."

His mother pursed her lips slightly. "All right."

The subject was closed. For now.

She rose, grabbed a bottle of wine off the counter, and poured herself a glass, leaning against the dark granite as she swirled the pale liquid. When she met his gaze once more, there was a softer look in her eyes. "You look tired."

She stared at him for several long moments and then crossed over, her hand falling to his chest, close to his heart. "You look tired in here."

Cain stared down at his mother and clenched his jaw. "Yeah."

"What's really going on with you?" Her blue eyes shadowed with concern. "And don't say 'nothing.' What happened in Barcelona was not *nothing*."

He sighed and moved away from his mother. Just thinking of the situation he'd left behind made him tense, and he ran fingers along the tight cord of muscle at his neck. Was it only twenty minutes ago that he'd been relaxed in the cocoon of Maggie's kitchen?

"You don't know the half of it."

"Then talk to me, Cain. Don't keep it bottled up inside. That's the worst thing you can do. It will make you ill, trust me."

Cain stared at his mother intently. He felt the words sitting in the back of his mouth, but his throat was tight. Spain had been a low point for him. The culmination of a lot of crap that had been building for months. The bitter taste of it made him grimace. "Barcelona was not good."

"Not good?" His mother frowned. "Cain, you threw a punch at one of your band members and knocked him off the damn stage. Nearly caused a riot. It's a hell of a lot more than not good."

Anger coursed through him swift and hard. "Blake had it coming. You can't expect to bang someone's wife without consequence."

Lauren's eyebrows rose in shock. "Blake was having an affair with Natasha?"

He nodded and glanced out the window into the darkness. In the distance, lights twinkled around the lake like shiny diamonds cutting through the black. His mother's windows were open, and a crisp, fresh breeze blew through the room. The rain from earlier in the evening had moved on, but the smell of its freshness lingered.

It was so quiet here. Serene. A far cry from the life he'd been inhabiting.

Damn, but he was tired of it all.

"Cain?"

He nodded. "Apparently he's the latest in a long line. I didn't know until after the divorce proceedings had started, or I would never have gone on tour with the bastard. Blake got drunk one night and it came out. A confession of his soul, I think he called it." Cain clenched his hands. "He should have kept his fucking mouth shut."

He felt his mother's warm hand against his arm. "So that's why he left the tour."

Cain's eyes were flat. He knew speculation had run rampant after the Barcelona incident—Blake had a drug problem, Cain had gone prima donna—but the plain truth was so much simpler.

"He crossed a line and was fired. Now he's suing BlackRock—which, I have to say, the record label isn't happy with. They want to pay him off and be done with it, but I'm not liking that train of thought."

"Oh honey, I didn't know." Lauren's brow furled. "But why would he sue you?"

"He's not stupid." He shrugged. "He knows the next album could put us over the top. Hell, everyone is expecting it. He's hoping to cash in. Blake's been there since the beginning. He's co-written everything with me and will make money off those royalties for years. But now he wants royalties from any future recordings… songs he'll have no hand in writing."

"He's blowing smoke. No judge would ever allow that to go through. He's being an asshole, angling for more money." She frowned. "Is Natasha putting him up to this? She still pissed that you broke it off with her?"

"I'm sure she's enjoying the attention. Her publicity machine will work any angle they can. Honestly, I don't give two shits about the money. I've never had buckets of the stuff, but have always managed to make a living.

That's not what I'm worried about..." His voice trailed off and his chest tightened.

"What is it?" His mother prodded.

"Nothing I want to talk about now." He pushed aside his dark thoughts. He'd deal with them later.

"Okay." Silence fell between the two of them, and then Lauren spoke softly. "How long are you staying here?"

He glanced down at his mother and felt a bit of the weight he carried leave him. "I don't plan on leaving anytime soon, if that's all right."

She looped her arms through his and rested her head against his shoulder. "That's more than all right."

"You catch anything?"

"Huh?" Cain turned to Mac and stretched out his long limbs in front of him. His feet were bare and he wriggled his toes, thinking that he hadn't been this relaxed in forever. The sun was warm against his face and shirtless chest, and the silence on the lake soothed his soul.

"Our boy's off in la-la land again." Jake grabbed the spot beside him as the boat rolled against the gentle swell of the water. "What the hell's got you so distracted?"

Long red hair, peaches-and-cream skin, and wicked blue eyes flashed before him.

"Nothing, I'm just enjoying the quiet."

It was Sunday, late morning, and the three of them had been out on the water for several hours. They'd spent most of Saturday cleaning up *Old Smoky*—the name given to the twenty-foot power boat Mr. Edwards had given to his twin sons on their fifteenth birthday. It sported a forty-five horsepower outboard and back in the day had had just enough room for the four of them, a case of beer, their fishing gear, and a couple of girls. Many a weekend they'd spent entire Saturdays out on the water fishing, drinking, smoking whatever they could get their hands on, and just shooting the shit.

God, to be that young again.

The four of them had been kings, with nothing on their minds but scoring as much tail as they could, hitting the best parties in town, and playing football. There'd been no responsibility—no limitations—only the open road of possibility to roam.

Cain ran his fingers along the edge of the boat. The cream and navy colors had long faded, beaten down by the sun. The damn thing brought back a lot of memories. His gaze rested on Jake and then slid to the empty seat beside him.

Jesse's spot. Yeah, a lot of memories.

"So, what's with the little redhead?" Mac popped open a beer and took a long drink before wiping foam from the corner of his mouth. "What's her story?"

Cain sighed. *Here we go.*

He glanced up. Mac's dark blond hair was already a shade lighter, and it was good to see him out of Armani and decked out in plain old cotton. He was bare chested and had gained a considerable amount of muscle since Cain last saw him. Mac had been hitting the gym hard. Hell, put him in a marine uniform and he'd be as badass as Jake.

Jake grinned. "Maggie? Raine's friend? The one with the kid?" Jake glanced at Mac. "Toss me one, will ya?" He settled back, his eyes boring into Cain. "So what the hell did I miss? You're home less than twenty-four hours and already scored the cutest thing in town?"

Mac laughed. "Some things never change."

Cain scowled at the two of them. "It's not like that."

Jake chuckled. "So tell me Cain…what it's like, *exactly*?"

He caught the look Mac shot at Jake, and his scowl deepened. "Drop it."

Truthfully, there was nothing to tell. The woman wasn't interested. After he made supper for Michael, she'd insisted he leave. She'd done everything but yank him by the arm and throw him out of her house. Said she'd set her alarm for every two hours so she'd wake up and promised that if the nausea continued, she'd go back and see the doctor.

Christ, he'd stood on her porch and listened to her turn at least three dead bolts behind him. If that didn't say "stay the hell away," he didn't know what did.

He'd left—reluctantly—and not because he'd been looking to score some action. Being in her home with her kid had been nice and simple and easy.

God, he missed easy. Normal.

"So, she shot you down?" Mac leaned back and smiled.

"What are we? Sixteen? Drop it." Cain sat up, ran fingers over his taut belly. Hunger pangs sat low in his gut, and he was ready to head back.

They were spending the afternoon at the Edwards place, relaxing and hanging out, just like old times. A barbecue was planned for later—a small, intimate affair—with his mother and Raine invited.

The Edwardses' loss was still raw, and they were mourning. Hell, they all were, but if Jesse's death had taught them anything, it was the need to hold close the things that were important. Family and friends. And that's what today was about.

Mac was supposed to head back to New York on Monday, and as for Cain, he'd finally called his manager the day before, after Charlie had begun hounding his mother. Figured he'd better, before rumors started to circulate that he'd died or disappeared somewhere over the Atlantic.

Their part in the tour was officially over. The Grind had picked up another act to continue with. After the Barcelona incident and Blake's abrupt departure, they'd had no choice—the Glasgow show had been done with a hired drummer. But as was the way of it in this day of celebrity, the incident, captured on YouTube and the like, had generated even more buzz.

He'd nearly started a riot, and it had only served to enhance BlackRock's profile. What the future brought was up to him, and as the weight of it pressed on him, Cain grimaced. His next move would be critical, and that begged the question, could he handle it on his own? His entire career had been linked to Blake.

Cain sighed and rubbed the scruff on his chin. Christ, he didn't want to think about that right now. For the moment he was free, not due in the studio until the fall. Seemed like a distraction was in order. Again his thoughts turned to Maggie.

He arched a brow at Jake and asked the question he'd been pondering since the day before. "When are you heading back to Afghanistan?"

Jake drained the last of his beer, crushed the can in his hands, and looked across the lake toward home. "I'm not." Jake's face was hard, his eyes dark as he turned to Cain. "We should head back."

The conversation was over, and Cain knew enough to let it go. "Sure. Sounds good." He cracked a smile. "It's not like we caught anything."

Several boats dotted the lake. The sun's intensity had increased in the last hour or so, and cottage country had come alive. The shoreline was dotted with a thick carpet of trees and the seasonal cottages that surrounded the public beach near the south side.

Jake turned their boat north, which was where his family's home was located. It was the premier spot on Crystal Lake, and the homes that claimed the north shoreline belonged to residents of the town who could afford to live there—which weren't many—or new money that had come to town from the city.

Cain grabbed his old worn and dog-eared Boston Bruins cap off the seat beside him and pulled it down onto his head. It looked like shit, but then, it had rested in peace, tucked away inside *Old Smoky* for years.

The ride to the Edwardses' took less than five minutes, and as they pulled up to the boathouse, he noticed a boy on the beach. A little guy with russet curls, pale skin, and bright green swim trunks. Behind him, up near the gazebo, a woman stood, hands shading her eyes as she glanced toward them, her long, dark hair drifting on the breeze.

His gut flipped and rolled like he was sixteen again, sniffing around the skirts of Shannon Graham, his first crush. He'd been pathetic then, and damn if he didn't feel a flush creep up his neck now.

Cain rubbed his jaw and let his shaded eyes drink

in the simple beauty that Maggie exuded. It was easy to do—the woman was wearing a black bikini. Not a skimpy number like the ones his ex used to favor. This one covered all the parts that should be covered, but as his gaze wandered her creamy flesh, he felt his groin tighten. Her breasts were a touch more than a handful—just what he liked—and though she was slender, her belly was softly rounded, the way a woman's should be.

But it was the bottoms that snagged his attention. *Hello*. They were boy cuts. Christ, there was nothing sexier than a woman nestled inside a pair of tight black boy shorts. She turned and spoke to Raine, and his eyes lingered on the soft swell of her ass, the length of her toned legs.

"Your little redhead sure as hell fills out a bathing suit." Mac smacked him on the back before jumping onto the dock.

Cain glared at his friend and ignored the snort Jake emitted as he leaped onto the dock and glanced toward the gazebo. Cain's gaze rested on Maggie, lingered on the miracle that was her boy shorts, and desire rushed through him, fast and hot. He clenched his teeth together tightly.

She sure as hell did.

Chapter 7

"You didn't tell me they were going to be here." Maggie tossed a towel onto one of the chaise lounge chairs and set her beach bag on the ground. She'd followed Raine to a shaded area beneath a large canopy near the beach, and they were settling in for the day.

"Who?" Raine glanced toward the boathouse and turned to Maggie. Her pale skin was translucent, paper-thin, and the smudges beneath her eyes shadowed a soft gray. Raine shrugged. "I didn't think it mattered."

Maggie turned away, rummaging through her bag for God knows what, but intent on looking busy. Occupied. Hard to do, when all she could focus on was the man who—she chanced a glance over her shoulder—was still looking in her direction. Her heart skipped a beat, and she knew she was blushing again.

Raine's eyes narrowed. "What's going on?"

"Nothing." Maggie answered too quickly, and she took a second to settle her nerves. "I just thought it was going to be a quiet afternoon, is all."

"Well, I don't think we're in for an orgy or anything, but if you want, I can check."

Maggie's head jerked up, and she laughed at the expression on Raine's face. The young widow was teasing, and it was nice to see. There hadn't been a whole lot of light moments in her life lately.

"It's fine." Maggie shook her head.

"If you say so..." Raine's gaze lingered, and the scrutiny made Maggie uncomfortable. She turned from the woman and grabbed a book from her bag along with a bottle of sunblock. It was approaching noon and already hot as sin. Sweat pooled between her breasts, and the breeze that rushed along the water whispered across her skin.

She applied a generous amount of the coconut-scented lotion and tossed it back into the bag. Michael had been greased up as soon as they arrived.

"Raine, glad you came for the day."

Maggie froze. *Cain.* His voice was low, the timbre electric, and her stomach lurched at the sound of it.

Raine smiled and glanced behind her. "I see you decided to stick around for a few days. Your mom must be thrilled."

He chuckled. "I don't know about thrilled, but it sure as hell feels good to be home. Been way too long."

"Ya think?" Raine answered drily.

Maggie felt his attention like a stroke of heat across her flesh. Goose bumps spread along her arms. "How's the head, Maggie? Your stitches giving you any problems?"

She ignored Raine's arched brow and slowly turned around. Cain stood a few feet away, his eyes hidden behind dark glasses.

The man sported a pair of black swim trunks that hung way too low on his hips. Did he do that on purpose? His chest and abs were perfection—this she already knew. She might have suffered one hell of a knock to the head, but the one clear image she remembered was of Cain. Her eyes wandered lower, to the "cut," that indent low on the hips that makes a woman's mouth water.

Wrong thing to do. Heat pooled in her belly again, this time accompanied by a sharp stab of something she didn't want to analyze. It left her flustered, and she was getting pretty damn sick of feeling off-kilter whenever Cain Black was around.

Stay above the neck.

Her face froze into a smile, or at least what was supposed to pass for a smile, and she shrugged. "I'm fine. Uh, everything is good...I...you know, slept and then my alarm...went off every couple of hours or so..."

Her cheeks darkened, and she glanced down at her toes. She sounded like a complete moron. What was it about the man that reduced her to a teenaged mess of awkwardness?

"Mom! Cain said he'd take me out on the boat later!" Michael's excited voice broke the spell.

She cleared her throat and nodded. "That's nice."

Cain removed his glasses and flashed a smile. "We can all go for a ride. The weather's perfect."

"No," she answered—a little too quickly—and winced at the note of panic in her voice. "I..." She smiled at Michael. "That's fine. You go, sweetie. Mommy wants to relax today."

Jake Edwards joined them, along with a tall, handsome blond man she recognized from the funeral. Jake's expression was subdued and somewhat aloof. Maggie's heart broke for the soldier. His loss was tattooed onto his soul, and there was no hiding his pain.

"Hey." Jake's gaze touched Raine before sliding to Maggie. "Glad you two could make it. I know my parents think a lot of you and your son."

"Thank you." She murmured. "It was nice of them to invite us for the day."

"Cain, do you want to see my fishing rod? Mom bought it for me for getting six As on my report card! I haven't tried it out yet." They all turned to Michael, and he shuffled his feet. "Actually, I've never even been fishing before, so I don't really know what to do."

Cain glanced her way, but she kept her eyes focused on Michael.

"Sure. Why don't we grab some lunch first. Did you get worms? I think we're all out." At Jake's nod, Michael's face fell.

"We didn't think about worms. Can't we just pretend?" His open smile tugged at her heartstrings.

Cain laughed. "There's no fun in pretending." He moved closer to her son and rested his hand on Michael's shoulder. It was a small gesture, but one that twisted her insides something fierce. "We'll hop in my truck after lunch and drive into town to get some bait. Sound good?"

They both looked at Maggie—Michael's face full of hope, Cain's unreadable.

"Can I, Mom?" Michael was near bursting, antsy. "I promise I'll sit in the back and everything." He looked up at Cain and whispered, "Air bags freak Mom out."

How could she say no?

"That's fine, Michael."

"Sweet!" He high-fived Cain. "I'll get my pole. I left it on the dock."

"I don't know about you guys, but I need some food." Mac turned toward the house. "Your mom make her potato salad?"

Jake shrugged. "I'm sure she did." His eyes lingered on Raine. "You coming?"

She shook head. "Maggie and I had a late breakfast."

"Did she eat?" Jake asked Maggie, his face hard. He looked like he was back in that dark place...the place he'd been when he first returned to Crystal Lake over a week ago. Gone was the lightness of the morning. Something had changed, and she shifted uncomfortably.

Truth was, Raine had barely touched her fruit salad, and Michael had finished it.

"Oh for God's sake, Jake. What are you, the food police?" Raine turned and shook out her towel. She grabbed a pile of magazines from her bag, mumbling under her breath, and flopped down onto the low-slung chaise.

Her skin was milky white, and the two-piece amber-colored suit she wore was retro—very forties in style and totally suited to her looks. With her hair piled on top of her head and the overlarge black sunglasses perched on the edge of her nose, she resembled a movie star from a long-ago era. She rapidly flipped through the pages, ignoring them as she settled into the chair.

"*Okay,* I'm gonna grab some grub," Mac said to no one in particular. Marnie and Steven were on the lower deck. The barbecue was lit, and the smell of burgers and dogs wafted on the breeze. He headed toward them.

Jake swore and followed suit, while Cain watched them, a frown replacing the smile he'd sported moments earlier.

"Is he..."

Cain's gaze swung back to her. His dark eyes were shadowed with concern.

"Is he all right?" The man's brother had just died—of course he wasn't all right. But there was something more at play, and Maggie had a feeling things were a lot more complicated than most people realized.

"No." He shook his head and looked behind her. "He's not." He exhaled and ran fingers along the back of his neck. "So you girls are good?"

Maggie nodded.

"Okay." His mouth crooked into a halfhearted, easy smile. "I'm going to grab a burger and then take Michael out on the boat. If you change your mind and wanna come with, just let me know. There's lots of room."

The last place she wanted to be right now was on a small boat with only a few feet between them.

"Thanks for taking him. He loves the water, but I just don't really have the time to get him out…between work and…" She shrugged. "Well, and the fact that I don't have a boat."

Cain smiled, a lazy, slow, seductive smile that started the old heart up but good. "Come with us," he said carefully, watching her way too intensely.

Her mouth was dry and she shook her head. "I'm… I'll," she stammered, "stay with Raine."

His grin widened.

"I have a book." She jutted her chin slightly, regaining a bit of her composure.

Cain looked down at her in silence. A breeze rippled the air between them, lifting long wisps of her hair into the wind. She tucked them behind her ear, and his gaze followed the action. Heat flushed beneath her skin as she looked up at him.

The look in his eyes set her heart beating even faster against her chest. So fast that it was uncomfortable. Electricity charged the air, and her breath hitched at the back of her throat. A vision of his mouth sliding across her neck flashed before her eyes, and she blinked rapidly in an effort to clear it from her mind.

"No problem. He's a great kid."

Cain turned, and for a few seconds Maggie stared after him, at the long, lean lines of his body. Heat curled inside her belly, and she dragged her eyes away, mad that the man was able to get under her skin so easily.

Maggie slid into the chaise beside Raine and opened her book, though the words blended into a mishmash of letters.

"So, what's going on between you two?"

"Sorry?" She turned to Raine.

"Cain? Something's going on between you two."

Maggie frowned. "I barely know the man, and from what little I can see, he's not exactly the kind of guy I'd ever consider dating." At Raine's sly grin, she said, "Not that I'm considering it or anything." Raine snorted, and Maggie's frown deepened. "With anyone, for that matter."

"Well, that's too bad." Raine flipped through her magazine. "You would be good for him, especially after his nasty divorce."

A few moments of silence stretched out long and thin, and even though she knew she should keep her mouth shut, Maggie couldn't seem to help herself.

"So what's the story with that?" she asked carefully, her eyes trained onto the book she held, though honestly, the words were a blur. "His divorce."

Raine settled into her lounger, wiggling a bit until she got comfortable. "He married Natasha Simmons. I'm sure you've heard of her; she's an actress from LA."

Natasha Simmons. That was a name she did know. An image of a tall, leggy blonde flashed in her mind. Bond girl?

"Really." She tried to sound disinterested but in fact was anything but. "So what happened?" she asked casually.

Raine sighed and closed her magazine. "I'm not sure. Cain's never really said, but you can bet it wasn't easy or clean." She grinned. "At least not according to some of the tabloid things I've read."

Something twisted inside Maggie. *Natasha Simmons*. The total opposite of everything that Maggie was. Not that she was interested or anything.

She looked over to where the boys were gathered. Lauren Black had arrived, and Cain stood beside his mother, his arm loose around her shoulder. It was obvious the two of them shared a special relationship, and he seemed so down to earth. It was hard for her to picture him with someone like the starlet he'd married.

"I've known them my whole life." Raine murmured. "The Bad Boys of Crystal Lake."

At Maggie's arched brow, Rain smiled. "That's what everyone called them after they were arrested."

"Arrested…for what?" Maggie sat straighter, more than a little interested in Raine's answer.

"That's a story for another day. Trust me, you wouldn't believe me if I told you." She smiled sadly. "They've always been more than friends, you know… more like brothers. It's good…" Her voice faltered, and a shuddering breath fell from her lips. "It's good they're together again."

Save for one, Maggie thought. God, life sucked sometimes.

Maggie settled back, the book forgotten as she watched Cain and her son. Michael chatted animatedly, his arms in the air, his whole body talking, telling a story as he held on to his fishing rod as if it was the most amazing thing in the world.

He looked up at Cain like he was some kind of god, and her chest tightened. Michael was getting much too attached to a man who'd come into their life by accident. That wasn't a good thing. Cain would leave for LA—his career pretty much demanded it—and that was probably for the best.

Cain glanced her way and smiled, his gaze lingering for so long his mother turned her way. Startled, Maggie lowered her eyes and shoved her sunglasses up onto her nose.

It would be better if he left sooner rather than later.

And not just for Michael's sake.

Chapter 8

Tuesday morning in Crystal Lake found the sun shining bright, and even though it was just past nine it the morning, the thermometer was creeping into the midseventies. Flowers were in bloom and the lake glistened as if precious gems floated on its surface.

Cain drove along Crystal Lake Road and headed toward town. His windows were down, and the fresh air, heavy with the scent of late spring, lifted his spirits as he navigated the two-mile stretch.

The lake was on his left, and the winding road was bordered on each side by colorful bands of black-eyed Susans and white daisies. In the distance, pine forests blanketed the entire area, painting the landscape a vibrant green.

It was a beautiful, picturesque kind of place and one he hadn't fully appreciated growing up. Such is the ignorance of youth.

The town had come into existence because of the flourishing lumber industry back in the 1800s. Crystal Lake was but one of many lakes and waterways that connected to the powerful Muskegon River. The Edwards family had garnered most of their wealth when the twins' ancestor Thomas Edwards, a lumberjack from the wilds of Canada, had arrived in the area with ten dollars in his pocket and a burning ambition to make a life for himself.

His hard work and keen mind had enabled him to push forward, and the Edwards Lumber Company had been born off the sweat of his brow and the blind determination in his heart. During its heyday, the lumber company had made him and a select group of individuals who'd laid down roots in Crystal Lake millions.

Those roots had taken hold with a tenacity that survived the downturn in the lumber business, and now, more than a hundred years later, the town was still home to the descendants of many of the first-wave inhabitants.

It wasn't a large town by any means, boasting a population of only four thousand souls when Cain had lived there ten years earlier. As he drove into town he noted they'd gained another thousand over the last decade—at least according to the sign on the side of the road near the old mill: Crystal Lake, Home of the Lumberjacks. Population 5,120.

He grinned as he passed the sign. Hoo-yah. Football was still king. He was glad to see that not much had changed and that those things that had changed were for the better.

He took his foot off the gas and eyed the old mill as the SUV rolled by. It was now a fancy gift shop with an adjacent pub-style restaurant. A patio filled with patrons jutted out into the water. Crystal Lake sported a tributary waterway that ran through town and dumped into the large body of water the town was named after.

Cain's gaze drifted overhead to the iron railway, and a vivid image of himself and the boys jumping off of it, just shy of the dam, brought another wistful smile to his face. It had been dangerous—stupid—but Christ, the high was one he'd never forget.

Large, stately homes from another era with huge oak trees guarding them welcomed him back, and he marveled at the feeling of déjà vu as he turned down Front

Street. It was short and ended at the water. Two young boys pounding the pavement furiously, with their skateboards and fishing poles tucked to their backs, rushed down the sidewalk to his left, swerving at the last minute as a couple of girls screeched in their direction.

They didn't break stride. They were on a mission—Michigan boys in search of water and fish.

He pulled into Lawrence's Tackle & Bait and cut the engine. The place was the last one on the street, a smallish brick building that had stood for nearly one hundred and fifty years. At one time it had been the post office, but when the downtown business district had sprung up across the bridge in the thirties, it had been taken over by the Lawrence family. It was *the* place to get bait and tackle, and over the years the family had added a variety of items to their inventory—everything from screwdrivers to shotguns.

Cain slid from his truck and grinned like a kid. Damn, but it felt good to be back.

He strode inside and took a few seconds to adjust his eyes to the dark interior. The smell of sandalwood oil, wood, bait, and fish greeted his nostrils. It was a sharp blend that hadn't changed a bit.

"Well, shit, Cain. You back already? Don't tell me you used up that bait you got on Sunday." Daniel Lawrence—a.k.a. Old Man Lawrence—moved from behind the counter. He'd been old for as long as Cain could remember, and though his gait was a bit slower than a decade earlier, he was still spry for a man in his mideighties.

Cain shook Mr. Lawrence's hand and nodded. "Yeah, and we didn't catch squat." Cain moved to the display of lures. "I think I need to invest in some new tackle."

Mr. Lawrence guffawed. "You lose your touch, Hollywood?"

Cain grinned. He hadn't been called that in years. "Naw, I think the fish have gotten smarter, is all."

The old man's faded eyes softened, his once-tall body slightly bent as he shuffled closer. "It's good to have you back, son. You been gone too long. This town takes care of its own, and eventually most who leave find their way back."

Cain glanced toward the colorful fishing lures, more than a little unnerved at the intensity behind those faded eyes.

"You take your time there. I'll grab you some bait."

Cain watched him shuffle down the narrow aisle and then proceeded to pick out several lures, including some new ones for Michael. He grinned as he thought of the boy. They'd had shit luck Sunday afternoon and had caught a few sunfish, which they'd thrown back in the water. Cain wasn't so sure if it was because the fish weren't biting or if he was just too distracted by thoughts of the boy's mother to concentrate on fishing.

He'd promised to take Michael out again tomorrow and wanted to make sure they were outfitted properly. The gear Cain had left behind at the boathouse—his tackle from years ago—was sad, and it was time for new.

"Here you go." Old Man Lawrence tossed a large container onto the counter and nodded at the lures in Cain's hands. "Good choice." His brow creased. "Why so many?"

Cain placed the tackle on the counter. "I'm taking a friend's son out for the day tomorrow."

"Uh-huh." The elderly gentleman pushed round

glasses up his nose and quickly packed the lures into a paper bag. "The O'Rourke woman's boy."

Cain wasn't surprised. Gossip and innuendo traveled faster than a speeding bullet in this town. That was something that was never going to change. "Yes, Maggie's son, Michael."

"She keeps to herself but makes it out to church service once in a blue moon. I guess she can't be all that bad." Mr. Lawrence peeked over his specs, his watery blue eyes narrowed thoughtfully. "A woman alone is a dangerous thing, especially one as pretty as that O'Rourke lady." The old man nodded, his expression serious. "Plus, she's got that dark red hair, and that can't be good."

Cain tried his best to keep the smile from his face. "How so?" He handed over some cash and waited while Mr. Lawrence's gnarled fingers navigated a cash register that was older than Cain.

"Well, son…" Cain held out his hand to accept the change that was placed into his waiting fingers. "She's either hiding something, or that red hair has made her unmanageable."

"Unmanageable?" What the hell was Maggie? A horse?

"This is the truth. Don't you know what they say about redheads?"

Cain was almost afraid to ask.

Old Man Lawrence lowered his voice. "They've got the fire of a witch inside them and can be one of two things."

Cain grabbed his bait. He couldn't wait to hear what his choices were.

"She can be the greatest pleasure you'll ever encounter, or…"

Cain struggled to hide a grin.

"She'll be the death of you…bad luck."

"Bullshit." He shivered as the damp air of the store rolled over his shoulders, and opened his mouth but closed it again.

The elderly gentlemen looked so serious that for a moment Cain didn't know quite what to say. All of a sudden Mr. Lawrence's face crinkled and he guffawed loudly, slapping his hand onto the counter as laughter rolled out of his mouth.

"I'm just teasing, son, though no one really knows much about this Maggie. She could be a serial killer for all we know…like a black widow."

The man had been watching way too many thrillers. Cain shook his head and smiled. "Take it easy, Mr. Lawrence, and give my best to your wife."

"I will. And Cain?"

"Yeah?" He paused in the doorway.

"Sure is good to have you boys back here."

He nodded but said nothing as he cleared his throat. He had a feeling he needed this town more than they needed him, but that was a secret he'd keep to himself.

Cain slid into this truck.

In the meantime, he planned on getting to know Maggie O'Rourke a whole lot better than anyone else in Crystal Lake. He slipped the SUV into gear and cranked the tunes, grinning as "Summer Nights," an old Van Halen song, erupted into the quiet.

Hell, yeah.

"Summer nights and my radio…"

And a girl with dark red hair.

Chapter 9

"Mom, is he here yet?" Michael's excited whisper penetrated Maggie's early-morning fog. It was Wednesday morning, just after five a.m., and she stifled a yawn as she took a sip from her second cup of coffee.

"He said five fifteen, sweetie. I'm sure he'll be here soon."

She glanced out the window into the dark. Whispers of fog crept along the road, ribbons of smoke that shimmered from the streetlight down the way. Cain was taking Michael fishing as promised, and apparently the best time happened to be at this godforsaken hour.

She'd been surprised when Cain called Tuesday evening to remind her he'd be by at the crack of dawn to take Michael out on the lake. It was another shot for her son to try the whole fishing thing, since Sunday afternoon had been a bust—they'd caught nothing. Obviously the man had meant what he said. Maggie had secretly hoped he was just being polite.

She'd wanted to say no, but couldn't come up with a reason good enough to do so. She wasn't about to ruin what would be a memorable day for her son because Cain Black made her uncomfortable. That was her problem to deal with.

Besides, he'd be leaving Crystal Lake soon enough, and with his departure, the enigmatic complication that was Cain Black would be gone.

Twin beams of light cut through the dark, and Michael jumped up and down. “He’s here!”

Her son clutched his pole, and Maggie tugged the edges of her robe together, suddenly conscious of the fact she was still in her jammies. The plain cotton robe fell to just above her knee, and Lord knows it covered more than her bikini did, but still.

Her hair was piled loosely on top of her head. She tucked an errant strand behind her ear and shuffled nervously, her bare feet cold on the worn hardwood.

A soft knock at the door startled her, which was ridiculous, considering she knew he was out there. With a dry mouth, she carefully unlocked three heavy-duty dead bolts and was able to jump out of the way before Michael yanked it open.

Cain’s eyes found hers immediately, and that familiar feeling—the one she’d grown to resent—hit her in the belly. It twisted and electrified her insides in such a way that it was hard to breathe. Heat crept along her skin, cajoling goose bumps from her flesh as the early-morning air slithered across her bare legs.

“Morning, Maggie.” His voice was low, warm, and her name rolled off his lips in an easy drawl.

He was dressed in an old pair of jeans and a white T-shirt with the Rolling Stones logo emblazoned onto the front. It was as faded and worn as his jeans, which fit every inch of his long legs like a glove.

His jaw was shadowed with day old stubble and he smiled, a lazy lift to his mouth, as he ran his fingers through the mess of hair atop his head. The edges of his shirt lifted, exposing a large expanse of his toned lower belly, and of course her eyes went *there*. To that delicious male "cut" that only served to emphasize his hips and abs.

Did he practice that maneuver? Was there anywhere else to look?

She dragged her eyes away and cleared her throat. His warm brown eyes were hooded, and he looked like he'd rolled out of bed minutes earlier. His smile widened even more, and her lips tightened in reaction. Cain Black was working it, but she wasn't in the mood to play.

"I've packed enough food for the both of you. Extra sandwiches, snacks, soda, and I tossed in a couple bottles of water."

"Did you put in my Snickers bar?" Michael asked hopefully.

Maggie rumpled his curls, kissed the top of his head, and nodded.

Michael glanced up at Cain. "We only have one, but I'll share, okay?"

Cain chuckled. "All right, but I warn you, Snickers are my favorite."

"Me too! I'd eat them every day, 'cept Mom says too much sugar isn't good for your teeth."

Cain winked. "Well, your mom would be right." He paused. "Is that your gear?"

Michael nodded and grabbed his small plastic tackle box and fishing pole.

"All right, buddy, we should head out."

"Sweet!" Michael ran past Maggie and was out the door, not one look back or kiss good-bye. Nothing.

"Make sure you call Mommy on her cell if—"

He'd already disappeared inside Cain's truck.

"—something happens," she finished lamely.

"Don't worry, he'll be fine. Trust me. I grew up on this lake."

Resentment flushed her body with a hot wave of heat as she met Cain's gaze once more. His eyes were dark, intense, and she flinched when his hand reached for her, but she refused to move away.

Maybe she didn't want to.

Cain paused, his eyes not wavering, and her tummy twirled crazily, as if hundreds of butterflies were having a party. Gently he pushed away the curtain of hair that had fallen from her ponytail, near her temple.

Her heart thrummed against her chest as his fingers grazed the bruise from her fall. His touch was soft, and an ache erupted inside as he caressed her there. It had been so long since anyone had touched her in that way. *Years*.

"Your stitches are looking good. I don't think there'll be a scar." The timbre of his voice had changed, an added depth that coated his words in silk. She swallowed and nodded, unable to answer.

His eyes lowered and settled on her mouth. The air around them thickened—it must have—because all of a sudden she couldn't breathe. She heard the catch in his breath as he exhaled and wondered if his heart was beating as fast and furious as her own.

Heat suffused her cheeks, but she couldn't tear her eyes from his mouth.

"So, the deal is…"

"What?" She glanced up into his eyes. "Deal?"

Was that her voice? All whispery and Marilyn Monroeish?

He smiled again, a slow, devastating grin, and for the

first time she noticed a tiny dimple near the corner of his mouth. His eyes glittered like liquid glass. "You got a grill?"

"You mean a barbecue?" she asked firmly. Good, Marilyn had left the building.

At his nod, she answered, "Yes."

"Great. Your son and I will provide the fish for dinner, you look after the fixings."

She opened her mouth, an automatic protest riding her tongue, but instead of making up some excuse, as she should have, Maggie found herself agreeing. "All right."

Cain paused, and she thought that maybe he was surprised. "Okay." He glanced toward his truck. "I should go." He took a step back and shrugged, his even, white teeth a flash in the dark. "Michael's waiting, but, uh, I'll see you later."

Maggie closed the door and leaned against it, her hand on her heart as she settled her nerves. She watched the beams of light from his truck creep across her walls as Cain reversed out of the driveway and headed toward the lake. She stared at Michael's Chicago Blackhawks cap. It lay on the floor. She picked it up, fingered the logo, and held it close to her chest before heading toward his room.

She'd just agreed to dinner with Cain. What the hell was up with that? A smile touched her lips, and her steps were light as she headed toward Michael's room. She wouldn't think about it. Wouldn't overanalyze what it meant, because it meant nothing.

It was just dinner, a special thank-you for taking Michael fishing.

Maggie disappeared into her son's room. It was time to make beds and get ready for her day.

On Wednesdays Maggie only had one client, Mr. Jackson, an elderly widower who lived on her street. He was a sweet man, and she knew he looked forward to her visits not only because he needed his house cleaned, but because he was lonely. His only child, a son, lived in the city, well over two hours away, and he no longer drove beyond Crystal Lake's town limits.

Mr. Jackson was a weekly client, so the house was kept up—an easy clean—but she still spent longer than necessary with him. He followed her around and chatted, and truth be told, Maggie enjoyed his company as much as he did hers. He regaled her with stories from his past, a time when he'd grown up on a large farm near the Canadian border. He was funny, witty, and a total charmer.

It was nearly one thirty when she finished, but Maggie still had time to run a few errands and be home before three o'clock. She'd decided a fresh garden salad would be perfect with whatever kind of fish the boys brought home for supper and at the last minute decided to make sweet potato pie—Michael's favorite.

By the time the fresh vegetables were washed and prepped and dessert was cooling from the oven, it was nearly five thirty. Maggie glanced out the window. Did she chance a shower?

A quick sniff under her arms had her shuddering. Hell yes.

Maggie crossed to the door and stared at the dead

bolts for a few seconds before peeking outside. Her neighbor Luke was on his front lawn, cell phone in his hand and his dog running madly around him. Sounds of children playing down the street could be heard. She hesitated. Bit her lip. Then quickly released all the dead bolts and unlocked the door. Michael had left without his key, and she didn't want him waiting on the porch if they returned while she was in the shower.

Maggie slipped into her room, where she spent an extra five minutes trying to decide what to wear. In the end, she pulled a pair of black three-quarter-length capris and a moss-green tank top from her closet, tossed them onto the bed, and hopped into the shower.

It was the fastest shower she'd ever had. For one thing, she hated that the front door was unlocked, and for another, images of Cain bursting into her room and finding her alone in the shower kept flashing through her brain.

Of course that would never happen, but still, the thought was enough to get her butt out in record time.

She dressed, combed out her long hair, and searched the top of her dresser for some mascara. She seemed to remember a tube lying around. She found it, had trouble unscrewing it, and when she pulled out the wand, she made a face and tossed the entire thing into the garbage. It was like cement. It *had* been that long since she made any kind of effort with her appearance.

Whatever. She was being silly anyway. She wasn't out to impress Cain Black.

Maggie busied herself in the kitchen, and it was approaching six thirty when she heard the sound of a motor in the driveway. She smoothed her hair, slowed her steps—didn't want to appear too anxious—and opened the door. Cain stood at the foot of her porch, Michael's wild curls nestled in the crook of his arm.

Her son looked like an angel—an exhausted one, for sure. His small chest rose and fell as he slumbered.

She moved aside and let them pass. Cain's hair was nearly as wild as her son's, and a smile tugged at her mouth as she closed the door behind them.

"He fell asleep on the boat," Cain whispered softly. "He didn't move at all on the ride home."

"I think maybe we should just put him in his bed." Maggie flicked the curl that fell against Michael's forehead. His long lashes swept low against his cheek, and his breaths fell in long, deep exhales. She was pretty sure he'd be out for the night. "It's this way."

Maggie led the way toward Michael's room and watched as Cain carefully laid her son on his bed. She couldn't lie. It was bittersweet, watching the man treat her son like a treasure. It was something his father had never done.

Cain doffed Michael's shoes and tossed them before grabbing the afghan that lay at the foot of the bed. He draped it across Michael's small form and stood back, staring down at him for a few moments.

His cell phone went off at that moment and he cursed, tossing a *sorry* Maggie's way before striding past her.

She closed the door to Michael's room and followed Cain into her living room. His back was toward her and he was talking rapidly into the phone, though his words were muted and she had no clue whom he was talking to or what it was about.

He slipped the phone into his pocket and turned. His

dark eyes were serious, his mouth set tightly, and Maggie got the feeling that his mood had just done a complete 360.

"Is everything all right?" she asked finally.

"It's good." Cain exhaled and rolled his shoulders. "Sorry we're so late. We just kinda lost track of time."

"Oh, don't apologize. I'm sure Michael had a great day." She shrugged. "Beats cleaning houses with Mom."

Silence fell between them. She heard the ticking of the clock from the kitchen, the slow, steady beat of it getting louder and louder as Cain stared at her, his expression unreadable.

"I gotta..." he began, and he swore under his breath as he shook his head. "I gotta go, Maggie. I got this thing...to take care of, and I..."

"Oh." She nodded quickly, swallowing a lump of disappointment as she moved to the door. "Of course, don't worry about it. Michael's out for the evening anyway, so..."

"I hope you didn't go to any trouble."

"No, not at all." She shook her head and glanced away. "I didn't really have time to do much." She shrugged. "Don't worry about it."

He was there, inches from her, his crisp, male scent teasing her nostrils as he took another step closer. He hesitated, but she kept her gaze lowered and moved aside. "I'm tired myself, so..."

"We'll do this again, okay?" His voice was gentle, cajoling, and for some reason that pissed her off.

She remained silent but nodded.

An awkward moment passed, and then Cain walked through the door and was down her front steps faster than a wino downing a bottle of booze.

He ran to his SUV and yanked the door open, grabbing for his cell again as he did so. He looked up as if it were an afterthought and crooked his head. "I'll be in touch." His phone was buzzing in loud, rapid bursts, and he hopped into the truck before she had time to answer.

Maggie closed the door, not sure what the hell had just happened. A shiver rolled over her arms and she wrapped them around her midsection, squeezing what bit of warmth she could before heading to the kitchen. She was suddenly cold, which was odd, considering the temperature was still in the high seventies.

The slow ticktock of the clock grated on her nerves. She glanced up at it and frowned. It was so...ominous. A sliver of sadness rippled through her, and she angrily shoved it aside. What was the point? And why did she care so much?

She sighed and crossed to the small table that had been set for three and stared down at the place settings. What an idiot. She'd even folded purple napkins into hats.

On the counter beside the dessert that had long cooled stood a bottle of white wine—an impulse purchase. She considered pouring herself a glass but carefully corked it instead and then cleared the dishes before tossing her now-limp salad into the trash.

Her appetite was long gone.

She turned out the light and stood in the early-evening shadows, lost in the silence that was her life.

Chapter 10

CAIN PULLED INTO THE PARKING LOT BEHIND THE COACH House, Crystal Lake's only bar that featured entertainment, and not the dancing kind either. Sal was too classy to have girls in there during the day, strutting their stuff, even though, surely, he'd make a killing. The Coach House was a large, rambling building on the edge of town that had absolutely nothing to do with its name. There was no coach and there was no house. There was only brick, mortar, and an aging expanse of blacktop. It had been a dive years ago, and as he glanced around he noted it hadn't changed at all.

He ran his hand across the roughness of his chin, thinking the five-o'clock-shadow look was getting old.

The Coach House had been the local watering hole they—the Edwards twins, himself, and Mac Draper—had claimed as a home base of sorts. It had an unlimited supply of booze, was sketchy enough that the atmosphere rocked, and most importantly, had live entertainment every weekend.

This was where Cain had honed his skills, both as a guitarist and a performer. It was the site of his first-ever live gig, the first place he'd gotten drunk, and the place where he'd lost his virginity to Shelli Gouthro. It had been a quick and amorous act performed behind the big oak tree on the far side of the parking lot.

He scratched his chin. It had been a hot summer night not unlike this one.

Christ, it seemed a lifetime ago.

He slid from the truck and stood for a few moments as his mind wandered to Maggie and the evening that could have been. Damn, he'd looked forward to spending the night with her.

His cell phone vibrated, shaking him from his thoughts, but he ignored it and made his way to the entrance. He knew who was on the line and quickly disappeared inside the bar, wondering how bad things were.

It was dark, but the smell of grease and beer hit him in the gut with all the subtlety of a brick wall. Cain could have been blind and deaf or half-asleep, yet he'd know where the hell he was. His mouth watered at the thought of a cold beer, burger, and fries. It was hours since he'd eaten.

"Cain Black! Holy shit, it's been a while."

He turned and shook the enthusiastic hand offered to him by Salvatore Nuno, owner of the Coach House. The man's head was as bald as he remembered, though his belly had grown…a lot. The jovial glint in his eye and the warmth that was reflected in his voice, however, was the same.

"It's good to be home, Sal."

The man's smile fled as he nodded toward the back of the bar. The place was half-full, a bit of a dinner crowd before the band took to the stage in a few hours.

"He's back there."

Cain's eyes narrowed, but he couldn't see shit. The dark corners were impenetrable, had always been, which was why they'd generally ended up hidden among the shadows. Old habits die hard.

"I'll bring you a cold one and some food, no?"

"Thanks, that sounds great." He patted Sal on the back and moved past him. Whispers followed in his wake, eyes clung to his back, as he threaded a path through the chaotic mess of tables that really had no rhyme or reason. Somehow it all worked.

By now his eyes had adjusted somewhat, and his mouth tensed as he made his way over to the last booth. Jake glanced up, and Cain slid in across from him.

"Sorry to tear you away from the little redhead." Jake's tone was teasing, but Cain ignored him, his eyes settling on the prone body next to him. Mac's head rested on his arms, though he faced the wall and Cain couldn't see shit.

"How is he?"

Jake took a long drink from his beer and carefully set the now-empty bottle on the table. He stared down at his hands and shook his head. "Not good. Though from what I hear, his father looks way worse."

"He got into it with Ben?" Cain grimaced. "He should have gone back to New York on Monday like he'd planned."

Jake winced. "No kidding, but he wanted to see his mother one more time. I guess his dad came home unexpectedly, and that's when all hell broke loose. The cops were called in, but Nick… You remember the running back from our team? Nick Torrent?"

An image of a large teenager with bad skin and an even badder attitude tugged his memory. The guy had been built like a Mack truck.

At Cain's nod, Jake continued. "Well, he was called to the scene, and Mackenzie convinced Torrent to bring him here instead of the hotel he's been staying at." Jake frowned. "That was around noon, and from what I can tell, he proceeded to get loaded until he passed out. Sal called me an hour ago."

Sal set a beer on the table in front of Cain. "Food's on its way." The bar owner's gaze rested on Mac. "His old man is the worst kind of bastard there is. I don't understand why Lila won't leave him. The kids have been gone for years."

Mac groaned and turned toward them. His eyes were still closed, but Cain saw that the right one was nearly swollen shut. Cuts and bruises marred his buddy's face, and he looked more like a prizefighter than an architect. Cain shook his head. The man was about as far away from Armani as you could get.

Seems the sins of the father weren't something Mac could outrun.

Cain took another swig from his bottle and glanced around. Equipment was set up on the stage—classic Marshall stacks, a Pearl drum kit, and three microphone stands. It was bare-bones, but seriously, all you needed.

"Who's playing?" He felt the itch deep down and eyed the stage with a hunger that surprised him, considering he'd just come off a ten-month tour.

"Don't know the name, but from what Sal said, a local band of pimply faced teenagers. Country rock maybe?" Jake shrugged, a smile crossing his face. "You wanna play?"

Cain finished his beer and slid back in his chair. He couldn't deny the thrill that shot through him at the thought. "Nah, I'd hate to intrude on their night."

"Intrude? Hell, if you got up there and played a song or two, they'd probably crap their pants, which is something they'd gladly do in order to brag that they shared a stage with the dude from BlackRock."

Sal brought over a plate filled to the brim with a large burger and fries—total heart attack on a plate—and Cain dug in hungrily while Jake ordered a couple more beers. What the hell, he was on vacation. Sort of.

"So, how did it go with the kid? You guys have better luck than we did?"

Cain nodded, swallowed, and washed down his food with a large gulp of cold brew. "It was good. We caught a full bucket of perch." He smiled. "For a little guy, he has stamina. Lasted nearly the entire day out on the water."

"Yeah, and his mother looks great in a bikini."

The rough voice came from nowhere, and they both looked at Mac in surprise. The entire right side of his face was swollen, while his chin was a mess of purple and black. Dried blood coated the corners of his mouth and crusted near his nose.

He stretched out his arm and groaned, then cursed when his frown caused even more pain. "I feel like shit," he announced to no one in particular.

Jake cocked his head and laughed. "Sorry to say, buddy, but you look even worse."

Mac leaned back into the corner of the booth and scowled at them. "I need a drink."

Cain arched his eyebrow and grinned at Jake as he motioned toward Mac. "You sure you want to go down that road?"

"Hell, yeah." Mac signaled to Sal. "I'm still drunk, so the way I see it, the only direction is up."

"That makes no sense whatsoever." Jake snorted and called for the bartender too. "But I think I'd like to go wherever the hell you're headed." He grinned at Cain. "When was the last time we got out of hand?"

"Hell if I know. It's been so long, I don't remember."

Mac leaned forward, his face dead serious. "It's time to make some new memories, my friends."

Salvatore came over with some cold ones, a look they knew all too well on his face—a cross between fear and trepidation, with a bit of anxiety tossed in for the ride.

"Now boys," he began as he set the beers on the table.

They echoed his words in perfect harmony but weren't able to coax a smile from the round Italian.

Sal cleared his throat and stood, arms crossed, eyebrows furled. "Let's not have a repeat of the last time you were together, all right?"

"Last time?" Jake glanced at Mac, and the two of them burst into laughter. It took a few seconds for the fog to lift, and when it did, Cain threw his head back and joined in. The memory wasn't exactly clear, but he did recall Jesse and Jake riding into the bar on the back of a black-and-white Holstein cow.

"I'm serious now. If I think things are going south, your butts are outta here." He turned to Cain. "I don't care that you're all Hollywood these days."

"Don't worry 'bout us, Sal." Jake winked. "We'll make sure to clean up any mess we leave behind."

Sal's eyes narrowed, though the ghost of a smile lifted the corners of his mouth. "Sure you will...but I swear, if I step into anything that remotely resembles a flaming pile of shit..." Sal shook his head and muttered all the way back to the bar.

The three of them sat in silence for a few moments,

each lost in a memory that was both comical and bittersweet. Cain shoved his empty plate away and grabbed his drink.

He stared at Mac, marveled at the mess that was his face, and lifted his beer in salute. Blood wasn't everything. He and Mac knew that better than most. As far as Cain was concerned, these two men were his family, and it felt damn good to be home again. Jake followed suit, and then Mac.

"To Jesse," Jake said softly. "May there be lots of beer, whiskey, Holsteins, and a big-ass pile of shit wherever the hell he is."

They emptied their bottles and ordered another round.

The sound of a drop D slid through the night and drew Cain's attention. It was a heavy note, an aggressive punch that signaled the band was definitely not country music. As always, it electrified him—the sound of a guitar—and his body thrummed with energy.

The band was on stage, setting up their guitars, making sure their mikes were in place, and generally doing a last check before showtime. A large mountain of a man had slid in behind the sound board set up behind the dance floor, and they did a quick sound check—nothing intense, just enough to get the levels right.

The band was a young bunch—Shady Aces, the banner behind them said. They were decked out in skinny jeans that hung halfway down their asses, a look Cain just didn't get. Who the hell walked around with their boxers on display? Their hair was greased up something good, their ears and faces covered in piercings and their arms adorned with tattoos. Total badass.

Their cocky attitude and arrogance fit the whole rock

thing, but he knew from experience all the posturing in the world wouldn't help if the talent wasn't there.

Cain watched from the shadows, enjoying his relative anonymity and the easy comfort of Mac and Jake. Five minutes later, when the band struck the first note of a raunchy, rocking blues tune, he was right there with them and down for the ride.

The kids had talent, and as their set progressed, their confidence grew, and it was reflected in the music. They played a good forty-five-minute set, and when it was over, the furtive glances in his direction told Cain they knew he was in the club.

He walked over to the boys, wanting to let them know how much he'd enjoyed their performance, and twenty minutes later found him onstage, a beat-up Fender slung across his chest and a grin that spread ear to ear on his face.

This was where he belonged.

He struck a chord, a bluesy, hard-rocking note that rang out into the crowd. It took everything the boys had to keep up to him. Cain was a pro. He'd been around the block more than once, and when he played his music, it was like an extension of his very soul. He knew how to work the crowd, and his larger-than-life personality took over the stage. There was no one else up there but him.

He caressed and cajoled runs, pulled heavy vibratos from the strings like all the legends before him. He was a mix of Hendrix and Van Halen and Stevie Ray. His whiskey-soaked voice soared and then came back to earth with the subtle nuances that only he could do. It was obvious to everyone the boy belonged onstage.

Cain and Shady Aces played for hours, and by the

end of the night, the Coach House was standing-room only. The news had spread via cell phones and text messages, and a lot of old familiar faces showed up.

The high was one that never got old, and later, much later, he and the boys continued to bond over a bottle of Jack Daniel's. Or two. They'd moved from beer to the hard stuff with ease, and Cain knew he'd pay the price.

Which he did.

Raine made sure of it

He woke up with harsh light sliding across his face and rolled over, groaning as his head thwacked against the wall. His mouth felt like it was full of cotton, and his cranium wanted to explode.

Shit, how many bottles of JD had they finished?

"You guys up yet? I have to head into the city, so if you want a lift to your truck, now would be a good time." Raine stared down at him, and he saw the lack of concern right away. She so didn't care that he felt like crap.

"How did we get here?" He was on a futon, fully dressed...hell, his boots were still on his feet. His mind was fuzzy, and a groan from across the room drew his attention. He propped himself up on his elbows and spied Mac sprawled out across a sofa.

"You boys called me to come get you last night, though I'm not surprised you don't remember. I brought you back here, because I sure as hell didn't want your mother to deal with two drunken losers at three in the morning."

Two?

Cain sat up, stifled a groan as he glanced around the room. "Where's Jake?"

"He didn't want to stay here and didn't want a ride either." Her voice held a slight tremble, but she thrust her chin and glared at him. "Jake doesn't seem to want to have anything to do with me since the funeral. Actually, he's been a complete ass for a long time now, way before Jesse…" Her voice trailed off and she shook her head. "I'm getting fed up with his attitude."

Cain didn't know what to say, so he kept quiet.

"Do you know what's up with him? 'Cause I don't think this has anything to do with Jesse."

It has everything to do with Jesse. And you. And Jake.

"Jesus Christ, Cain, what the hell happened last night?" Mac staggered to his feet, effectively cutting into an awkward conversation, and Cain winced at the sight of his beat-up face. It looked much worse this morning—the swelling and mottled bruising was harsh in the early-morning light. He could only imagine what it felt like, considering Mac's head must be pounding as badly as his.

"I have no clue what happened to your face, Mackenzie, but the alcohol didn't help." Raine shook her head in disgust. "What did you do? Get all jacked up and pick a fight with someone bigger than you?"

"Nope." Mac smiled at her, though his eyes remained frosty. He pointed to his face. "This would be courtesy of my father."

Shocked silence fell on the room, and Raine glanced down at Cain. "Dammit, Mac, I'm sorry. I didn't know."

"Don't worry about it." Mac winced as he stretched his arms. "I'm sure I look like absolute shit, but Ben's hurting worse than I am. At least I hope he is."

Cain looked at the ground and exhaled. Somehow he doubted that. Mac was in pain, and it had been building inside him for years, layer upon layer. It's just that his scars, the deep ones that mattered, lay beneath his flesh, hidden from view.

"Well, guys, I have an appointment I can't miss, so if you want a ride..."

Cain stood and nodded. "Sounds good, and thanks for coming to the rescue, Raine."

Her eyes never left Mac. "No problem." She turned then, her eyes questioning. "So, Sal was saying you're doing the big benefit concert over the long weekend?"

Cain stopped dead in his tracks. "What?"

She laughed, her glee echoing into the silent house. "The football field is in dire need of a redo complete with a new stadium, so they've organized a big event on the Fourth of July. Salvatore said you agreed to headline."

Christ, he must have really tied one on the night before.

"I can't..." he began, and then stopped. Why couldn't he? He was in no rush to get back to LA.

"I'm thinking about hanging around for a few weeks."

Cain turned to Mac in surprise. "How's that gonna work with your job?"

"That's the beauty of computers, my friend. I can work from remote locations and get my stuff done." He shrugged. "Truth is, my load is light this summer, and I haven't had a proper vacation in years. I've got weeks coming to me. I might take them now." His eyes narrowed. "See if I can't convince Mom to leave, maybe come back to New York with me."

"The Booker's cottage is for rent," Raine offered. "You know, if you were serious."

Mac looked at Cain, and a grin split wide across his sorry-ass face. "You in?"

Maggie crossed his mind just then, and that familiar tightening in his chest followed suit. He was in no hurry to leave, but renting a cottage? Hell, he hadn't thought that far ahead, but if he stayed...the possibilities were endless.

Maggie O'Rourke just might be the distraction he needed.

A smile split his face, though it was followed by a wince as pain radiated along his skull. He didn't hesitate.

"Hell, yeah."

Chapter 11

MAGGIE ENTERED LAUREN'S HOME WITH SOME trepidation. She assumed Cain was gone—his truck wasn't in the driveway—but still she was wary. The thought of running into him wasn't one that pleased her.

It was early Friday, just before noon, and God help her, but she'd thought of nothing but him since Wednesday evening. It wasn't all good either. She didn't know what stung more, the fact he'd ditched her so easily or that she'd been obsessing about it like a fifteen-year-old. She'd been riled up ever since and filled with a truck-load of emotion.

She'd cut off *those* kinds of feelings so long ago that at first she didn't know what the heck they were until it hit her. She'd *wanted* to spend the evening with him. Not because he'd taken her son out and treated him to a day on the lake. Not because he was easy on the eyes and had a killer smile. She wouldn't even go near the six-pack of abs he sported. It was more than that.

Maggie liked the way he made her feel. She liked how his eyes darkened to a deeper shade of chocolate when he looked at her. It made her belly curl with heat, and that was something she hadn't felt in a very long time.

Of course she realized nothing would come of it. Musicians, especially rock musicians, didn't mix with women and children. Everyone knew that, right? But still, for those few moments when her body reacted in that way—hot, filled with awakening need—she knew that she was still alive. She knew that somewhere, buried beneath the layers of pain, hurt, and betrayal, there was a part of her that thrived, a little bit of the old Maggie.

And it felt wonderful. It gave her hope.

Maggie issued a soft hello, but there was no answer. The house was silent, empty. On Fridays, Lauren volunteered at Shady Oaks, the retirement home near the lake, so depending on what time Maggie arrived, there was a pretty good chance she wouldn't see her.

If you see Cain, tell him I said hey, and can you please remind him he promised to show me how to clean those fishes?

Michael's excited chatter rolled around her head as she busied herself putting away the fresh linens Lauren had left for her. Her son had slept the entire night after Cain brought him back and hadn't stirred from his bed until nearly eight the next morning. Since he was a boy who was up with the birds most days, she knew he'd been exhausted.

She smiled. Exhausted, yes, but in a good way, and as soon as he'd woken, it was nonstop chatter.

She'd heard every minute detail of his day with Cain. About how he'd taken Michael out on the lake to a "secret" fishing hole he used to go to as a little boy.

It was a secluded stream where the fishing was particularly good.

It was the most awesome place he'd ever been.

Cain was one of the coolest dudes he'd ever met in his whole entire life.

Even cooler than Tommy's dad, who was a sports broadcaster in Detroit.

Her smile faded as she crept down the stairs that led to the basement. It was damp, as basements are, and she rubbed her arms rapidly, trying to spark a bit of warmth in her blood.

Lauren had left a note indicating she didn't need to clean downstairs, but she had towels to put away.

Maggie crossed to the small office, the scene of the crime, so to speak, and knocked rapidly—just in case. There was no answer.

She opened the door and was hit by the scent of pine cleaner, an intense odor that tingled her nose sharply. She flipped on the light, and her eyes swept over the newly cleaned carpets. They looked brand new. There was no blood, no evidence of her unfortunate header into the corner of the desk.

The room was tidy, nothing out of place. There was no luggage, no clothes or personal items that spoke of a guest. There was…nothing.

She'd already been upstairs and knew the guest rooms hadn't been used. Cain must have left for LA after all without so much as a good-bye. Michael would be disappointed, but he would get over it and as far as she was concerned, it was probably for the best.

Maggie crossed to the bathroom and stowed the towels on the shelves and paused, her fingers trailing along the soft blue material as she glanced around. She caught a whiff of *him*—a subtle caress of his scent that lingered in the air.

She whirled around, but there was no one there. Maggie swore under her breath and turned out the light. *Get your head out of the clouds*. She still had the kitchen to deal with, and if she didn't get a move on, Michael would get home before she did. His friend Tommy was back from sleepover camp, and Michael had been invited to Tommy's house for the afternoon.

The computer monitor on the desk flickered, and she glanced at it as she walked past. Her hand reached for the door, but then a thought popped into her head, one that had her turning back toward the desk.

No, you don't need to torture yourself.

But what was the point of common sense if you couldn't ignore it?

Before Maggie could stop herself, she'd crossed the room and stared down at the computer screen. She didn't have one at home—she just couldn't afford the extra cost of Internet and all that went with a computer. Michael hadn't complained, and quite frankly, if he needed to work on one they went to the library.

She tapped the mouse, and the screen flickered once more before the Google home page appeared. Maggie bit her lip and glanced over her shoulder like a four-year-old about to put her hand in the cookie jar—for the tenth time. What the hell was she doing? She exhaled and before she could change her mind clicked on Images and typed "Cain Black BlackRock."

The monitor flooded with pictures of the band—studio shots and live ones as well. One stood out. An image of Cain. He was shirtless—skin glistening and sweat soaked—a guitar in his hands and jeans impossibly low. Maggie clicked, and the photo filled the screen.

Her cheeks flushed fast and hard as if a shot of fire had erupted across them. Her heart leaped in her chest, beating against her rib cage in quick, heavy falls. That a picture could get such a reaction from her was startling, but nevertheless it had.

The shot was incredible. Cain's eyes were closed, his fingers spread out along the fret board. The tattoo on his forearm was sexy. It lent an allusion to danger, and for some reason she liked that. Behind him, blues and purples lit his body in an eerie glow as mist curled around his legs. It was beautiful, fantastical, and yet it was his face that riveted her attention.

He looked like he was in ecstasy. As if everything he'd ever wanted was in the gold-top instrument that he was making love to.

She studied the angles of his face, the strong jaw and incredible lips. His hair was wet, curled across his brow, and hung in wild waves around his face. It wasn't fair. That so much masculine beauty was packaged into one man.

Maggie's palms were damp, and she swept them across the front of her T-shirt before clicking on more photos. A thought struck. She refreshed Google Images and typed "Cain Black Natasha Simmons."

There were a ton of Cain and his wife, or rather ex-wife, Natasha, intimate moments stolen from public events and even more from his everyday life. At the grocery store, Starbucks, walking along the sidewalk, and kissing her neck as they ate dinner at a café.

They made her uncomfortable, and she closed the image window, heart in her mouth as she searched articles.

Page after page loaded of items related to Cain Black, his music, his women, and his purported wild sex life. Something about Barcelona popped up, but Maggie had no desire to read about his sexcapades with some beautiful Spanish model or socialite. One article claimed he'd been engaged to a relative of the queen. Maggie clicked on it and several pop-ups filled the screen, all of them images of Cain shirtless, sweaty—sexy as all hell. Every time she tried to close one, another would appear.

"Shit." She bent over, and panic hit her in the chest as she clicked in rapid succession, but nothing happened. At this point there were at least seven windows open.

"You've got to be kidding." The screen was frozen. "Dammit!"

"Anything I can help with?"

Maggie swallowed and closed her eyes.

This. Could. Not. Be. Happening.

"No, I'm good." If only she could click her heels together and disappear. "Don't come close…I'm, ah." She sounded like an idiot.

What the hell was he doing here?

She opened her right eye, and her heart sank. It didn't just sink, it fell into her gut, and a wave of nausea followed suit. *Oh God*. The screen was plastered with photos of Cain, yet one line glowed neon green. It flashed over and over and over: "Naked shots of Cain Black, click here *NOW!*"

Frantically she searched for the power button, but it was too late. He was there, beside her, his tall body bent forward, his eyes seeing what she saw.

"I…" She shook her head and wanted to die. If the floor had opened up and sucked her into the bowels of hell, she'd have been happy.

He moved closer still, so close she felt the heat of him against her clammy skin. Her insides were on fire, yet her teeth chattered crazily from the cold that racked her frame.

Or it could have been the abject humiliation that riffled through her body with all the subtlety of a steam engine that left her shaky.

"Here, let me." She inched aside, hung her head, and glanced away. "It's my old computer, and the damn thing freezes all the time."

No shit.

"Best thing to do is a reboot."

Cain cut the power and turned to her, his eyes glittering pools of liquid ebony. He leaned against the edge of the desk, legs spread, and Maggie blushed, realizing she stood between them. She moved, wanting to step back, but his arm shot out, and his hand—those long, warm fingers—closed along her forearm.

"Don't."

With that one word, underlined by a huskiness that tugged at her insides, Maggie froze. All sorts of feelings rushed through her, physical and emotional. Hot and cold. Fear and anticipation. Crazy and even crazier thoughts twirled through her mind. Images of tongues and skin and heat and those damn eyes.

An ache formed in her gut and spread, infiltrating every single cell in her body until she trembled.

She stared at him in silence, but he was too intense, and she lowered her eyes, watched the beat of his pulse at the base of his neck instead. It seemed safer somehow.

The air was thick like molasses. It had to be—she couldn't breathe.

"What do you want to know, Maggie?" His voice was like butter, thick and silky at the same time. She shuddered as his fingers slid along her arm to pull her in closer.

Danger lurked in the air, encircling her in a mad embrace she couldn't escape. Maybe she didn't want to. But that would be crazy, wouldn't it?

They were inches apart, and she inhaled the rich aroma that was all him. Wrong thing to do. It was incredibly male, tangy, full of spice, and it got her head spinning the way one too many glasses of wine did.

"Ask me anything," he challenged. "I have nothing to hide."

Her mouth was so dry, Maggie didn't know if she could speak. She cleared her throat, very much aware of the fingers that caressed the delicate area between her palm and her wrist. Each time his forefinger rubbed there, a little piece of her liquefied, melted, and burned. She felt she should push away and get as far from Cain Black as she could.

What was she doing? This road she was on was dangerous, she knew this, but Maggie felt unable to get off.

"I don't..." She shook her head, not knowing what to say. On one hand, she was mortified that he'd found her online, ogling pictures of him like a freaking teenager. On the other, his abrupt dismissal the other night stung more than she wanted to admit.

Then there was Michael.

She was confused and felt impotent with her inability to act. She'd kept her feelings locked away for so long now that it was foreign, this deluge of emotion. She was afraid to follow her wants and needs. Those kinds of things led to a dark place.

Her head shot up as a sliver of clarity cut through the fog. "What do *you* want?"

Cain remained silent, but something changed. She

felt it. His pulse was faster, and his breaths fell in shorter, quicker spurts. Danger solidified and wrapped itself around her tight as she struggled to make sense of her emotions and get words out of her mouth.

"You said I could ask you anything," she started in a rush. "Why are you…?" She shook her head, felt the burn in her stomach surge as a wave of anger thrust through her. "Why are you doing this?"

"This?" he asked silkily, *dangerously*. His gaze swept along her arm from where his hand held her still and up to her chest, where he lingered a little too long. She felt her nipples harden, felt them strain against the tight confines of her T-shirt. A shiver rolled over her body, and she exhaled shakily as he slowly lifted his eyes and looked directly into hers.

He moved again and tugged on her gently until she was against him, tight between his legs with her hands upon his chest.

At that moment Maggie was aware of many things. The length of his lashes as he stared down at her. The golden flecks that shimmered behind the dark brown of his eyes. The accelerated beat of his heart beneath her fingers.

The thick bulge that filled his jeans and burned against her hip.

"Why am I doing this?" he asked once more, his voice husky as he lowered his head. His warm breath tickled across her flesh as ripples of desire rolled through her trembling form.

Maggie closed her eyes. She stopped breathing. And maybe the world stopped spinning, because it felt like the ground had shifted beneath her and she was falling.

His hands claimed her hips, and he turned her so that she was flush against him. So that every inch of her from the waist down was pressed into his body.

So that the place between her thighs, that hot, moist part of her, rubbed against him in a way that ached.

A groan fell from between his lips, and she shuddered as his mouth skated across her neck to settle beneath her earlobe. He nuzzled her there, and everything inside Maggie erupted in a red-hot wave of need that was so intense, her legs surely would have buckled if Cain's strong grip hadn't held her firm.

His hands slid upward until he cupped her head and fingers slid along her jaw in a smooth motion. He forced her to look up at him once more. "Ask me again what I want," he said hoarsely.

Maggie closed her eyes. This was so wrong. To feel this way about a man like Cain Black. He was way out of her league. "What do you want?" she whispered.

His breath was on her face once more, caressing her skin like small whispers of magic. The ache inside was so intense it was painful.

"The answer's real simple, Maggie."

God, the way he said her name.

"I." He kissed her cheek and her legs did give out, but his hands were there, and she clung to him. "Want." His mouth slid to her temple, where his tongue darted out to taste her there. He nibbled his way down to her mouth and hovered above her lips, with only a whisper of heat between them.

She opened her mouth, felt the anticipation that tingled inside her body and was weak from the weight of it. She was coming apart, and the man had barely touched her.

It had been so long since she felt this way. On the cusp of desire and rank with its effects.

"Open your eyes, Maggie." His voice was so low, she barely heard him. But the feel of his hands on her face was urgent, and his muscles bunched against her palms as he shifted beneath her.

She opened her eyes and ate the groan that sat at the back of her throat. Cain stared down at her as if he was starving. As if he needed her to breathe.

His right hand slid into her hair, and his lips brushed the softness of hers. His eyes never left hers as he whispered against her mouth.

"I want…you."

Chapter 12

Cain stared down at Maggie and struggled to keep it together. She was killing him. He'd never had such a need, such an insane desire, for a woman before. *Ever*. And Lord knows, over the past ten years he'd seen a hell of a lot of them in all shapes and sizes.

He swallowed thickly and nuzzled her neck, loving the warm scent of her, the soft feel of her.

He'd swung by the house to see his mother—had totally spaced and forgotten she volunteered on Fridays—and at the last moment decided to come inside on the off chance that he'd find Maggie.

Find her he did.

Bent over the desk in cutoff jean shorts, her toned legs and round ass shown off to perfection. He hadn't seen anything that hot in ages—Daisy Duke had nothing on Maggie O'Rourke—and it had awakened a truckload of fantasies that had immediately gone south. Way south. Way *hard* south.

She whimpered beneath him, and he groaned at the sensation left behind as she rubbed along the length of him. His already-straining cock tightened until the exquisite pain threatened to erupt.

He cupped her chin and breathed into her mouth.

"I want…you."

His lips grazed the softness of hers, teasing and coaxing until she opened beneath him. His mouth moved over hers, and he claimed what he'd wanted for the last week. The fragrant silk of her hair surrounded them, and his fingers tangled in their folds as he deepened the kiss. His tongue invaded and stroked, and the taste of her was intoxicating. His hands traveled the length of her body until he rested upon her sweet round ass.

She whimpered again, a soft feminine sound that went straight to his gut. He clenched everything and groaned into her mouth. Christ, he hadn't been this horny since Shelli Gouthro had pulled him from the Coach House all those years ago. Back then it had been all about getting laid, but this…this was so much more.

Maggie kissed him back, a full-on surrender, and for the longest time he held her, his mouth drinking from hers, tasting, suckling, as his hands roved as much of her as he could reach. He couldn't help himself. She felt way too damn good between his legs.

Her hands crept up to his neck. The touch was hesitant, unsure, and that alone drove him crazy. When was the last time he'd been with a woman who wasn't the aggressor? He couldn't remember.

Cain lifted her into the air, coaxed her legs around him, and leaned back against the desk as her arms encircled him fully. Holy Christ, but she was every fantasy he'd ever had and more.

He groaned into her mouth. This was going way too fast. He wanted her. Badly. But he wasn't about to have sex with Maggie on a desk in his mother's basement. She deserved more than that. He wanted to *give* her more than that.

"Hey," he whispered against her lips. "Babe, we need to stop now, or I'm not gonna be able to."

Maggie pulled away slowly but lowered her eyes. She trembled against him, and something about how she looked tugged at his heart in a way he couldn't recall feeling before. He wrapped his arms around her tightly and rested his chin on her head as she tucked into his embrace just like she belonged there.

For several long minutes there was nothing but silence broken by their quick, jarring breaths and frantic beating hearts. Eventually she relaxed in his arms, and for the moment it was enough.

Cain exhaled a long, shuddering breath. "So," he said, "I need to apologize for the other night." Maggie squirmed in his arms, and reluctantly he let go, hissing softly as she slid along his body until she was standing.

Her long red hair had fallen loose from her ponytail and hung about her heart-shaped face like a curtain, the deep color a perfect foil for her creamy skin. Her eyes were luminous, like pools of liquid navy, but it was her full lips, bruised from his mouth, that drew his attention.

They were marked. By him. And there was something primal in that that he liked.

Her tongue slid along her lower lip, and he couldn't take his eyes off her. "You don't need to..." She shook her head and looked up at him. "Michael had an amazing day, and I'm grateful you were able to give him that. If you could just..." She glanced away.

"If I could..." His hand reached for her, but she took another step back so that she was out of his reach.

"If you could just call him or something before you leave, I think he'd really appreciate it." A small smile claimed her mouth. "He seems to think you're a big deal or something."

"Before I leave?" He looked confused and took a step toward her.

Maggie frowned and made a wild gesture with her hands. "To go home. Your stuff is gone. I thought you'd already left for LA, but obviously you're heading off soon."

Hell, no.

"Would you miss me?"

She looked surprised at his question. "I…" she stuttered and shook her head. "No, I just—"

"You're not getting rid of me that easily," Cain interrupted and took a step forward until he was inches from her. She didn't move away this time. "I'm not going anywhere. Mac and I have rented a cottage not far from Jake's parents."

"Mackenzie Draper?"

He nodded. "He's the reason I bailed the other night. Some stuff happened, and Jake called. I don't want to go into detail, but…" He needed her to understand. "He's like family to me, and I had to leave."

"You don't owe me an explanation."

"Yeah, I do, and technically I owe you more."

"More?"

"I promised your son I'd show him how to clean the fish we caught, but since I had to do it right away, I'll get around to teaching him next time. But I still owe you a meal, and the fish is on ice, so…"

Her scent teased his nostrils as he gazed down at her. Maggie opened her mouth, but his finger was there before she could speak. For a split second, an image of her lips encircling him—and he wasn't thinking about his finger either—rushed through his mind. The bulge between his legs thickened even more, if that was possible.

Christ, but he had to be stronger.

"You can't say no."

She arched an eyebrow and removed his finger from her mouth. "If I want to say no, I will," she challenged.

Little minx. Cain smiled wickedly and leaned toward her, his mouth close to her ear. "Here's the thing, though, Maggie. You don't want to."

"How do you know what's in my head? What I want and don't want." She was annoyed now, but he was totally okay with that. He liked that she had spunk and didn't roll over onto her back for him.

"Woman, I just kissed you. Trust me. You don't want to say no any more than I want you to."

Maggie stared at him for a moment, and then her chin jutted out. "I don't make a habit of associating with felons."

Okay, he hadn't seen that one coming.

"You think I'm a felon?"

"Raine told me you and your friends were arrested. I'm not sure I want that kind of influence around my son."

Cain swore under his breath. The woman was looking for an excuse to blow him off, and Raine had just handed her one.

"Are you saying Raine lied?"

"No."

"Oh." She looked surprised.

"We were arrested when we were seventeen." Cain moved closer to her, loving the way her tongue darted out to moisten her lips. Lips that he wanted to taste and kiss and do all sorts of things to. "Me and the boys: Jake, Jesse, and Mac. It was quite the crime."

"What did you do?" Her voice was hushed, her eyes wide.

He stared at her for several long moments until her eyes widened in trepidation and her breath held, waiting for his next words.

"You have to understand we didn't mean for it to happen." He shook his head, his expression serious, his tone somber. "Hell, we were just kids really."

"Seventeen isn't exactly a kid," she said carefully.

"No, it's not, and we should have known better." He sighed. "And I suppose we should have known it wouldn't have ended up any other way than it did." He shrugged. "Not with Jake involved. Hell, he even lured Jesse to the dark side, and Jesse was always the guy who said no."

She bit her lip and for a second, and he was mesmerized by an image of her tongue sliding along his skin.

"What happened?" she asked softly.

"I can't lie or sugarcoat. It's a matter of public record that we kidnapped him in Indiana—"

"Kidnapped! You can't be serious."

He continued on as if she hadn't said a word. "Like I said, it wasn't my idea, but shit happened, and we kidnapped the bastard in Indiana, which was our first mistake, because anyone who watches *Law & Order* knows you should never transport a body across state lines."

"A body?" Her eyes narrowed slightly.

"Sure, you didn't think they called us the Bad Boys for kicks, did you?" He tried to look solemn, but it was hard because she looked so damn cute. "He had one hell of a trip, that's for sure. We showed him things…things he'd never have seen down there in Indiana. We showed him Michigan the way it's supposed to be done. We took him all over the county, out in the boat, and then, uh, attended a few parties where he met a lot of fine local girls. Hell, he was so damn popular, Seth Daniels used up at least two disposable cameras, 'cause everyone wanted their picture taken with him. Of course, that was before we buried him."

"Buried." Her brow couldn't arch any higher.

He nodded.

"You buried him," she said again.

"Yeah, Ronald."

A small crease furrowed Maggie's brow. She opened her mouth to speak but then closed it. She waited a moment, shifted her weight.

"You're bullshitting me."

"No, I'm not. Of course, if he'd have just come with us nice and easy-like, I'm sure it wouldn't have gotten so complicated. As it was, Jake used his powers of persuasion, and it was a piece of cake."

"Powers of persuasion."

Cain nodded. "Bolt cutters, to be exact." He sighed, a long exaggerated noise. "Eventually the law caught up to us, or rather Jesse. Two detectives showed up at the Edwardses' door and he led them to where we'd buried him." Cain grimaced. "Jesse was willing to take the fall for the rest of us, but we couldn't let that happen, especially since it was really Jake's idea. So we all came forward."

Maggie looked confused and then slightly horrified. He had her.

"It wasn't pretty, and the story made headlines in all the local papers. We were legends." He grinned. "They called us 'the Hamburglars' in Indiana."

"What?" Her tone was slightly pissed off and nearing more than a little annoyed.

"Yep, we buried Ronald McDonald out by Varini's

garbage dump, but he looked pretty damn good when we dug him up, considering he'd been buried beneath a bunch of crap for eleven months."

"You stole a Ronald McDonald and buried him for eleven months."

"It was a high school prank, and sure we got into a lot of trouble, but it was worth it. Hell, they still talk about it." He laughed. "The damn thing was so big, it's head and feet stuck out the windows of Jake's Civic all the way home. Can you imagine? Those big honking feet? That goofy smile?"

"Really?" she said drily, and he knew she was trying her hardest not to laugh. "Sounds like a blast, but you have a record, so I don't think it was that smart."

He shook his head. "Nope. I'm no criminal. The charges were thrown out and the arrests expunged from our records, so you don't have to worry I'll be a bad influence on Michael."

His hand closed around her wrist, and her energy tingled along his flesh. It was a connection unlike any he'd had before, and the thought of exploring it was like a physical ache. "So, you coming?"

Maggie muttered something under her breath. He couldn't quite catch it, but thought he heard the words *arrogant* and *bastard* and maybe *dumbass*.

She did however follow him from the office.

"I have to finish up your mom's kitchen." They'd just cleared the stairs and stood in the foyer of the house. Sunlight filtered into the large open space from the floor-to-ceiling windows on either side of the door, and it haloed Maggie in a wash of light that took his breath away. Her hair was on fire, her skin luminous.

Maggie tapped her toe and nodded toward the kitchen. "I'm not done here, and honestly, I'll be a while, so tonight is probably not good."

"I'll help you."

"No!" She shook her head and moved away from him. "*No.*" She swore loudly several times and this time made no effort to mute her words. No longer annoyed, she was angry.

"I don't need your help. I'm a maid, Cain. I clean houses to pay my bills. I clean your mother's toilets, and I scrub her floors. I clean half of Crystal Lake, for God sake. *That* is what I do." She threw her hands up in the air and took a few steps away from him. Her chest heaved and her cheeks were flushed with heat.

He had no idea why she was getting so worked up, but he sure as hell liked it. She was sexy when she was mad.

She turned, and he was surprised at the unshed tears that hovered behind her eyes. "I'm not a model or a movie star or a groupie or… I'm none of those things, Cain. I'm a maid and a mom, and I don't get what this is. What you want." She exhaled, and his insides twisted and melted at the look on her face. "What *is* this, Cain? What do you expect to happen between us?"

He knew she was confused. Hell, so was he.

"I don't know," he answered truthfully. "But I think it could be something special and real. In my world, *special* doesn't come around a whole hell of a lot. It's hidden beneath layers of greed or ambition. So when it does…" His thoughts turned to Jesse and Raine and all that they'd lost. "When it does, you need to grab hold of it, or you're a fool."

Cain walked past her. "I'm helping you clean this

kitchen, and then I'm going to drive you home. You're going to sit outside with a glass of wine and relax while Michael and I prepare supper." He glanced over his shoulder and grinned. "That's what this is, right now, at this moment."

"That was cool, and good thing Mommy decided to stay on the deck, 'cause all those slimy dead fish would have totally grossed her out."

Cain laughed. "Well, good to see you've got the stomach to be a fisherman." He winked. "And next time I take you out, I promise I'll teach you how to clean them."

Maggie's voice slid between them. "Michael, make sure you use lots of soap and scrub beneath your fingernails, please."

The kid looked up at him, eyes wide. "See? She sees everything."

Cain grinned and glanced back at Maggie. She sat in a chair on the deck, and as promised, a glass of wine had been provided. Cain had brought all the fixings, salad, and potatoes. Of course, the salad had been premade at the grocer, and the potatoes were in fact a container of store-bought potato salad, but hell, it would do.

Michael scurried off to wash his hands, and he followed suit. The fish had been cleaned and were ready to go on the grill.

"I made a lemon sauce for the fish." Maggie handed him a cold beer and reached for her glass of wine. "It's in the small container by the barbecue along with foil and tongs."

"Thanks, lady." He winked, loved the flush that stained her cheeks, and headed toward the barbecue.

Maggie's yard was a small oasis that was a perfect example of "size doesn't matter." It was a space meant to hang out and relax in. A large oak tree provided shade to nearly a third of the space, and there was an oriental waterfall in the corner that provided a Zen-like touch. The honeysuckle that crept along the back wall was fragrant, the scent hanging heavy in the warm June air. A small vegetable garden was tucked away in the far corner of the yard, and colorful flower beds overrun by petunias and geraniums crept along the foundation of the house.

It was pretty much paradise as far as he was concerned, and Cain hummed to himself as Michael helped prepare the fish. They arranged the fillets neatly on the foil, doused them liberally with the marinade that Maggie had provided, and covered them so they'd cook.

It felt good to do this. To do something for someone else. For too long he'd been on his own, and for the first time he realized that the few years spent with Natasha had never brought out this need in him. The need to put someone else first.

Being back here in Crystal Lake was about as far away from the life he'd built as he could get. But he was okay with that. In fact, he was beginning to suspect he needed a shot of something *real* in order to survive the future.

He took a long drink from the cold beer in his hand and glanced back at Maggie. She was someone he wanted to worry about. Someone he wanted to do things for.

"This smells so good, it's making my tummy rumble." Michael laughed and rubbed his belly. Every single piece of anxiety that lived in Cain had left him. As if a leak had sprung inside his body, he was light and stress-free.

He felt like a damn king.

"Sure does buddy, and it's gonna taste even better than it smells."

The boy's forehead creased into a frown. "Is it because we caught it? So it's fresh? Cause I never smelled anything this yummy."

He ruffled the top of Michael's head. "This is gonna be the best fish you've ever had, and it's because you worked for it. Anything worth having in life has to be earned."

Michael nodded, and his little face screwed into a frown as he kicked at the ground. "Miss Lauren is your mom, right?"

That was a 360-degree change in conversation. Cain nodded. "Sure is."

Michael glanced up, eyes wide, mouth set in a serious line. "Where's your dad?"

He stared down at the boy. *Good question.*

"I don't know, Michael." Cain busied himself with the fish, rearranging the fillets in the foil before covering them again. They were almost ready. "My dad left when I was a little guy barely five years old and never came back. He could be anywhere, I suppose." *Or dead.*

"Oh." Michael shoved his hands into his pockets and kicked at the ground once more. "We're the same, then."

"Yeah?"

Michael shook his head and glanced toward his mother. "I don't have a dad anymore either."

Cain didn't know what to say. The tone of their conversation had changed, and no longer were they two guys grilling some fish. Michael was sharing something pretty damn heavy. It was shadowed in his eyes and evidenced by the rigid set of his small shoulders.

Cain was curious. He'd assumed Maggie was divorced, a single mom. He hadn't considered the possibility that she was a widow.

He knew nothing about Maggie or where she came from. Nothing about the man she'd had a child with. He pursed his lips and took another swig of beer. Something hot flashed through him, a sliver of jealousy he had no right to feel.

But it was there nonetheless. He didn't like the fact that another man had tasted her, had held her, and created life with her.

What the hell was up with that?

"You guys ready yet? I've got the table set." Her voice startled them both, and a frown slid over her face. Maggie had crept up on them and stood a few inches from her son, but her focus was on Cain. "What's going on? Am I interrupting?"

Michael shook his head but didn't answer.

Cain put his hand on the boy's shoulder, flashed a smile at his mother. "We're good, and your boy's hungry, so..."

They ate on Maggie's small deck. There was just enough room at the table for the three of them. The fish was tender and tasty, as were the sides. It was cozy, intimate, and the bottle of wine went down smooth as silk.

The sun set in a blaze of reds, oranges, and gold. Cain

settled back and enjoyed the view. He'd seen the same sun set hundreds of times and had never given it another thought. But tonight, here with Maggie and her son, he thought that it was pretty much perfect.

Chapter 13

"You've got a weird look on your face. Is everything all right?"

Maggie busied herself with the small stickers she held and ignored Raine's question.

"Or does the weird look have anything to do with the fact that you and Cain spent the night together."

"We didn't…" Maggie began and shot her a dark look. "We did *not* spend the night together."

"Whatever," Raine teased as she followed behind and priced the goods Maggie had stickered. The two of them had volunteered to help out with a massive garage sale organized by the football team. It was one of several money drives that were in place in order to raise funds for the new stadium that had been proposed for the local high school. It was being held along the banks of the river that ran through town, and at the moment the entire area resembled a country fair, with booths set up and displays everywhere.

The event had been organized weeks earlier, and Maggie was happy not only that Raine had come out to participate, but that her mood was light.

"That's not what I heard."

Actually, Maggie could do without the teasing.

"Well I don't know what you heard, but whatever it was is wrong. Cain and I had dinner together, but that's it." She made a face. "And how could you hear anything anyway? It's been less than eight hours since I saw him."

"Lady, you don't understand the network that exists in this town. Someone *sees* something and *tells* someone else, and then next thing you know it's on the front page of the *Lake Herald*." At Maggie's look of panic, Raine giggled. "Well, maybe not the front page."

Raine held up a large velvet painting of a half-naked woman lounging underneath a tree on an equally gaudy chaise. She made a face. "My God, this is like a bad version of Rose's portrait in *Titanic*." She giggled. "Free?" She wrote something on the sticker and moved on to the next item. "So you *did* spend the night with Cain."

Maggie bit her lip. *Stay in your good place*.

She flipped a braid behind her shoulder and bent over to place a sticker on a box of stuffed animals. They were near the north end, not far from the dam, two of a slew of volunteers. Though it was just past six in the morning, the air was already sticky. It was going to be a hot, humid day.

"We had dinner at my house. That's it."

"All right, *I* believe you, but I just thought you should know what the rest of Crystal Lake thinks."

"Maggie!"

She glanced up as Lori Jonesberg jogged toward them.

"Here she comes! Quick, run while you still can!" Raine whispered, and then busied herself with a stack of books.

Lori was an attractive brunette—for the moment. As owner of A Cut Above, the local salon, her hair color changed frequently. She was a few years older than Maggie, and her family had lived in Crystal Lake for generations. Her husband was the fire chief, her children the local sports superstars, and she herself was like a tornado in human form.

Maggie groaned as she straightened and pasted a smile to her mouth that she so did not feel.

Lori paused in front of them, her face split wide in a grin. "My God, girl, you need to spill. I heard you and Cain Black are an item?"

Maggie glanced at Raine, who smiled wickedly and turned back to whatever it was she was pricing.

Lori's salon was the hub of Crystal Lake, and she was very much the queen bee. It was gossip central. If you wanted to know who was sleeping with whom or who was having money problems or whose so and so had passed, you made an appointment for a haircut. Guaranteed, you'd leave the salon with lighter pockets, but your head would be filled with all the latest news.

Maggie smoothed her tank top and pretended to pick some lint from her shorts. Anything to avoid the probing brown eyes that stared at her with rabid glee.

It was pretty bad that Lori already had the scoop and her salon hadn't even opened for business yet. Too bad her information was wrong.

"Lori," Maggie said carefully, "I don't know what you heard, but—"

"Oh my God, Maggie. It's all right. Snagging someone like Cain isn't anything to be ashamed of. Lord knows you've been a nun since you arrived in our little town. No one can blame you for wanting a little of what he's got going on." The woman winked as if they were sharing a secret or a confidence that she was privy to.

"Lori, you're wrong about this!" Panic nipped at her

heels. She didn't want the entire town thinking she was having sex with Cain Black. "We just had dinner, nothing more. He took Michael out on the boat, and we ate the fish they caught. That's it." Exasperation colored Maggie's voice a deep husky tone, but as a flashback of Cain kissing her—her legs wrapped around his midsection, her body pressed against his—flashed before her, a blush settled onto her cheeks, and that was something she couldn't hide.

"Sure, hon." The woman winked. "The thing is, Cain Black doesn't just do dinner, if you know what I mean." She shrugged. "I wouldn't worry about it. I mean, the worst people can say is, you're using your son to snag one of the Bad Boys. Kudos for picking the sexiest one."

Maggie was speechless.

It was at that exact moment Cain arrived with Jake and Mac in tow. When she saw Mackenzie, all thoughts of Lori and her outrageous comments fled.

Mac's face was a mottled mess of cuts and bruises, and his right eye was swollen and black. She thought of Cain's words, of the "family trouble" that had called him away Wednesday night, and her heart softened. Maggie knew what it was to bear the brunt of someone's perverted version of love.

She also knew the physical scars would heal, but it was the mental ones that needed tending the most. The healing process was so much longer and more complicated.

"Lori." Cain's one word had the beauty queen literally prancing in her inappropriate heels.

"Cain." The woman batted her eyes like a pro. "Nice to know you're sticking around. I hear you're playing the big concert scheduled for the Fourth of July weekend."

The woman dripped sugar like it was honey, but her tone changed quickly as she spied Mac.

"Good Lord, Mackenzie, I heard you got into it with Ben the other night." She sounded horrified.

"I'm sure you did, Lori." Mac walked past them toward Raine, while Jake hung back, though his eyes followed his friend.

Maggie glanced up at Cain. His eyes rested on Lori, so she was able to study him unobserved. Something fluttered in her chest as she took all of him in. He was dressed in a faded black T-shirt, one emblazoned with A Farewell to Kings across the chest. He wore the board shorts she'd seen him in at the Edwardses'. The ones she knew barely hung on to his hips. Her mouth went dry at the thought, and she wanted to look away but couldn't.

His tattoo drew her eye, an intricate design of music notes and what looked like gems—rubies—and though it was something she'd never do herself, she could appreciate the beauty.

Cain said something funny, and her heart lurched as he smiled at the woman. His grin was wide, it was warm, and it was genuine. Maggie wanted it for herself and frowned as that thought jumped into her head.

Lori leaned in close to Cain, whispered something in his ear, and then winked at Maggie. She made a dramatic turn and left, her long, skinny legs teetering as her four-inch heels stuck into the soft grass.

"So"—Cain's eyes swung her way—"put us to work."

"You didn't say anything about working the garage sale last night." Her thoughts found their way out into the open, and she blushed as his smile deepened.

"Nice surprise?"

Maggie clutched the pad of stickers in her hands and cleared her throat. She ignored his comment mainly because even though it *was* a nice surprise—if she wanted to be honest—he sure as hell didn't need to know. "Actually, Luke Jansen is in charge." She glanced past Cain. "He's over there."

Cain's smile faded somewhat, but he nodded. "Sure. Is Michael here?"

"He's around somewhere. Most likely with his buddy Tommy."

"All right. Let's do this." He nodded to Jake. "And then later"—he winked at Maggie—"we can play."

Mac groaned, a scowl hardening his features into a painful grimace. "Why the hell I let you talk me into getting up this early on a Saturday to come here is the question of the day, my friend."

"Suck it up." Cain tossed a smile her way. "I'll find you for lunch, all right?"

Heat shot through her belly and settled down *there*. That he could do that to her with just a smile was insane. Her heart sped up, and her breath hitched at the back of her throat.

I don't know. I think this could be something real. His words echoed in her head like a whisper.

A glimmer of hope nestled in her chest, a schoolgirl musing, and she found herself smiling in return as he nodded and then jogged toward Luke, with Mac and Jake close on his heels. The three of them—the Bad Boys, as they were called—had the attention of nearly everyone at the park.

Including Maggie.

"Okay, tell me again how he means nothing to you?"

Raine stood beside her, black marker in hand, though she followed the men's progress as well.

Maggie didn't say a word. Mostly because there was nothing to say, at least nothing she wanted to say out loud. In the space of less than two weeks, Cain had insinuated himself into her life, her thoughts, and her feelings. For the moment, she had no clue what she was going to do about it.

She decided to think about it later. Which was easy to do, considering the bombshell that Raine was about to drop in her lap.

"So, I went into the city yesterday."

Maggie continued to sticker the mountain of toys in the section they'd been given. She looked at Raine. The young widow was pensive, her brow furled in concentration as she carefully wrote out prices. Her complexion was pale even with the wash of sun that caressed her.

Maggie sensed the conversation had just become serious.

"I had an appointment with a specialist." Raine continued to price the toys as she spoke. "A fertility specialist." Her dark eyes sought Maggie's, and she paused, letting the pain inside show briefly. Raine's bottom lip trembled, and she took a second to compose herself before continuing. "I'm thinking of having a baby."

Maggie's jaw dropped. Okay, she knew the young widow was hurting and hurting bad, but this was insane.

"A baby," Maggie repeated, kind of stunned.

Raine's eyes shimmered in the sun, the unshed tears like misty diamonds. "Jesse's baby." She laughed, but the sound was bittersweet and held no hint of joy. "We froze his sperm before he shipped out the last time he was home on leave. I didn't want to. I thought it was creepy and unnecessary since, you know, he'd be home again, but Jesse insisted." She bit her lip and exhaled. "It's as if he knew he wasn't coming back."

Maggie didn't know what to say. All around them, volunteers were setting up for the sale. Conversations floated on the air, talk of the baseball game and barbecues or what plans had been decided for the rest of the weekend. Small stuff. Life stuff.

All of it paled in comparison to what the young widow was struggling with.

"The night that Jake called… I remember him telling me that Jesse had been hurt. Really bad. And before he even had a chance to say he'd passed, I thought of what Jesse and I had done." Raine exhaled and glanced around. "I knew before he said the words." She shuddered. "I knew Jesse was gone, and I was so angry at him."

Raine took a second to compose herself, and Maggie's heart broke at the struggle she saw. "I'm still angry, and even though I know it makes no sense, I feel like…when he donated his sperm he was giving up. That it was an omen." Her voice rose. "Everyone thinks I'm mourning Jesse, that my days are filled with thoughts of him and what we had and what we lost, but they're wrong. You know what the truth is?"

Maggie remained silent.

"The truth is, all I've been thinking about is the fact that he'd want me to have his baby, and I don't know…" Maggie bit her lip and held back tears of her own. "I don't know if I want to do it, and that makes me feel like a total bitch."

"Raine, you need to take some time. Now isn't the moment to make a decision like this. Jesse's death still hasn't hit you, but trust me, it will." Maggie gave her a hug. "Everything is still so fresh, I'm sure some of it doesn't seem real. A baby is a huge commitment, and I wouldn't advise anyone to try it on their own."

Raine's shrugged. "You seem to be doing a great job with Michael."

"I had no choice."

"I'm sorry." Raine whispered.

"You *do*, but you need to take some time. Step back and look at it when your emotions aren't all over the place. You haven't even grieved your loss. So don't do anything rash, because once a child is conceived, that baby is for keeps."

"Hey, you girls all right?" Luke Jensen, Maggie's neighbor, cut into their moment. "Can I get you guys coffee or anything?" The paramedic looked from Maggie to Raine questioningly.

Raine shook her head and moved away as Maggie began to sticker a fresh lot of toys. "We're fine."

Luke's gaze lingered, but then he moved on.

She spied Cain hauling out boxes of stuff from a small trailer that had appeared out of nowhere. He'd taken off his T-shirt, and his muscles rippled beneath the sheen of sweat that coated his skin. He turned suddenly as if he knew she was staring at him. Their eyes connected, and the physical jolt that shot through her body was scary. In that moment she knew. This man would break her heart if she let him.

She needed to forget about him. And she needed to do it fast.

Mac was tossing the stuff out to him, cursing as he did so and complaining about the pain along his jaw—a jaw his father had marked with his bare fists. Jake moved things along, though the soldier kept glancing in their direction, his gaze seeking Raine, his eyes filled with pain and hunger.

Were they all right? Luke's question echoed inside her head.

Yeah, Maggie thought, *we're all just freaking peachy*.

Chapter 14

To say the garage sale was a success would be an understatement. The weather had cooperated, spilling sunshine and heat onto the field, encouraging the crowds to come early and spend heartily.

The townies were out in full force, and the influx of weekenders and a good number of folk who'd traveled from the city was impressive. The executives who'd organized the event were happily counting their cash, and by noon a good amount of the donated items were long gone. They'd been packed into cars and trucks and trailers and taken away, hopefully never to be seen again.

Cain watched Maggie from across the park.

She was still with Raine, though the toy section they'd been in charge of was very much depleted. She stretched her arms above her head and rolled her shoulders. The tank top she wore emphasized her full breasts, and her legs, with their delicate calves and toned thighs, were once more shown off to perfection.

With her hair hanging in braids, she looked like every man's fantasy schoolgirl, and the kicker? She wasn't working it. At all. Just watching her drove him crazy.

Cain groaned and ran his hands across his chin. Even now, here among the families and town folk, in this very public place…all he could think about was her. About having her alone and naked.

He was hard like a geek teenager with no control, and

his groin tightened even more as she rubbed the back of her neck, which in turn pushed those delectable breasts tighter against the thin fabric of her shirt.

Her soft curves, hesitant touch, and the flare of passion he'd coaxed from inside her the afternoon before played over and over in his mind. He hadn't wanted a woman this badly in years. Hell, not even Natasha had touched him the way Maggie did.

It wasn't just physical either. Sure, she was easy on the eyes and had a body that made his mouth water, but it was so much more than that. Her laughter was contagious, her shy wit captivating, her affection for her son quick and sure.

He loved watching her interact with Michael. The mutual respect and love the two of them shared made him feel empty when he considered what filled his life.

And yet there was so much he didn't know. Cain's eyes narrowed as he continued to study her. She was a mystery, this woman, and one he fully intended to unlock.

"You got a thing for her." Mac handed him a bottle of water and chugged his own back. "Bad." He tossed his empty bottle into the recycle bin behind them. "Weird, 'cause she's not your type."

Irritation pinched Cain's mouth and he glared at his friend. "How the hell would you know what my type is?"

Mac laughed, a loud, hearty chuckle that turned several heads, including Maggie's. "You've dated models and singers and married an actress and, uh..." He tossed a wicked smile at Cain. "Let me see, there's the whole groupie thing, which honestly I don't know much about, but I can only imagine."

"Well, maybe my tastes have changed." Cain scowled at Mac and shoved past him.

Luke Jansen strolled up to Maggie and Raine, but Cain's course was set and he didn't deviate from it. He clenched his teeth and glared at the large paramedic. The bastard didn't give up.

"There you are, Cain." The paper-thin voice stopped him cold. Just like back in the day.

Mrs. Lancaster, the pastor's wife. He had a sudden urge to look behind him, to make sure trouble wasn't following in his steps.

He turned quickly and smiled at the little woman before him. She was barely five feet tall, her round frame draped in a blue and yellow print dress that looked as if she'd grabbed it from one of the donated clothes hampers, and her feet were encased in black rubber boots. In her arms she held a basket of daisies that were as white as the perfectly coiffed hair that was pulled back into the tightest bun imaginable.

Cain grinned. Time had stopped at Mrs. Lancaster's door and left the lady exactly as he remembered. Boots and all.

"How are things, Mrs. Lancaster?" he asked politely. He glanced behind her, and his mood darkened when he spied Luke a little too close to Maggie for his liking.

"Oh my goodness, they're just fine." The woman beamed at him and adjusted the large basket in her arms. "I was thrilled when Lauren told me you'd decided to prolong your visit home."

He nodded. "Yeah, it feels good to be back. You need help with that?" Cain asked.

"Oh no, dear, I'm on my way home. Must help Frank

prepare tomorrow's sermon." She paused and cocked her head. "It would be awfully nice to have you sing in church again."

For a second Cain was speechless. He hadn't sung in service since he was a teenager. In fact, it had been just as long since he had stepped inside a church.

"Don't look so horrified." The woman winked and smiled. "You might be surprised how good it feels to come back to the fold. Lord knows, the corruption you face every day must wear you down. All that sex and drugs and..."

Rock and roll?

"Well, I'm sure you know what I mean." Her faded blue eyes narrowed. "Crystal Lake will energize your soul and fill your spiritual well, Cain. If you let it." She rearranged the daisies and glanced toward Maggie. "It works miracles."

With that, the slight woman turned and headed toward the parking lot. She disappeared into the throngs of people milling about, and Cain felt the tension on his shoulders leave in a swoosh.

He'd never had a problem with authority figures—teachers, principals, police officers, and so on. But that woman, that small bundle of godliness, had always managed to penetrate his defenses, and after all these years, she still made him nervous as hell.

As if she knew something he didn't.

He continued on toward Maggie, his steps sure, his strides long. Luke glanced up and narrowed his eyes as a frown crept over his features.

"Black," Luke said.

Cain ignored him. No one called him Black. Not even Mac or Jake.

"You ready to get out of here, Maggie?"

Her eyes were wary, and for a second he thought she was going to protest. "I…" she began, but Luke cut in.

"She'll be here for a while."

Anger shifted beneath his skin, and Cain flexed his fingers before glancing toward the paramedic. "Really." He gestured behind him. "Seems to me you've got a ton of help, and since Maggie was here before the crack of dawn setting up for this sale, I think she's good on the volunteer front, don't you?"

"What's up?" Raine asked as she slid a marker behind her ear and tossed a toy into the reject bin.

"We're heading back to the lake." Cain flashed a grin. "You coming?"

"Is Jake going back?"

Her question surprised Cain. He shrugged. "I assume he'll make his way over. He's already left to go meet his father."

Raine rolled her shoulders. "Okay, sounds good. I need a break." A smile crept over her pale features. "Here comes Michael."

Michael was running full tilt, his legs pumping hard as he raced toward them, his friend Tommy steps behind. "Cain!" He waved several large sheets of paper in the air. "I found them."

Shit. Cain felt Maggie's eyes on him but ignored her.

Michael was puffing hard as he slid to a stop and grinned at them all before handing over his precious cargo to Cain.

"Thanks, buddy. We'll be leaving soon. Did Tommy clear it with his folks?"

The fair-haired boy with Michael nodded. "My dad

said it was okay as long as Maggie is there, because then he'll know that no shenan..." He scratched his head. "Shenanig..." The kid's brow furled and he turned to Michael.

"Shenanigans."

Tommy grinned. "Yeah, that's the word. None of that will be happening."

Cain hid a grin. "All right, then." Nice to know his reputation as a hell-raiser was intact.

He chanced a glance at Maggie. The wariness had returned to her face—big-time—along with a hint of annoyance. *That* he sensed clear as day. "Can I talk to you?" It wasn't a question. It was an order. Her lips were tight, her features even tighter.

Hell, yeah, she was annoyed and bordering on pissed, which meant that... Christ, he didn't know what it meant. He just knew he liked it. This interaction with her, no matter if she was happy or angry. As long her gorgeous blue eyes were focused on him—he cracked a smile at Luke—and no one else.

He followed her until they stopped several feet away. "What's up?" When in doubt, play dumb.

She opened her mouth and then closed it again, her gaze moving past him and then back. She spied the paper in his hand, arched her brow, and nailed him with a look that said *What the hell?*

"Why did Michael bring you my illustrations? Those were donated to raise funds for the sale."

"They did."

"They did what?"

"They raised funds for the sale."

"Really." Sarcasm touched her voice, and he grinned.

"Yes. They fetched a good price."

"What's considered good?"

"Five hundred dollars."

Maggie's mouth fell open again, and he groaned softly as the urge to grab her and kiss her *hard* rushed before him in Technicolor porno. Long red hair, entwined limbs, and that soft, full mouth. Shit. He hardened instantly and shifted, groaning inwardly as he did so.

Her color was high, the normally pale complexion a soft blush.

"You paid five hundred dollars for a few drawings I donated." Disbelief rang in her voice.

"That would be correct." He glanced down at them for the first time. They were colorful pieces featuring a young boy, an older girl, and the biggest, fattest tabby he'd ever seen. The scene looked fantastical, whimsical almost, and was good. Really good.

Michael had told him that his mother drew—that she was working on a children's book and had donated a few sketches she wasn't going to use. That was enough. He'd had to have them.

She stared at them for a good long while, and a shadow fell over her face. In a second her mood went from annoyance and anger to…well, if he was honest, it looked like she was afraid.

That stopped him cold. Shit. He didn't want her to think he was stalking her or anything. That would be creepy. "Hey, I didn't mean—"

"What are you doing?" she interrupted in a whisper. "We can't…you can't…"

She *was* afraid. But she didn't have to be.

"We can." Cain took a step closer until her subtle

scent teased his nostrils. Until there was only a breath of air between them. His eyes were intense as he stared down at her. "I don't know about you, but that kiss yesterday… I can't stop thinking about it…about how I want to do so much more to you."

She lowered her eyes, but his hand moved to her face, and he was encouraged when she didn't pull away. In fact, she leaned into his palm. The movement was subtle, but it was there, and it gave him hope.

His thumb skated across her bottom lip. "I want to put my mouth on every single inch of your body." Totally forgetting about everyone else, Cain slipped his forefinger between her lips and bent low. "The things I want to do to you, Maggie, are driving me crazy, and I can't get the images out of my head. Yesterday was just a teaser. You have no idea what I'm going to do to you when I get the chance."

She tugged away and he let her move, her breaths falling fast and hard. Her nipples stood out in stark relief against her top, and Cain knew she was as horny as he was. Thank God he'd worn his loose-fitting board shorts, or everyone within ten feet would know the state of what was going on between his legs.

"Look, I'm sorry if you think I used Michael to get you to agree to come out to the beach." He smiled, and damned if he wasn't working it. Just a little. "I just thought he'd like to hang out with his buddy." Cain glanced around. "And really, it's another perfect beach day."

Her eyes were stormy again. Just like the night he'd met her.

"I'll be honest, Maggie. I don't know what this is between us or where it's going. The only thing I'm sure about is that I've never felt this way before. All twisted and frantic and"—he grinned—"horny as hell." Something passed between them in that moment, a look in her eyes, an answering need.

Cain decided to put it all out there. "I want to know what you think about before you fall asleep." His eyes smoldered and his skin was hot. He lowered his voice and moved closer, loving the way she bit her lip. "I want to know *who* you think about when you're alone in the shower. What makes you laugh and what makes you scared." He had to make her understand. "I want to know *you*, and I want you to know me, because that kiss that we shared? That connection? It doesn't come around every day, and I sure as hell want some more of that."

Cain held out his hand. "You do too. I can feel it. Live in the moment Maggie. There's nothing wrong with that."

He was suddenly aware of the others milling about several feet behind him. It was a reality check, and he cocked his head, effectively dousing the erotic images in his mind. "You coming?"

She stared at him for several long seconds, and just when he thought he'd blown it, Maggie exhaled, squared her shoulders, and put her hand in his. She didn't say a word.

But that was all right. She didn't have to.

Chapter 15

ARE YOU OUT OF YOUR EVER-LOVIN' MIND?

Maggie could ask herself that question until she was blue in the face, and she wasn't sure the answer was the one she wanted to hear. Which would be…hell, yes.

It was nearly three in the afternoon, and she watched her son frolic along the beach with his friend Tommy. Out on the lake, boats and Jet Skis zipped by, their clean lines cutting through the blue water and leaving a white froth behind them. Along the shore private beaches were occupied, kids and adults enjoying the sun and water. Families building memories.

She and Raine were parked on the dock near the boathouse, the water lapping at their feet as they dangled them in the cool water.

She glanced up at the cottage several hundred feet away. This was such a beautiful spot, with the cottage nestled among a canopy of forest that ran along the shoreline. Pine and spruce crowded together and stood like soldiers. The house was rustic, built with reddish-brown logs and resembling a cabin out of the past. It was an A-frame, and the entire front facade was a solid wall of windows. A long veranda ran the length of the structure, which boasted a couple of reclining chairs and a rickety table. In the corner, resting against the railing, was an acoustic guitar.

The house was plain in comparison to the Edwardses'

home or Lauren's, but then, it was truly a cottage and not meant for year-round living.

She sighed and tried to relax, but it was next to impossible. She and Cain had danced around each other for the last few hours—covert glances, stolen smiles that hid secrets. She'd wanted to ignore it, wished it didn't affect her so, but at the moment, her body was buzzing with anticipation. She couldn't help it. Every time he looked at her, she felt a jolt of energy slice through her body. It was unnerving.

She ran a hand along the back of her neck. The action pulled her tank top tight across her chest, and she bit her tongue and hissed. Her nipples tingled and her belly clenched.

Cain was right. There was no way around it. This thing between them was palpable. It was alive inside them both. God, the thought of his hands on her body was enough to drive her to distraction.

Not once in the entire time she had been in Crystal Lake had she entertained the idea of being with someone. She'd been content to carve out a life and look after her son. Heck, for the first few months it was all she could think about. She'd arrived with five thousand dollars and not much else. It had taken everything in her to set up a house and keep things normal for Michael.

If she was honest, she'd given up on the possibility of a relationship long before she left Savannah. The twisted thing that her life had become had left her no choice, really. It had beaten her down and snuffed out the flame.

And now there was a glimmer of *something*. Would it be worth it? To open up and experience Cain Black, even if it was just for a short period of time?

She heard him inside the cottage whistling to himself as he prepared meat for the barbecue. Mac was helping, or rather drinking beer, while Cain prepared. There was something dark inside his friend, a wounded soul that she could relate to. Maggie didn't know the details of his life, but she thought that maybe he drank a little too much.

So far, Jake hadn't shown up.

"When's Jake heading back to Afghanistan?" she asked. Good. This was good. Think about other things, and maybe the longing that hung in her belly and warmed the softness between her legs would go away.

Raine sighed and kicked her toes into the water. Little minnows swam crazily, darting in all directions. They looked like what was going on inside her belly.

"I'm not sure. He's not exactly talking to me these days." Raine splayed her hands out along the deck, and Maggie frowned, noticing for the first time that the young widow had removed her wedding band. "We had an argument the other day, and things aren't good."

"Oh. Sorry to hear that."

Raine pushed her hair behind her shoulders and leaned back, her eyes closed as she drank up the sun. "I don't want to talk about Jake or Jesse or the phantom baby." A ghost of a smile touched her pale lips. "What the hell is going on between you and Cain? And don't tell me nothing, because seriously, he's eating you with his eyes."

Raine straightened and glanced at her, and a giggle fell from her lips. "I don't ever remember seeing him so"—she shook her head and made a weird face—"so freaked-out over a woman."

"Freaked-out?"

"I see the way he looks at you, and it makes me think of being sixteen again and how I felt when I first realized I was in love."

Maggie nearly choked. "Love? Um, I think you're getting way ahead of yourself. I've barely known him two weeks."

"Oh I know. I didn't mean… It's just…" She shrugged and looked out over the water as her face fell and her chin trembled. "If I could go back in time, there are so many things I'd do differently—"

"Raine, you can't think like that," Maggie interrupted.

"Oh don't get me wrong. There's a lot I *wouldn't* change. But the thing that scares me most is the thought of never feeling like that again. The innocence, the hope, and the endless possibilities. We had it all. I don't want to lose that. I'm scared that *that* part of me will dry up, turn to dust, and fade away like it never existed. That I'll forget what it feels like to connect with someone so intensely that it hurts." She turned to Maggie, her eyes filled with glassy tears. "I'm twenty-eight, and I'm scared my life is over. If I have this baby…" She sighed, tucked a long strand of hair behind her ear, and looked back out over the water. "We were kings back then and didn't know it. We had no responsibility and the world at our feet."

"You miss him."

"I miss all of it."

"You're young. Don't give up." Maggie winked. "Love will find you again."

"So says the woman who's afraid to date." Raine's eyes narrowed. "I know there are things in your past that have scarred you too, but Maggie, you need to listen to your own advice. Cain's a good guy, and from my perspective, I'm not afraid for you. He won't break your heart. He's not that guy." Raine glanced toward the cottage. "It's Cain I'm worried about."

Maggie was stunned. She didn't know what to say.

"Why would you..." she began. Anger stirred in her gut. Okay, the woman was newly widowed, but hell, that didn't give her the right to freaking say whatever was on her mind.

"Don't take it personally, Maggie. But I've known Cain my whole life, and as much as people would like to think he's a player, he just doesn't do casual."

"Really? I find that hard to believe." The pictures she'd seen the day before ran through her mind, and with them, a tingle of jealousy. If she were being honest.

Raine shrugged and rose. She offered her hand, and Maggie pulled herself up until she stood beside the small brunette. "Believe what you want, but you'll see...he's one of the good guys, and when you finally realize that? Promise me you'll let him go, because unless you're willing to walk away from whatever the hell has damaged you, he'll get hurt."

Maggie didn't know what to say.

Raine sighed heavily. "And then we'll have to listen to song after song about the pain of his tragically broken heart. Seriously, you can't do that to us." There was a teasing undertone to her voice, but Maggie knew the woman was serious.

The smell of steak on the barbecue drifted toward them. Maggie glanced up at the house and smiled as Lauren waved down to her. Jake was with her, and he nodded in their general direction, then disappeared around the corner where the barbecue was located.

"Mom! Is it almost time for supper? We're starved."

Michael and Tommy came running up the beach. She decided to put aside Raine's words and concentrate on the here and now. The young widow longed for a past that would never be hers again. Maggie had no desire at all to revisit hers.

Cain stretched back and watched his mother and Maggie converse. They were on the deck of the cottage relaxing, sipping hot chocolate. Dinner had been great, the steak tender, the wine smooth, and the company… His eyes rested on the redhead. The company was perfect.

Raine had grabbed a ride home with Jake, and Mac had disappeared soon after the plates were cleared. Draper had claimed he had somewhere to be, but Cain suspected it was more that a visit to the Coach House was needed in order to drown his demons in a bottle of vodka.

He sighed. As long as Mackenzie stayed away from his father, he'd be okay.

Dusk was settling, and he'd built a bonfire near the beach. Michael's buddy Tommy had just left—his father had swung by—and now it was just the two of them. Michael threw some branches he'd collected onto the flames, and they watched the tiny embers that flew into the air like fireflies. "Do you have marshmallows?" Michael's eyes widened hopefully.

"Sure do. My mom brought a bag with her."

"Awesome. Do you have wieners?"

"Dude, you just ate an entire T-bone, and you want more meat?"

Michael giggled. "I make the best SpiderDogs ever."

"Maybe a midnight snack, if you're still up."

Soft feminine laughter drew their attention, and Cain's heart jumped at the sight of Maggie laughing at something his mother had said. The woman could change the world with that smile.

"Do you hate your Dad?" Michael asked suddenly. His foot sifted through the sand, his eyes fixed on his toes as if they were the most interesting thing in the world.

But Cain knew better.

"Hate?" He shrugged and settled back onto his elbows. "That's a pretty strong word." He thought about it for a few moments. "I don't think I hated my father. Even when he was home, he wasn't really around. I was more hurt and disappointed, I guess." His eyes closed, and once more he saw the little boy that he'd been. Waiting. Always waiting. "That first year after he left, I thought every night would be the one."

"The one?"

"The night that he'd come home, back to me and my mom. But it never happened, and eventually I gave up."

Michael slid in beside him, and Cain moved, gave the kid some room. The boy nestled against him, and something hit him in the gut that he wasn't expecting. A rush of emotion that was both a need to protect and something else entirely.

It was the something else entirely that he wasn't real sure about.

"I hate him." Michael said quietly. "My dad. I don't want to see him ever again."

Cain was silent. He had no idea what to say, but one thought spoke loudest in his mind. Maggie's ex was alive. Somewhere out there.

"He used to hurt my mom." Michael's voice trembled.

Cain glanced up at Maggie. He couldn't see her face anymore—the shadows had grown long—but he heard the soft lilt to her voice, that Southern roll that he'd come to adore. He saw the elegant curve of her hand, an artist's hand, tuck a stray curl behind her ear. His heart leaped into his throat, and anger tightened inside him. His fist clenched, but he remained silent.

"I used to hear her crying at night sometimes, and once it was so loud, so…sad that I wanted to make her feel better." Michael's chin trembled, and Cain's fist unclenched. "I snuck into their room…" His fingers crept onto the boy's shoulder, and Michael glanced up then, his huge blue eyes glistening with tears. "I saw him hit her." Michael made a fist and shoved it in the air between them—a small, angry fist that trembled. His face darkened, the cheeks flushed a ruddy color. "His hand was like this, and he hit her on her arm and then on her face." Michael shuddered angrily and swiped at the tears that fell from his eyes. "Over and over," he whispered.

Something twisted inside Cain, something dark and deadly.

"Hey, it's all right buddy. We don't need to talk about this right now." Cain rubbed Michael's shoulder, trying his best to keep his voice neutral and calm. It was hard. He was fucking livid. He needed to focus on the boy.

And yet how did you wipe away that kind of pain?

Michael plunged forward, and Cain realized the best thing he could do was listen.

"I was so scared that I ran back to my room and hid in the closet, but he found me." His voice lowered until it was barely a whisper. "His face didn't even look normal. It was all red and angry and scary."

Michael kicked his foot, and his little hands were clenched so tight, the knuckles were white. "He tried to hurt me too. Said I was a little snot-nosed bastard who didn't deserve anything." Michael shuddered. "The police came and took him away before anything really bad happened."

Cain's gut rolled over. Shit. He'd had no idea. But it sure as hell explained a lot. The wary look that had been in Maggie's eyes the first few times he met her. How she'd cowered when he tried to help her after she fell. She'd thought he was going to hit her.

"What happened after the police came?"

"We left and came here."

Cain let the information settle for a bit. "Have you talked to your father since you've been in Crystal Lake?"

The boy shook his head. "No." He looked up at Cain and was anxious. "I'm not supposed to talk to anyone about him. You can't tell my mom I told." His chin trembled, and Cain squeezed his shoulder.

"Hey, we're good. I won't say a word."

"Swear on the Bible?"

"A whole stack."

"Okay. Mom says it's our private business and no one needs to know. I think she's scared..."

Cain frowned, unease sliding through him. "What's she scared of?" He asked the question, but he knew what Michael was going to say before he opened his mouth.

The boy's small shoulders hunched forward as if he

were trying to draw what warmth he could from the fire. "She's scared that he'll find us and then..."

"Then what? It's okay. You can tell me."

"He'll hurt us. I don't want him to hurt my mommy," Michael blurted before burrowing into his side. The boy shuddered and shook against him. It was obvious he was scared, and for a moment, red-hot anger coursed through Cain.

His arms went round the boy, and he pulled him in as close as he could. His gaze traveled back up to Maggie. His heart pounded hard and fast, and he clenched his teeth together tightly.

The thought that anyone could hurt her or Michael filled him with such rage, he wasn't sure he could speak. To think this little guy had seen such violence against his mother made him sick, and to think of Maggie on the receiving end left him feeling weak. So he took a few moments. Envisioned his fist connected with the slimy coward's face many times over. It might not be the right thing to do, but it sure as hell made him feel better.

"That won't happen."

"Promise?" Michael whispered.

"Yeah." His chest welled with the hot flush of emotion inside him. "I promise."

What the hell was he doing? Cain knew he was about to cross a line, but he didn't care. Maybe he should. Who the hell was he to be promising her kid that everything would be all right? He ignored the inner voice of reason. The one that months, or even weeks, earlier would have been enough to send him packing.

Cain nodded toward the fire. "How 'bout some marshmallows?"

Chapter 16

"WHAT ARE YOU DOING, CAIN?" HIS MOTHER'S TONE was sharp, and he knew that he was most likely in for it. She'd been dying to get him alone ever since she arrived and found Maggie and her son at the cottage. He glanced back toward the lake, but it was hidden by the dense grouping of birch trees that lined the driveway next to the cottage.

It was late. Michael was asleep, curled up near the fire in a large comforter he'd found inside the cottage. Mac had returned, dropped off by a taxi, and he'd crashed in the back bedroom almost immediately. A quick, slurred "Hey" and he'd disappeared.

He'd left Maggie by the fire too, and he thought of her there, with the moon low across the water, a breeze in her hair, and the glow of the embers reflecting on her skin. Things had changed between them today. Their connection. It wasn't subtle. It was potent, and he knew she felt it as deeply as he did. Anticipation sat in his gut, twisted his insides so badly he was short of breath.

He wanted to hold her—make love to her—protect her with a ferocity that he'd never felt before.

"Cain? Did you hear me? Are you all right?"

He turned back to his mother. "I'm good." His arms crept round her shoulders, and he kissed her solidly on the cheek, a grin softening his face. "Really good."

Lauren stared up at him, a frown marring the perfectly

arched eyebrows and darkening her eyes. "So this thing with Maggie..."

"Mom, let's not go there. We're both adults, and I think Maggie is a lot stronger than you give her credit for. I don't know what this *thing* is, but I know what it's not." He stepped back and opened the car door for his mother. "It's not casual, and it's not easy or ordinary or simple. Its fire and excitement and a whole bunch of stuff I can't even explain."

His mother cocked her head, a slow smile on her lips. "You sound like a writer."

"It's what I do," he snorted, and then paused. "I think I'm ready."

"Ready?" Lauren prompted. He heard the concern, the worry, and wondered who it was for. Him or Maggie?

"To fill in the holes." He shrugged. "To maybe live for something or someone other than me or the band."

His mother looked surprised. Confused maybe.

"Okay." Lauren slid inside the car and glanced up. "*Okay,*" she repeated. "Just be careful, Cain. You're stepping into a complicated situation, one that involves a child and who knows what else."

He clenched his jaw tightly, his thoughts darkening as he thought of what Michael had shared with him earlier. Complicated? Hell, yeah, but he was ready for it.

"Don't worry about me." He kissed her once more and patted the top of the car. "I get that you're concerned, but you don't have to be. I love you."

Lauren put the car into gear. "I love you more." She reversed out of the driveway, and he watched the glow of her taillights disappear around the bend.

Cain headed back to the fire, his steps light and sure.

"Hey." Maggie glanced up at him. Her eyes were huge jewels that glistened in a face as smooth and creamy as ivory. The wind had messed with her hair so much that the long, tangled waves hung down her shoulders in crimson ropes. She looked delicate, hauntingly beautiful.

He wanted to talk to her about her situation, about her ex and what all of it meant, but he knew he needed to be careful. He didn't want to spook her. Didn't want to do anything that would send her packing.

Cain cleared his throat and glanced at Michael. The boy was out cold. A day of fresh air and water was nothing to be messed with. "I guess we should get him home…or you could stay if you want." He nodded toward the cottage. "There's room."

"No," she answered quickly. "No, we should go." Maggie stood and shivered. It was damp, and the fire was nearly out. She was still in her tank top and shorts, and he knew she was cold. "Thanks for everything. It was really…" Her eyes widened as she stared at him, and he knew his desire was there for her to see. How could it not be? He felt it in every cell of his body. The need to hold her was that intense.

She licked her lips and he groaned inwardly. "It was really nice."

She was whispers and smoke and sex.

Cain took two steps and grabbed her into his arms. He gave her no choice and held her close, though he couldn't stop his hands from running along her frame until they rested in the hollow of her back. Her skin was bare there, cool to his touch, and he smiled when he felt a tremor rush beneath her flesh. She was rigid at first, but then relaxed against him. Her head rested just under his chin, and he was content to hold her. To breathe her in and keep some part of her inside him.

The night caressed them. It was filled with the scent of the outdoors as a soft breeze slid across their skin. Crickets chirped incessantly, and in the distance, lights twinkled across the water. Laughter echoed into the air, traveling miles along the lake.

Maggie shifted, her arms creeping up to his neck, and he groaned as his cock pulsed painfully between his legs. He'd had a hard-on for days now, and the ache wasn't going away anytime soon.

He pulled her with him, away from the slumbering child and fire, into the darkness. There were no words, just a need that clawed at him. Did she feel it too? This insane urge to crawl inside someone's skin? To feel their every thought, emotion, and desire?

Maggie shuddered against him and moaned softly as he cupped her chin. He looked into her liquid soft eyes and ran his finger along her jaw.

"I can't believe it's taken the entire day for me to get you alone." Shit, it sounded like such a cliché, but it was true. It was as though the damn universe had conspired to keep them at arm's length.

She swallowed, ran a nervous tongue over her lips. They shone under the moon's glow, and he couldn't take his eyes off them.

"We're not really alone," she whispered.

He had no idea what had just come out of her mouth. In fact, all he thought of was her lips on his body, trailing a line of fire down his stomach and even lower. Images of that perfect, plump mouth wrapped around the aching hardness between his legs and her long hair bundled in his hands left him weak.

Cain felt like he was coming apart, and he'd barely touched her.

"I want you, Maggie, so bad it hurts. If I could have you here, right now, I would." His voice was rough, heavy with desire and need.

Her mouth hung open, and he thought she was probably shocked at his bold statement. He didn't care. He lowered his mouth and groaned into her, his tongue going deep, probing the hot wetness inside as he kissed her long and hard and thoroughly.

She tasted like cinnamon and chocolate, and when her tongue met his, when that first tentative stroke tingled inside his mouth, he melted. She was everything at that moment. The air he breathed, the blood that pumped through his body, the thoughts that crowded his brain.

His hand splayed across the roundness of her ass, and he pulled her in as tight as he could, loving the heat that spiraled out from his stomach to clutch him hard. He tore his mouth away and sought out the valley between her breasts. Her skin was damp, heated, and that scent he'd been craving, that unique signature that was all hers, tingled in his nose.

Such a rush of possessiveness rolled over him that he was momentarily stunned. It was as if she'd been imprinted onto him somehow. He not only wanted her—and wanted her badly—he wanted no one else to touch her. Ever.

Maybe that thought should have been enough to stop him cold. But it didn't.

The sounds that erupted from deep in her throat drove him crazy. He felt every single one of them rip through him, and he licked, nibbled, and suckled her there, low in the crook beneath her ear. She shuddered against him and groaned softly. It damn near undid him.

"I need to see you." His voice was harsh, his breaths ragged.

"Michael..." Her voice was so low, he'd barely heard her.

"He'll be fine."

Cain brought her with him, back a few feet, and they tumbled onto one of the low-slung lounge chairs near the beach. The vinyl was cool, wet from the water and the night's dew. They didn't care. Their hands were grabbing, tugging, twisting, and he rolled onto his back, gazing up at her in wonderment as she ripped at his T-shirt.

The moonbeams from above dusted her head in an eerie glow, gave her an ethereal quality that was breathtaking. Her lips were parted, their bruised softness swollen and sexy as hell. He sat up with her straddling his lap, and he threw his shirt onto the ground.

"I'm a goddamn mess for you, Maggie."

Her hands were near his stomach, the fingers circling the flesh that lay open to her. She licked her lips again like the temptress she'd become and adjusted her body. Her hips slid across his groin, causing just enough friction to elicit a hiss.

"Touch me," he whispered, teeth clenched.

Her gaze focused on him, the edge of her tongue peeking out as her hand slowly moved. His breath hitched at the back of his throat, and he gripped the sides of the lounge chair, his knuckles white. Her touch was like a whisper of feathers, tracing and touching, teasing.

She moved once more, the apex between her legs hot against his upper thigh. When she closed the heat of her palm across his cock, he couldn't help himself and swore. "Holy Christ, Maggie."

A playful smile swept across her mouth as she began to massage him in a slow, methodical motion that had his balls aching for relief. He hissed. "You gotta stop, babe. You're moving too fast—"

"I don't want to."

Her words stopped him cold, and he groaned as her free hand crept along his abs until she leaned forward and braced herself above him. She continued to knead and roll her palm across the hard length of him, and when she closed her mouth over his nipple and began to suckle, he tightened even more and for a moment thought he was going to literally explode in her hand.

"Sweet fucking Jesus."

Her hand moved faster against him, rubbing and grasping, all the while gyrating her hips along his thigh, and the heat of her burned him. His right hand crept up her rib cage and held her in place, while his left sought out the heat between her legs and he mimicked her motions, his palm firm against her softness.

She stared down at him, mouth open, panting, as his fingers rubbed along the crevice there. She looked wild, untamed, and when her fingers slipped inside his shorts to grasp his cock—when it was skin on skin—he groaned and paused.

His heart leaped into his throat, and the pressure inside was fierce. He wanted nothing more than to throw her to the ground and bury himself inside her. He could do it too. She was there, riding along with him and, from the dampness in his palm, as horny as he was.

A whimper escaped from between her lips as he continued to rub along the inside of her legs, fingering and teasing until he slipped inside her panties. When his fingers found the wetness there, he didn't wait but plunged two long fingers inside her slick warmth.

She screamed. Not a surprised, holy-shit kind of scream, but a throaty, sexy noise that drove him crazy. "Cain, I—" He moved his fingers, massaging her tight sheath with quick, sure strokes, and she moaned.

"Maggie..." Christ, he couldn't even finish his thoughts.

He closed his eyes and let her hold him as he continued to minister his own form of torture. He bit his lips as her thumb massaged that sensitive skin beneath the head of his cock, and his chest rose and fell in rapid jerky motions. When he didn't think he could take any more, he squirmed, sat up straighter, and grabbed the hand that was inside his shorts to hold her still.

Cain stared into her eyes, those large liquid pools of ocean, and time stopped. She was the most beautiful thing he'd ever seen. Her tongue was caught between her teeth, and her skin shone with the silvery sheen of sweat. He shifted and coaxed her toward him, claimed her lips in a whisper of a kiss. It was all about touch and emotion and communicating without words.

He knew she was as worked up as he, and that if he wanted, he could have her right now. But for the first time in his life, he wanted more than just a quick screw. He wanted more than the pleasure of a physical release.

He *would* have Maggie, but he wanted it to matter.

Cain broke off the kiss, and his fingers settled into the thick hair at her nape. He couldn't believe he was about to do this again but…

"We gotta stop Maggie," he murmured hoarsely, "or I won't be able to."

She dropped her forehead to his chest. His right hand slid up along her back, and he tugged until she relaxed and collapsed against him. She was shivering, and he held her tightly, loving the way she fit into his arms like the last piece of a puzzle.

For the longest time, Cain held her, stroked her hair, and reveled in the feel of her. Darkness enveloped them in a secret embrace, with only the soft glow of the moon on the horizon as witness. The crickets still chirped, the frogs croaked incessantly, and in the distance a loon called, its song sad and mournful. The breeze that slid across the lake was cool, and after a while she shifted and whispered against his skin, "I should get Michael home."

Her hand slid into his as he rolled off the lounge chair and stood. Cain's arms wrapped around her shoulders, and he kissed her forehead, his fingers lingering along the bare flesh of her arms.

"Let's go," he said softly.

The fire was nearly out, and Cain lifted Michael into his arms, blanket and all. He kicked sand onto the embers and followed Maggie through the dark to his truck. They rode back to town in silence, the powerful engine purring through the quiet and filling the space between them.

When they arrived at her house, Maggie unlocked the door for him, and Cain stepped through, her son tucked securely in his arms. He headed toward Michael's room and deposited him on his bed just like he'd done a few nights earlier.

The little head of curls moved, and Michael yawned. His eyes fluttered and opened slowly. "I had fun today," he murmured.

"That's good." Cain ruffled the top of his head while Michael uttered something unintelligible before sliding into Sandman's embrace once more.

Cain took a second, tugged the blanket up to Michael's chin, and then followed Maggie out to her small porch. He turned, his hands gripping the overhang as he stared down at her. "So," he began, and her head snapped up as if she was startled, not expecting him to speak. She was nervous, her tongue flicking along the edge of her lips, and he felt a sharp answering tug once more.

Christ. It wasn't fair, what this woman could do to him without even trying.

She crossed her arms over her chest and exhaled. He reached for her and caressed her cheek before his fingers sank into the thick hair and he cradled her head.

"So, Michael tells me he's going camping with Tommy's family this week."

Maggie nodded, a slight frown marring her forehead.

"When's that happening?"

"Tuesday." Her voice was one shade past a whisper.

"Okay, Tuesday it is." It was Sunday. He could wait until then.

"Sorry?"

Cain smiled and brushed her mouth with a soft kiss. "I'll pick you up at five." He let go and stepped off her porch.

"For what?"

"What else? A date."

"Cain, wait! I don't...are you sure that's a good idea? I mean, we'd be in the public eye and..." She exhaled and ran her hands through her hair. "We'd be seen."

Cain cocked his head and laughed. "Well, holy shit. I think this is the first time a woman hasn't wanted to be seen with me."

"No! It's not that, I...I just..."

She was jumbling her words up, and he fought the urge to kiss her senseless. The woman was adorable. Her mouth sinful. What an amazing combination.

"Is it Michael? You don't want him to know we're seeing each other?"

She lowered her eyes.

"Don't worry about him. He'll be fine, I promise." He paused and smiled wickedly, loving the way her tongue touched the edge of her teeth as she glanced up at him. "Maggie, we have unfinished business, you and I." Her chest heaved, and that damn tongue was at it again. If he didn't know better, he'd think she was the biggest tease this side of Detroit. "I'm taking you out for dinner, where I will do my best to charm the hell out of you"—he narrowed his eyes—"and then we're going to get naked together."

She opened her mouth but closed it again without uttering a word.

"The things I'm going to do to you, Maggie, just might be illegal in some states."

Cain turned and headed toward his truck, keys jangling in his hands loosely. "Make sure you get lots of sleep," he tossed over his shoulder. "Because you're sure as hell gonna need it."

Chapter 17

"Do *NOT* CUT ANY OF THAT HAIR OFF!"

The loud words startled both Maggie and the hairstylist who held a good chunk of Maggie's hair between her fingers.

It was Monday afternoon, later in the day, and A Cut Above was buzzing with clientele, stylists, manicurists, and shampoo girls. The shop was located downtown, near the clock tower, just east of the town hall. Out front every single parking space was filled, and the sun glanced off the windshields, blinding anyone who cared to look.

Maggie's one client of the day, Annabelle Jenkins, was done—her three-bedroom bungalow only took a few hours—and on impulse, Maggie had decided to treat herself to a pedicure *and* a haircut. It had been months since she had anything done with it. In fact, the last time her locks were trimmed, it had been a work of art created by her son.

Lori Jonesberg appeared in the mirror behind her, her expression focused, intense. "I've had a cancellation, Sandra, so I'll look after Ms. O'Rourke. The clean towels have just been delivered and need to be put away."

Sandra stepped back and let Maggie's hair fall from her fingers. "Sure, Lori." The tone was respectful, but Maggie caught the narrowed eyes before Sandra disappeared from view.

Lori's fingers threaded into Maggie's hair, and she

lifted the heavy weight, checking the ends thoroughly before letting the tendrils fall again. "I'll have to take about an inch off the bottom but no more." Her dark eyes crinkled. "They look damn good, considering you use the cheapest product on the market."

"I…" Maggie started.

"It's all right. You don't have to thank me. I really did have a cancellation." Lori winked before turning to one of the girls behind her. "Grab my tray and bring a coffee for Maggie."

The young teen scurried to do Lori's bidding. The owner of A Cut Above was petite, standing five foot five in her four-inch spikes, but she was a dynamo nonetheless. Maggie studied her in the mirror. She was also no longer a solid brunette. Lori's chic cut was now dyed a deep chestnut with blond and red highlights.

"I heard the garage sale did huge business." Lori's gaze was still focused on her hair as she spoke.

"Uh, yes, Luke said they raised a significant amount of money."

"That's good," Lori murmured as she cocked her head to the side and lifted a piece of Maggie's hair. "So what are we doing today?" Lori frowned as she studied Maggie's head.

"I thought a cut?"

Lori shook her head.

Maggie bit her lip "Maybe? I was thinking something different. I've had it long for years, and I"—she shrugged—"thought that a change could be good." At Lori's frown, she arched an eyebrow in question. "Or not?"

"No." Lori shook her head again. "No, we're not going to take much off. Trust me on this."

Okay. Maggie was a little unnerved at the sudden attention and the woman's desire to make her over.

The young teen appeared at Maggie's side just then and handed her a steaming cup of coffee. She rolled up a tray beside Lori and left as quickly as she'd come.

"We're not?" Maggie asked.

"Nope." Lori leaned in close to her ear. "Guys like Cain, rockers? They like their women to have long hair."

Heat stained Maggie's cheeks as a slow grin rolled over Lori's face. The woman tugged on her hair. "They need something to hold on to, you know, when—"

"Lori," Maggie interrupted, embarrassed.

The petite brunette laughed and reached into her tray. "Don't get your knickers in a knot. I'm just teasing." She cocked her head, and their eyes met in the mirror. "I'm right, mind you, but if you don't want to talk about the fact that you're having sex with Cain Black, I'm fine with that."

"I'm not," Maggie sputtered, suddenly aware of the glances and whispers aimed in her direction.

"Honey, don't bother denying. Because if you haven't done the nasty yet"—Lori held up a large swath of hair—"you will." She fingered the piece, let it drop, and smiled at Maggie. "I'm going to add a few layers to give you some shape. Your color is gorgeous, but we'll add some highlights, some blond and a few darker pieces. It will make the texture shimmer and add depth."

Rebecca Stringer-Hayes strode into the salon at that moment, spied the two of them, and walked over. "Lori, I was hoping for a quick trim." The blonde's gaze lingered on Maggie, a cool smile in place as she adjusted her large bag across her shoulders. It was Gucci, and not a knockoff either.

Lori shrugged and secured a cape around Maggie's neck. "The salon's busy, Rebecca. We don't have a lot of slots for walk-ins."

"Kate Andrews told me she had to cancel."

"She did, which is why I'm working on Maggie."

Rebecca was irritated. Her glossy lips pursed tight and her foot tapped rapidly on the tile floor. "And how long will that take?"

"Long enough. If you're desperate for a trim, sit in my chair, and Sandra will be more than happy to snip away."

"But Sandra isn't my person. *You* are." The whine was nasal, and Lori grimaced.

"I suggest you make an appointment then. I have one or two openings the week after next."

Rebecca stopped tapping her toes and gripped the edge of her purse so tightly, her knuckles were white. "You can't fit me in for a trim." Disbelief colored her words in a throaty layer, and Maggie shifted in the chair, uncomfortable with the other woman's behavior and the interest they were creating.

Lori swore under her breath. "No, Rebecca, I can't."

"Fine, but if you have a cancellation before then, I want it." Rebecca turned and then paused, her voice loud as she glanced over her shoulder. "I need you to stay later tomorrow, Maggie. The grout in the bathrooms is horrendous, especially around the toilets, and they'll need to be scrubbed by hand—all four of them."

Irritation flared inside her. Maggie looked at Rebecca through the mirror and shook her head. "I don't visit until Wednesday afternoon, Rebecca."

"Whatever." Rebecca waved her hand in a dismissive gesture. "Just make sure you do them when you come. They're a disgrace."

Rebecca left the salon in a cloud of perfume and attitude. Maggie watched her go, amazed at how much of a cliché the woman was. Blond, skinny and…

"She's always been a bitch. Don't let her bother you."

Maggie glanced at Lori in surprise.

Lori grabbed pieces of foil and pinned a large chunk of Maggie's hair on top of her head. "Seriously. That one was born high on herself, and she'll never change."

The heat that sat in Maggie's cheeks spread. She didn't want this. She couldn't *afford* this. Like a mind reader, Lori patted Maggie on the shoulder and leaned in close once more.

"Don't worry about the cost. I'll only charge you for the cut. Besides, it's all you booked for." She shrugged. "Not your problem I feel like playing around with your head."

"Why are you doing this?" Maggie was curious. It wasn't like they were great friends. They were acquaintances, had been on a few school trips together with their children.

Lori's face softened, and she spread some of the mixture along a piece of hair before securing it inside the foil. "Most people would be shocked to know this, but I'm a fairy-tale kinda girl." She grabbed another piece and began applying the mixture. "You just seem like someone who could use a Prince Charming in her life. And if he happens to be a rocker with to-die-for abs and a killer smile, well, that's all the better, don't you think?" Lori pinned that piece up and grabbed for another. "Oh, and before I forget." Lori made a face and looked at Maggie's toes in horror. "We're going to redo the color. Pink passion is for old ladies. Just sayin'."

Approximately two and a half hours later, Maggie left A Cut Above humming a tune, her steps light. Her hair was layered and highlighted with funky chunks of peekaboo color that shimmered as the wind picked up and lifted the tresses into the air. Her toes were no longer pink, but sported a vibrant navy color—one that she totally loved and kept admiring as she slowly made her way toward the bus stop.

Maggie shouldn't have been surprised when she nearly mowed over someone—or rather not someone, but Jake Edwards. He'd just exited the bank, and she sidestepped at the last second, barely missing him.

She turned back. "Oh, Jake, I'm sorry. I..." She stopped talking. His eyebrows were furled, all scrunched up as if he was deep in thought. He nailed her with a look that was not happy. In fact, that was an understatement. Jake Edwards looked pissed off and angry as hell.

"Do you have a minute?" His voice was as sharp as his features. His mouth was tight, and she shifted beneath his steady gaze. For whatever reason, Jake Edwards made Maggie nervous. He was like an elastic band strung way too tight, and she had a feeling he was going to snap. *Soon*.

She glanced at her watch. "Uh, it's late, and Michael's home alone. I really need to get his supper on."

Jake strode toward her and grabbed her elbow. "Good. I'll give you a lift. We can talk on the way."

Okay, he was kinda scaring her now.

Maggie yanked her arm from his. Granted, the man had been through an unbelievable trauma, but that sure as hell didn't give him the right to manhandle her or order her around.

"I can get home on my own, thanks," she answered stiffly.

A flurry of emotion rippled across his features, and he ran his hands through the short crop of hair atop his head. The motion drew her eyes to the tattoos on his arm. They were strange symbols she couldn't place, but one she knew—Gemini, the sign of the twins.

"I'm sorry, Maggie. I don't mean to come across like such an ass. I just really want to talk to you about something." He frowned and pointed to a truck parked up the way. "It's important."

Was he going to warn her away from Cain? Did he think she wasn't good enough for his friend?

"God, I'm screwing this all up." His dark eyes settled on her with a cold intensity that made her swallow and want to step back. "It's about Raine and her cock-and-bull idea to get pregnant."

"Oh." She hadn't seen that coming, and for a second was at a loss for words. "I don't—" She started to shut him down cold, but stopped at the bleak look that crossed his features. Something inside her softened. She wasn't wholly sure of what his relationship with his brother's widow entailed, but from what little Raine had said, she knew it was complicated. She also knew his feelings for the widow ran deep, and she wasn't sure they were all that appropriate. "Jake, I don't feel comfortable discussing Raine's personal business with you."

His mouth shut tight and his eyes glittered. "So it's true then," he growled. His hands fisted and he shook his head. "Is she fucking crazy?"

He slowly unclenched his fists and let out a long

shuddering breath as all emotion disappeared from his face. "All right then. Whatever," he muttered.

A horn honked, and his name was shouted from the passing vehicle. Jake smiled and waved, but it was false. There wasn't anything light or happy in his eyes when they returned to Maggie. "I'm sorry if I came across like an asshole. She just..." He frowned and shook his head. "Raine pushes all my buttons, ya know? And she's not thinking straight right now. Having a kid is huge. Hell, she can't even look after a goddamn cat, for Christ sakes. Who the hell do you think has Casper?"

Casper was the large white cat that lived at his parents' home.

"Why don't you tell her that?" she said softly.

Jake stared down at her for several long minutes and then shrugged. "Nah, it wouldn't do any good. Raine always does exactly what she wants, and there's no one who's ever been able to convince her otherwise except Jesse. And he sure as hell ain't around."

Maggie didn't know what to say to that. She hoisted her purse onto her shoulder and took a step toward the bus stop. "I'm sorry," she said simply. "I have to run, Jake."

"Hey, I'm still good for a lift. Sorry about being all crazy and shit. It's been a long few weeks." The sad attempt at a smile tugged her heartstrings, but Maggie shook her head.

"Thanks for the offer, but I like the bus."

"You sure? Cain would kick my ass if I didn't ask, or at least he could try." Jake tried to make the situation light, but it only led to an awkward silence.

"I'm good, Jake, and I hope..." She cleared her throat of all the emotion that sat at the back of it and hoped he knew how sincere she was. "I hope you find some peace soon."

He cocked his head, dug his hands into the front pockets of his jeans, and shrugged. "That's something I gave up on a long time ago. But thanks."

She caught her bus with minutes to spare and walked through the front door of her home into the waiting arms of her child. He'd spent the day at Holy Trinity, the local church, participating in the youth group, and he'd been dropped off an hour earlier. Maggie held her son close, even as he squirmed and tried to wriggle from her grasp.

"Hey, your toes look cool. They're like the color of Harry."

She glanced down into his expressive face, and tears filled her eyes as the love she felt for her son hit her in the chest. She cleared her throat. "Harry? My toes remind you of… Who's Harry?"

"He's a fish." Michael giggled. "Tommy's fish."

Maggie snorted and ran her fingers through his curls. "Tommy has a fish?"

Michael followed her into the kitchen. "Yep, his name is Harry, and he's a Chinese fighting fish. He's so cool, and Tommy's brother Zachary told me that he can't have any friends in his tank because they'd kill each other."

"Oh, Harry sounds just lovely." Maggie made a face and reached in the fridge for the casserole she'd baked that morning.

"He's not lovely. That's a sissy word, Mom. He's a fighter."

"Aha." She spooned some of the casserole onto a plate and threw it in the microwave. "Grab the milk, honey."

By the time Michael had fetched the milk from the fridge and poured himself a glass, she had a steaming plate of food on the table.

"So, you didn't forget that I go camping with Tommy tomorrow, right?"

"I didn't forget." That was an understatement.

Her son opened up for another mouthful and paused, spoon frozen in midair. "His mom is picking me up in the morning. They want to be at the campsite by lunchtime."

"What time will Sharon be here?" The butterflies started almost immediately. Tomorrow. No child. Date night. Cain.

Maggie twirled the fork around her plate, not really hungry but thinking she should at least make the effort.

"Right after *Batman*."

She smiled at her son. *Batman* was his favorite cartoon, and he watched it every morning. "All right, so I think when you're done eating, you should hit the shower and get that out of the way before bed."

"Yep, and I'll pack my bag too."

"Good idea."

"Mom?"

Maggie gave up on the casserole and rested her chin in her hand. "Yes?"

A grin spread wide across his face, and her heart jerked, full of love as she gazed into his twinkling eyes. "I like your hair. You look extra pretty tonight."

She rose from the table and dropped a kiss on his forehead. God, how she loved him. He was her life, and at the moment, her life was pretty much perfect.

Chapter 18

Cain slid his '68 Gibson Les Paul across his lap and leaned back in the chair as he looked out over the pristine blue lake in front of him. It was another gorgeous summer day, the breeze was slight, and the water was dotted with boats pulling skiers and tubers alike.

His long fingers slid up the rosewood fretboard, and he absently picked at the low E, caressing the note into a fullness that came naturally to him.

For as long as he could remember, the guitar had been an extension of his arm. His mother had given him an acoustic when he was eight. She'd gotten it free at a garage sale, along with a bunch of how-to magazines.

Cain had felt an immediate connection to the instrument. He'd tossed the magazines and taught himself how to play. It became an obsession, something he did every day, and for a child of eight, that was saying something. From then on, his life consisted of music, football, and his buddies.

All of it had led him to where he was today.

The notes he pulled from those six strings and the melodies he created were like magic. He lived for the thrill of creating something unique. He wrote songs from the heart, hard-rocking tunes, and soulful ballads. His unique voice—a blend of whiskey blues and hard-edged rock—bent and colored the melody in a way no one else could.

Cain Black sang the way he did everything else—at full tilt and full of passion. He'd never been afraid to put it out there…but would he be able to write without Blake? Would he be able to come up with the words that would blend perfectly with the melody? Did he have it in him?

These were sobering thoughts, and he frowned as the lightness he'd enjoyed for the morning disappeared. He'd done his best not to think about the band and what was in store for him when he returned to LA.

Christ, if he couldn't carry his weight—write songs that were hits—would his dream be over before it had a chance?

He strummed a few more chords. Blake was the lyricist—had always been that guy. Could Cain do it?

"That something new?"

Mac strolled onto the deck, dark glasses covering his eyes and two days worth of beard shadowing his jaw. His *GQ* hair, however, looked perfect.

"You look like shit." Cain ran a pentatonic scale, fingers flying over the strings, and shook his head. "How much vodka you throw back last night?"

Mac stretched and groaned. "Too much."

Cain wanted to say more but decided to keep his mouth shut. Truthfully, he was worried about Mackenzie and thought that maybe he was hitting the sauce a little too heavy. But as Jake had pointed out the night before, Mac had always done things his own way and, if pushed, tended to hit back.

It was better to let him deal with his demons on his own terms, and if things got messy, they'd intervene.

"So what's on for tonight?"

Cain's fingers stilled. "I'm taking Maggie out for dinner."

"The little redhead."

Cain nodded.

"The little redhead of the sexy little boy shorts."

"Yeah, that would be the one."

Mac sank into the chair a few feet away and took a bite out of a large green apple. "So what do you got planned, Romeo?"

Cain's fingers plucked out a soft melody—one filled with major notes, happy notes, and grinned. Oh, if he could only share the images in his mind.

"I thought I'd take her to Jack's Hut."

"You're kidding me, right?" Mac removed the shades from his face and shook his head. His eyes were bloodshot and he looked evil, with his forehead crinkled in disbelief. "Jack's Hut is a dive. Why don't you take her to Le Rouge at the Pine Resort? I've heard their food is phenomenal."

"Nope. Jack's Hut is more my style." Cain snorted. "Besides, I don't speak French."

"You're gonna blow it. This girl is going to think she's not worth your time."

Cain rose from his chair, the Les Paul cradled carefully in his hands. "Thanks for your concern, but I've got it covered." He nodded. "I've got a couple errands to run in town, but I'll be back later for a shower. What's Jake got planned? You guys hooking up?"

Mack finished his apple and shrugged. "No clue. I've got some work to do, a few loose ends to tie up on my last project, and I might swing by the Edwardses' later. He's not going back to Afghanistan—you knew that, right?"

Cain nodded. "Yeah, he told me, gave me some technical term about the last surviving child that got him out of the rest of his tour."

"Something's up with him and Raine. It's not good."

"Was it ever? I mean, for Jake?"

Mac grimaced. "It's more than all that old shit." He sighed and rubbed the back of his neck. "God, we're a sorry-ass bunch."

Cain flipped his middle finger in salute. "Speak for yourself. My immediate future is looking pretty damn fine."

"Don't rub it in."

Cain disappeared inside and put the guitar back in its case. The Goldtop Deluxe was his pride and joy. He'd bought it privately from a collector, had paid a hell of a lot for it, but didn't care. It was signed by Les Paul himself, the legendary guitarist and designer of the instrument, and honestly, he'd have paid triple what he had.

It was nearly noon. He grabbed a bite to eat, pulled a T-shirt over his head, and slid into a pair of jeans. His clothes had finally arrived a few days earlier, and he was thankful to have his own stuff and not have to borrow Jake or Mac's shit. He'd only brought a few things with him when he arrived for the funeral. Hell, he hadn't planned on staying longer than a few days, and sure there was a stash of clothes at his Mom's, but most of it was old and ratty.

Springsteen was on the radio, "The River," blasting through the speakers as he pulled out of the driveway and navigated up the narrow lane. Tall evergreen trees bordered the road and gave the impression of deep woods. With the lake behind him and cottages hidden like a secret, Cain welcomed the absolute wash of peace that surrounded him.

His mood was light as he drove toward Crystal Lake, and it didn't take long for him to cross the small bridge that led to the northern side. He hadn't been downtown yet and whistled as he feasted his eyes on the new and improved center of town. It had had a complete redo, with an emphasis on quaint, an obvious attempt to lure the tourists who spent their dollars and propped up the local economy. All the storefronts had new facades, and the light standards that lined the streets resembled something out of Dickens's England.

Cain pulled into an empty space in front of the Rose Garden and cut the engine. The sidewalks were full, couples strolled hand in hand, and he was happy to see the town thriving.

The bell that tinkled when he walked through the door of the Rose Garden alerted the woman behind the counter that she had a customer. Mrs. Avery pushed her glasses higher up her nose and smiled heartily when she spied him.

"Cain Black! I heard you were in town. So nice to see you." She moved from behind the counter, beaming.

"Hi, Mrs. Avery." He nodded. "Feels good to be back."

She shook her head. "It's Mary. I feel silly having a grown man call me Mrs."

"How's Frank?" Her son Frank had been a bit of a hell-raiser back in the day. He was a few years older than Cain, and they'd played ball together a couple years.

Mary's face glowed. "Oh my goodness, he's wonderful. His wife, Robin Travers…remember her? She's about to have their third child—a boy! They've got two girls, so we're quite excited about this little one."

Son of a bitch. Frank Avery—the punisher, as he'd been called on the field—was a dad.

"That's great. Give him my best."

Mary's eyes crinkled in her plump face, and she laughed. "I will, but I'm sure you're not here to talk about Frank. What can I do for you?"

"I'd like some flowers delivered this afternoon, if possible."

"Sure, that won't be a problem. Do you know what you want?"

Cain smiled and nodded. "Tulips if you have them. Deep red ones."

"Let me check the cooler. I think we might be able to help you out."

Mary popped back out after a few moments. "I've got two bunches, and if we need more, my supplier is due in a few hours, so we're in luck."

Tulips were simple and elegant and totally Maggie. She'd mentioned they were one of her favorites, a little tidbit he'd stored away.

"Can you arrange them in a container of some sort? I'm not sure what she has."

"Of course."

Cain reached for his credit card and handed it over.

"Is there a specific time you'd like these delivered to your mom's?"

He signed the receipt. "Ah, they're not for my mom. I want them delivered to Maggie O'Rourke. Not sure of the proper address, but she's renting Old Man McCleary's house."

If Mary Avery was surprised, she didn't show it. "Why yes, I know Maggie. Lovely girl, and that son of hers is such a polite young man."

"Great! Thanks for this, and hopefully I'll see Frank around."

Mary's pale hazel eyes were intent as she stared at him. "What would you like on the card?"

"Nothing." Cain turned. "She'll know who they're from."

One down, two to go.

He decided to leave his truck parked where it was and walked to Jack's Hut, which was located at the end of the main drag. It was exactly what the name implied—a small dwelling with a thatched roof that looked out of place in northern Michigan. But the beer was cold, they served the best damn wings he'd ever had, and he was hoping the jukebox still worked.

The owner owed him a favor from way back, and he was kind of hoping it wasn't too late to cash in.

Twenty minutes later he'd finished his business at the Hut and crossed the street, his eyes fixed on the Super Drug Store that was up the way.

Large glass automatic doors slid open for him, and Cain walked inside. A wall of cool air greeted him, and it felt damn good. He glanced around. The place hadn't changed at all. It still held that antiseptic scent that, if inhaled for too long, was nauseating.

The store was well lit and busy. Shit. He kept his head low and cursed the fact that his trusty Bruins cap was on the seat of his truck.

He paused for a moment, not liking the uncomfortable feeling that settled in his belly. It had been so long since he ran an errand like this that he felt like a damn teenager. With Natasha there'd been no need, and while on tour, well, there were always roadies to do this sort of thing.

Cain slid through the aisles, his focus on the last one to his right. If his memory was correct, that's where the condoms were. And Lord knows his evening wouldn't progress the way he wanted unless he was equipped. He somehow didn't picture Maggie as the type of woman to keep a box full of rubbers by her bed.

He sidestepped an elderly man—"Sorry"—and peeked into the aisle. Yep. There they were. Right beside the jock-itch powder—and Mrs. Lancaster. Her pink and red dress was damn hard to miss, but it was the white hair and black rubber boots that gave her away.

He groaned inwardly and glanced at his watch. It was now nearly two in the afternoon. He'd told Maggie he'd pick her up at five. Time was running out, and though he'd have liked nothing better than to grab them and go, there was no way in hell he was going to pick out a shiny box of condoms while Mrs. Lancaster stood inches away.

He scowled. And really, why the hell were the boxes so damn shiny anyway?

He headed down the next aisle, not really focusing on anything and hoping like hell Mrs. Lancaster would leave already.

"Hey Cain." It was Dave Edmonds, his old football coach. The gravelly voice was distinct though not as robust as he remembered.

It seemed his delicate mission was going to be interrupted by every damn person he knew. Figures.

The man shuffled over from the pharmacy counter,

and they chatted for several minutes about the weather, football, music, and the upcoming fundraiser. Coach Edmonds had aged, but his humor was as sharp as ever, as was his opinion, which was strong on most every subject imaginable. He thought Cain's music was crap and that he'd be more successful if he had a banjo in his band. And a fiddle.

"Well, sorry to bother you, Cain. I'll let you get back to whatever it is you're doing."

He shook Coach's hand and then gestured crazily. "Thanks, I'm just trying to find the right ones..." His words trailed off as Cain took a second to glance at the shelves in front of him. They were crammed full of products—feminine products, to be exact, in all shapes, sizes, colors, and—he cringed—wings. What the hell? His eyes narrowed. They even had them for thongs?

Coach Edmonds frowned and shook his head, a weird look in his eyes. "Sorry. This is beyond my scope. I can't help you with this." Coach took a step and paused, laughter underlying his words. "Good luck with that."

Cain grimaced and nodded. "Yeah, thanks." He waited until Coach was gone and crept to the end of the aisle, a smile widening his mouth as a memory rushed through him.

The first time he ever bought condoms, it had been a group effort. He'd come in with the boys—Jesse, Jake, and Mac. It had been late, a Friday night. The Super Drug was open until midnight, and they'd waited till Brenda Borstrano had left for the night, leaving only one of their schoolmates at the register. If not, she'd have spread it all over town that the Bad Boys were rubbering up.

They'd had no clue what to buy and in the end had

grabbed a box of every kind that there was. Size large, of course.

He smiled at the memory. They'd spent a small fortune, and as it was, most of the condoms they bought had never been put to use. Even then their dreams had been larger than their reality.

Cain pretended to walk by the aisle, shot a covert glance toward his prize, and was happy to see that Mrs. Lancaster had moved on from the jock itch. He turned quickly and headed straight for the rack of condoms. His eyes scanned the variety that was there, and for a second he was that kid from back in the day. Confused and entirely way too excited.

He had no idea there was so much to choose from, mostly because he'd only ever had straight-up, normal condoms.

Where to start? Christ, there were glow-in-the-dark condoms, flavored condoms, studded-for-his-and-her-pleasure condoms, and warming condoms. *Warming?*

Shit. He grabbed the closest one and raised an eyebrow at the name emblazoned along the side of the box in bold neon green, Rough Rider. It was somehow… appropriate. A grin cracked his face and he chuckled. It was one of the studded brands. Why the hell not?

Another box caught his eye. He hesitated and then grabbed it too. He'd never even heard of a vibrating condom ring before, but hell, it couldn't hurt to try. He smiled wickedly at the thought. It sounded very interesting.

He turned and nearly ran over Mrs. Lancaster. The woman was scrunched near the display of antifungal creams, and there was no way he was getting around her. He was about to head the other way when she spoke.

"You played football, didn't you, Cain?"

He glanced down at the box in his hands and froze. The neon color seemed to pulsate beneath the harsh fluorescent lights above. Damn, anyone other than her and he'd have been fine. But Mrs. Lancaster? The pastor's wife?

"Cain, are you deaf, my dear?"

He turned, kept his right hand behind his back, and smiled. "Mrs. Lancaster, sorry, didn't see you there." He nodded. "Sure, I played some ball."

"You ever get the jock itch?" She straightened and peered up over her glasses.

"No, ma'am." He chuckled. "I never had a problem in that area."

Her eyes narrowed. "Hmm, well, this isn't common knowledge, so I'd appreciate it if you could keep it under your hat, but my Franklin sweats a lot."

Okay, that's not what he'd been expecting to hear. "Ah, sorry to hear that, Mrs. Lancaster."

"Yes, well, it's been his cross to bear"—her eyebrow arched—"so to speak." She pointed toward the display behind her. "I Googled it."

"It?"

"Jock itch. He's got this rash, and it's something fierce to behold."

"Oh."

"Playing football and all, I thought you might have a suggestion as to which antifungal cream or spray is better." Her face was screwed up into an intense frown, as if this was a life-and-death decision. "There's powder too, but I'm just a little confused."

"Sorry, Mrs. Lancaster, I don't know which is the

best, but I'm sure they're all equally effective." He shrugged. "Maybe a cream?"

Or a shot of something in the ass? He hid the smile that accompanied that thought.

She nodded. "Yes, that's what I was thinking." She shrugged. "He's an old man with an itch. This can't be rocket science."

"Well, I've got to get going, so..."

She grabbed a tube of cream and chuckled. "Goodness, of course. I'm sure you've got much more important things to do than discuss such a thing with an old lady."

Cain let her pass, his face hot. He swore everyone in the damn store was staring at him. He clutched the box in his hands tightly. Mrs. Lancaster kept up a pleasant chatter all the way to the front cashier, and he followed behind.

"I hope Pastor Lancaster feels some relief soon." He smiled tightly. Crap, Rebecca Stringer was heading his way. He needed to get the hell out of the store.

"I'm sure he'll be fine."

Cain stepped by her and stood just beyond the cash register, his intent to inch past.

"I'm sure he will, but Cain, you might want to pay for those before you leave." Her gaze moved to his hands, and she smiled, a devilish twinkle in her eye. "Stealing is a sin, son, among other things."

He looked at the shiny black box in his hands and swallowed. Not cool to be caught by the pastor's wife with a box of big-ass studded condoms, and a vibrating condom ring to boot.

Rebecca was nearly to the cashier, a determined look

on her face. His blood pressure rose significantly. He so didn't want to deal with her right now.

"Do you want to..." Mrs. Lancaster motioned in front of her. "I'm sure you're in much more of a hurry than I am. Why don't you pay for your purchase first." She winked and whispered, "You might want to ask for a paper bag, though you should know they charge a quarter for them now."

He forced a smile and clutched his Rough Riders.

Sure, he'd get right on that.

Chapter 19

MAGGIE HAD CHANGED AT LEAST SIX TIMES IN THE LAST half hour, and at the moment, her bedroom was a disaster. Clothes were strewn everywhere, and shoes littered the floor. She didn't have a whole lot in her closet, so the mess represented most of what she owned.

Her fingers smoothed the soft lines of the skirt she wore. She'd forgotten about it, mostly because she'd had no reason to wear it for the last few years. It was an older piece, but hugged her curves in exactly the right way. She glanced around. The mess was worth it. She felt sexy, anxious, and excited. Things she hadn't felt in years.

Her hair was loose, fell past her shoulders in a curtain of crimson that she'd carefully straightened. The subtle highlights Lori had added shone like slivers of gold, and when she turned her head, her eyes were luminous, emphasized by the new makeup she'd purchased.

It was amazing how a little bit of mascara coupled with dark, smoky shadow made her eyes pop. Light blush across her cheekbones and some gloss on her lips, and she was good to go.

The skirt was a wraparound, plain black and short, falling halfway down her thigh. She'd joined it with a soft green silk halter and black sandals that she'd borrowed from Raine. She was braless and a little nervous about the fact, but she didn't have one of those fancy crisscross halter bras.

Her fingers ran over her chest lightly, and her nipples hardened, their rigid tips very much in evidence. She thought of Cain's hands on her and blushed when she thought of how boldly she grabbed him between the legs. He'd felt so big and strong.

As the image lingered, the slow, heavy ache she'd been fighting for days intensified. Good God, she had no need for color on her cheeks. Her natural embarrassed tone would be more than enough.

A stab of fear shot through her, and she blew out a nervous breath. All she could think about was sex. With Cain. Her mind had been filled with erotic images of him since Sunday night, and she groaned as her hands rested against her heated cheeks.

She couldn't do this. She was no practiced actress or knowledgeable model. Heck, she only knew of one way to do it. What if Cain expected something…spectacular? What if there was some new way to do it that she'd never heard of? Some weird, kinky thing that was all the rage with rockers and models and…

You sure as hell had no problems with inhibitions the other night.

The thought snuck into her mind and her blush deepened.

The things I'm going to do to you, Maggie, just might be illegal in some states.

His words echoed in her head, coiled around the heat in her belly, and kick-started her into action. Cain would be here any minute.

She grabbed the pile of clothes off the bed, stuffed them in her closet, and threw the shoes in as well. She could deal with putting them away properly tomorrow. A giggle escaped, and she made a face. If only her clients could see her now.

Her gaze fell to the red tulips on the small nightstand beside her bed. They'd arrived a few hours earlier. A classy arrangement in a beautiful crystal container. There was no card, but she knew who'd sent them. It was a simple gesture but one that meant more than Cain could know.

Tulips had been her mother's favorite.

After straightening up the mess of makeup in her small bathroom, she slipped into the delicate black sandals and straightened the corner of the comforter. The bed was a king-size monstrosity and filled a good portion of her room. It had come with the house, as had most of the furniture. The mismatched sheets she had didn't exactly fit properly, but it had never been an issue.

Because she'd never had a man back to her house before.

Maggie bit her lip. Should she change them? Did it matter?

She took a step toward the bed and froze as the doorbell ripped through the silence of her home. Her heart beat a furious rhythm, and her skin rippled with another wash of heat. She shivered from a violent chill and hated the way her stomach tightened, full of nerves.

For one second she considered staying put, pretending she wasn't home. What if people started talking? What the hell had happened to her need to lay low and blend in?

The bell sounded again, and she closed her eyes. Was it so awful to want something special for herself? To want Cain as much as she did? Her resolve faded as the doorbell echoed once more.

"Don't be a coward," she whispered, and followed

the fading echo of the bell out to the small foyer. Her tongue darted across her lips nervously, and she yanked the door open before she lost the nerve.

She was sure the birds still sang, that Mrs. Johnson's lawn mower still mowed, and the laughter from the children a few doors down still echoed in the street. And yet she heard nothing.

Everything faded away like fog rolling across the road in the early morning. Just like in the movies. There was nothing but Cain. He was larger than life, and in that moment, she could acknowledge wholeheartedly he was the sexiest man she'd ever laid eyes on.

His long legs were covered in faded denim, while casual Doc Martens adorned his feet. He wore a white button-down shirt. It was formfitting and emphasized his wide shoulders and tapered waist. His sleeves were rolled up, and his tattoo peeked out at her, a vibrant picture against his darkly tanned skin.

Her eyes slowly traveled up to his face, and the breath caught in the back of her throat. His hair was still damp as if he wasn't long from the shower, and the slow smile that spread across his mouth left her weak. It spoke of secrets and desires and promised all sorts of naughty things.

Shit.

"Hey." His voice was husky, low.

"Hi," she answered, and took a step back. "Do you want to come in or…" Maggie didn't know what the heck to say. She hadn't been on a first date since she was sixteen. But back then things had been different. Expectations were so not what they were tonight.

"I think we should just go." His eyes glittered, and his smile was full-on devastation. "You look…" His eyes caressed her body with one hot look, and he leaned down close near her ear. "Amazing." His breath tickled the side of her neck, and Maggie's mouth went dry. She swallowed, a gut reaction, but nearly choked.

"Let me grab my bag."

She knew his eyes followed her, and it took a lot of willpower to walk in a calm, controlled manner. She grabbed the small bag Raine had dropped off with the shoes. "Okay, I'm ready."

Cain smiled and stood to the side. "I hope you're hungry." Maggie nodded, but as her belly rolled once more, she doubted she'd be able to eat at all.

She turned the lock and followed him to his SUV. He opened the passenger door and stood back, though his fingers caressed her bare back as she stepped inside. He leaned across and secured her seat belt, and from the wicked look he gave her, Maggie was pretty sure it had just been an excuse to rub his arm across her breasts.

She'd barely been able to contain the hiss that slithered along her tongue.

She fingered her small bag nervously as Cain backed out of the driveway. Luke Jansen was on his front lawn, tossing a ball to his golden retriever, Shelby, though his gaze was fixated on the SUV.

Maggie waved, and Luke paused, ball in hand, his expression hard. He didn't return her wave.

"He'll get over it."

She glanced at Cain. "Sorry?"

"Jansen. He's got a thing for you."

"Oh, I don't know about that. I mean, he's asked me out a few times, but it just...he's not..."

"He's not for you?"

She fingered the edge of her skirt. "He's nice enough and all, but no"—she glanced at him—"he's not my type."

He smiled, and her heart quickened. "Good to know."

Cain turned down onto Main Street. "Mac suggested I take you to Le Rouge for dinner."

"Oh, I've never been." Which wasn't surprising, considering one entrée probably cost more than what she made in a day.

"I hope you're not too disappointed if we don't."

Maggie shrugged. "I don't eat out a lot, so I'm not particularly fussy where we go."

Cain maneuvered his truck around a parked car that was half in the street and drove down the main drag of Crystal Lake. He pulled into an empty spot in front of a smallish building that stood alone. Above the door was a plain wooden sign: Jack's Hut. It looked out of place among the elegant buildings that surrounded it.

"This place might not look like much, but trust me, it will be a great. Jack's been around for years."

"It looks cute." Okay, Le Rouge might have been a bit on the grand side. She didn't expect to be wined and dined, but this place looked a slight cut above fast food. *Very* slight.

"Hey, we can go to Le Rouge if you want." He flashed a smile. "I just thought our first date could be more… low-key…intimate."

Cain used his hands a lot when he talked, and she focused on them. The fingers were long, and as they slid along the steering wheel once more, she thought of them on her skin, traveling up her belly. Touching her breasts. She closed her eyes and swallowed a groan. She so didn't care where they ate.

"Hey, you're not disappointed, are you?" His concern was genuine, and she shook her head, her hand reaching for the door.

"I'm just happy to be with you." The admission slipped from her mouth without thought.

Cain jumped from the truck and was at her side, his hand reaching for hers, enveloping her own into his warmth. He pulled her close, held her against him, and she felt his arousal. He leaned down and brushed his lips across hers. "Let's go."

Her heart skipped a beat as she read the "Closed" sign that hung in the window. Inside, the lights were dim. "Are you sure they're open?"

Cain nodded, a sly smile on his face. "Positive."

They escaped the warm summer evening into the dark, cool interior of Jack's Hut. It took a few moments for her eyes to adjust, and when they did, her mouth hung open, a soft "Oh" on her lips as she gazed at the room in wonder.

The place was empty, candlelit, and filled with small vases of tulips that were set upon every available surface that could hold them. Music drifted from a jukebox in the corner, blues by the sound of it, sexy notes layered between the rich, throaty vocals of some unknown goddess.

In the middle of the room was the only table. It was set for two and held a small bucket of ice filled with Coronas.

Cain's face lit up like that of a little boy on Christmas morning. "Now this"—he glanced around—"this is more my style."

A tall man appeared from the back pushing a cart laden with food. Maggie sniffed a host of aromas and was surprised at the hunger pangs she felt. Considering she'd been full-on nauseous only a short while earlier, things were looking up.

Chicken wings, garlic bread, and nachos.

The gentleman was solid, with a full head of shockingly black hair and bushy eyebrows to match. His bare arms were powerful and loaded with tattoos, some of which were not exactly appropriate.

"Cain! I just finished." The man's dark eyes landed on her, and his smile widened. He walked toward them. "You must be Maggie."

She nodded. "Hello."

"I'm Jack. Nice to meet you." He tossed a set of keys to Cain and shook his hand. "Lock up when you leave, and throw the keys back in through the mail slot. I've got an extra set at home."

"Thanks for everything." Cain followed Jack to the door and locked it behind him. He glanced back at Maggie. "Last chance to change your mind. I can make a phone call and get us into Le Rouge if you prefer."

She couldn't take her eyes off him. The setting didn't matter. *He* was what mattered, and if she could have him to herself, with no prying eyes, then all the better.

"This is perfect." And it was.

His warm hand was on her back as he escorted her to the table. Small, spiky shivers of desire leaped across her flesh at his touch.

Cain opened two bottles and handed her a cold Corona. "Do you want a glass? I can grab one from behind the bar."

Maggie shook her head. "I'm not really a glass kind of girl." A smile crept over her mouth. "The bottle is fine."

He held his Corona aloft, and Maggie raised hers as well. "To our first date," he murmured.

The next three hours flew by. Cain shared a good many details about his life, and she found herself fascinated at the stories he told of faraway places she'd only seen in magazines and of the funny, crazy, and sometimes disturbing intricacies of living out of a suitcase for months at a time.

He told her about growing up in Crystal Lake, of the good times he'd shared, of the Bad Boys, and of the lost one, Jesse. Maggie was enthralled and touched, and laughed until her belly hurt.

By the time they were done eating she was totally under his spell.

"I see why you're the front person in your band." She paused, enjoying the way the candlelight danced in his eyes. "Why all the women are thrilled you're home."

Cain cocked his head and smiled. "And that would be because..."

Maggie lowered her eyes and ran her fingers along the empty bottle of beer in front of her. "I'm sure you're a great musician—"

"You're sure?" he interrupted with a laugh.

"Well, I'm not familiar with your music, but I think it's safe to assume you've got talent." She smiled and shrugged. "But I think it's probably more than just the fact that you write good songs."

He leaned closer. "So tell me what you really think."

"I think you could charm the pants off just about anyone without even trying."

Silence fell between them for several long moments, and then he spoke, his voice so low she barely heard him. "There's only one person I want to charm tonight, and she sure as hell ain't wearing pants."

The jukebox had long finished, and the candles flickered in the dark. His eyes were intense, and she felt the change in the air. It was like a physical touch, a caress, and a shudder all at once. He grabbed her hand, his touch gentle and hot. Maggie watched, her breaths falling in jerky spurts as he lifted her fingers to his mouth and slowly licked the last remnants of sticky sauce off them.

The ache between her legs erupted in a single shot of urgent need, and she bit her lip, her eyes never leaving his.

"I think we're done here." His voice was rough.

Maggie stood, and when he held out his hand, she slipped hers inside his large grasp, loving the way he pulled her into his body. She felt like she belonged, and the thought was one that soothed and calmed and fanned the flames of desire at the same time.

"Let's go."

Outside the early-evening sky was shot through with reds and golds. It sliced through the dark that loomed on the horizon—a beautiful, mad palette of color. The sidewalks were mostly empty, though the few patios scattered downtown were filled with patrons.

When they reached his truck, Cain's hands slid along her waist, and he brushed his mouth against hers, a quick, probing touch that was over much too soon.

And yet it nearly took her breath away.

"Let's get you home," he murmured against her mouth.

The ride back to her house was silent; the air was charged with an energy that slithered along her body and left her trembling. Maggie gripped her purse tightly, forced herself to relax, but it was hard.

Cain pulled into her driveway and hopped out of the truck in a quick, fluid movement. She already had her door open, but he helped her down. His touch was sure and possessive. It lingered and burned.

His hand didn't leave hers, and when she fumbled for her key, he grabbed them from her purse, unlocked her front door, and followed her inside.

The silence of her home was so loud, she was sure he heard her heart banging against her chest. Lord knows, it pounded in her ears furiously enough. For a second she felt dizzy, weak, most likely panicked, but then he was there behind her, his body heat searing the bare flesh of her back.

Cain's arms slid around her rib cage and he held her for the longest time, so tight she felt every inch of his hard frame. His breath was hot against her neck, and when he nuzzled the sensitive area beneath her ear, she groaned.

His right hand slid up and cupped her breast as he continued to trail small kisses along her neck. "Oh Maggie, the things I'm going to do to you..."

Gently he turned her in his embrace. Her eyes focused on the pulse that beat in his neck. The rhythm was as mad and frantic as hers. It hit her then. He was just as affected as she. That knowledge filled her with a confidence she'd never felt before.

Slowly her eyes rose.

"So you said the other night." She licked her lips and trailed her fingers along his chest until her hands were splayed across his shoulders. "I was a good girl and took your advice."

"You did?" His chocolate eyes glittered.

She felt saucy. Dangerous. Powerful.

Maggie nodded and stood on her tiptoes so that she could whisper in his ear. Her sensitive nipples scraped along his chest, sending shards of desire spiraling across her flesh.

"I got a full night's sleep, which I guess is a good thing." She paused, felt his hardness against her stomach. "Because I'm not expecting to get any tonight."

Maggie wriggled out of his arms and kicked off her shoes. She turned slowly and headed toward her bedroom, well aware of the man left behind.

Chapter 20

Cain had never seen anything as hot as Maggie O'Rourke. And he'd been around the block. She was Jezebel and Monroe and an angel all rolled into one sexy package.

He followed her down the hall like a dog in heat and was at her side seconds after she entered her bedroom. The room was dark, with long shadows flickering along the wall.

He watched her for the longest time. Let the pressure build. The passion and need. And then he crossed to her bedside and switched on the small lamp that was there.

"I need to see you," he whispered.

Maggie's huge eyes glistened like liquid glass. Her mouth was parted; her chest rose and fell rapidly. Elegant fingers, the tips a deep shade of navy, tucked a strand of hair behind her ear, and he noted the slight tremble.

She was nervous.

For the first time in a long time, he could say that he felt the same.

"Let me see you," he said again.

A slow, sexy smile claimed her lips, and she walked toward him, her movements graceful, like a cat's. Maggie stopped a few inches from him, and her sweet, exotic scent teased his nostrils.

His desire raged, and he panted from the effort it took

to hold himself still. Every single muscle in his body was tense, hard, and he ached to hold her.

Her hands rose, and she reached behind her neck. Her head tilted to the side, and a long curtain of hair momentarily covered her face. When her hands fell once more, so did the silky green fabric, and slowly she tugged it down over her breasts until she was bare to him.

"Jesus," he whispered. Her breasts were creamy, the dusky rose nipples hard. They were perfect, fully rounded, and begged to be touched.

Maggie's eyes never left his as she continued to tug the fabric down to her waist. She carefully untied her skirt and seconds later stood like a goddess in nothing but a skimpy, sexy-as-hell black G-string.

Cain shifted his legs in an effort to alleviate the pressure between them. He was so hard that he was afraid he'd blow early and they'd both be shit out of luck. He needed to take it down a notch. He ran his fingers through his hair and exhaled.

"You are beautiful, Maggie."

Her eyes shimmered, and she licked her lips, her small tongue darting out quickly. "I..." Her chest heaved. "I've never..." She looked up at him and he saw her heart, her soul, reflected in her eyes. She crossed her arms across her chest and his heart swelled. "I've never done this before. I mean, I've done *this* but not with anyone other than Michael's father. Never," she whispered.

He reached for her. "I know." He paused. Something shifted inside him, a pull at the very core of his soul. She was unique and wonderful and sexy as hell. She touched him like no one before, deep down where it mattered.

This night wasn't about him or the fact that he needed to be inside her so badly it hurt.

This was about Maggie and his desire to put her on a pedestal and give her everything that he could. He wanted to put her needs and desires above his. And he'd start right now.

Her lips parted and he lowered his mouth, claimed the mouth that had teased him all night. She tasted like sin, and he probed deeply, loving the way she melted against him as his tongue danced along her softness.

He kissed her long and hard until his bones liquefied and his heart pounded heavy inside his ears.

"Holy Christ, woman, you're tearing me apart." His hands slid into the thick curtain of hair that fell to her shoulders, and his mouth nibbled along her jaw until he reached her delicate ears. She shivered in his embrace as his left hand slid down her body, cupped her hip, and urged her tight against the hard bulge in his jeans.

He turned, sat on the bed, and lifted her easily so that she straddled him. She groaned and moved back and forth across him, her softness hot and damp against his cock. He tightened even more and gritted his teeth as she continued to writhe against him.

"Slow down, babe," he whispered, loving the whimper that fell from her as she halted. "Or this will be over before it begins."

His hands cupped her breasts, and his mouth finally claimed a turgid peak. He closed around her and suckled gently at first and then harder, with much urgency. Her breast swelled against him, and he massaged the other, taking his time so that he could enjoy her fully.

"Oh Cain," she breathed.

His name on her lips, the passion that colored her voice—it filled his chest with an emotion that grabbed him hard. He licked the hard, puckered nipple and turned his attention to her second breast. Minutes later, she leaned against him, her arms on his shoulders, her breaths rapid and harsh.

Slowly his hands caressed their way down to her hips, and he held her for several moments, teasing himself with the feel of her heat on him. Carefully, he moved her so that she lay on the bed.

Her huge eyes stared at him in silence as her breasts rose and fell rapidly. Her knees were bent, and his eyes rested upon the small silk patch that hid the treasure he sought.

Cain stood and doffed his shirt. Hell, he might have broken a few buttons in his haste but didn't care. His fingers made quick work of his belt, and his jeans and shoes followed until he stood by the bed buck naked, with a raging hard-on and a rabid desire.

He slid alongside her and claimed her mouth once more, this time a tender sweep, more of a tease than a taste. Cain stared down into her eyes and kissed her nose, her cheeks, and her forehead.

"Remember what I said, Maggie?"

She nodded, eyes not wavering, though she remained silent. His hand trailed down her chest and settled upon her belly. Muscles moved beneath her flesh as he splayed his large hand across her.

He smiled, a wicked glint in his eyes, and his fingers moved lower. When he slipped inside her thong and probed the soft wetness there, she bit her lip and groaned.

"Don't close your eyes, Maggie." He needed to see her, see the pleasure in her eyes. Pleasure that *he* gave her.

She whimpered beneath his ministrations but held his gaze steady. Cain took his time, his long fingers massaging, teasing, until she was slick with need. When he slid two fingers deep inside, she bucked her hips slightly and he smiled. God, she was tight. He bent lower and whispered against her mouth.

"Relax, babe." He moved slightly so that he lay across her, rotated his fingers inside her, and when she jerked crazily, he paused and then rubbed the sweet spot in a steady, thorough motion until she quivered.

"Oh God, Cain." Her hips gyrated in a jerky movement, and he claimed her mouth once more as she came. Her orgasm rippled through her, and he felt every nuance of it. When it faded, when his fingers ceased their magic, he broke the kiss and spoke, his tone husky.

"I'm just getting started."

Maggie stared up at Cain in wonder. She'd never been this aroused before. Ever. She wasn't sure she'd ever had an orgasm before, at least she didn't think so, and she was pretty sure that if she actually had to think about it, it hadn't happened. Maybe she'd had a baby orgasm or a twinge, but nothing like this.

His hard, muscular body strained against hers, and she knew how close to the edge he was riding. Heck, she'd seen him. He was huge and hard and so ready.

He dropped another kiss on her and moved away. For a second she felt bereft as cool air slid along her body.

But then he dragged her thong down, leaving her fully exposed, and her breath caught in her throat at the dark look of desire that hung on his face.

A slow, wicked smile claimed his mouth, and he slid to the floor so that he was on his knees. *Between her legs*. His hands were on her thighs, and he gently pulled them apart. Cain tugged her forward until her butt was on the edge of the bed, and she squeezed her eyes shut as she felt the heat of his breath against her inner thigh. *Oh God*.

His mouth was down there. So close.

She'd never done this. She wasn't a prude by any means, but Michael's father had never taken his time with her. Sex had always been a quick, furious joining, and then it was over. Their repertoire hadn't included anything but the missionary position.

Cain's fingers slid along her thigh, and her first instinct was to close her legs, but the gentle pressure he exerted won over. "Relax, Maggie." His words tickled so close to her *there* that she blushed. And when his fingers began their assault once more, she whimpered.

Which turned into a full-on groan as his tongue slid inside her most secret spot. He teased and tortured until she couldn't stand it anymore. Her inhibitions flew right out the window, and her legs relaxed until she was fully open to him. Until she could enjoy what he was doing and revel in her sexuality. Her hands found their way into the thick waves that framed his face, and she held him steady as he suckled and teased and stroked until her body erupted into another orgasm, one that liquefied her and left her weak and panting.

"Cain, I..."

She didn't have time to finish—not that she could begin to vocalize her thoughts—because he flipped her onto her belly and hoisted her butt in the air. "I can't hold back, babe. I want to, but I can't."

Maggie was still dazed, vaguely heard the ripping of foil, and then his hands were on her ass. His right hand massaged the roundness before sliding up to the dip at the base of her spine at the same time his left was there at her sex, probing and teasing.

She felt him against her back, the heavy, hard weight of him, and turned her head slightly. "Cain, I don't know if I can—"

She didn't finish. Because she couldn't speak. In one thrust he was deep inside her. Stretching her open as he slid in and then paused. She trembled with anticipation as the heat of her passion thrummed through her body. It was electrifying, wonderful, and totally hot.

"I knew it," he whispered against her back.

She could only nod. There were no words.

"I knew you'd feel like heaven."

Cain moved slowly in and out, and each pass sent shock waves of pleasure rippling along her skin. She was on fire, her belly was tight, and the pressure that built inside once more was unlike anything she'd experienced.

It was intense and biting and painfully exquisite all at once.

His breaths fell rapidly—she heard them like hard bursts of energy—and he lifted her hips into the air, held her at a different angle as he increased his rhythm.

"Damn, woman, but you were made for me."

His words thrilled her, and she cried out as the pressure inside gripped her hard. There was no noise—save for whimpers of pleasure, the creaking of her bed, and the sound of flesh on flesh. His strokes were firm, controlled, and when he upped the rhythm, she was right there with him. They came together in a shattering orgasm that left her weak, breathless, and completely done.

They collapsed back onto the bed, his heart pounding at her back, a melody that was in sync with her own. Cain's arms never left her. He pulled her into his embrace, and she rolled onto her side and tucked her head into his chest.

She didn't want this feeling to go away, to fade into memory as if it had never happened, so she closed her eyes and visualized every moment that she could, every touch and sound and smell.

Silence enveloped them in long, gentle waves. She listened to his heart, traced the hard ridges of his abs, and didn't know what to say. There were no words to describe how she felt. *Satisfied*, *content*...they didn't cut it.

"Are you all right?"

Maggie nodded. She wasn't sure she could speak just yet.

"You're one hell of a woman, Maggie." His hand was gentle as he traced the line of her hip and stayed there in a possessive caress. She loved the feel of it. Of him beside her. Of his scent in her nostrils. She loved the ache between her thighs, the one that spoke of loving and of belonging.

"So beautiful," he continued. Cain nuzzled the side of her neck, and the hand on her hip gripped a little harder. He paused and stretched his body so that he could reach over the bed.

He fumbled for something, and her eyes ate up the beautiful lines of his body hungrily. He was hard again, and already an answering ache stirred within her.

When Cain turned back to her, he grinned and held up a small package in his hand. The look on his face was a cross between that of a boy on Christmas morning and a man about to take what he wanted.

Her mouth went dry, and her belly did that little flip she'd grown accustomed to. His desire was raw and echoed what she felt inside.

"What's that?" Her voice was throaty, seductive.

His grin was wicked. "It's a condom ring thing. A *vibrating* condom ring."

Okay, she wasn't expecting that. "Oh. I've never..."

He peeled the wrapper back and winked. "Me neither"—he leaned toward her—"but I'm thinking we're going to like it."

Chapter 21

SUNLIGHT FILTERED THROUGH HER BEDROOM WINDOW, casting thin beams of gold against the drab gray walls. They mimicked the pattern of Maggie's cheap window coverings, missing slats and all. The blinds were crap, but for the most part they did their job.

Cain was next to her, and she relished the warmth of his body. He was relaxed with one of his arms thrown over his head, legs sprawled wide. He appeared younger as he slept, softer. It was amazing, really, how his features aligned perfectly. God, she could spend hours just looking at him. He was simply beautiful.

Maggie's back kinked and she moved slightly, a groan slipping from her lips as her body protested. Her muscles were stiff, and parts of her ached. *A lot*. *Those* parts of her. She giggled. It was a good pain, but nonetheless a glaring reminder of her lack of experience and the fact that she hadn't been intimate in a very, very long time.

A blush stained her cheeks as her mind wandered. Oh, the things he'd done to her. The things she'd *let* him do to her. A smile crept along her mouth as she traced his chest, though it soon fled as reality set in.

She felt the weight of it, that reality, pressing on her chest. This wouldn't last. How could it? He'd be leaving at some point this summer. The man lived in Los Angeles, and his career would call him back.

A single mom with a kid didn't figure into that, but still…

Don't go there, Maggie. Don't fantasize about a future that doesn't belong to you.

She sighed and relaxed in his embrace. Who was she kidding? The baggage she'd hidden away, the stuff from her past that she'd shared with no one…that wasn't going anywhere, and besides, she wasn't naive. Cain Black didn't belong in her world any more than she did in his.

She'd done a bit of research, and she knew BlackRock was on its way up. Their last CD had garnered a lot of attention from the public and critics alike, and there was a lot of buzz about the next record. Cain would fly as high as he let himself and go where his career took him.

When he left—and he would leave—whatever *this* was between them would end. She needed to pull up her big girl pants and get with the times. But that nagging doubt remained. The one that said this wouldn't end well for her.

Maggie gave herself a mental shakedown. She needed to be realistic. Modern women had affairs all the time and for a variety of reasons. They took what they needed and moved on with no guilt. No strings.

"Hey, why the frown?" Cain stretched and hugged her close, his hands roving her body, fingers seeking, caressing. He kissed her forehead. "No frowning allowed unless…" The lightness of the moment left as his voice trailed into silence. He cupped her face between his hands, his eyes intense as he studied her. "You don't regret last night, do you?"

She shook her head. "No," she whispered.

Cain leaned toward her and brushed his mouth across hers, then back again, this time parting her lips and kissing her with such tenderness that it brought tears to her eyes. When the kiss finally ended, she was sprawled across his chest, and she felt the hard length of him pulsing against her belly.

He traced her mouth and smiled. "Good, because I sure as hell don't." And then his mouth was on hers again, tasting, stroking, with an intensity that surprised her.

Maggie pulled herself up until she was perched above him, a sly smile falling across her face at the look of absolute need in his eyes. His hands claimed her breasts, and as his mouth closed around a turgid nipple, she closed her eyes and gave in. She would take this ride are far as she could, and she'd damn well enjoy every minute of it.

No regrets.

Her small kitchen table was laden with food. Scrambled eggs, home fries, toast and jam, fresh strawberries, and juice.

"Wow, you really are the king of breakfast." Maggie grinned at Cain as she settled down across from him, a slight wince crossing her features.

"Problem?" he asked, a naughty smile on his face as he reached for the fruit and helped himself to a generous amount of eggs and toast. He knew exactly why her bottom was sore.

"Nope."

Cain spread a liberal amount of jam on his toast and the smile never left his face.

They settled into an easy conversation, one that ebbed and flowed with laughter and wit. Cain was smart and funny and had a biting sense of humor that she liked. He was also damn sexy to look at first thing in the morning.

His jaw was shadowed with stubble, but it only emphasized his sensual mouth and classic cheekbones. His brown eyes glittered as he laughed, and his hair, that thick sexy head of hair, begged to be toyed with. He was dressed in boxers, which was something every girl should experience at least once in her lifetime.

"More coffee?" he asked.

Maggie nodded. This was foreign to her. Being waited on, looked after, coddled even…so not in her daily handbook.

"What you got planned today?"

She stretched, hissing softly at the aches and pains. "I have a client this afternoon."

He poured her another cup of coffee. "Good job you didn't have one this morning."

Maggie inhaled the rich aroma and took a sip. "I canceled."

A slow grin spread across Cain's face. "Pretty confident, weren't you?"

"I…" Once more her cheeks darkened, and she glanced down at the steaming cup of java in her hands.

He leaned over and dropped a kiss on her forehead. "I'm just teasing, though if you took the afternoon off, I'm sure we could find *something* to do."

"I can't."

Cain nodded toward the window above her sink. Sunlight bathed the yard in a warm glow, and the vibrant blue of the sky was breathtaking. "It's going to be another great day." He moved around the table and it took everything in her to avoid staring at the perfection that was his abs. The hard, smooth flesh and the dusky covering of dark hair that pointed downward, toward his…

"We could go out on the boat. I could borrow Jake's." His hand slid behind her neck, and the familiar rush of heat along her skin began in earnest. "I know a place where we can skinny-dip—"

"Cain, some of us have to work. I can't cancel another client in order to continue with this…this sex marathon."

His eyebrow shot up at that.

"First off, it wouldn't be right, and secondly, I have bills to pay. I don't have a money tree growing in my backyard. I clean houses and my kid eats. I know it's not your thing, but that is my reality." Gone were the warm fuzzies as an unfamiliar feeling of anger filled her.

His face hardened for a second and then relaxed as he leaned against the table and stared down at her.

"I understand your reality just fine, Maggie. I sure as hell wasn't born with a golden spoon in my mouth. I had a lot of lean years, played a lot of dives, slept in shit holes that weren't fit for most animals, let alone the human kind. Hell, there were weeks we had no money for food. It was just us and our music." He shrugged. "Sure, things are better now. The band's doing well, and I've made a decent living for years writing songs for all kinds of artists. I don't own a yacht or anything"—he flashed a grin—"*yet*. But I do all right."

"It's not the same thing, Cain." Maggie rose from the table and began to clear the plates. "You only had to worry about yourself. I have a son."

He was silent as he helped put away the leftovers

and then grabbed a tea towel while she washed up their dishes. The lightness of their morning had vanished like water leaking from the tap. The intimate back-and-forth of lovers was no more. Cold reality had set in, and Maggie couldn't lie, it was much too early for the bubble to burst.

She wanted the easiness of dawn. The comfort of his arms and body.

Cain leaned against the counter—his boxers lying dangerously low on his hips—with the damp towel draped across his shoulders. God. The man didn't even have to try, and he looked like a walking commercial for Axe. She could picture it now. Hoards of women crashing through her door, slipping in through the windows, crawling over each other in an effort to get to him.

"Do you have family, Maggie?"

His question surprised her. "I..." She grabbed the towel off him and draped it over the drying rack. She wasn't going there with him. With anyone, for that matter. *Family*. Her family was...

"Hey, I didn't mean to upset you." He reached for her, but she sidestepped to avoid his touch. She knew the power that was in his hands, and at the moment she felt vulnerable. She'd be no match.

"I'm not upset."

"I think you are."

"You don't know me well enough to know if I'm upset or not."

"I think I do."

"Jesus Christ, Cain." She whirled around and pushed a large chunk of hair off her face. "That's bull! You don't know anything about me."

"Well, you're right about that Maggie." He pushed away from the counter and took a step toward her. His face was no longer relaxed—his eyes were narrowed, his mouth tight. A muscle worked its way along his jaw, and she knew he was angry. "You have a habit of keeping people at arm's length. I've known you for what, three weeks?" He shook his head. "And the only thing I know for sure is that you've raised one hell of a kid, that you're independent, focused, and that the sight of you in that tank top is making me insane."

"Cain, I don't… There are things…"

"Maggie, its okay if you want to keep secrets or leave your past behind. Or run away from whatever the hell it is back there that's got you so spooked that you're afraid to trust. I get that." He took a step toward her. "But don't assume that this is casual for me. Don't assume I don't want to know every single detail about you. What makes you tick, where you come from, what your dreams are."

"We had sex, Cain—"

"Ya think?"

She ignored his smile. "Lots of sex, but still, you can't expect me to believe this isn't something you don't do all the time. You're guitar singer guy. Apparently a pretty good one too, so I'm sure this kind of situation—"

"Situation?"

God, he isn't making this easy. She blew out hot air. "Casual sex marathons." She winced as she said the words. It made everything about the evening before cheap. And it wasn't.

"Nothing about last night was casual…at least not for me." His eyes flashed, and Maggie was uncomfortable with the direction of their conversation. "I'm not that guy, Maggie. If I was, I'd have hightailed it out of here last night after our third round, met the guys at the Coach House, and told them how you're the best lay I've had in years."

She bit her lip and looked away, more than a little shocked at his direct words. "There's nothing spectacular about me, Cain. I'm just an average woman—"

"You are *not* an average, everyday woman." His fingers crept up to her cheeks, and he cradled her head between his large hands. "I don't know what reality you're living in Maggie, but it sure as hell isn't mine."

The dark of his eyes expanded, their lash-framed beauty intense as he stared down at her. "You leave me breathless."

He pulled her into his embrace, and Maggie rested her head against his chest. She was too weak to protest, and why would she? Why would any woman in her right mind push away someone like Cain? Why was she trying so hard?

She inhaled his scent, reveled in the comfort and feel of him, and the moment would have been perfect, except Shelby, Luke's dog, decided to exercise her right to bark. And bark. And bark.

"What was that?"

Cain looked down at her. "What?"

"Didn't you hear that noise?"

He shook his head and glanced out the window into her backyard.

"No, it came from the..." *Shit!* Maggie slipped from Cain's embrace and dashed to her front room. She peeked out the window and saw Tommy's mother, Sharon, opening the passenger door of her Volvo. The top of Michael's curly head bopped into view, as well as Tommy's fair one.

Sharon was parked behind Cain's big SUV, and Maggie ducked as the woman glanced toward her house. She felt like a child caught with her hand in the cookie jar. Pretty damn ridiculous, considering she was an adult. In her own home. But still, this wasn't good.

"Oh my God, Cain. Michael's back. I wasn't expecting him until tomorrow." Her heart was in her throat. "You need to hide. He can't know you're here." Oh God, this could not be happening.

The one time I decide to have someone stay over, I get busted by my own kid.

Cain peeked through the window and stood with his hands on his hips. She saw the smile and knew he wasn't nearly as concerned as she. "He's gonna know I'm here, Mags. That's my truck in your driveway."

The blood drained from her face. The hard reality of her night of sin stared right back at her, and the view left her sick to her stomach. Crap. She hadn't thought of the fact that Luke, Mrs. Nichols across the street, and now Sharon would see Cain's vehicle in her driveway.

In the morning.

Where it had sat all night. All night while she was having sex. With Cain. A sex marathon.

She groaned. If the entire town didn't know what had transpired at 45 Linden Street the night before, they'd surely know about it soon. Superman himself would be jealous at the speed at which news like this would travel.

"You need to get dressed." She pushed Cain toward her bedroom. "Hurry! And..." Her mind whirled in twenty-five different directions. "You just stopped by because—"

A knock sounded at the door, and Cain disappeared down the hall, but not before she caught sight of the wide grin he sported.

Maggie exhaled, smoothed the mess of long tangled hair that fell over her shoulders, and opened the door.

"Sharon," she exclaimed as if totally surprised, "is everything all right? I wasn't expecting you until tomorrow."

"Mom! Is that Cain's truck? Is he here?" Michael pushed past Tommy's mother and dragged his buddy along with him.

"Michael John O'Rourke, don't be rude. Stay where you are." *Please don't go toward the bedrooms.*

She turned back to Sharon, denial on her lips, but dropped any pretense of lying almost immediately. The woman was staring at her with an all-knowing look, her eyes doing a quick once-over from the top of Maggie's disheveled hair to the bottom of her fancy painted toes.

"But is he here?" Michael asked.

"He stopped by to help me with something."

Was that a snort?

She eyed Sharon closely.

"Help you with what?"

Oh God, was her own seven-year-old going to put her through the ringer?

"A plumbing issue." *Seriously? That's the first thing that comes to mind?* She cringed as the words escaped her mouth and glanced at Sharon. *Okay, that was definitely a snort.*

"Hey, Michael, I wasn't expecting to see you, buddy." Cain strode in the room fully dressed—thank God—though his attire was definitely dressy for an early-morning call. Of course Michael and his little friend would never know the difference, but Sharon sure as hell did.

Maggie may as well have taken out an ad or rented a billboard: Yes, I Had Sex with Cain Black Last Night.

Cain turned to Tommy's mother and offered his hand. "Nice to meet you, Sharon, isn't it? I knew your husband from high school, but you're not from around here, right?"

"Oh no." Sharon giggled like a schoolgirl.

Maggie watched a host of emotions flicker across the woman's face. *Unbelievable*. Give the man five seconds and he could turn anyone to mush.

"I met Roger in college. I'm originally from Detroit." Her smile vanished and she turned to Maggie. "Which is why I'm here. We had to cut our camping excursion short. I got a phone call, and my father's ill, so Roger and I are heading to Waterford, which is where he's in the hospital. I was hoping maybe Tommy would be able to stay here with Michael. I don't have any details about my father other than they rushed him in an hour ago."

"Of course." Maggie nodded. "I have a client this afternoon, but I'll figure something out."

"Thank you so much, Maggie." The relief was evident in her voice. "I'll call you later when I know what's going on, but either Roger or I will be back for Tommy. I just don't know when."

Maggie followed Sharon out onto the porch. "Don't worry about it. He'll be fine."

"Tommy, you be good for Maggie, all right?" Sharon yelled back into the house.

The boys disappeared, and Cain followed the women

outside. He leaned against the porch railing, and she felt his gaze on her as she walked Sharon to her car. Luke was outside, ready to head out for the day, his burly frame draped in the dark colors that the EMT officers wore. He avoided looking in her direction even as he backed out of his driveway. And nearly ran into the ditch.

Luke's tires squealed as he peeled down the street, and her brow furled in irritation.

She glanced back at Cain. His face was split wide in a grin, one that managed to increase her irritation while making her hot and fluttery at the same time.

Maggie sighed inwardly.

In the harsh light of day, her simple world had just ramped up to complicated.

Chapter 22

"What are you now, a professional babysitter?"

Cain glanced up and had to shade his eyes from the sun as he shrugged. "Just helping Maggie out."

Jake dropped his butt into the chair beside him and spread his long legs out on the dock. It was early afternoon. The sun was a brilliant ball of fire, and the heat was intense.

"Where's Mac?"

"He needed to scan and email some documents back to his office in New York, so he went to town, the library, I think." Cain was on the dock adjacent to the boathouse, his tall frame in shadow as the boys played in the water, roughing around and generally making a lot of noise.

"So…" Jake cracked a smile. "How'd it go last night with Maggie?"

Cain set his guitar beside his chair and shrugged. "It was good."

"Good." Jake repeated.

"I had a really good time."

"That's it. Just good."

"Yup."

"That's all you're gonna share."

Cain's eyes narrowed. "Yeah"—his eyes narrowed—"it is."

Jake's mouth opened wide. "Holy shit."

"What?" Cain settled back into his chair.

"Man, are you in trouble."

"Trouble?" He grabbed his guitar again and strummed a few chords. "How so?"

Jake stretched his arms out and rested them behind his head. "This girl means something to you, and that, my friend, means trouble. You crossed the sacred line of just sex. You're now in the land of sex with consequence."

"Since when did you become so damn cynical?"

"Don't get your panties in a knot, it's an observation. I'm just saying, the little redhead obviously means more than a quick lay to you. But she comes with baggage, in case you weren't looking past that tight little body and mess of red hair."

"Baggage," he said drily.

"A kid."

Cain frowned. He didn't like the analogy. He glanced at Jake, but the soldier was focused on the boys. Michael was wrestling at the edge of the water, his buddy Tommy in a headlock, as the two of them struggled to get the upper hand. They rolled over and both went under, and a few choice words that neither one of their mothers would ever want to hear followed them down.

"God, they seem just like us." Jake sighed and rolled his shoulders.

"Yeah."

"You ever think about having kids?"

Cain stopped playing. He glanced at Jake and set the guitar down once more. To say he was surprised at the turn in conversation would have been an understatement.

"No, never." He scratched the stubble along his jaw. "Natasha wanted one before the ink had dried on our marriage license, but I was dead set against it." He kept his eyes on the boys. "God, if we'd had a child together, it would have been a disaster." He eyed his friend closely. "You?"

Jake's face was hard. "Nah. That's one hell of a commitment, which is why..."

"Why what?" Something was up. "What the hell's going on, Jake?"

Jake scowled. "Raine wants to have a kid."

"A kid." Cain let that settle a bit. This was serious shit.

"A goddamn kid." Jake shook his head. "She's clearly nuts."

Cain couldn't lie. He was shocked. "Raine wants a baby? With who?"

Jake ignored his question. "The girl can't even look after a fucking cat. How the hell is she going to raise a kid on her own?"

"Back the truck up." Cain swung his legs over the side of his chair. "Who the hell is she having a kid with?"

"Jesse."

Cain was dumbfounded and confused.

"Jesse froze his junk before we shipped out last time. It's all he talked about"—he snorted—"having a kid with Raine. He made me promise that if anything happened to him, I'd look after her." Jake shook his head. "It's like he knew he wasn't coming back, and he just dumped this crap on me anyway."

"Shit." Cain didn't know what else to say.

"Exactly." Jake exhaled, his eyes still on the boys.

"Is that why you're not going back to Afghanistan?"

Something changed then. The energy around his friend darkened. Jake's hands were clenched, his body no longer relaxed. The eyes that turned to Cain were flat—emotionless.

"I'm not going back because I'd be a detriment to my unit. The shit that happens over there, it changes you. Makes you crazy. Do stupid things."

Cain didn't push it. He wasn't clear on the circumstance surrounding Jesse's death. All he knew was what Mac had confided. That Jake had witnessed Jesse's death, but that was about it. His friend was in a dark place, and considering his feelings for Raine, he wasn't hopeful Jake would snap out of it anytime soon.

"So, what are you going to do?" he asked instead.

The boys ran along the beach like crazy people, their hands weapons as they pretended to shoot each other. Michael glanced over, and the smile on the kid's face did something to Cain. His chest swelled with an emotion that was becoming a little too familiar. It was warm and fuzzy and *protective* all at once.

Shit. This must be some of that consequence Jake was talking about.

"I gotta do something. All this downtime is driving me crazy. Too much time to think." He paused and then muttered, "Too much time to remember." Jake looked out over the lake. "I'm thinking of diving into the construction project for the new football field and stadium. They want a state-of-the-art facility, and Dad's company won the bid." He shrugged. "I've always been a hands-on kind of guy. Mac might be on board to design the thing."

"That's not what I meant."

Jake glanced his way, his eyes narrowed, his mouth tight. "I didn't think so," he said drily. "I don't know what I'm going to do about Raine. She's stubborn as hell, and personally I think she's crazy to even consider having a baby on her own." His eyes darkened, and a bleak look crept into his features. "I don't know if I can be the one to be there for her."

Why the hell would Jesse put that on his brother? He had to have known Jake's feelings for Raine ran deep. Or maybe that *was* the reason.

"What about you?" Jake asked, the heaviness of the moment gone. It was eerie how the man could switch gears so quickly. "You gonna tell me what the hell Barcelona was about?" Jake stared at him expectantly. Cain saw no reason to sugarcoat.

"Blake was fucking Natasha."

"Shit, that's low."

"Yeah."

"You should have given him the boot after decking him."

Cain leaned back. "Agreed." He paused. "She called a few hours ago—Nat."

"What did she want?"

Cain shook his head, still surprised as hell himself. "Said she'd made a mistake about Blake and the divorce. All of it. According to her, I should give her a second chance, 'cause apparently we're soulmates, she just didn't know it till now."

Jake grimaced. "I hope you told her where to go."

"I did."

"Good. So what are your plans?"

Plans. The future. Cain had no clue.

"I'm here at least until after the Fourth of July. Not due back in the studio until the fall."

"So, you're heading back to LA after the big"—Jake made quotation marks with his fingers—"stadium show?"

Cain's thoughts turned to Maggie. Was he? Could he leave just like that? Did he even want to? The idea left him more than a little unsettled.

"I'm not sure what my plans are. I need to get some new material written or..." He ran fingers along his temple and sighed.

"Or what?"

"I'm screwed...the band is screwed."

Jake grinned and slapped him on the shoulder. "Well, you better get your ass in gear and get writing."

If only it were that easy.

"Cain! Look what I found." They both turned as Michael came running up the beach, a large bass dangling from his hand. The little guy stopped inches from them, his small chest heaving and his face flush with excitement. He pushed wet curls from his face with his free hand and shoved his prize up high. "Look how big it is! I never saw a fish like this. What kind is it?"

"Dude, that would be a *dead* fish." Jake chuckled.

Michael frowned, wrinkled his nose, and giggled. "I know its dead. It stinks worse than Shelby when she's wet."

"Who's Shelby?" Jake teased. "I sure hope that's not your girlfriend."

"Nope." He giggled. "I like Kristen Blake. Shelby is Luke's dog," Michael answered.

"Who's Luke?"

"Jansen. He's Maggie's neighbor." Cain offered.

Jake's eyebrows rose questioningly. "Jansen...full-back Jansen from football?"

"That'd be the one."

"He's a paramedic, and he gets to drive a big red and white truck." Michael inserted. "He likes my mom."

"Really?" Jake's smile was now wide.

"Yep, but I don't think she wants him to be her boyfriend. She likes Cain." The kid grinned shyly.

Jake snorted, but Cain ignored him. "It's a bass, Michael."

"It's really cool." Michael waved its scaly hide in the air. The dead eyes looked like round black buttons that had been dried out. "Bigger than the ones we caught the other day."

"Maybe we should toss it up into the bush." Cain tried to hide his grin but wasn't totally successful.

"Sure." Michael yelled to his friend, "Tommy, we got a mission!"

Cain watched the two boys scamper off toward trees that surrounded the cottage and picked up his guitar once more. His fingers ran along the strings, picking out an upbeat melody. The acoustic sang beneath his touch, and he changed the rhythm slightly, incorporating a bluesy feel with some heavy fills.

"That something new?"

He nodded. "Yeah, been working on it for few days."

Jake sat back into his chair. "Sounds good, so what's the issue?"

"I've always been the melody guy, ya know? I just...I don't do lyrics."

"You've got to suck it up and focus." Jake's voice was matter-of-fact.

"Yeah."

"You'll get it done."

The two of them settled into a certain kind of silence that only they could enjoy. It was full of ease and a comfort that had been years in the making.

Cain grabbed some snacks and watched the two young boys indulge to the point he knew he'd be in trouble. He somehow doubted Maggie would be impressed with the chips and soda he'd provided.

Mac rolled in around three thirty, and Cain jumped up. He wanted to pick up Maggie when she was done at work. She'd be finished around four, and he intended to get there before she hopped the bus.

He pulled a T-shirt over his head and slipped into a pair of sandals. The woman had been stubborn this morning, insisting she'd take the bus as always—refusing a ride—but he was determined she ride home in style.

She was at Rebecca's, and he knew exactly where the house was located. According to Jake, she and Bradley Hayes had bought the house at the end of Maple Avenue. It had once belonged to the mayor of Crystal Lake and in its day had been a real showpiece. He was quite sure with Hayes's family money it had been restored to its original splendor.

His mouth tightened at the thought of Maggie working for Bradley Hayes. He'd always been a dickhead, and his wife, Rebecca Stringer, was a grade-A bitch. He didn't want to think about the abuse Maggie sucked up in order to survive. She was right. He couldn't relate to her day-to-day life.

His gaze wandered to Michael. Years ago, if someone got in his face, he'd told them off and moved on. End of story. There was no groveling, no sucking up in order to make some cash.

A sobering thought, that. He wasn't sure he was a big enough person to deal with some of the crap she did.

"I'm off to grab Maggie. You guys watch the boys till I'm back?"

Mac saluted him. "Sure can do."

"Not me, I'm outta here." Jake stood and stretched out his legs. "I feel like I've been standing still for days. I'm gonna hit the gym, burn off some energy. What are you guys doing later? Thought I'd swing by the Coach House. Ran into Salvatore the other day, and he said Texas Willie's in town."

"Texas Willie?" Cain laughed. "Tell me how it's possible that son of a bitch is still alive."

Jake shook his head. "I have no clue. I'm sure his brain is fried, though it hasn't affected his guitar playing any." He shrugged. "According to Sal."

"I'm in." Mac threw a football toward the water. "Let's play fetch, boys." Michael and Tommy took off at a run, their legs and arms pumping hard.

Cain started toward his truck. "You guys mind if I bring Maggie?" He didn't wait around to hear their answer. He didn't care. Texas Willie, his buddies, and his girl. Sounded pretty damn good to him.

Fifteen minutes later he pulled up to Rebecca Hayes's house and cut the engine. The driveway was a fair size for in town, with majestic oak trees lining either side, providing enough shade to keep the blacktop as dark as the day it had been paved. He supposed the leaves were a bitch in the fall, but that was a small sacrifice.

He took a moment to savor the place. The grandiose style had been refurbished to suit the period in which it was built, the late 1800s, and Cain would give credit where it was due. Bradley had done a great job. It was one of the oldest homes in Crystal Lake, and when he was a teen, it had been an abandoned wreck—a flophouse for drunken parties and *the* go-to place to bring your girlfriend for sex. Well, that and the Wyndham place.

He exited his truck and glanced around. There was some new money on the street. Most of the homes were in great shape, and he noticed a lot of minivans and SUVs in the driveways. The sound of children's laughter echoed from someone's backyard.

It was…nice.

He turned. A brightly colored ball rolled toward him with a little girl fast behind it. He scooped it up and threw it to her.

"Thanks." With a quick smile she darted back to where she'd come from.

A male voice cut through the gentle quiet, and he turned back toward the house. Bradley was walking down the drive toward him, waving furiously, as if they were long-lost buddies. Cain gritted his teeth and nodded to him as he moved up the drive.

"Cain! What the hell? This is a surprise. Come in for a beer." Hayes was dressed in swim trunks and nothing else. His ruddy complexion was in dire need of sunblock, and sweat beaded his forehead. He'd grown soft, his body reflective of a life of leisure. Bradley looked just like his father, down to the slightly thinning hair and accompanying paunch. "Rebecca didn't say anything about you swinging by."

"I'm good, thanks, and Rebecca didn't know." Cain nodded toward the house. "Is Maggie done?"

Surprise crossed the man's face but was gone just as quick. His eyes narrowed slightly, and Cain didn't care for the calculating look that crept into them. A slow grin spread across his face. "So it's true." He laughed and shook his head. "Didn't doubt it for a minute."

"Sorry?" Cain's eyes narrowed. He knew what was coming even before the words left Bradley's mouth.

"Dude, you're banging the maid."

Chapter 23

"What did you say?" He clenched his hands and squared his shoulders. *Son of a bitch*. His anger was instant, the burn hard.

"I..." Bradley laughed nervously. He'd overstepped and realized it too late.

"First off..." Cain took a step forward. He enjoyed the fear that he saw in Hayes's eyes. He had at least four inches on the man, and while Bradley had gone soft, Cain was lean, in shape, and at the moment very, very pissed off. "Don't ever call me dude. Got that?"

"Sorry." Bradley shook his head as a silly grin crept over his features. "I didn't mean..."

"And secondly," he interrupted, "I'm not *banging the maid*. What are you? Fifteen? What I do in private and who I do it with is none of your goddamn business. Same goes for Maggie."

"Look, I meant no offense."

"Your kind never does."

"Hold on a second, Cain." The man's bravado had returned. He puffed out his chest and sucked in his gut. "It was a stupid comment, but really, don't you think you're overreacting a bit?" He smiled then, like they were buddies sharing a secret. "Christ, I don't blame you. With that Southern accent and all that hair, she's pretty damn hot. Hell, if I could nail that piece, I would, but come on, she's a fucking maid in a town that you'll be saying good-bye to in a few weeks, and you've been with Natasha *fucking* Simmons, for Christ sake."

Cain's anger erupted, washed through him in a cold fury, and he was barely able to keep it together. In that moment he wanted nothing more than to pound his fist into Bradley's face. Pulverize his nose and shut his filthy-ass mouth. His hands fisted, and he took a step forward but froze when a small gasp caught his attention.

Cain glanced toward the house, and his heart rolled over at the sight of Maggie a few feet away. That she'd heard most, if not all, of the entire exchange was evident. Her face was pale, and hurt shadowed her eyes.

Rebecca was a few feet behind, and to her credit, a look of embarrassed shame colored her cheeks a deep rose.

But it was Maggie's huge blue eyes that tore at him, and he turned to Bradley, his voice calm, though the underlying anger was clear. "Apologize to Maggie right now, or I'll kick your ass all over Maple Avenue."

The threat was real, and Bradley knew it. Cain Black was one of the Bad Boys. Their reputation was legendary.

Bradley turned to Maggie, though the bastard didn't have the balls to look her in the eye. "I'm sorry if anything I said offended you," he said stiffly.

She strode past him without a word and jumped into Cain's SUV.

Cain looked at Bradley in disgust. "You're an asshole. I'd find someone else to scrub your floors. She won't be back."

He didn't say anything until they'd turned onto Main Street. Maggie sat stiff as a board, her hands clutched tight to a small bag.

"Are you all right?"

Maggie nodded but didn't reply.

"Maggie, talk to me. What that dickhead said back there...he's just...you can't let a small-minded loser like him upset you." Shit. Was she going to pull away now because of someone like Hayes? The thought twisted his guts.

Her fingers relaxed and she leaned back into the seat. For a few seconds she was silent, but then she turned to him. "He's just saying what everyone in town is thinking, Cain. He doesn't have the manners to keep it to himself like everyone else."

"Maggie, that's ridiculous."

"I don't care," she said softly.

"What?" He pulled over onto a side street. There was no way he could drive and talk to her at the same time. Not when the conversation was so intense.

Maggie turned toward him. Her eyes still shone with the glimmer of tears. "I don't care what the gossip is, or what someone like Rebecca or Bradley thinks." Her voice was tremulous, the soft lilt that caressed her words exquisite. "I deserve a bit of happiness, Cain, and if being with you gives them the power to point fingers"—she shrugged—"I won't let that bother me."

He undid his seat belt and slid toward her. "Babe, you gotta know, what he said, about Natasha—"

"Shh." Her fingers were on his lips, and she leaned into him. "I don't want to talk about your ex-wife."

Cain gathered her close, inhaled her scent as she nestled in his arms, and for a few moments felt absolute peace. Everything about her felt right.

"I want to take you out tonight," he murmured next

to her ear. She shivered in his arms, and he shifted his body. He was hard, ached for her with an intensity that was painful.

"What about Michael and Tommy?" She turned, and he thought that he could look into her eyes forever. They were dark, luminous pools of navy.

"Already looked after."

"*Really.*" Her eyebrows knit together. Damn, but her eyebrows were perfect.

"I called Sharon on her cell, and her husband is picking them up. They're not heading back to the campground, but Michael's been invited for the night. They're going to pitch a tent for the two of them in the backyard."

"Oh." She sounded unsure, and he was afraid he'd overstepped.

"I didn't think you'd mind, considering they were supposed to be together until tomorrow."

"That's fine. How's Sharon's father?"

"He's good. Apparently it was a small stroke, but he's expected to make a full recovery."

"So"—her fingers crept along her chest—"two nights in a row. That's a record for me."

"Good to know." He chuckled.

"If we're going out, I'll need to shower."

The thought of Maggie naked and wet in the shower did all sorts of crazy things to him. "That sounds like an amazing idea." He nuzzled her neck and smiled at the groan that slipped from between her lips. "I could use a shower myself."

"Well, what are we waiting for?"

Holy hell, but she set him on fire. Cain grabbed her

mouth with his. He cupped her face between his hands and marked her with a deep, passionate kiss that left them both breathless when he finally pulled away.

"Let's go," he said hoarsely.

He made it back to Maggie's in record time, and the two of them were like giddy teenagers—all fumbling hands, tearing of clothes, and the mad, insane, *desperate* need to be together.

Hot water mixed with passion made for a hedonistic experience. Cain took his time and cleaned every single inch of his woman. He lathered and stroked and kneaded and massaged until she trembled against him. He was man enough to admit to a certain amount of pride in the fact that he'd coaxed several orgasms from her as he did so.

And when he finally drove his body into hers, when her legs were wrapped tight around his waist, her breasts crushed against his chest, and the heat of her surrounded him in a warm, wet sheath, he experienced something he'd never known before. Complete and utter surrender.

He felt like…he'd just come home.

"Oh Cain, that was…" She was breathless, and he kissed her bruised lips.

"Yeah." He wrapped her in a towel and carried her into her bedroom. "It was."

She giggled and wrapped her arms around his neck. Cain loved the sound of her laughter.

"Dammit, Maggie, we should just stay here and eat and have sex and then eat some more."

"And have sex?"

"Sounds like a plan."

She walked to her dresser, and his eyes followed

the smooth, easy lines of her body. She was petite, but had a dancer's body—lithe and fluid. He felt a twinge below once more—her ass was damn fine to look at as well.

"We should hurry up. I want to see Michael before Sharon's husband picks him up." She slipped into a pair of pink boy-short undies and he groaned. Christ, it wasn't fair what a little slip of lingerie could do to a man. "Where are we going?"

"What?" He dragged his gaze from her delectable body.

"Tonight? Where are we going?" She bit her lip. "I don't know what to wear. Not like I have much choice but..."

He crossed to her, stooped, and closed his mouth around one of her nipples, teasing the peak into a hard pebble as his tongue stroked.

"God, Cain, if you keep this up we won't make it out the door, and I need to see my son." She pushed him away with a grin, though her heightened color told him all he needed to know. As much as he couldn't keep his hands off her, she felt the same.

"The Coach House."

"What was that?" she asked.

"It's where we're going, so dress casual. Jeans are fine. Promise me something though." His grin was wicked as he feasted upon the perfection of her breasts.

"I don't make promises until I know the consequence." Her eyes flashed, and he welcomed this saucy side of her wholeheartedly.

"Promise me you won't wear a bra, and as for the *consequence*..." He laughed at the expression on her face and pulled her close for one more kiss. "The consequence," he murmured against her mouth as his hands reached down to cup her butt, "will be a repeat of last night...if you're up for it."

Maggie had never been to the Coach House. In fact, until a few hours ago she hadn't been aware of its existence. She glanced around. Her initial reaction? She wasn't missing much.

It was dimly lit, with the requisite neon beer signs strewn about—Budweiser and Miller the most popular—and a small stage tucked into the corner. The smell of stale beer and fried foods filled the air, and even though it looked less than respectable, she had to admit the atmosphere was upbeat, the energy and vibe electric.

She sat next to Cain. They were in a booth that gave them a clear view of the stage, and she'd been told it was theirs—as in the Bad Boys'. And though she'd never been one of *those* girls—the kind that clung to their men with rabid glee—she totally loved the fact that his arm was draped around her shoulders.

It made her feel like she belonged to someone, and that was something she hadn't felt in years.

She noticed the looks, the whispers, nudges, and pointed fingers, but didn't care. For the first time in a long time, Maggie relaxed and was worry-free. She accepted a cold beer from Cain and took a long drink, loving the desire she saw in his eyes when he looked at her. Desire he made no effort to hide.

She'd taken him up on his dare and wore a low-cut fitted black vest—with no bra—and she'd matched it with her only good pair of jeans. They were old, well-worn, but fit her curves snugly, and though they were low in the waist, Maggie had no problem showing off her trim belly.

Something *he* would have flipped over. She shuddered at the thought of Dante, Michael's father, and tucked it away immediately. She wasn't going there, not tonight.

"So Maggie, where are you from?" Mac smiled. "I detect the sultry South in your voice."

She set her beer bottle on the table and turned to Cain's friend. Mackenzie's bruises and scrapes had pretty much healed, but none of them detracted from his good looks. In fact, they gave him an edge that a good many women liked, judging from the looks he'd garnered when they walked in. The man was golden sun, piercing green eyes, tall athletics, and as charming as Cain.

He was also smart. His intensity made her uncomfortable, though she smiled in return and kept her voice light as she answered. "That would be correct."

"Whereabouts exactly?"

"What is this, twenty questions?" Jake interjected. He was seated opposite them and had taken his eyes off the entrance long enough to join the conversation. Raine had indicated that she might stop in for a drink, and he was noticeably on edge.

Mac glared at Jake. "It was just one question, and for the record"—he turned back to Maggie, a wide grin on his face—"I want to know a little more about the woman who's turned Cain into the guy who holds hands and fills Jack's Hut with a freaking boatload of tulips."

The lights dimmed even more, and a loud growl of approval rushed through the crowd. Cain squeezed Maggie's shoulder and whispered into her ear. "Don't mind Mackenzie. He gets a little intense sometimes."

But she caught the unspoken questions in his eyes. He wondered about her past, and so he should. They were sleeping together. His life was pretty much an open book, but hers…was closed.

There was no way she was opening up that can of worms, not with Cain.

"You all right?" He leaned over and swept his mouth across hers.

She nodded and whispered, "I'm fine." It was scary, really, how good she'd become at lying.

His dark eyes studied hers until she glanced away.

A man strode onto the stage. He was tall, lean—all legs—and wore a wide-brimmed cowboy hat perched at an angle on his head. His T-shirt was emblazoned with the name Texas Willie in crimson.

He flashed a toothy grin to the audience and picked up his guitar, his arms all sinew and rope. The man looked to be in his early forties, though Maggie had a feeling he was probably younger. He had the look of a person who lived on the edge, and the goatee that adorned his thin, pale face only emphasized the fact.

He glanced in their direction, piercing black eyes crinkling as he smiled, tipped his hat, and bellowed into the mike. "Well, what do you know, Mr. Hollywood is in da house." The crowd erupted as he strummed a power chord and the rest of the band took their places.

Cain held his beer up in acknowledgment and grinned.

"Just so you know, my friends…" Texas Willie began to play a blues melody that was raw, catchy, and real. "Hollywood isn't the only one who can rock it!"

Texas Willie's announcement brought another round

of cheer, and the band threw themselves into the first song of what was to be a rollicking, blues-heavy set.

The music infiltrated the space around them. Its infectious melody slid over her skin, and though she tried, Maggie couldn't relax. Mackenzie's eyes touched hers a little too often, and she felt as if everyone in the bar was staring at them.

Raine didn't show, and Jake's frosty attitude grew colder as the evening progressed, but Cain…he was lost in the music, and it was a beautiful thing to see. His foot tapped to the beat, his fingers thrummed along the top of the table, and his head bopped to the rhythm.

When a slow, seductive melody slid into the dark, Cain grabbed her close and they moved onto the dance floor, her small frame tucked into his. His arms cradled her, his large hands splayed possessively across her back and in her hair.

It was dark out here, and the invisible cloak of anonymity slid over her skin, allowing her to enjoy the moment. She didn't feel the heat of prying eyes or the unanswered questions that Mac had posed.

They moved together, a sensual shuffle of fluid limbs, straining muscles, and a constant need that was a physical ache. The music was hypnotic: sex and candy rolled into one hell of an erotic number. Cain's mouth slid down her neck, and the world fell away. In her mind there was no one but him.

His lips skated across hers, and he whispered hoarsely, "Let's get out of here."

Suddenly Maggie froze as Bradley Hayes's words echoed in her mind. What the hell was she doing? Could her heart afford for her to be so selfish?

"What are we doing, Cain?" She stopped dancing, and the two of them stared at each other while all around them bodies moved and slid and touched in the near dark. She licked her lips nervously.

Cain's hands crept up to cradle her cheeks, his eyes intense and passion filled as he gazed down at her. "What are you afraid of, Maggie?"

"Nothing." *Everything.*

"Are you sure?"

She glanced up at him and her heart lurched. His dark eyes studied her intently. She saw his hunger, his desire, his need…for her. In that moment she made a decision. One she prayed she wouldn't regret. Maggie leaned into his hands as her own crept up, and she threaded her fingers through his.

"I'm not sure about anything," she whispered.

He bent low until his forehead touched hers. "You can be sure of one thing."

"What's that?" His hands were on her ass now, and he held her tight to his hips, his erection resting against her belly.

"You can be sure that I'm going to make you whimper and beg for"—he ground his groin against her, and the ache between the folds of her sex intensified—"this." He was breathing hard now. "You ready?"

She was so not ready for any of this, but the devil who sat on one of her shoulders took over, and her fear was silenced.

Maggie nodded, and the two of them turned and left without saying good-bye to anyone.

Chapter 24

Cain shifted beside Maggie and didn't take his eyes from her. He cradled her close, enjoying the warmth of her body and the feel of her in his arms. She was relaxed, had been thoroughly loved more than once, but still a soft frown settled between her eyebrows.

Like the previous night, she'd tossed and turned, mumbled things he couldn't understand. He knew she was holding back the part of her that was scared, and even though he wanted her to let him in, he was afraid to push. She needed to come around on her own. She needed to learn to trust him with her secrets.

He sure as hell didn't like it, and every time he thought of the bastard who'd dared to touch her, he was filled with impotent rage. What he wouldn't give for a chance at this guy's ass.

He'd been sleeping at her house ever since Jack's Hut, and that was a few weeks ago. Hell, after that first night together there was no way he was going to sleep anywhere else. They'd fallen into a kind of relationship he couldn't define—one based on the physical, but there was an ease to the way they reacted to each other. They spent every minute together that they could, and he was more than a little embarrassed to admit that he'd become *that* guy—the one that sneaked out of her house under cover of night. Like a damn criminal.

Shit, if the guys in the band could see him now. He'd been reduced to skulking around like some horny teenager afraid to get caught with his pants down.

Maggie sighed and nestled deeper into his arms as he pushed back the hair at her temple. He didn't care. It was worth it.

The window was open, and he inhaled the fresh, cool air that blew in on the breeze. The smell of fresh-cut grass still lingered. Mowing the lawn was a chore he'd been more than happy to do and one that had pissed off Luke Jansen something fierce. Especially when he tossed the shit his dog left behind back onto Luke's lawn.

He stretched and settled against her softness, content and happy. The sun was making its way upward, and early-morning gray illuminated Maggie's bedroom.

The clock beside her bed glowed 5:30, and he knew it was time for him to leave. While Michael was an early riser, usually up before seven, this morning Cain was headed to Detroit, and if he wanted to beat traffic, he needed to be on the road by six. Dax Jones, his bass guitarist in BlackRock, had agreed to participate in the fundraiser on July Fourth. His flight from the United Kingdom was due to arrive this morning.

"You're awake," Maggie murmured against him. Her arms crept across his chest. Sleep clung to her eyes, their blue depths mysterious and sexy as she looked up at him. "I don't want you to leave."

He kissed her nose and shifted once more. "Trust me. The last thing I want to do is get out of this bed, but Michael will be up soon, and I've got to get my ass in gear and head to the airport." The silky skin beneath her eyes was smudged, light bruises that signaled either a lack of sleep or something else entirely. "Are you okay? You didn't sleep well last night."

She glanced away, and unease slid through him as he continued to study her. She picked at the blanket, her elegant fingers nervous. Something was up.

"I'm fine, I just..."

"Just what?"

"I worry about things that I probably shouldn't and..." She bit her lip, attempted a smile. "Never mind."

That got his attention. Cain sat up. "What's going on, Maggie?"

She pulled the blanket up across her naked breasts and ran fingers across her temple. "Nothing. I said drop it."

"I'm not going to drop it. Something is obviously bothering you, and I want to know what the hell it is."

That heavy weight on his chest, the one that had plagued him for the last few days, was back. It had always been Cain's experience that when his world tipped too far into good, it usually bottomed out and swung back the other way. Like a little slap in the face to remind him that it didn't matter to the big guy upstairs who the hell he was.

She exhaled and sat up to face him. Her hair hung in crimson ropes around her shoulders, and with sleep still heavy in her eyes, her skin makeup-free, she looked like a damned Lolita. His body hardened instantly. She was like a drug he couldn't get enough of, and he felt a twinge of anger at the thought of how she affected him.

At the control the woman possessed, whether she knew it or not.

Cain rolled his shoulders and tried to relax.

"I'm just... Michael is getting attached to you, and I'm a little worried about what's going to happen when..." She paused as if gathering her thoughts, and then she spoke in a rush, as if the words tasted bad. "When you leave Crystal Lake."

"You're worried about *Michael.*"

She frowned. "Of course I'm worried about Michael. I'm his mother. It's my job to worry."

Cain stared at her for several moments. "And what about you, Maggie? Would you miss me if I wasn't around?" He didn't know how tense he was until he let go of the sheet clutched between his fingers.

Something flickered in the depths of her eyes. She held his gaze for several seconds and then looked away. "Are we really going to have this conversation now?"

"What conversation?" He didn't like where this was headed and cursed himself for opening a can of worms.

She shrugged. "We both know you'll be leaving eventually. The question is, when? After the fundraiser? At the end of July? Maybe you'll stay until August or September. I don't know. It's not like you've shared your plans with me, but you will leave us behind."

His mother's words echoed in his head, and he winced, more than a little pissed because there was truth in her words.

"Maggie—"

"Don't, Cain." She shook her head. "Seriously, you don't have to say anything. It is what it is." She smiled, a tremulous, beautiful smile. "I have no regrets, if that's what you're thinking. None. I just...I don't want Michael to be hurt when you leave."

She sounded like she'd already said good-bye, and

it pissed him off. How the hell did she know what he thought? What he felt or wanted?

Fuck, he didn't even know what the hell was going on in his head.

"What if I don't leave?" he asked, the words slipping out of him before he had a chance to grab them back. He didn't like this serious turn. The bubble was about to burst, and he had a feeling the next few minutes were going to be a turning point in his relationship with Maggie. Whether it was good or bad was the question of the day.

She looked at him as if he had two heads. "Of course you're going to leave. You don't belong in Crystal Lake."

Her words lit the fuse that had already sparked. "How the hell do you know where I belong? Are you a fucking mind reader now?" His words were harsh. He threw off the covers and slipped from her bed, searching for the jeans he'd thrown off the night before. The floor was a tangled mess of their clothes.

Clothes that had been torn and tossed in haste, because at the time all they could think about was getting naked and having sex. Maybe that's all he was to her. Wouldn't that be ironic? *He* was the quick lay, the rocker stud who would eventually go away.

Maybe that's what she wanted.

"I didn't mean anything by it, Cain, I just..." She stared at him, obviously confused. "I don't know what you want me to say."

Cain slipped into his jeans and grabbed his shirt off the end of the bed. Once he had his boots on, his anger had tempered somewhat but not enough to take the bite out of his words. "The truth would be a great start."

Her cheeks flushed pink at that, and she sat up straight, the sheet falling dangerously low. "The truth? What are you talking about? I've never lied to you."

"Because you haven't *had* to."

"What's that supposed to mean?"

"It means that I don't know shit about you, and obviously that's the way you want it."

Her eyes flashed, and he knew she was angry. She opened her mouth to speak, but he didn't give her the chance.

"Where do you come from?"

"What?"

"You're from the South, that's obvious. The night we met, Rebecca told me you were from Savannah, I think." Her lips pursed tightly at his words, and she clutched the blanket up tight again. He pierced her with an intense look. "Is she right?"

Maggie stared at him in silence, and the anger inside him festered. It wasn't rational, what he felt—the resentment that rushed through him—and that fed the frustration even more. He wanted her, but he didn't know what the future held. Why couldn't they just enjoy each other and take this thing day to day? Why did everything have to be hard?

"What are your parents' names? Are they alive? What's your favorite color? Do you have any siblings? Why do you draw?"

She shook her head, "I…"

He didn't give her a chance but plunged forward. "Who the hell is Michael's father? Is he in the picture at all?"

"*That* is *none* of your business." She slipped from the bed, the blanket held tight to her chest. Her face was flushed, and he saw the sheen of tears that filled the corners of her eyes. It killed him to see her like that. To know that he'd been the one to upset her. But hell, all he was asking for was a little honesty. Was that too much to expect?

"I think you should leave."

"I was already leaving, Maggie, but this isn't over." He turned and opened her bedroom door. "Because I'm coming back, and we're going to finish this conversation."

He left without another word and slipped out of her house in silence. Luke Jansen was putting out his garbage as he drove by, and the urge to flip his middle finger in the guy's direction nearly won out. He did, however, manage to keep his cool and ignored the man instead.

He left town and hit the open road, trying his damnedest to clear Maggie from his mind. After a while the silence settled him somewhat, and he cranked the tunes, tried to lose himself in the melodic strains of U2 as he sped down the interstate, but it was no use. By the time he arrived at airport he was wound tight and his mood was dark.

He kept his head down—no sense scaring all the little old ladies with his scowl—and was relieved when he spied Dax Jones with relative ease. He was glad to see him, glad Dax had agreed to play for the benefit, and for a moment his spirits lifted. The tall Brit was among a posse of people who'd just cleared the baggage area, but he stood out like a sore thumb. How could he not? With his shock of midnight-black hair, pale skin, myriad tattoos, and red and white plaid jeans, he wanted to be noticed. His T-shirt proclaimed God Save the Queen, and the Union Jack adorned the top hat that rested upon his head.

"Cain, you look like utter crap, mate."

Cain smiled, aware that they were garnering a fair share of interest. "Nice to see you too, Monk."

"Hey, let's not start up with that bit, eh?" Dax grinned and slung his bass over his shoulder.

Cain said nothing, though his grin said it all as he grabbed the other bag offered to him. Monk was a nickname Dax had earned on their last tour with the Grind. The story was pretty damn funny and a lot raunchy, involving Dax, two strippers, a judge, a principal ballerina from the Prague ballet company, and a monk.

"I'll go easy." Cain nodded. "This way."

The two of them made their way through the terminal, and by the time they'd reached Cain's truck it was late morning.

"We got time to stop for a drink? I'm fecking thirsty, mate."

Cain backed out of his spot and pointed the SUV toward the highway. "It's not exactly happy hour yet, my friend, though I do have a full fridge of beer back in Crystal Lake." *And a woman I need to see.*

"But do you have cider?"

"No, but I'm sure we can track some down."

Dax relaxed in his seat and sighed. "I'm bloody tired, so don't mind if I close my eyes."

"Go ahead. Get some sleep. We've got a couple hours ahead of us."

"And Cain?"

"Yeah?" He glanced at the Brit, not liking the sly smile that graced his mouth.

"You look like bloody hell."

"So you said."

"I can't wait, then."

Cain wondered if he was going to regret asking Dax to come back to the U.S. He'd forgotten how annoying his riddles were.

"I said I can't—"

"I know what you said Dax, but what the hell did you mean?"

Dax laughed and settled back into his seat. "I can't wait to meet the woman who's managed to tie your underknickers in a knot."

Chapter 25

Maggie dried the last of the supper dishes and put them away. She placed the damp dish towel over the drying rack and glanced around her small kitchen. A crystal vase of purple tulips so dark they appeared black stared back at her from the table. They'd been a gift from Cain.

The table had been set for two tonight—the first time in the last several nights. She hadn't heard a word from him since he left this morning, but maybe it was for the best.

She sighed and glanced down the hall toward the bathroom. The shower had stopped. "Michael, make sure you brush your teeth. I left clean pajamas on your bed."

His answer was muffled, and from the sound of it, his mouth was full of toothpaste. She wandered into the living room, tossed a magazine into the rack beside the sofa, and stared out the window. The sun was still bright, even though it was nearing nine in the evening.

She spied Luke out front, bringing his garbage cans back in from the road, and swore under her breath. "Dammit!" She'd been in a daze this morning and had forgotten to put hers out. She wrinkled her nose. With this heat, her little shed out back was going to smell. *Huge*.

"All done, Mom."

Maggie turned and walked over to her son, doing the inspection dance as she checked behind his ears, sniffed his hair, and eyed his fingernails. He giggled. "Do I pass?"

She brushed his damp hair back and kissed his forehead. "With flying colors. Good job, sir." Maggie gave him a hug. "Twenty minutes and then bed, all right?"

He nodded and plunked himself on the sofa. "Mom?"

Here it comes. Maggie's gut tightened. "Hm?"

"How come Cain didn't come for supper? He loves your cucumber salad."

She pasted a smile to her face and shrugged. "He was busy, honey. He had to go and pick up a musician friend of his." She watched his face closely. Her son was smart and didn't miss much.

"Dax Jones?"

"Yes, I think that's his name."

"Cain told me he's from across the pond and that he speaks funny." His forehead furled. "Like David Beckham."

"He's British, sweetie, so yes, he'll have an accent."

"Oh." He shifted a bit. "Did I tell you Cain asked me to play with him in the charity football game? It's supposed to be father and son, but"—Michael shrugged—"he said it didn't matter. We're going to be on the same team with Tommy and his dad."

"Yes, I think you mentioned that a *couple hundred times*."

As one of the fundraiser events, a charity football game had been organized, with a host of alumni and their children. It was to take place in the afternoon on the Fourth, just after the parade.

"Tommy's dad said that Cain was a really good football player, like he could have gone to the NFL and everything!"

"Really," she murmured, sliding onto the sofa beside him.

"Yep." Michael nodded. "Tommy's dad said Cain has the Midas touch, whatever that is, and that he's one lucky son of a—" Her son's face froze, and then he giggled. "Well, you know what I mean."

"Yes, I do," she said drily.

"So"—Michael bit his lip—"is he, like, your boyfriend?"

Okay, she hadn't been expecting that. For a second Maggie was speechless, and though her first instinct was absolute denial, she watched her son closely and spoke, deciding honesty would be the best bet.

"I'm not sure. Would it be weird if he kinda was?"

Michael's face screwed up. "Weird? No"—he shook his head—"Richard Masterson's mom has three of 'em."

"Three?" She blinked, thinking she'd heard him wrong. He was quite serious, though, and nodded, his damp curls bobbing against his forehead.

"Yep, but it's supposed to be a secret, because one of them is married to another lady."

All right then. Maggie tousled his hair. "Well, you'd better keep *that* to yourself. Time for bed."

Michael gave her a hug, and she held his body close. She didn't want to let him go, and when he began to squirm, her arms fell away reluctantly. "You want a story?"

His tired eyes brightened. "'Cozy Land'?"

Maggie grinned and nodded as he slipped from her arms and dashed toward his room. Cozy Land was a magical place that little boys and girls went to just before Sandman grabbed them and pulled them into slumber.

A child could be anywhere in the world…or be anything. In a pirate boat out on the Caribbean Sea. A whale rider off the coast of Australia. A tea party on a bank of clouds. Every night in Cozy Land was different. It was a product of her imagination and had grown as her stories evolved. So much so that she'd started to write them down and draw accompanying illustrations.

Michael loved the stories, and it was her secret ambition to get them published one day. Just one dream in a long line of yearnings.

That would be her Cozy Land.

Maggie followed him to bed, and they snuggled together for almost forty-five minutes until his head bobbed forward and didn't recover. She would tell him the rest of his Cozy Land adventure the next night. She was pretty sure he'd want to know what happened after the tree house in the Amazon rain forest had begun to float into the air.

She tucked him in and kissed him on the forehead before closing the door to his room.

The quiet of her home was deafening, something she hadn't noticed for a while. She wasn't in the mood for television, and even the thought of writing or drawing didn't excite her. She was out of sorts. Restless.

She closed her eyes and reached for the throw blanket. God, she felt like a dark cloud was hanging over her.

Maybe it was just a cloud of self-pity. Or maybe she just missed Cain.

Maggie rested her head back and closed her eyes. She'd never been in an adult relationship before. Her marriage didn't count. That relationship had been unhealthy. The only good thing that had come out of it was Michael. So the notion of give-and-take was a little foreign to her. She understood Cain's frustration with her, but it wasn't easy for her to open up.

No one knew the details of her marriage, of her life… of the many disappointments and losses she'd endured.

Some of them had speculated. Lauren and Raine certainly knew her past wasn't all puppies and rainbows. But they didn't *know*.

Did Cain deserve that sort of trust? She'd let him into her home, into her *bed*, so why was it so hard for her to open up to him?

What was the point? That was the real question.

Maggie sank into the sofa and tried to find some warmth. She'd never be free of her past, and she knew she should break it off with Cain before things became more complicated than they already were.

She must have dozed off, because when she woke later, her house was in darkness. She stretched and rubbed the sleep from her eyes, groaning softly as her stiff muscles protested. A soft knock sounded at her door, and she froze.

It was Cain. She knew it.

Her body shifted inside; it felt like a dose of shock therapy had been discharged. She was all kinds of excited, sick, and scared—at the same time. *This* was her body's reaction to Cain. It was like radar, only instead of producing a blip, she got nauseous.

Her heart pounded so hard, a wash of heat rushed over her skin, but she tossed the blanket aside and crossed to the door. She opened it before she had the chance to chicken out.

Cain stared down at her in silence. He filled the space around her, and though he hadn't even touched her yet, she felt him like a physical force.

"Maggie, I..."

She didn't let him finish. Her arms were around him, and her lips reached for his. Searching, seeking his warmth and strength...his soul. She didn't care about anything other than the man in front of her. She kissed him as if she was starving. As if he was the only thing that could save her.

His hands slid down her body, and he hugged her to him, murmuring words into her ear, though honestly, she had no clue what he was saying. All she knew for sure was that the anxiety and fear that had settled into her body for the day were gone.

Seconds later, or maybe it was minutes, he gently pushed her inside and closed the door behind them.

"I meant to call earlier, but I got hung up with Dax. I'm sorry." Cain exhaled. "After the way things were left this morning, I didn't want you to think…" His dark eyes shone. "I didn't want you to think that I wasn't coming back."

Her heart constricted. This morning he'd promised they'd finish their conversation. "Cain, I don't want to fight."

His hand caressed her cheek, and she leaned into his touch like a flower seeking the sun. "I don't either. I just need to be with you." He shrugged. "I can't explain it any other way." His hands crept around her waist. "This must be what a junkie feels like when they're jonesing for a hit. You're my drug of choice, Maggie."

Cain lifted her with ease and sank onto the sofa with Maggie across his lap. She rested her head against his chest, listened to the heavy beat of his heart, and for the first time all day felt peace.

Cain drank in her scent, her softness, and her surrender.

He'd had one hell of a day. Anything that could have

gone wrong did. As soon as he returned to the cottage with Dax, he'd been called to the football field because his input was needed on how the stage was to be built. Planning something on this scale should have been easy, but in a small town, nothing ever was. Too many hands in the pot led to wasted time. In the end, he'd called Mac, and the job was finalized.

Though that had led to discussions about production—sound equipment and lights—and he'd driven nearly fifty miles to the closest city in order to make sure the proper gear was reserved for the Fourth. He'd lucked out and had been able to finagle Pat Rossi—a guy he'd worked with in the past—to do sound and lights, and only had to throw in an extra case of beer to seal the deal.

He'd hightailed it back to Crystal Lake and had come straight here, anxious because he hadn't been able to call Maggie. His cell had died, and his charger was nowhere to be found.

Cain kept her close, his hand caressing her cheek. He loved the small upturn in her nose, the way she leaned into his touch. His arms tightened around her, and his chest constricted something fierce. This little firecracker had come to mean a lot to him in the past few weeks. What *was* he doing? His arms tightened, his breathing quickened.

"Her name was Rose."

"Sorry?" he murmured.

"My mother." Maggie pulled away and glanced up at him, her blue eyes shadowed and sad. "Her name was Rose," she whispered.

Chapter 26

"MAGGIE, WE DON'T HAVE TO..."

A long shuddering breath escaped her lips as she nodded. "Yes. We do." She paused and nodded. "I do."

Her eyes misted, and a sad smile tugged at her mouth. Maggie fingered a long strand of her hair, twirling it slowly as she lay in his arm. "She had dark red hair just like mine." Her brow furled briefly as if she was remembering. "Maybe a bit lighter, but it was beautiful, and her skin was the color of alabaster." Cain stilled, nestled his head into the crook of her neck as she continued.

"She had freckles. Lots of freckles. She didn't care for them, I remember that. She used to put this special lotion on her face and arms every night. Something she bought from the Avon lady. It was in a green container that she kept by her bed, and I remember the writing was pink. I think she thought the cream made her freckles less visible. My dad called them magic bits of fairy dust." A soft sigh escaped her lips as she settled into his arms. "I used to trace them with my finger. She thought I was crazy because I loved them."

"She sounds beautiful."

"She was. Everyone loved her." Maggie closed her eyes and smiled. "She laughed a lot and loved to dance. We'd crank the stereo and twirl around the living room to her favorite bands, like Pink Floyd and Lynyrd Skynyrd."

"The classics."

"Yes. Being from the South, my dad was kind of horrified she wasn't all bluegrass and stuff, but Skynyrd was about as country as she got."

Maggie shivered in his arms, and he ran his hands along her shoulders, keeping her close to him.

"'Free Bird.'"

He barely heard the words, and when she began to sing, goose bumps erupted along his skin.

"'If I leave here tomorrow'"—she inhaled and continued, her voice tremulous—"'would you still remember me?'"

Cain's chest tightened with an unfamiliar feeling, and suddenly he knew where this was going.

"She died when I was fourteen. Cancer."

"Babe, I'm sorry." Cain heard the pain in her voice.

"Me too," she whispered. "It was cervical, and at first we thought she'd be all right, ya know? It was scary, all her treatments. The chemo and radiation, and then she had surgery. But she got better." Her fingers traced circles along his arm, and for a few seconds there was silence. "She got better," she whispered fiercely.

Cain was quiet. Hell, he didn't know what to say, but he figured she didn't want that. She needed him to listen.

"We had one more summer." Maggie blew out a long breath and rested her head back against his chest. "She gained her weight back, and her hair grew into this really cute pixie cut. Mom tried to cram so much into that summer, I remember being kind of resentful. There were times she wanted to do stuff and I…I ditched her." A long shuddering breath fell from her lips. "I ditched her," she whispered painfully. "I wanted to chill, to hang with my friends. I mean, my mom was better, she wasn't dying anymore…it was all good."

She paused, and his heart broke for the little girl that she'd been.

Maggie shook her head slowly. "Except it wasn't. The cancer came back in the fall, and it was meaner, stronger, than before. It had spread to her bones, and she went downhill so fast. I tried to help her the best that I could. I'd sit on the sofa and hold her puke bowl when she was sick, arrange her pillows so she was comfortable. I'd dress her, wash her and…when we were alone I'd crank her tunes, and we'd sing them at the top of our lungs like two crazy people."

"Oh shit, Maggie." She was crying now, tears flowing down her face, falling like drops of rain onto his arms.

A few moments passed, and she cleared her throat and wiped her eyes. "She passed a week before Christmas, and when she died she took my dad with her."

"What do you mean?" Cain was puzzled.

"My father disappeared. He stopped living. He started drinking, and after a while he just gave up on everything. His job, his friends. Me." She paused. "He hated me."

What the hell?

"Why would he hate you? That doesn't make sense."

She bit her lip and fingered the edge of a throw blanket. When she spoke her voice was barely above a whisper. "He told me once when he was drunk that he couldn't stand the sight of me."

"Oh babe, that's rough, but I'm sure he didn't mean it. People say a lot of stupid things when they're in pain. Throw alcohol into the mix, and it's ten times worse."

She nodded. "I know he didn't mean them, not really. But they hurt. *Really hurt*. He was broken, you know, and I…I was a constant reminder of why. Every time he looked at me, he saw her, and it must have killed him."

He kissed the top of her head. "Maggie, we don't have to…you don't have to do this."

She turned in his arms, and he was struck silent at the fragile beauty that he held, though really, he knew that was a smoke screen. Cain believed that Maggie O'Rourke was the strongest person he'd ever met.

"At first we just learned to live without communicating all that much. I threw myself into school, and he drank his way to the bottom of every bottle he came across. When we lost the house and moved into an apartment, I thought my life had bottomed out." She shook her head. "I was wrong. He lost his job and started drinking his way through whatever money we had. I tried to help out…got a job waitressing, but it wasn't enough, and besides, the more money I brought into the house, the more he drank. When I was sixteen he told me to go. To leave and not to come back. He said I could apply for social assistance like all the other welfare girls did and get my own place on 'baby alley,' which is where a lot of young mothers lived."

Something cold thrust its way inside him—anger for this faceless man who'd abandoned his child like garbage.

"What did you do?"

Her eyes were puffy, her skin blotchy, from crying. "I left," she whispered. "And I haven't seen him since."

"Christ, Maggie. I had no idea."

"Oh God, I've never"—she shuddered—"I've never shared this with anyone, not even…"

"Who?"

"Michael's father," she whispered.

Cain waited for her to continue, but she didn't. He was surprised at how disappointed he was that she didn't trust him enough to share everything. She closed her eyes and he held her.

Later, much later, he heard her whisper, "Thank you."

"I didn't do anything." His fingers pushed a long strand of hair off her wet, heated face.

"It feels good to be free of that secret."

Cain carried Maggie back to her room and slid into bed with her. She turned on her side and settled her body against his. He held her for a very long time, listening to her breathe, and was nearly asleep himself when she murmured, "Green."

"What was that, babe?"

"My favorite color is green."

With that heartfelt admission, he was a goner. In that moment he knew there was no one else for him but Maggie. She'd claimed his heart without even trying.

He inhaled her scent and kept her close.

There was still a ways for them to go. Her trust was a fragile thing. Maggie was holding back. There was the whole question about Michael's father. He knew about the violence but nothing else. Where was the guy? Had they been married? Were they divorced?

But as his mother used to say, baby steps…you have to crawl before you can walk. Damn straight.

Cain would do whatever it took to release Maggie from her demons. Even if it meant crawling to hell and back.

Chapter 27

THE SMELL OF SAWDUST FILLED THE AIR ALONG WITH the sound of hammers and saws—a handyman's paradise.

Cain's cell phone vibrated. Again. It had been going off intermittently, and he couldn't ignore it anymore. He grabbed it from his pocket and stared at the LA exchange. It was Natasha, and from the looks of it, she'd called at least a dozen times over the past hour.

"What's up?" Jake paused on his way by, arms full of lumber. It was early afternoon, Thursday, and they were in the middle of building a suitable stage for the festivities on Saturday. So far the job was going well, considering. The "too many hands in the pot" thing hadn't become a detriment—yet.

"Nothing."

Cain pointed toward Dax. The Brit had insisted on helping build the stage, and Cain wasn't so sure it was a good idea. If he didn't lose a finger it would be a miracle. "No, that's plywood. Mac needs the lumber from the other pile for the frame."

The Brit made a face, cursed a string of foul words before turning around, and dumped his load of plywood in favor of the heavier framing lumber. Cain's cell phone rang once more. He swore, powered it down, and slipped it into the front pocket of his jeans.

Screw Natasha. He didn't have time for her bullshit.

"Everything all right?"

He turned to Mac. "Right as rain." He nodded to the skeleton of a stage. "So, we on schedule or what?" The plan was to get the staging built Thursday, and then Friday the production was to arrive. Sound check and all the final details had to be dealt with before Saturday.

Mac nodded. "Pretty sure we'll get it done." Mac's eyes narrowed. "As long as your British peacock manages not to screw things up."

Cain snorted. *Peacock* was about right. Dax's choice of wardrobe was somewhat eccentric, to say the least. He'd arrived at the site wearing Union Jack pants—leather Union Jack pants, no less, in this heat—a silk dress shirt to match, and his infamous top hat. White cowboy boots finished the ensemble. Dax wasn't exactly the type for manual labor. But his heart was in the right place.

Michael and Tommy ran by them, arms waving madly as they dragged a cooler in their wake, off to dole out some cold drinks to the workers. Maggie had let Cain take the boy for the day, and the two kids were having a blast.

"So, things with Maggie are good, I take it?"

Cain followed Mac to the staging area. He grabbed a hammer and adjusted the sack of nails that hung from his waist.

"Yeah, things are good."

"So what are your plans?"

"Plans?"

"How long you sticking around?"

"We've got the cottage for the summer, Mac."

"That's not what I meant."

Cain chuckled and followed Mac to the stage. Most of the framing was in place; it wouldn't take long to finish.

"I know what you meant, and I don't know what I'm going to do." He shrugged. "It depends."

"On what?"

His answer was simple. "Maggie."

"Shit." Mackenzie grinned. "You're so gone."

Cain said nothing.

"You're totally gone for her."

Cain turned to the task at hand and nodded. "Yeah, I guess I am."

The rest of the afternoon flew by, and it was nearly five when they called it a day. The stage wasn't fancy but it was solid and, thanks to Mac, had been designed so that it could be broken up into sections, rolled away, and stored for future use.

Things were moving along, and Cain was in a great mood. They'd ordered pizza and wings—Cain's treat, courtesy of his buddy at Jack's Hut—enough to feed all the volunteers who'd stuck around to the end. Michael sat at his side happily stuffing pizza into his mouth. Tommy and his dad had left a few hours earlier. They were heading into the city to visit his grandfather, so it was just Cain and the boy.

He glanced down at Michael. He was fine with that. In fact, he was more than fine with that. The kid had managed to burrow into his heart in pretty much the same way his mother had.

He stood and stretched, worked out a kink in his neck. His muscles protested, but he liked the burn. He was in shape, but it felt good to get his hands dirty again. Nothing like an afternoon of hard physical labor to soothe the mind and work the body. It was good to get back to basics.

"Who's that?"

Cain followed Jake's line of vision, and his mood darkened. Instantly.

Son of a bitch.

A man lurked near the edge of the field, but it wasn't the man who angered Cain as much as what he was carrying. A camera. A big honking camera. He glanced down at Michael. Christ, if he'd taken the kid's picture…

"Michael, you stay here with Salvatore, okay?"

Had this been what Natasha meant? She'd called him several times the week before because she wanted to visit. The woman was insane. He'd finally told her that he'd met someone, that her pipe dream of hooking up with him again was ridiculous. She'd been livid and had threatened to ruin his summer.

He'd cut her off and hadn't thought anything of it. The woman had blown steam throughout most of their marriage, and it had never meant anything. But the paparazzi? They had no interest in him per se, and the only reason they'd be here was if Natasha had pointed them in this direction.

He'd fucking kill her.

"You need help dealing with this asshole?" Jake clenched his hands and stood.

"I'm good."

Cain strode toward the interloper, his features blank, though inside his anger roiled. He was pissed and really didn't have time for this shit.

The paparazzo fiddled with his equipment and, from what Cain could tell, was most likely packing up for the day, which meant he'd gotten what he came for. Cain's anger spiked. Children were hands-off, and if this guy had crossed that line, he was going to be one sorry son of a bitch.

As he got closer, Cain frowned. He recognized the slimy bastard. Dirk was his name. He was the asshole who'd sold pictures of him and Natasha on their honeymoon. The man was a weasel with no moral integrity at all.

He was nearly upon him when Dirk turned, his pinched features tightening into what was supposed to be a smile, but Cain took it for what it was. A big *fuck you.*

"Give me the camera." Cain wasn't playing around.

Dirk's long hair hung in dreads halfway down his back. His caramel skin was as fake as the hair he'd paid huge money for. His skinny arms hung like pencils at his side, the camera held loosely in his long fingers. He was such an arrogant little prick.

Cain's hands fisted and he squared his shoulders.

"Dude, it's a free country. I'm just out taking shots of"—he sneered—"the scenery. No biggie."

"Give me the camera, *now*." He spit the words out.

Dirk took a step back, and the pencil-necked douche's eyes narrowed as he glanced behind Cain. "Cute kid. Secret love child?"

Cain's temper exploded, and he lunged forward. Dirk was surprised. In all their previous encounters, Cain had never reacted this way.

But then, he'd never had a child to protect.

His hand closed around the camera, and he yanked it easily from Dirk's fingers. Dirk tried to twist away, but he was no match for Cain. Cain's fingers dug in, and he had him by his shirt.

"Hey, you can't…"

"I can and I will." Cain was inches from his face. There was no mistaking the level of anger that he felt. "I suggest you get your ass out of town and don't come back."

"What's going on here?" Jake asked, his voice light. Deceptively so. The soldier's muscles bulged as he flexed his arms. "We got a problem, Cain?"

A squeak escaped Dirk's lips as Cain applied a touch more pressure, and a flash of satisfaction rushed through Cain. "I think we're good." He pushed the paparazzo away and studied the camera in his hands. After retrieving the memory card, he asked, "Does this have an internal hard drive?"

Dirk shrugged, his thin face screwed up something fierce as a wave of red colored his sunken cheeks.

"You know what? Doesn't matter. I'm taking this."

"You can't—"

"Don't push me. That kid's face is not going to be plastered all over some trashy mag because you think you have the right to take his picture." Cain leaned forward, and Dirk stumbled backward.

Smart man.

"Call Natasha. I'm sure she'll be more than happy to replace your equipment." There was no surprise, and Cain knew he was right to surmise Natasha's involvement. Hell, she'd probably sold them out on their damn honeymoon for the publicity alone.

Dirk glared at him and opened his mouth, but Jake interrupted. "If you were smart, you'd be gone already."

Dirk's gaze dropped to the camera Cain held, and it took everything inside of Cain to refrain from smashing the damn thing in his slimy, sweat-slicked face.

"Are you deaf and dumb?" Jake frowned and took a step forward.

Dirk searched through the front pockets of his jeans for a set of keys, a smile Cain didn't much care for on his face as he jangled them between his fingers. "Doesn't matter anyway, the cat's out of the bag."

"What the hell does that mean?"

Dirk was surprised. It was obvious. He laughed and then stopped abruptly. "You don't know? You haven't seen the pictures?"

Cain's heart sank.

"Shit, they broke this morning and are all over the Net. *Hollywood Scene* published them." Dirk's face screwed and he sneered. "I've been here for longer than a week. You do the math."

Son of a bitch. "Get out of here."

Dirk heard the warning in Cain's voice. This time he was smart. He turned and muttered, "Whatever," and then disappeared into a gray van parked along the street.

Cain grabbed his cell. He moved a few feet away and, as the signal gained strength, was able to bring up his browser. He Googled Hollywood Scene and frowned. They were notorious for their exposés. Treated celebrities like dirty laundry and regularly hung them out to dry with their pants down for the entire world to see. He didn't know why they'd be interested in him, but was sure the angle centered around Natasha.

When the site came up, his gut churned at the headline.

"Natasha Simmons's Ex-husband and Mystery Woman Get Hot and Heavy."

"Shit, this is not good." He shook his head, afraid to click on the link that would enable him to see the images.

Maggie was going to freak.

He glanced back to Michael and hit the link, his eyes not leaving the boy as it loaded onto his device. His world was about to crash and burn. He felt it, and there wasn't a damn thing he could do. As he scrolled through the pictures his gut churned and his face went white. When he'd seen every single one of them, his body thrummed with anger. He was flush with it.

He'd love to put his hands around Natasha Simmons's throat and—

"You all right?" Jake stood a few feet away.

What the hell was Maggie going to say when she saw the photos? She'd be pissed for sure. Cain shook his head. "No. I'm not."

A crow cawed in the distance, its eerie screech somehow an omen.

He turned to Jake. "Can you take Michael back to the cottage and give Dax a ride too? I have to talk to Maggie before she sees these, if she hasn't already. I have a feeling it's going to get ugly."

Jake nodded. "Sure. Call me later and, uh, good luck."

"Thanks." He stared down at the camera in his hand. He sure as hell was going to need it.

Chapter 28

MAGGIE SHOULD HAVE KNOWN HER HAPPY PLACE, that soft bubble of bliss, would never last. She should have known that it would inflate into a mess of gigantic proportions—one that would leave her on the floor, wrecked, and virtually frozen with fear at its demise.

But when a train derailed and came at you full tilt, you didn't always see it. And when you did…sometimes it was too late.

And that train ran you over.

Twelve hours earlier…

Maggie woke up with a tulip near her pillow and the scent of Cain all around her. The imprint of his body was like a picture on her sheets, and she closed her eyes, imagined him there beside her. It wasn't hard to do. The man's charisma was like a physical entity. He bled into everything he touched.

Maggie nestled into the blankets and noticed a folded note beside the tulip next to her pillow. She grabbed it and read it quickly before folding the small piece of paper and sinking back into the bed. She thought of his arms and the comfort he'd offered the night before. Of his strength and desire to protect. She'd never felt so coddled or cared for. Not ever.

The shell that slithered along her skin, that invisible force field she used to keep everyone out, had been cracked. She'd shared some of the pain that lived inside her, and the weight of those secrets was gone.

It gave her hope that the other stuff, the dark secrets that she hoarded, would one day lessen and ease her burden.

Maggie's alarm clock glowed six a.m. in the early-morning gloom. She stretched, and though she would have liked to linger, she threw back the blankets and jumped out of bed.

It was going to be a busy day. She had two clients on the books, and according to Cain's note, he would be by around seven thirty for Michael. A bunch of volunteers was meeting at the football field in order to get the stage built, and he'd promised to keep her son busy.

He'd ended the note with a promise to keep *her* busy later on.

Maggie grinned and slipped into the shower. Twenty minutes later she had coffee on, and when Michael shuffled his sleepy head down the hall, it was nearly seven thirty.

Michael had just sat down to eat his breakfast when there was a soft rap at the door. Her heart lurched and her cheeks flushed.

Cain.

"I'll get it." Michael almost tripped in his effort to get to the door, and Maggie stared after him, anticipation rolling inside her when she heard Cain's voice.

The two of them entered the kitchen, and her heart swelled. Cain was dressed "blue collar"—white T-shirt, old worn jeans, and work boots. His hair was damp, his chocolate eyes warm, but the smile that greeted her—that lazy, slow smile—was hot. Her heart leaped as she settled on his mouth.

Michael chatted animatedly, his arms moving violently as he described a scene from latest *X-Men* comic.

"Did you hear what I said, Cain?"

He nodded to Michael. "Sure, buddy. Wolverine kicked ass." His eyes remained focused on her.

Michael sat down and grabbed his spoon. "No." He shook his head. "I was talking about Gambit." He giggled. "But that's okay, I know you're making those weird faces at my mom."

Cain chuckled and ruffled Michael's head and then helped himself to a cup of coffee. He sat down, and the three of them chatted about their plans for the day and the upcoming weekend. There was an easy, comfortable flow that settled around Maggie's shoulders that maybe cracked that facade a bit more.

It felt like…they were a family.

Cain insisted on giving her a ride to her first client's house. Mr. and Mrs. Felkes lived in small, brick bungalow not far from Rebecca Hayes. They were a sweet older couple who shared their space with three cats and two litter boxes.

They were also curious about the large SUV she arrived in. When Maggie admitted that Cain Black had given her a ride, Mr. Felkes decided to spend the majority of the morning regaling her with stories of Cain's high school days. Felkes was a retired English and history teacher and had taught all four of the Bad Boys.

It was funny, really, how they were referred to in this way. It was as if they were legendary, like Butch and Sundance, or Billy the Kid and his gang.

Maggie finished up at the Felkeses' and caught the bus to her afternoon client. The Monroes were away on vacation, so it was a quick run-through, really—dusting, and vacuuming and mopping the floors. By three thirty she was locking up and heading home. It was a bit of a jog to the bus stop, and as it turned out, she had lots of time. It ran every half hour, and she missed the four o'clock by minutes.

Figures. Now she was stuck waiting until four thirty.

She'd just exited the bus downtown when her cell rang. Maggie wanted to hit the grocery store on her way home and pick up a few essentials—she was out of milk, eggs, and bagels *again*. Funny how a man in the house put a dent in the food budget.

"Maggie, where are you?" It was Raine.

"I'm downtown, why?"

There was a pause at the other end, and Maggie frowned. Something was wrong. She could feel it.

"I… What are you doing downtown?"

"Getting a few groceries."

Again with the silence.

"So, you're in the Super Saver? Like right now?"

"Yes, I just walked in. What the hell's going on, Raine? Why are you being weird?"

Maggie perched the phone on her shoulder and moved out of the way of a few shoppers. She was in the dairy aisle and needed breakfast fixings. She grabbed a carton of eggs and a block of cheese. She didn't the need the cheese, but it was on sale, and she was, if anything, a super saver when it came to shopping.

Janice Hopkins, mother to one of Michael's classmates, stared at her from the milk section, and when Maggie smiled, the woman looked away as if embarrassed and fled toward the produce aisle.

Maggie stared after her, and that's when she noticed Rebecca Stringer pointing her way, giggling behind her hands as she chatted with a woman Maggie didn't know.

"Maggie, I know this is going to sound strange, but can you just leave the store and I'll meet you in front?"

What the hell is going on?

"You want me to leave the store." She was getting weirded out.

"Yes."

"As in, drop whatever I have and just leave the store."

"I know it sounds crazy, but, uh, yes, I need to talk to you before . . ." Raine's voice trailed off, and immediately Maggie's internal radar roared to life. She heard it inside her head, pounding out an alarm that was in sync with her fast-beating heart.

"Before what?" Maggie turned her back to Rebecca, suddenly convinced every single person in the store was either staring at her or talking about her behind her back. She was uncomfortable and filled with inexplicable fear that her world was about to crumble.

She lowered her voice and hunched her shoulders. "Raine, seriously, what the hell is going on? And don't say 'nothing.'" She chanced a look at Rebecca once more and winced at the venomous glee that was in the woman's eyes as she continued to stare.

"Maggie, I'm almost there. Can you please just drop whatever you have and meet me out front?"

Rebecca had a magazine clutched between her fingers, and her friend grabbed it from her and opened it wide. The cover was bright crimson, the headline bold black and white.

She read it clearly from where she stood: "Natasha Simmons's Ex-husband and Mystery Woman Get Hot and Heavy."

The blood drained from her face. *Oh God.*

"Maggie, are you there?"

"I..." She couldn't speak. It felt like a box of cotton balls was stuffed down her throat.

"Maggie, you're not near the cash registers, are you?" Panic filled Raine's voice, but Maggie wasn't listening. She pushed her cart to the side, abandoned it, and walked toward the front of the store, her cell phone still held against her ear. People moved out of her way. Some stared. Some didn't. Some opened their mouths to speak and then closed them rapidly when they got a good look at her.

Did she look psycho? Deranged? Unhinged?

She reached the magazine section and nearly lost her lunch. *Hollywood Scene* stared back at her, the bold headline big enough for a person half-blind to see. The cover sported a picture of Maggie and Cain, bodies close as they danced together at the Coach House. Her face was upturned, mouth open for his kiss. His hands were in her hair and on her face, and he held her as if she belonged to him.

It spoke volumes.

She nearly dropped her cell and heard Raine's frantic voice as she tossed it into her purse.

Maggie grabbed the magazine and made her way

over to the self-serve register. After scanning the item, she paid for it and, ignoring the whispers and eyes that followed her, walked through the exit to head blindly into the parking lot.

She didn't stop walking until she crossed the length of it and stood beneath the shade of an oak that bordered Main Street. There was a bench a few feet away, and she sank onto it, the magazine between her fingers as she fought to keep her nausea at bay.

Carefully she opened it and flipped through the pages rapidly until she came to the center spread.

Her breath hitched. She choked. It was so much worse than she'd even thought possible.

There were several photos, ranging from candid beach shots to a few more of them dancing together inside the Coach House. But the largest photo drew her eyes—hell, there was no way to ignore it. The text beneath it was salacious and made her sick.

> *Natasha Simmons's newly divorced ex, rocker Cain Black, has been hiding out in his hometown of Crystal Lake, Michigan, since his tour ended abruptly last month when Black punched bandmate Blake Hartley onstage in Barcelona. Cain Black returned home to attend the funeral of an old schoolmate, a soldier who was killed in Afghanistan. He's said to be devastated. Looks to us like Mr. Black's new girl toy has done a lot to ease his broken heart. Wonder what his ex, Natasha Simmons, thinks of this mystery lady? Wonder what his girl toy thinks of the fact Simmons has expressed interest in*

> *reconnecting with her husband, claiming "he's the man for me. He just doesn't know it yet. He'll figure it out and come back."*

She clutched the magazine tightly and stared at the photo. It was an intimate shot. Cain was shirtless, his back to the camera as he looked up at her. His face was in profile, and it was obvious that it was him. She was in her skimpy black bra, her hands on his shoulders as she gazed down at him.

Her hair hung loose, and the expression on her face was one of longing, anticipation, and lust.

Two things were very clear. First off, she was identifiable. No question there. And secondly, the picture had been taken *from her backyard*, with a lens pointing in toward her bedroom.

Heat flushed her cheeks, and she bit her lip. She remembered that night. She knew exactly what had happened after the picture was taken. The ick factor alone—that someone had taken photos without her knowledge—was enough to make her sick, but the thought that they'd spied and seen things… Seen her and Cain together? She couldn't comprehend that.

Maggie closed her eyes as she tried to calm her nerves and the fear that was growing inside her. *Hollywood Scene* was a major trash magazine and was in every grocery store from coast to coast.

Oh God, they have a show…a half-hour recap on television every night at six.

Maggie stood, dropped her purse in her haste, and scooped it up quickly, throwing the magazine inside as she glanced down the street. Bus stop. She needed to get to the bus stop. She had to get home so that she could think.

So that she could plan.

There was no question that Michael's father, Dante, would see the pictures. The only question was, how much time did she have before he came after her? Days? Weeks? Or was it already too late?

The fear she felt for Michael was paralyzing. She let it claim her soul, but only for a moment. She needed to remember what it felt like. She'd become too soft, too complacent. She needed to feed from that fear.

Maggie wiped away the tears that had gathered in the corners of her eyes and walked rapidly toward the bus stop. She checked her emotions and froze them in place, her body going into battle mode in much the same way it had when she fled Savannah a year earlier.

Minutes later she hopped the bus, kept her head low, and sank into the seat just behind the driver. They pulled away from the curb as her cell phone chimed once more. She grabbed it and saw Cain's number, and her heart shifted, the pain so intense, a whimper escaped from her lips. Everything had changed in less time than it took to wash her kitchen floor.

But had she really expected the fantasy to last? She'd played with fire, and only a fool would believe the burn wouldn't hurt.

Maggie threw her cell back into her bag without answering.

She couldn't worry about Cain. He was a big boy.

She'd worry about herself later too. At the moment her only concern was Michael.

On second thought, she reached for her phone and

hit speed dial. Raine answered before the second ring. "Maggie?"

"I need you to do a favor."

"Where are you?"

"I'm on my way home. Can you do something for me?"

"Maggie, of course, anything."

"Cain has Michael. Can you get him and bring him home?"

"But Maggie, you need to talk to Cain."

"I *need* for my son to be home. Can you get him or no?" She was abrupt and didn't care.

Raine sighed. "I'm heading out of the parking lot from the Super Saver now and will swing by the football field."

Maggie tossed her cell into her bag and stared out the window. In the distance dark gray clouds were blowing in. Angry clouds filled with menace. How appropriate.

The train had just derailed, and there was no doubt in her mind. She was about to get run over.

Chapter 29

Cain saw Maggie about a minute before she realized he was there. He'd parked in the driveway but had spent the last five minutes pacing up and down her porch, trying to get rid of the nervous energy that hung low in his gut.

She moved up the street, her steps quick, her head bowed. A large bag hung off her shoulder, and she was hunched forward as if trying to ward off something.

He cursed, pissed at himself. He'd let his guard down. A lame-ass move, and now she was going to pay for it.

Maggie glanced up then, and he clenched his hands at the look in her eyes. It was back. The deer-in-headlights thing was back, and it was his fault.

"Where's Michael?" A hint of panic rolled beneath her words. Her Southern accent was much more pronounced, and she couldn't hide her fear.

"Jake took him back to the lake, but Raine knows he's there. She called me."

Maggie blew out a shaky breath, and her expression changed. It wasn't so much that her features physically moved. It was subtle, like a shadow creeping across her eyes. She squared her shoulders and marched up her narrow walkway, shoved her way past him, and unlocked her front door. She slipped inside, and he followed, wishing she'd at least yell. Throw something. *Do* something.

The silent treatment left him uneasy.

She let her bag fall to the ground, and a copy of *Hollywood Scene* slipped out. He stared at the cover, wincing again at the bold headline.

"Maggie, I'm so sorry. I don't know what to say. I had no idea there were paparazzi in town. Hell, why would I? They've never followed me before unless Natasha was around."

She walked into her kitchen without a word, and again he followed. Two wineglasses were pulled down from her cupboard, and she filled them with some merlot left over from a few nights back.

She treated herself to a generous gulp and moved away from the sink, leaving his glass behind. The unease in his chest tightened, gripped him in a band of tension that made it difficult to breathe. His eyes followed her as she slipped out the back door and disappeared into her yard.

Still without uttering a single word.

Cain grabbed his glass and downed the entire thing. He traced her footsteps down the stairs until he stood a few feet from her.

Overhead the gray clouds that had blown in earlier filled the sky, and he thought that maybe he'd felt a big raindrop. Maggie sipped her wine and leaned against the railing that led from the small deck down to the grass. She looked small, vulnerable, and he wanted nothing more than to hold her, just like he had the night before.

He felt like the biggest ass ever. Bringing this load of crap down onto her world.

Ignoring him, she walked to the back fence, her hands trailing along the yellow honeysuckle as she wandered toward the small waterfall in the corner.

"Maggie, I—"

She shook her head, held her hand up, and with the flick of her wrist he was silent. Cain watched her, hating the hopeless rush of emotion he felt. But he respected her parameters and hung back.

She slowly undid the clip atop her head, and a silken wash of crimson fell over her fingers as she gently shook out her hair. The wind had picked up, and he watched transfixed as her long tangles floated on the breeze.

She wandered over to the other side of the yard and stopped midway between the back fence and her house. She bent down and picked up something and then she froze.

Cain moved forward until he was able to see what she held—a cigarette butt. He frowned and watched her carefully.

"He stood right here," she said, her face tight. "And I never knew."

Cain followed her line of vision and cursed as he stared at the dark patch of window that belonged to her bedroom. She was talking about the dirtbag photographer.

"Maggie, I'll sue the bastard."

"What's the point in that? The damage is done. I'm just trying to understand what kind of person would sneak into someone's backyard and take pictures of them through their window." She hugged her arms around her body and shuddered. "It's invasive, perverted, and just…wrong."

"You'd be surprised."

She turned then, her eyes angry, their blue depths as dark as the clouds above them. "I don't want to be surprised. I have a little boy to look out for, remember? Being surprised isn't a good thing."

"Maggie, I know what you're thinking."

She shook her head and laughed, a short, harsh sound that didn't belong on her lips. "You have no idea what I'm thinking. Trust me."

He took a moment and then tried again. "This story will be big for a while, and then it will blow over. They'll move on to the next sorry son of a bitch. And then the next one. It's the way the machine works."

She looked away, and he felt her withdrawal like a physical slap. It pissed him off. That she could just turn off like that.

"Maggie, I know you're upset, and rightly so. But let's put things into perspective here."

"He stood in my backyard and pointed a camera into my window." She shook her head and her voice rose. "What if he'd held something else? What if it had been a gun pointed in my window?"

"Okay, you're getting carried away. A gun? Seriously? I'm a guitar player, for Christ sake, not the president." His chest tightened as he glared at her. She was blowing the entire thing out of proportion.

"For now." She muttered.

"What do you mean for now?" What the hell was she getting at?

Maggie rounded on him, her face flushed with anger. "Where do you think you'll be a year from now, Cain? Here? With me?"

"A year from now?" He sputtered.

"Because that would be wrong." She continued as if he'd never said a thing. "These past few weeks have been a fantasy. Those pictures in that trash magazine aren't real. They're fantasy, nothing more. A year from now, you won't be here and you won't be with me."

"How the hell do you know what I want?" He ran hands through his hair, his thoughts twisted, confused, and just plain fucking mad.

Maggie shook her head. "I don't know what you want, Cain, because we've never talked about it, but I do know one thing." She blew out a hot breath. "I have a son who needs to be protected."

"Maggie, nothing will happen to Michael. I'd never allow it."

"*You'd* never allow it?" She set her empty glass on the small patio table near the barbecue. "Let me be clear about this. *I'll* never allow it. I'm his mother. You're just..."

His pulse spiked as a new wave of anger rolled over him. "I'm just what?"

She stared at him, her eyes huge as several fat drops of rain fell from the sky. "You're the man I've been screwing, and as of now, it's officially over. We can't do this anymore, Cain." Thunder rolled in the distance and lightning streaked across the horizon.

"Can't or won't?" he snarled, his anger erupting.

"I won't do this anymore."

"Maggie..."

But she'd closed off. Retreated. Frustration and anger churned madly, feeding his dark mood. He blew out a long, hot breath and took a moment. He couldn't lose his temper. That would push her further away.

"Maggie, you need to take a step back. This isn't as bad as it seems." He tried to keep his voice calm and neutral, but the panic parasites were burrowing deep.

"I disagree. In fact, I *strongly* disagree, and I think

it's going to get much worse than it is today. It may seem like no big deal to you, but we're looking at this from two entirely different perspectives."

"They're pictures, Maggie. This will blow over."

"Blow over, my ass." She shook her head. "Maybe for you, but not for me."

Cain looked away. He didn't know what to say. How could he make her understand? It *would* blow over. This kind of thing always did.

He lowered his voice. "Maggie." She was going to run. He could feel it. "Why don't we discuss what this is really about? Because I sure as hell don't believe you're this upset over some pictures. What are you afraid of? Your ex-husband?"

She was surprised, her mouth half-open and eyebrows furled. She stared at him for several long moments, her mouth pinched tight. "I can't talk about this anymore. I need you to leave."

"I want to talk about it."

"I don't care what you want, Cain. This isn't about you or me." She thrust her chin forward. "It's about my son." She inhaled a ragged breath. *"My son."*

He'd been dismissed. "So that's it." Cain's nostrils flared, his eyes flattened, and he clenched his mouth so tight that pain radiated along his jaw. "Just like that."

"Look, Cain, I don't have time to hash this out." She shook her head, her eyes huge in her pale facc. "I've got a lot to think about."

"I'm not leaving, Maggie. Tell me about your ex-husband and what he did to you."

"Dante is none of your business."

The energy in the air crackled, and lightning rushed

across the sky once more. Raindrops splattered onto her face and body, the large drops leaving fat, dark circles on her clothes. *Dante*. He had the bastard's name.

"Michael made him my business."

"Michael? What do you mean?" Her chest heaved, and she glanced away. He knew she was fighting for control, and it broke his heart to see her so upset.

She ran trembling fingers along her temple.

He decided to lay everything on the line. What the hell did he have to lose? "I know he abused you, laid his hands on you and hit you." She flinched as he spoke, as if every word uttered slammed into her the way Michael's father's fists had. She clenched her fingers so tight around the delicate crystal glass, he was afraid it would shatter.

"Why would you…how would you…?" She struggled to finish her sentence, and if he could have done anything to wipe away her pain, he would have. She swallowed thickly.

"Michael told me."

Her eyes widened, and silence stretched between them. "No." She finally whispered. "But Michael, never…he *never* saw…" She looked away, her body and voice trembling.

Cain fought the urge to grab her into his arms. He wanted to offer comfort but at the same time was afraid to drive her away. A fragile connection had been forged and it wouldn't take much to break it.

"Oh God."

"Maggie, let me help you. Tell me what it is you need, and it's done. I can't be there for you if you don't let me in."

"I never knew that he saw." Her voice broke. "What kind of mother am I? *I never knew*."

He reached for her—he couldn't help himself. His hands slid along her shoulders, and he pulled her close, grateful that she let him. Maggie's head tucked just under his chin, and he breathed in her unique scent, loving the way she melted into him. She belonged there.

She belonged to him.

A steady fall of rain slid down their skin, but the two of them were oblivious to the storm that raged. She didn't move, and he made no effort to drag her into the house. The water washed over them, a cool balm against their heated flesh. He closed his eyes and held her, hoping, wishing, it would take away her pain.

After a while she stopped trembling, and her hands pushed at his chest. "Let me go, Cain."

Reluctantly he released her, but there was something in her voice that made him wary. That ball of fear inside him churned heavy as she took a few steps and turned to him.

"Raine will be here soon with Michael. I need you to leave."

"I'm not leaving."

She brushed wet hair off her face, but there was no expression in her eyes. It was as though the tap had been closed and the water had run out. She was blank. Already gone.

"I'll allow Michael to play in the charity football game with you, because I know how much it means to him, but after that we're done. I can't handle what happened here today, Cain. It's too much."

His anger spilled over. When had this woman gained

such control over his emotions? "So, you're willing to toss our relationship into the garbage because of a few pictures? I thought you had more backbone than that, Maggie. I guess I was wrong."

She took two steps toward him, her small form humming with anger. "I guess you really don't know me at all then."

"It's kind of hard to know someone when they're constantly shutting you out." He frowned. "Do you want to know what I think?"

"Not particularly."

He walked toward her. "I think you're using Michael and your ex as an excuse to run away from something pretty damn special."

She glared at him but remained silent.

"You've got trust issues. I get that, Maggie, but there comes a moment when you have to let go of that crap, or else..." His tongue got all tied up. How could he make her see?

"Or else, what?"

"You'll end up just like your old man, alone, bitter, and wasted." She flinched at his words, and he knew they'd cut her deep. "Don't you want to be happy, Maggie?"

She stared at him in silence for a good long while, and Cain thought that maybe he'd just crossed a line. But damn, she pulled his pin easier than anyone had ever done before, and he wasn't about to apologize for being right.

"I want you to leave."

Unbelievable.

"So that's it." He frowned darkly and took a step toward her.

"That's it."

"I don't get a say."

She shook her head. "No, you don't."

The back door flew open, and they both looked toward the small deck. Michael stood just inside, the grin on his face dying as he stared down at both of them. His curls were crazy, surrounding his head in a halo—a result of the humidity and rain.

He pushed away the stubborn wave that hung in his eyes and stepped onto the deck.

"Why are you standing out in the rain?"

Maggie made a noise, a soft painful whimper, and Cain stepped forward.

"Your mom was just coming in."

"Oh." Michael's eyes were glued to his mother.

"Thanks for all your help today, buddy."

Michael nodded, but his face paled as he stared at Maggie. "Are you all right, Mom? You don't look so good."

Maggie walked past Cain and enveloped her son. "I'm fine, honey."

"Is Cain staying for supper?"

Maggie kept her head lowered and whispered, "No. Cain was just leaving."

Cain's mouth thinned at her words, but he remained silent. No sense in causing a scene in front of Michael. That would only alienate her more, and this sure as hell wasn't the kid's problem.

"Why?" He wriggled out of his mother's arms and looked up at Cain, his expression serious. "Are you guys having a fight?"

He clasped the kid on his shoulder. Forced a smile. "I gotta run buddy, but we're still on for Saturday, right?"

"I think so." Michael glanced at his mother. "I want to play."

Maggie nodded and Cain winked. "Good, I'll see you then."

He let himself out the back gate even though everything inside him screamed that he should stay and hash things out. But what was the point? Maggie needed to cool off, and hopefully she'd come around tomorrow.

He hopped into his truck and sat there for a long time, his thoughts whirling. What the hell had just happened? When Cain finally fired up the engine, it was dark. The rain had stopped, though everything was misted in a film of slick water.

He glanced in his rearview mirror. Fog crept along the road, and it mingled with the steam that rose in the air from the still-hot blacktop. The storm had brought a wave of cold air, and it had cooled things down considerably, though the surface still held the sun's heat. Slowly he backed out of Maggie's driveway and headed toward the main drag, which would take him back to the lake.

He felt empty, confused, and pissed off.

What a cliché. It had all the makings of a number one fucking hit.

Chapter 30

Maggie watched the glowing red of Cain's taillights disappear, and though he was finally gone, it did nothing to make her feel better. She stepped back and let the silky fabric of the window covering fall back into place.

Her chest hurt. Her head. Her heart. *Everything* hurt.

All she felt was sadness. Incredible, bone-crushing sadness. The anger was still there, but it was burrowed beneath her pain and the impending feeling of doom.

In the space of a few hours her life had been turned upside down yet again, and this time there was no one to blame but herself. She'd known Cain Black was trouble the moment she laid eyes on him.

She should never have let him in.

And now Michael was going to pay for her mistakes, for her weakness and loneliness. For her selfish need to be loved by a man.

Maggie closed her eyes and tried to ignore the fact that she'd even thought of the word *love* in regard to Cain.

"Did Cain finally leave?"

Maggie moved away from the window and nodded at Raine. Her body felt like it was two steps behind. Like she was moving out of sync.

There was too much going on in her brain—thoughts of plans and backup plans—of leaving and getting as far away from Crystal Lake as she could. She slid into the large purple and green plaid chair that was kitty-corner to the sofa and picked at a bit of stuffing that had escaped the seam along the armrest.

Raine sat with feet curled beneath her, piping-hot cup of tea in her hands. Her dark hair was pinned loosely atop her head, and she was dressed in ratty clothes—oversized T-shirt and loose track pants—that were splattered in beige and teal splotches of color. It was something Maggie hadn't noticed until now.

Raine pointed toward the small table beside Maggie's chair. "I brought you a tea as well."

Maggie scooped the warm mug into her hands and took a sip, relishing the heat as it slid over her tongue. But still she shivered. She knew it was going to take a lot more than a warm drink to drive away the stark cold inside her body.

"Have you been painting?" she asked, thinking the question sounded lame and desperate—but she so needed a bit of normal right now.

Raine frowned, took a sip of tea, and settled into the sofa. "Are we really going to talk about my sad attempt to freshen up the spare room?"

Maggie stared at the brunette but remained silent.

Raine's expression softened. "I'd like to know what's going on in that brain of yours, because I can see the wheels spinning, and I'll be honest, Maggie, it's kinda scaring me." Raine took another sip of her tea and leaned forward. "It's never good to react to a situation when you're upset. Believe me, I know."

Maggie said nothing, because deep down, Raine was right. She just wished she didn't feel like she was already behind. That she needed to be gone from Crystal Lake like yesterday.

"You can't dump Cain because some pervert snapped a few pictures of you guys together."

"This isn't about Cain."

"No?" Raine settled back into the sofa. "What's it about, then?" Her tone was conversational, but the glint of interest was sharp.

Maggie stared down into her teacup. Steam rose from the surface, but it did nothing to thaw the ice in her veins. She grasped the cup tighter, so tight her knuckles cracked and her skin burned from the heat. She wanted to smash it against a wall. She wanted to scream at the top of her lungs, pull her hair out, and break something.

Mostly, she just wanted to curl up into a ball and cry.

She did none of those things. Instead she looked Raine in the eye and spoke. "I'm leaving town."

"Leaving town?" Raine sputtered. She'd obviously not been expecting to hear that. She wiped a few drops of tea off her chin. "What do you mean? To hide out? Where will you go? Shit, Maggie, if you really feel the need to get some quiet over the next couple of days, come and stay with me."

"Thanks for the offer, Raine, but that's not what I meant." Maggie ran fingers across her forehead and winced as pain lashed across her skull. She was well on her way to a lovely migraine.

"You don't understand. As soon as I can, probably Saturday afternoon, Michael and I are leaving Crystal Lake, and we're not coming back. I should leave tomorrow, but I can't take Saturday away from my son."

Raine was shocked. Her mouth opened, but no sound

came out. She took a sip of tea, her eyes never leaving Maggie, and when she spoke her voice was tremulous.

"But that doesn't even make sense. Don't you think you're overreacting? Just a little bit?"

Maggie gazed across the room at Raine. An image of Dante—his face twisted in rage, his skin tight, and his fists flying—crossed her vision, and she blinked rapidly to clear the image. She shook her head. "No, I'm not overreacting."

Raine studied her in silence for several long moments. "What are you not telling me, Maggie?"

Maggie's eyes shifted to just beyond Raine. She heard the shower running and knew that Michael would be a while. Could she trust Raine? Would it be all right to share some of this burden and confide in a friend?

A shudder racked her frame, and Maggie realized her clothes were still damp, from being outside and so was her hair. She leaned over and grabbed the throw blanket off the corner of the sofa and wrapped it around her shoulders. She couldn't get sick. There was too much to do.

"I didn't come to Crystal Lake because I'd planned on it—because I had family close by or friends here. I'd never heard of this place until..." She exhaled and paused for a second. "I let Michael choose our destination, and do you want to know how we did that?"

Raine nodded slowly but remained silent.

"He closed his eyes and pointed at a map. A travel map I took from his father's car. It was a tiny red dot in a sea of dots, but there it was, Crystal Lake. *That's* why we came here. I figured if we chose some random town, it would make it that much harder for us to be discovered."

Maggie saw the moment as if it were yesterday. The police had just taken Dante away, and she knew her window of opportunity was small. His daddy's money would have him out by noon the next day.

Michael's finger had directed their fate, and they'd left Savannah within the hour, armed with two large bags of clothes and the stash of cash she'd been hoarding for the last few years.

"Who are you running from?"

Maggie sighed and swirled the liquid around in her cup. So many confessions had fallen from her lips in the last few days.

"Maggie?" Raine prodded.

"My husband, Michael's father."

Silence greeted her admission, and Maggie glanced up into Raine's eyes. They were colored dark with concern.

"So, this man is dangerous?"

Maggie's eyes narrowed and it was hard for her to stay calm. "If he finds me he will take Michael away, and there is no way in hell that I'll allow Dante anywhere near my child."

"Maggie. It doesn't have to be that way. He can't just take your child away, especially if he's been"—Raine's voice softened—"abusive toward you or Michael."

"You don't understand." Maggie's words were bitter. "Dante's family is powerful, well established. They have a lot of money. I have nothing to fight them with."

"You'll never belong to anyone else, bitch. When I get out of here, I'm going to make sure you understand just how much you belong to me. And don't think of running. That didn't work out so well for you last time."

He leaned in close. She could feel the heat of his breath against her cheek, and her gut roiled, full of nausea.

"Because if you do, I will find you and I'll make sure your son never sees you again. You're nothing but trash, Maggie. Garbage that I rescued from the gutter. Remember that. What judge would award custody of that little snot-nosed bastard to someone like you? An uneducated, pathetic excuse for a woman?"

Dante's words echoed in her mind, his voice crystal clear as if he stood beside the chair, whispering his threats into her ear.

"Maggie, are you all right? You're as white as a ghost."

She shook the darkness from her mind and focused on Raine. "No, I'm not all right. Nothing about this situation is right." She shot up from the chair and threw the throw blanket behind her. "Dante is a monster. One who ruled my life for almost ten years, until I finally..." Her eyes filled with tears as the memories of that last night washed over her.

"What happened, Maggie?" Raine asked gently. "What made you leave?"

She bit her lip, let the anger inside build, and it filled her with power. "He went after my child, that's what happened. I wasn't enough to take the edge off anymore, and he went after Michael." Angrily Maggie wiped moisture from her eyes. "I'm sickened at the pathetic, weak person that I was. I can't believe that I let him tell me what to wear, where to go, what to make for dinner. He dictated every minute of my life."

Maggie crossed to the window once more and looked into the darkness. "I know this is going to sound weird, but I guess in a way I should thank him."

Raine set her cup down and crossed to where she stood. She threaded her arm through Maggie's. The comfort, the soft touch, did wonders, and Maggie welcomed the bit of peace that came with it.

"Why would you want to thank him?" Raine asked quietly.

"I wasn't a strong person back then, and as awful as it sounds, if he hadn't taken a run at Michael—" Her voice broke, and she took a second. "If he hadn't come after Michael, I might still be there."

"Whatever reason you had for leaving doesn't matter, Maggie. What does matter is that you *did*. You found the strength to take your son out of a bad situation, and you started all over in a town where you knew no one." Raine's arms enveloped Maggie into a hug. "That is not the description of a weak soul. That is a person with balls. Huge, freaking elephant balls."

"Well, I'm going to need those balls." Maggie replied.

"Maggie, *stay*. And if he shows up, fight him. You've come this far. If you leave, that just means he's won. Why would you let him win?"

She opened her mouth to retort, but Raine cut her off.

"I know you're scared, but you have friends here. A lot of friends who will do anything for you. And then there's Cain. I'm sure he'd love the chance to kick your ex's ass."

Maggie took a step back. Okay. Raine had lost her marbles. "I've known Cain for not more than a month. Why the hell would he want to get involved in my mess?" She snorted. "Because we're sleeping together? That's ridiculous."

Raine smiled and shook her head. "Of course not." Her grin widened. "It's simple. He loves you."

Maggie stared at Raine in shock, and when she finally

found her voice, several seconds had ticked by. "You're crazy. He's never...we've never..." She moved away, her eyes drawn to the darkness outside.

We've never said those words. She'd never *allowed* herself to go there, to even consider the intensity of her feelings and what they meant.

"I'm not crazy." Raine stood beside her again, her dark eyes filled with a sadness that wasn't there before. "I see the way he looks at you. The way he touches you as if you belong to him. The way he gets annoyed when Jake or Mac take up too much of your time. He might not even realize it yet, but he does love you, and you feel the same way."

"I don't...we barely know each other. Love takes time, and besides..." Maggie needed her to understand. "It doesn't *matter*. Cain isn't part of this equation. I'm leaving. It's my only option."

Maggie's watched the petite brunette as she leaned against the sofa and crossed her arms across her chest.

"You can't measure love by time, it doesn't work that way. You can't predict when or who or when..." Raine's eyes widened and Maggie saw the pain reflected in their depths. "It just is." A shimmer of tears glistened at the edges, and Raine wiped them away impatiently. "It can last a lifetime if you're lucky. Or it can last a week. It doesn't matter, so long as that one moment, that *special moment* in time that existed just for the two of you is the most amazing, crazy, awful, scary, and wonderful moment ever."

Maggie's eyes misted as she listened to Raine. She knew the young widow was talking about Jesse. Her loss was still so fresh, her pain palpable.

"You don't know how lucky you are, Maggie. To have that chance. To matter to someone."

The two of them stared at each other in silence until Michael appeared. He was dressed in his Batman pajamas, his hair slicked back and skin glowing from the shower. He stifled a yawn, and it was obvious that he'd had a full day.

"Go to bed, honey, I'll be in shortly to kiss you good night."

"No TV?"

Maggie shook her head and pointed to the hall. "No."

"Okay." He smiled at them. "Night, Raine."

He disappeared back down the hall, and Maggie followed Raine onto the porch. The night lay heavy against everything, its dark embrace full of a cool freshness that was a relief from the heat of the last few days.

Crickets chirped, their excited chatter echoing from inside the hidden places along the ground, and in the distance voices drifted on the breeze.

"Raine, you can't tell anyone what I just shared with you." Maggie's eyes pleaded. "Promise me."

"I won't." Raine hugged her tightly and then whispered into her ear. "But be smart. Listen to what I said. Don't throw away a future with Cain until you've talked to him. Because if you leave without sorting things out, the regret will eat you up. Maybe not right away, but trust me, you won't escape it. You'll never know what could have been, and you *will* break his heart as well as your own."

Raine pulled away, her expression dead serious. "And coming from someone whose heart has been ripped out of her chest…I gotta say, that would be tragic."

Chapter 31

The smell of coffee penetrated the fog inside his head and slowly brought Cain around. He groaned and rolled over, cursing as a twinge of pain ran across his shoulders. God, he'd slept like absolute shit, if he'd slept at all.

His muscles were stiff. Really stiff, though he supposed manual labor would do that to you. He flexed his arms and cursed. Guess he wasn't in as good a shape as he'd believed, though to be honest, the mattress was a piece of crap—it was like sleeping on a slab of concrete—and this had been the first night in weeks he'd actually slept on it.

He missed Maggie's bed and the feel of her warmth against his body. The way she burrowed into his side as if she were a part of him—*that* feeling was something he wanted to know every damn morning.

Arm flung above his head, he stared at the ceiling and frowned. He was still pissed off. He should have stayed. He should have refused to leave until they'd had it out, but then…if he'd pushed things, forced the issue, it might have made the situation worse.

Maggie needed some time to process. She'd come around. He hoped.

Cain groaned and rolled out of bed.

Maybe he was in too deep. His feelings had grown over the last several weeks. He knew it. She *had* to know, and it frustrated the hell out of him that he didn't know where he stood with her. Quicksand was easier to navigate than the mystery of Maggie O'Rourke.

Cain rolled his neck and swore under his breath as another wave of pain crossed his shoulders. He gritted his teeth. There was no damn way he was going to accept they were done.

Cain followed the scent of coffee and moved toward the open-concept kitchen located opposite the bedrooms. It was the focal point of the cottage, with a large island and lots of greenery. The cupboards were old, probably oak, but someone had decided to paint them bright yellow, which wasn't so bad, except they clashed horribly with the burnt-orange countertop and purple pottery that was strewn everywhere.

He glanced to the right. The wall of windows allowed the lake to come inside the space, and he spied Mac down on the dock, reading the morning paper. His eyes narrowed. Or was that *Hollywood Scene* in his hands?

"You look like shit, mate."

Cain grabbed a mug from the cupboard, filled it with some hot brew, and took a sip. Dax grinned at him and raised his glass in a mock toast. He was in his boxers—Union Jack, no surprise there—and his pasty white skin glowed in the bright sunlight that streamed in from the window above the sink. His thick, dark hair was all over the place, and a day's worth of stubble graced his chin. He didn't have his contacts in, and with his overly large horn-rim glasses, he was about as far away from a rocker as you could get.

If their fans could see him now…but then again, Dax had a certain charm all his own that seemed to transcend whatever his particular look was. Cain had decided long ago that it was a British thing.

"I may look like shit, but at least I'm not sparkling like some vampire wannabe," Cain said drily.

Dax snorted. "Hey, the whole vampire thing works for me. The ladies dig that kind of shit, no matter what age they are."

Cain took another sip of coffee. "I'm sure they do."

Dax hopped up onto one of the stools and rested his elbows on the island. "Was nice seeing your mom again."

Cain was silent. His mother had stopped by the night before. She'd tried discussing his situation with Maggie, but he'd refused to engage. How could he? He was still trying to figure things out himself.

"She's pretty damn cute, eh? Your little bird."

Cain wandered over to where Dax sat, a frown on his face, when he spied *Hollywood Scene* in front of the Brit. It lay open to the center spread.

"Christ, does everyone have a copy?"

"Dunno. Mac brought a few of 'em back last night."

"That figures."

Dax whistled as he glanced down at the pictures, and Cain's face darkened as he glanced at the magazine. In the picture, Maggie's face spoke volumes.

He grabbed it from Dax, ignoring the blast of curse words that fell from the Brit's mouth, and studied the picture closely.

She looked sexy as hell with her hair, that long silky mess of hair, all over the place. Her breasts nearly spilled from the lacy bra she wore, and he remembered how he couldn't wait to get her out of it.

It was a picture that any man would find erotic. Sexy.

But right now? As he gazed down at it, all Cain focused on was the look in her eyes. There was softness there—a surrender in their depths that hit him in the gut.

Maggie *looked* like he *felt*. It wasn't about sex for her. Not in that moment. It was about love.

Cain ran his hand across his jaw and let the magazine fall onto the counter. Holy Christ.

He didn't just want to be with her. He *loved* her. Real, true, I'd-freaking-die-for-you love. The realization washed over him with the strength of a jackhammer, and he slid onto the stool beside Dax and set his mug onto the counter.

He sang songs about this stuff all the time, but until now he'd never experienced it. Not like this. His marriage to Natasha had been a huge mistake, one where lust had been mistaken for love. This thing with Maggie was on an entirely different level.

"Are you all right?" Dax asked.

"No."

"Ah." Dax closed the magazine. "So, should I be worried then?"

"No."

"Okay, but you're a bit peaked, mate, and sorry to say it's not a good look for you."

"What?"

"I said you look like shit."

"I love her."

"What was that? You're mumbling into your cup."

Cain glanced toward the Brit and grinned. "I love her."

Dax took a sip of coffee and arched his brow, a huge grin on his face. "Well, that's nice for you. *Really nice*. The question is, mate: What are you going to do about it?"

"About what?" Jake barked.

They both glanced up as Jake walked into the kitchen. The tall soldier was dressed in running shorts and a T-shirt covered in sweat. His muscles bulged and his veins stood out in stark relief. He tossed an empty water bottle into the recycle bin beside the island and stared at them both.

"You guys gonna fill me in?"

Cain rubbed his eyes and glanced up at his friend.

"Never mind." Jake crossed to the coffee machine and grabbed a mug from the cupboard. "I'm thinking this has to do with Maggie?" He emptied the carafe and leaned against the counter.

Cain remained silent.

"You love her."

Hearing Jake say the words so matter-of-factly pretty much cemented the entire notion. Cain nodded. "Hell, yeah. I think I might have fallen the moment I laid eyes on her at Jesse's funeral reception."

Jake lowered his eyes and stared into his cup. "That's good. Jesse'd be happy for you." Jake chuckled. "Hell, let's be honest, he'd be riding your ass big-time. He always thought that you'd be the guy with a posse of women. Like Hef and his bunnies." The soldier grinned. "Glad to see he was wrong."

"Well, mates, I'd love to sit around and discuss Cain's love life, but we've a show to put together, and time's running out. So what's the plan?" Dax looked at him expectantly, and for a second Cain blanked.

"Uh…" He frowned.

"Fundraiser. Music. Football?" Dax slid from his stool. "Ring a bell?"

Cain glanced toward the clock. It was nearly nine

now, and they needed to finish a few things before they'd be ready for production setup, which was scheduled for noon.

Cain grabbed his mug and finished his coffee. "We should get going. There's a lot left to do."

Jake nodded. "All right. I'm going to run home, change, and I'll meet you guys at the field."

"On your way out, tell Mac we'll be leaving in ten." Cain caught the wince the Brit tried to hide as he placed his mug in the sink. "A little sore this morning?"

"Bloody hell, I didn't expect to be getting my hands dirty. Dammit man, I hope I can play my bass tomorrow."

"Nothing a good hot shower won't cure."

"Right."

Mac entered the cottage and tossed his magazine onto the counter. "So, lover boy, we heading out soon?"

Cain grabbed the magazine along with the one Dax had been reading. He looked at Mac and frowned. "You got any more of these hiding around?"

"Nope. But I hate to tell you this. They're everywhere."

"No shit." Cain's lips thinned. He was in for it, and so was Maggie. He just hoped the people of Crystal Lake went easy on her.

"You going to see her today?"

Cain nodded to Mac. "Damn straight. As soon as we get everything organized for tomorrow, she's my first stop."

Mac's expression changed—the joker was gone. "Good. That's good." He sighed and stretched out his long limbs. "We're a sorry-ass bunch…the Bad Boys of Crystal Lake. Unlucky in love. It would be nice to see one of us get it right."

Cain frowned. "Jesse got it right, from the get-go."

"Maybe so, but that relationship left scars." Mac's eyes darkened and he shook his head. "I'm worried about Jake, and what the hell is Raine thinking? A baby? Personally, I think he'd be better off shipping back to Afghanistan."

Cain was stunned. What kind of crazy ass shit was this?

"Why the hell would you want him to go back there, to the place where he watched his brother die? Away from his friends and family? That doesn't make sense."

Mac was quiet for a few seconds, and then he spoke. "At least over there he's got an outlet for his anger. He can use it, hone it, and let it eat the pain. Here? It will just fester and grow, and being around Raine won't help him at all. I'm telling you, it will be ugly when he finally explodes." Mac looked away. "Trust me. I know what the face of ugly feels like, and the scars don't ever go away."

Cain sighed. "It's too early for this shit."

"You're right. Forget I said anything." Mac moved toward his room. "I'm going to grab my shades, and we should head out to the field."

He watched Mac disappear and then headed back to his own room for a quick change. There was no point in showering. Not with all he had on his plate today.

He grabbed his cell and tried Maggie's number, but there was no answer. Shit. He needed to hear her voice. Needed to know that things were going to be all right. He pocketed the cell. He'd have to keep trying.

Twenty minutes later he was on his way to town. As luck would have it—at least the kind of luck that followed him around these days, which was bad—everything was behind schedule. The production equipment and crew didn't show until nearly two in the afternoon, which was good, considering it took them nearly that long to get the finishing touches in place, the power supply being a major headache. The wattage hadn't been sufficient as is, but an electrician was called, and the problem was solved. When the heavy cables—long electrical snakes—were finally run, it felt like a small victory.

The volunteers kept their heads down, and no one ribbed him about *Hollywood Scene*. For that Cain was grateful. He wasn't in the mood to discuss the fallout. Roger, Tommy's father, was one of the volunteers, and though Cain wanted to grill him about Michael's whereabouts and Maggie, he kept quiet. There was no use in putting him on the spot.

The stacks of speakers were put in place, two towers on either side of the stage. The rigging that held the lights was hoisted into the air, across the front of the stage, and a one-row of lighting was placed behind the drum riser.

All the musical acts were to use one set of equipment to make things easy. The amps—Marshall stacks—and the drum kit were ready to go, but it was a slow process getting everything in place, the instruments properly miked, and ready to go.

Texas Willie and his band were helping, as well as several other local acts, including Shady Aces. They were all participating in the fundraiser. It made for a few frustrating moments, and it took Cain's raised voice, with the reminder that this was a charity event, not an MTV appearance, for the boys to settle in and work together.

When the first note was hit at sound check—his

guitar singing out into the gathered crowd—he didn't feel pleasure as much as relief.

But by then it was nearly six o'clock.

Cain had been trying Maggie's cell phone the entire day. Not once had she picked up. She didn't have a landline, so he had no other way of getting in touch with her. The pressure in his chest, that feeling of doom that had dogged him all day, hit hard. He'd tried Raine several times as well and had had no luck there either.

He'd just packed up his Les Paul when he spied Jake.

"I'm heading to Maggie's now. Sorry to do this again, but can you get Dax back to the lake?"

"I think a bunch of us are heading to the Coach House first, but I'll make sure he makes it home safe. We wouldn't want a drunken Brit roaming the streets of Crystal Lake, especially in that getup."

Dax sat on the edge of the stage with his bass, his fingers flying over the frets as he slapped and pulled the heavy strings. The instrument, one meant for rhythm, sounded melodic in his hands.

He'd kept the horn-rimmed glasses instead of his contacts and once more sported white leather pants, flashy red boots, and a vintage Def Leppard T-shirt. There was a circle of locals close by, mostly women, all of them eyeing the Brit with adoring, shy smiles.

"I don't think you need to worry about him, Jake."

"Probably not." Jake tapped him on the shoulder. "I hope things work out with you and Maggie."

"Thanks."

He was starting to panic. *Where the hell are you, Maggie?*

Chapter 32

"Mom, are you mad at Cain?"

Maggie chewed on her lip as she looked across the table at her son. He'd just shoveled a second helping of meat loaf into his mouth and stared at her expectantly.

What to tell him? He was smart and knew things were wrong. She didn't want to lie, but the sad fact was that the truth would hurt him. And for the moment, she couldn't do that to her son.

Not yet, anyway.

She wanted to keep him in that bubble of safety and happiness as long as she could, because she knew in the next little while, those big blue eyes of his would be filled with sadness, confusion, and most likely anger.

Maggie had kept him close today, taken him with her to her clients' homes. So far he'd been spared the details of the magazine, and she wanted to keep it that way until she had a chance to talk to him about it.

Mrs. Landon had been more than happy to keep Michael occupied while she cleaned her bungalow, and in fact had entertained her son while Maggie slipped uptown to her bank.

She'd quietly emptied her account and kept her eyes to the ground. She didn't want to talk to anyone and had nearly made a clean getaway until she literally ran into Mrs. Lancaster, the pastor's wife.

The woman had gently clutched her hands. There'd

been a certain calmness that flowed from Mrs. Lancaster into Maggie's body, an energy that soothed Maggie's tired and scarred soul.

The two of them had stood for several minutes on the sidewalk, Maggie in her work clothes and Mrs. Lancaster in the rubber boots she loved so and a dress that was green and red, just like a Christmas tree. When Mrs. Lancaster had finally spoken, it was anticlimactic. "Where are you off to in such a hurry, Maggie?"

Maggie had suddenly been filled with fear of the unknown, a terrifying, soul-wrenching fear. She had no idea where she was going. None. *Could* she do it again? Did she have the strength to take Michael and run? She'd shaken her head and yanked her hand from Mrs. Lancaster's grasp.

"I'm sorry, I'm just really tired." Which of course was an understatement of epic proportions. Maggie Grace O'Rourke was exhausted. She'd hopped on the Cain Black Express, and it ran full tilt. Now that the damn thing had derailed, she was lost.

The pastor's wife had smiled and spoken, her words soothing, her tone gentle. "You're not lost, child. The day you set foot into Crystal Lake is the day you found your way home." She'd winked, like the mind reader she was. "Remember that."

"Mom? Are you all right? You've got that weird look on your face. The one where your eyes get all crinkly."

Michael's voice penetrated her thoughts, and Maggie gave herself a mental shakedown. She needed to keep focused. Be sharp.

"I'm fine, Michael, and no, I don't think we'll be seeing Cain tonight. He's pretty busy preparing for the football game tomorrow and the concert." She gave him a smile, a horrible, fake thing that slowly faded as Michael's dark eyes stared back at her.

He didn't believe a word she'd said.

He picked at the veggies on his plate. Carrots. Usually his favorite. "Did you and Cain have a fight?"

Maggie pushed her plate away. She couldn't pretend to eat, any more than she could pretend that things were okay. "Cain and I..." she began and stopped. What the hell was she going to say to her son? She needed to say something, to prepare him, because there was a very good possibility that he'd be exposed to the nastiness of the trash magazine in the morning.

"Did you have a fight because of the pictures?"

Maggie stared at her son in shock. How in the hell did he know about them? He'd been with her all day. Lauren had been home when they arrived to clean her house, but she was positive Lauren Black would never discuss something like that with Michael.

"What pictures are you talking about?" Her mouth felt like it was filled with sawdust, and she barely got the words out.

Michael rose from the table and disappeared into the living room. He came back a few seconds later, *Hollywood Scene* clutched between his fingers. He carefully placed it on the table in front of Maggie and moved closer to her.

She stared down at the offending piece of garbage and barely held back the rage that was inside. She itched to tear the damn thing to pieces but held off. She couldn't lose it in front of Michael. She just couldn't.

She turned to him, her fingers lifting his chin so that

she could stare into his eyes. The huge balls of liquid blue shimmered, and she saw the questions, the confusion, in their depths. "Where did you get that, Michael?"

His mouth twitched, and he shuffled his feet as his eyes dropped. "Don't be mad," he whispered.

"Honey, why would I be mad? Just tell Mommy the truth, all right?"

She was scared, imagining all sorts of crazy things, different ways he could have gotten his hands on a copy. A stranger handing it to him on the bus when she wasn't looking. Someone leaving it on their porch. A prank by one of his friends.

"I saw it in your purse."

"What?"

"It was sticking out, and I thought it was a comic, and then I saw Cain on the cover."

Maggie groaned. She'd tossed her bag as soon as she let herself into the house the night before. And there it had stayed until Michael found it.

His fingers kneaded the edge of the table nervously.

"It's okay, Michael. You did nothing wrong, honey. It was my fault for leaving it like that. Did you…did you look inside?"

Maggie held her breath, felt the stab of pain that rushed across her chest as if she'd been laced with a whip. The thought of Michael seeing that center shot made her ill.

He shook his head. "No. I just looked at the cover and knew it wasn't a comic, and then I stuffed it in the book rack."

Maggie stared at her son in silence. "Okay."

"Are you mad at me?" His voice trembled, and she

grabbed him to her chest in an instant. His arms slid around her waist, and she held her son as if he was her lifeline for as long as she could. Her chin rested on his curls and she whispered, "No, I'm not mad at you. I'm proud that you're brave enough to tell the truth. But I have to tell you something."

Maggie exhaled and set Michael back a bit so she could look into his eyes. "There are more pictures inside that magazine, honey. Pictures of private stuff…of Mommy and Cain. Do you understand what I'm trying to say?"

"Like the one on the cover? Of you guys kissing?"

Her cheeks flushed red, and she nodded. "Kind of."

Michael shrugged. "Mom, that's not a big deal, not for adults anyway. Bobby Terio's sister has tons of pictures of herself on Facebook, *kissing* pictures and some in a bikini." Michael's face wrinkled into a comical grimace. "They're gross."

"Oh, so you've seen them," Maggie asked, not too impressed.

"Well, just once. But we got caught, and Bobby's mom disabled the Facebook, so now his sister can't show off her kissy-face pictures anymore."

Maggie stared at her little boy in awe. He didn't know the whole story, of course, but still she felt so much better knowing he hadn't been freaked out at the sight of her and Cain together.

Of course, he hadn't seen the center spread, but judging from his reaction, Michael would be more grossed out than embarrassed.

"Okay, but this is a little different. Someone took those pictures without my knowledge and put them in that magazine. Honey, that magazine is sold in most grocery stores. They even have a television show on every night. Do you understand what I'm trying to say? Your friends might see them, and some of them might tease you tomorrow."

"My friends all think you're pretty. They won't care." Michael looked away, and his hands fisted into tight little balls at his side. "You're afraid of him, aren't you? That he'll see."

At first Maggie didn't know what Michael meant. "Cain? No, honey, that's silly. And trust me, he's already seen them."

"I meant my dad."

Cold spread along her body in rapid flashes that left her shaking. Maggie's heart broke as she stared at her son. It broke into little pieces. That a seven-year-old boy could be that intuitive was astonishing. She thought of Cain's confession the night before, and her heart swelled again as she thought of that last night in Savannah.

And of what Michael had witnessed and never shared with her. Her little boy had dealt with all of that on his own. She felt…defeated.

"I don't want to leave Crystal Lake, Mommy."

She didn't know how to respond. Michael was much too observant and smart for such a young boy. Maggie didn't want to lie, so she remained quiet.

A soft knock echoed into the house, and they both jumped.

Michael recovered first and ran to the living room, and by the time Maggie cleared the kitchen, Cain stood in the middle of her house, his dark eyes upon her, his hand on Michael's shoulder.

Her son leaned into the man the same way she did when he was next to her. As if their bodies needed him in order to function.

He looked tired, her musician. His clothes were dirty—no doubt from a full day out at the field—but it was his eyes that grabbed her attention. They looked *haunted*.

Maggie swallowed and felt her throat tighten. It was like looking in the mirror.

He turned to her son and ruffled the curls on top of his head. "Hey, is it all right if I talk to your mom for a bit?"

Michael nodded. "Sure. I have a book I wanted to read anyway." Michael glanced back at her. "Is that all right, Mom?" She nodded, still unable to speak, and watched him disappear down the hall toward his bedroom.

"I tried calling, but you didn't pick up." Cain ran his hands through his hair and stared at her.

"Oh." She finally found her voice. "With everything that happened yesterday, I forgot to charge my phone."

"I hope you don't mind that I came over." He took a step closer to her. "I know you told me it was over last night and to stay away, but Maggie, I—"

"Cain, I don't know if I can do this." She was so confused.

He held his hands up. "I won't take long. I have to get something off my chest, and I need for you to know where I stand. Because I sure as hell don't have a clue as to where your head's at, Maggie. Maybe you'll share that with me soon, I hope you will, but for now I just want you to listen."

Maggie slid onto the edge of the sofa. She had no energy left at all and was pretty much running on fumes.

"I love you."

Maggie's chest constricted at his words, and even if she wanted to respond, there was no way that she could. It was impossible. The part of her brain that controlled vocal chords had just taken a trip south, and she was speechless.

Cain stared at her from a few feet away, his tobacco-colored waves wild, tinged with new streaks of sunlight. His dark eyes glittered, their depths filled with emotion. She tore her eyes away and her gaze fell to his mouth. That was the wrong thing to do.

He had a way of making a woman forget, and with the stakes this high, Maggie needed her wits about her. He didn't give her a chance, of course, because he plunged forward and paced across her small living room as he spoke.

"I've said those three words to a few women in my day. I've sang them every single night on stage, but until now, I can honestly say I've never really *felt* them. It's so damn easy to say you love someone, because they're just words. *I love you*. Three little words. But it's the feeling behind those words that's hard. It's the feelings that make them matter."

Cain paused inches from her. She held her hands tightly in her lap when all she wanted to do was lose them in the thick waves at his nape and pull him close.

"Do you believe in fate, Maggie?" It wasn't a question really, because he plunged forward without giving her a chance to answer. "I do. I believe that everything happens for a reason. Karma is real and will either bitch-slap or embrace you when you least expect it. I believe that there are people who come into our lives for different reasons. Some leave, and there are others that are meant to stay. *Keepers*."

He moved closer still until the warmth of his breath caressed her cold skin. But he didn't touch her. He didn't need to. His words were physical. They slid across her skin and settled into her soul.

"I've got several guitars back in LA. Some are worth a fair bit of money, but only one of them means the world to me and is a keeper. It's the guitar my mom gave me."

His hand reached for her, and she leaned her cheek into his palm. "I don't know if I'm making sense, but that's what you are to me Maggie, a keeper. I need you in my life."

He was breathing heavy, and when his hand left her cheek, taking his warmth with it, she whimpered softly.

He stared at her long and hard, and when he spoke there was a surety to his words that grabbed her, that made her believe. "I know you've got secrets and pain and a whole bunch of shit I know nothing about. But I'm not going away. I want to make this work…this thing we have between us. And yeah, my life might be different than Luke Jensen's or Doctor Harding's, but I think we could make it work. I think we should at least try." His ran his fingers through his hair, a gesture she'd come to love. "You have to know I'd never do anything to hurt you or Michael."

"Cain, I—"

"And the pictures… I should have known Natasha would pull something crazy like sending the damn paparazzi after us."

He nodded toward her window and tossed a set of keys onto the table beside the plaid chair.

"You know where I stand. I want you to take some time and think about what I said. About us. About being honest with each other and sharing everything. Will you do that?"

Maggie nodded in silence.

"Good, but fair warning. I'm pretty damn relentless when I want something."

Her heart skipped a beat at the look in his eyes.

"I want you and Michael." He shrugged. "It's that simple. I'm leaving you my truck, so there's no excuse for you not to come out to the football field."

Cain's eyes smoldered, his gaze resting on her mouth, and she thought that maybe he'd come to her. She found her body leaning forward, anticipating. Instead he turned and left her to the quiet of her home. Maggie sank back to the sofa and touched her mouth. He hadn't kissed her, but she felt a burn nonetheless.

She closed her eyes and fought the hot and cold that claimed her body in waves.

What the hell just happened?

Chapter 33

MAGGIE SLEPT IN.

When the sun began to rise in the sky, when those first golden rays cut through the dark Michigan night, she was dead to it all. She lay on her side, cuddling a large pillow in much the same way she'd clung to Cain every night that he was in her bed.

Her small bungalow was silent, and it wasn't until nearly nine thirty that she rolled over and opened her eyes a crack. She winced, not used to the bright sunlight that shone into her room. She'd been so tired the night before that she'd barely managed to get her teeth brushed, had pulled on a T-shirt and bottoms and crawled into bed without closing the blinds. Considering a pervert had been in her backyard only a few days ago, not a smart move, but one she'd blame on exhaustion.

After Cain left, she'd done a lot of soul-searching, and she realized a few things about herself. Not all of it good.

Cain was right. She was using her past as a shield to keep him away. How could she not? Everyone who mattered to her had left, either physically or emotionally.

Then Dante had come along, and at first things had been great. Like a starving urchin, she'd clung to him for the love and emotional support that she'd lost. She'd fancied herself in love with him, had been blind to the monster that lived inside of him, and in the end he'd pounced on the bruised young woman she was and broken her spirit.

But he'd also given her something wonderful…a child to love and to take care of. A child to keep safe and happy. Michael was her reason for everything.

But what kind of example was she really? Hiding in Crystal Lake? Afraid to stand up for herself…to stand up for Michael.

She wanted to believe that she was better than that. She had to be better than that, or what was the point?

She'd lain awake for hours, and when she finally fell asleep a decision had been made.

Maggie rolled over, saw the time on the clock and shrieked, rolled over once more, and promptly fell out of her bed. She landed on the floor, and her head barely missed the corner of the bedpost.

Crap! They were going to miss the parade!

Her cell went off as she stumbled down the hall, and she skipped the bathroom, her bare feet shuffling along the hardwood as she headed into the kitchen. She'd remembered to plug in the damn thing the night before, at least, and it was working.

She didn't have caller ID and hoped her disappointment didn't ring too loudly when she answered and heard Raine on the other end.

"Maggie, where the hell were you yesterday? I called, like, twenty times, drove by your place, and you didn't answer. You weren't there." Accusation rang in her voice, and Maggie winced.

"Raine, I'm sorry. My phone was dead."

"Your phone was dead. Unbelievable."

"I forgot to charge it. I'm sorry."

"Don't do that again. After everything you said the other night, I was afraid you'd packed up and left without so much as a good-bye."

Michael appeared, sleep still in his eyes and his curls a mad-looking cap of tangles. "Hold on, Raine."

Maggie kissed her son quickly and pointed to the bathroom. "Why don't you go and shower now. We don't want to miss the parade."

His eyes lit up, and a wide grin spread across his face. "Okay. Can I grab a granola bar first? I'm hungry."

She nodded. "You still there?"

"Yes." Raine paused. "So, you sound like you're in a much better place than you were the other night."

"I am." *Lord, you have no idea.* "Cain came by last night."

"He did." A hint of naughty entered Raine's voice, and Maggie smiled. "Is he there now?"

"No, he was only here for five minutes."

Maggie walked back to the living room and stared out the window. Cain's truck still sat there. She glanced down at the keys on the small table. It had been real.

"Oh."

Maggie smiled as she grabbed his keys and fingered the large black and silver fob.

"Are you going to tell me what happened, O'Rourke, or am I going to have to come by and shake it out of you?"

"He told me that he loved me." Her words rushed from her in a whisper, and hearing them once more made it all the more real.

Silence greeted her confession, and after a few seconds, Maggie spoke again. "Raine?"

"Yes, I'm still here. What did you tell him?"

"Nothing. He didn't give me a chance. He gave me the night to think things over. He wants me to be sure about how I feel."

"And how do you feel, Maggie?"

I love him.

"Mom, I need to talk to you."

Maggie's smile fled when she glanced down at her son. His tearstained face looked up at her, and she felt her heart crack at the sight.

"Raine, I gotta go. I'll see you later."

Maggie tossed her cell onto the kitchen counter and scooped Michael into her arms. His small body trembled against her, and he fought to control the sobs that were burrowed inside him.

"Baby, what's wrong?" She ran her hands along his cheeks and tugged gently so that she could look into his eyes. What the hell had happened in the shower?

A long, shuddering breath was released, and he was finally calm. One single tear glistened along his eyelash, and she kissed it away.

"I'm sorry, Mommy. I was in the shower and started to think about how much I was going to miss Tommy and this house"—he shuddered and pointed outside—"the birdhouse out back, and Cain…and I got really sad." He wiped his eyes. "I'll even miss Shelby, and she poops all over our grass."

"Oh Michael, I'm so sorry. Honey, I did a lot of thinking last night." She tightened her arms around him and drew him close to her chest. "It would be wrong to leave right now, to run away and start over because we're afraid of…your dad." Maggie struggled to breathe as a wash of emotion flooded her. "I don't want us to live in fear."

A hiccup escaped from Michael, and a tremulous smile crept over his face. "We're gonna stay in Crystal Lake?"

She kissed him, gave him a big hug, and didn't let go. "I can't think of any other place I want to be."

Maggie cradled Michael's face in her hands and stared down into his dewy eyes. "Cain told me what you saw." Her lip trembled, but she refused to cry as her thoughts turned to the past. She forced herself to speak. "I want you to know that what happened between me and your father wasn't healthy, and I'm so sorry that you had to see some of that ugliness." She searched his eyes and felt him stiffen. Dante had never reached out to his son. Never touched him the way Cain did.

"What if he finds us?" Michael whispered.

Maggie stared at her son, at the classic lines that defined his features. He was very much like Dante, and he'd grow into a handsome man one day. Thank God, he'd never inherited the mean streak and blackness that lived inside her husband.

Just thinking about Dante made her sick. He represented so much that was unfinished in her life. So much that she'd run from. She glanced at the clock. She'd deal with that mess, but first, a parade.

"Don't worry about that. Today is football and Cain's concert, okay?" She kissed him once more, her hands lingering on his shoulders as she steered him toward the fridge. "I think you need to eat some breakfast while I shower, and then if we hurry, we'll make the parade before it reaches the end of Main Street."

Michael's face lit up and he nodded, his curls bobbing and the one that she loved straying over his brow.

He pushed it away impatiently. "Awesome! And then we're going to go to the football game, right?"

She smiled and headed toward the shower. "Yes, so dress appropriately."

Maggie had the fastest shower of her life, though she was careful to make sure her legs—among other things—were shaved and smooth as silk. She towel-dried her hair and left it to hang in long waves. She didn't have the time or inclination to straighten it. Besides, Cain loved the wild look, and today, for him, she was all over that.

A light gloss on her lips and a bit of mascara and she was good to go. She pulled on a pair of boy-short undies and then slipped a light, airy halter dress over her head. It had been an impulse purchase a few weeks earlier, a markdown at the Dallas Boutique, which was a small shop downtown.

Maggie loved the feel of it and twirled in a circle, letting the skirt swish around her legs, the hem stopping just above the knee. The warm green color complemented her dark hair and the light tan she'd acquired over the past few weeks.

She felt beautiful.

An image of Cain flashed before her eyes and filled her with such a gentle wave of longing and need that she paused. Her heart pounded, and her chest was tight, filled to the brim with so many things—excitement, possibility. *A future*.

She glanced up and caught sight of herself in the mirror. Slowly her hand rose, and she pushed several strands of hair away from her face. Was it the light streaming in from the window that made her eyes so luminous and her skin glow?

Her fingers fell to her lips, and she smiled a full-bodied smile full of happy. The lightness she felt *inside* was visible in her reflection.

Maggie leaned in closer. Nah, it wasn't the sunlight. She was in love. Totally and completely in love.

She glanced at the clock once more. "Michael, we need to leave, or we're going to be late." *And I need to see Cain.*

Her flat white sandals were beside the bed. Maggie slipped her feet into them and angled her foot so that she could see them better. They weren't fancy. They were old, well made, and comfortable. She shrugged and grabbed her purse from off the dresser.

Maggie glanced into her son's bedroom on her way down the hall, but it was empty. His pajamas were strewn across the floor, and several books lay scattered about as well, which was odd. Michael was a neat freak, just like his mother, but she supposed the excitement was too much.

She smiled. She'd tidy it up later.

"Michael, make sure the back door is locked, all right sweetie?" Her son was near the kitchen, his back to her, his body decked out in sports attire—purple, green, and white. "Hurry up, babe. We don't want to be late."

He made a weird sound and turned, his face so pale that his freckles stood out like cinnamon dust. His eyes were huge saucers, and his fists were clenched to his sides, where they trembled uncontrollably. Instantly her internal antenna erupted into a scream, one so loud that she winced, though her gaze never left her son.

He opened his mouth, but nothing came out.

A telltale stain darkened the front of his shorts, and

her eyes dropped to the small puddle on the floor. The scent of urine hung in the air. He'd wet himself.

Her son was terrified.

Her fingers loosened and her purse slipped from them.

"Michael..." she whispered. "No."

But she knew. Hadn't she been expecting this? Wasn't playing with fire dangerous?

A shadow moved behind him.

Her voice trailed into silence, and for a moment she thought that maybe her heart stopped beating. She felt like she'd been punched with Thor's hammer, and it took everything inside Maggie to keep it together and not lose it in front of her son.

"What are you doing out here, Maggie? In this small town of nothing. Raising this boy without my influence and doing a piss-poor job, if you don't mind my saying."

A tall form slid into view. Dante looked at his son in distaste. "Shouldn't the little bastard be toilet trained by now?"

The man's chiseled features were model perfect. Straight nose, high cheekbones, and classic jaw. The dark eyes and skin, mingled with midnight black hair, added an edge that he liked to exploit.

It was July Fourth, hot as hell, and he was dressed in black slacks and a long-sleeved V-neck shirt. The cut was tailored, expensive, and emphasized his lean but powerful build. One he worked hard to maintain.

He smiled then, and the handsome face disappeared. It morphed into the monster she remembered, and Maggie hated the fact that the fear inside exploded into something paralyzing.

In less than a minute, he'd managed to transport her

back in time. Back to that dark, desperate place she'd been running from for the last year.

And she feared that this time there'd be no escape.

Chapter 34

THE CLOCK TICKED IN SLOW, METHODICAL TIME. *TICK… tock…tick…tock…*

It echoed from the kitchen, and for a moment, it's all Maggie heard. There wasn't room for anything else inside her head—her thoughts disappeared, all emotion stopped.

She had no clue how long she stood there like a zombie, but eventually the clock faded and she became aware of many things.

The labored sound of her lungs as she inhaled quick, shallow breaths.

Michael grinding his teeth—a nervous gesture he hadn't done in over a year.

The contents of her purse scattered all over the floor.

The heavy smell of Dante's cologne. The smell of fear.

And the absolute silence from outside, which was the most terrifying sound of all.

She was alone. There was no one else. All her neighbors had gone to the Independence Day parade downtown. Not even Luke's dog, Shelby, could be heard, and usually a strange vehicle was more than enough to set the dog barking madly.

Maggie glanced toward Dante. He was staring at her, watching her closely, his dark eyes glittery with a frenetic energy that was off. Her stomach heaved as a slow smile spread across his face.

In that moment Maggie knew that if she wasn't smart,

she wouldn't be leaving this house alive. She had a child to protect, and right now that's all she focused on.

Dante didn't say a word as she crossed to Michael and grabbed him close. Her son shook and clutched at her fiercely as he whispered near her ear.

"I'm sorry I let him in…I thought it was Cain." His voice was so small, so full of remorse, that Maggie had to take a minute to push back the tears that threatened.

Be smart.

Her only thought and concern was Michael. Dante would never let him leave, and she knew she needed to get him out of the house. If anything happened to Michael…

She cleared her throat and gently tugged his fingers from her shoulders so that she could look into his eyes. "I want you to listen to me and do exactly what I say. It's important." At his nod she continued. "Go to your room, and you know those big headphones that I'm always yelling at you to turn down?"

She saw the confusion in his eyes, and when he would have glanced back to his father, she grabbed his chin. "I want you to put them on and listen to your music as loudly as you can. Turn the volume up and just…listen."

Would he know what she meant? The headphones were outside in their small shed, where she'd banished them a few days earlier. He could get them…if he climbed through his bedroom window. The screen could easily be knocked out.

"Can you do that for me, Michael? Find your headphones?" Her grip tightened on his shoulders. Oh God, she needed him to understand. She needed him to escape.

She turned Michael before Dante had a chance to speak to him and pointed him toward his room. "Go."

She bent down and kissed him quickly before whispering, "You know where they are."

She watched her son hesitate, and everything inside her screamed so loud that she winced.

"You heard your mother, boy. Go to your room. She and I have unfinished business."

Michael stumbled and then ran the rest of the way. Maggie didn't breathe until she heard his door slam shut.

And then she turned to face her past.

Dante's eyes narrowed as he glanced around the home she'd made. "So, this is where you've been hiding out." He gestured toward the living room. "It's a dump."

She shook her head, though the denial died on her tongue as he moved closer.

"What was that?"

Maggie flinched, though she didn't move.

"You don't agree?" He cocked his head and studied her for several moments, slowly moving over every inch of her body. When his eyes returned to hers, she began to panic. They were black with anger, hatred, and something else.

Something insane.

"You look like a whore in that dress, with your tits nearly hanging out. Is that what he likes? The bastard you've been fucking?" His words lashed at her, but she kept her eyes lowered.

"Lift your dress up." His voice was flat.

She glanced up as everything inside her stilled. "Dante, I don't..." Fear clogged her throat as his lips drew back in a feral snarl.

He took a step toward her and squared his shoulders, his hands fisted into deadly weapons at his side. "Lift... your...skirt."

She stared at him in silence. What game was this?

But then what did it matter? She'd do whatever it took to protect Michael. To give him enough time to escape.

Maggie fixed her eyes onto the pulse at his neck and let her hands fall to the soft material at her hips. Carefully she gathered the material into bunches and slowly pulled it upward until the hem was near her crotch.

"Don't stop now." His voice had changed. It was thicker. Darker. She recognized the tone, and it made her sick.

She closed her eyes as she tugged the hemline higher, until her underwear was bare to him.

She broke out in a cold sweat as the old fear—that all-consuming, paralyzing fear—stole over her once more. Her teeth started to chatter. She was so cold. It was well into the eighties and her house wasn't much cooler, yet she felt as if she were standing in the middle of a frozen wasteland.

Suddenly he was behind her, his breath against her neck, and she nearly doubled over as a wave of nausea rolled through her stomach.

His fingers gripped her arms, and he pulled her back so that she was flush to his long length. He was aroused—she felt his erection against her back and wanted to scream. Wanted his hands off her. Wanted the smell of him out of her body.

"You never dressed like a whore for me." His hands crept around and he grabbed at her breasts roughly, pinching her nipples through the cotton until she whimpered. "Never wore sexy panties or went braless."

He ran his tongue along her neck, and she bit her lip, trying her best to keep quiet. She knew the more she struggled, or screamed, or cried—the more excited he got.

"You never wore your hair down or smelled this good."

Dante seemed to forget that he was the one who'd chosen her wardrobe. Her hairstyle. Hell, he was the one who'd bought her undergarments.

"Do you fuck like a whore now, Maggie?"

His touch made her skin crawl, and it took everything inside her to remain pliant in his arms.

His hand slipped inside the halter top of her dress, and she wanted to die as he ran his thumb over her nipple. As he cupped her breast and squeezed it brutally.

His mouth was near her ear. "I'm going to fuck you, Maggie. Once more for old time's sake, and then I'm going to take my son, and you will never see him again."

Dante's words set off something inside of Maggie—like a pin had been pulled, releasing a rush of emotion. Even though it was the wrong thing to do—she needed to stay calm for Michael—she began to struggle. She kicked and tried to bite his hand, but she was no match for his strength.

He clamped his hand over her mouth and dragged her down the hall toward the back of the house. Toward her bedroom.

She stopped struggling as they passed Michael's closed door, and though her mind was circling fast, she was losing hope that she'd find a way out.

He yanked on her hair, and she yelped as he threw her onto the bed. Dante was breathing heavily, and the weird fire in his eyes—the one she'd noticed earlier—was brighter, more frantic.

Maggie pushed her hair from her face and stared up at him, her chest heaving as she tried to calm herself.

Dante glared at her and flexed his fingers. "On the floor."

"Dante, you don't have to do this." Oh God, he was going to rape her, and there was nothing she could do to stop him. He'd beaten her in the past, but he'd never forced himself on her.

She was going to be sick.

"Get on the floor." His hand was on his belt, and she glanced around the room wildly. "And bend over like the bitch you are."

She froze, and for a moment nothing happened.

Then he growled like an animal and grabbed for her foot. Maggie kicked toward him and tried to scramble away. She didn't see the fist flying, and when it connected to the side of her skull, for a few seconds she saw stars.

"Mommy!"

Michael's terrified cry ripped into her soul. Dante turned toward her son, his fist raised, his body thrumming with violence.

Maggie reacted on instinct and grabbed the glass vase full of tulips that was on the nightstand by her bed.

"Michael, run!" she screamed.

Michael's little white face stared at her in horror. "Run! Now!"

He turned and darted back down the hall, and when Dante would have run after him, Maggie swung the vase with all her might.

She hit him near his shoulder and knocked him off balance, but it wasn't enough. And as she scrambled forward—her only thought to get between Dante and Michael—he slammed his fist into her stomach.

"You goddamn bitch!"

And then she was on her back, gasping for air.

"You never learn. I wouldn't have to do that if you would"—he bent over her—"just fucking listen."

He flipped her onto her stomach and hoisted her hips into the air. "It's time I taught you a lesson."

Chapter 35

"I'M GOING DEEP!" CAIN ARCED HIS ARM AND THREW the football high into the air and then took a step back to watch as Mac ran his butt off in order to catch it.

It was good to know his arm still had it. It was also good to know that Mac's long legs had lost a bit over the last few years.

He took a long drink from his water bottle and wiped sweat from his brow. It was around eleven in the morning, and the parade had just finished. A good-sized crowd had already gathered at the football field, all of them anxious to watch the game and stay for the concert that would start later in the afternoon.

Everywhere he looked, American pride was in evidence—the Stars and Stripes rippled in the breeze, and most people wore red, white, and blue. Cain sported an old T-shirt with Uncle Sam on the front—a favorite he'd dug out of the Edwardses' boathouse. Good God, the clothes he and the boys had left behind made him cringe, but there were the odd gems among the bunch.

And then there was Dax. The Brit had decided to forego leather pants—thank God—at least for the morning, but was still decked out in his usual Union Jack garb. Even his kneesocks sported the British flag. *Kneesocks*, for Christ sakes.

There was a new intensity to Dax today. Turns out he was quite the footballer back home, and he'd stepped up and offered to play in the charity game. His game face was fierce, and Cain hoped the man knew today's game was for fun and that there'd be kids involved. That's all he needed. A wackjob Brit, taking out a line of ten-year-olds.

Cain scanned the crowd, looking for that familiar splash of crimson that made his heart jump. But so far he hadn't seen her. Nervous energy kicked in, and he shook out his limbs.

They would come. There was no way in hell Maggie would let Michael miss the game.

"Cain, there you are!"

He turned and smiled as Raine pushed her way through a large group of spectators.

His smile soon faded when he realized Raine was alone.

"Where's Maggie?"

Raine shook her head. "I don't know. I talked to her this morning, and she said she'd be at the parade, but I haven't seen her yet." She reached into her purse. "I'll try her cell again."

"Don't bother. I tried five minutes ago, and it's not in service."

Raine frowned. "That doesn't make sense."

That feeling in his gut—the one that said shit was about to hit—twisted hard, and Cain clamped his jaw tight. Something wasn't right.

Raine twirled in a circle, shading her eyes from the sun. "She was so excited and happy this morning."

Cain stopped Raine and hoped he didn't look like the lovesick fool that he felt inside. "She was?"

A slow smile claimed her mouth, and Raine punched him lightly in the chest. "Of course she was. She couldn't wait to see you." Raine giggled and continued to scan the crowd. "I'm not sure why, of course."

Jake joined them at that point, breathing hard, his T-shirt drenched in sweat.

"Damn, you look like you jogged all the way from the lake." Cain was worried about the soldier. Jake didn't say much these days and spent most of his time pushing his body to the extreme.

"I did."

"Are you crazy?" Raine frowned. "That's dangerous in this heat."

Jake shook out his limbs and grabbed Cain's water bottle. "This is nothing, compared to the heat over there." They both knew he was referring to Afghanistan.

"Well, you're not over there anymore, and these kinds of stunts will land you in the hospital." Raine's hands were on her hips, and to say that she was angry would be an understatement. "Did you hear what I said? You can't be pulling that kind of crap. It's not fair to those of us who are worried about you."

Jake took a long drink, wiped some excess water from his mouth, and glanced down at the petite brunette. His expression was hard, his eyes flat.

"I think you're confused on two fronts. A, I don't give a shit what you think, and B, I'm not Jesse, so don't lecture me."

Cain grimaced and walked away, giving the two of them some privacy. He didn't like being a spectator to the private stuff going on between them.

Luke Jansen was a few feet away. He'd traded his paramedic uniform for football gear and was limbering up with stretches.

"Jansen!" Cain shouted.

Luke turned, though his smile faded when he spied Cain.

"Have you seen Maggie?" Cain strode toward him. "She should have been here by now, but I can't find her, and her cell is off."

Luke shrugged and anger riffled through Cain at the look of satisfaction that was etched into his face. "Jansen, I know you want to bust my balls, and trust me, you'll get your chance on the field, but right now I'm concerned about Maggie."

"Concerned," Luke answered drily.

"Yes. *Concerned*. It's not like Maggie to say she'll be here and then not show." He'd always been the kind of man to listen to his gut, and right now this gut was saying things were wrong. Way wrong.

"Well, maybe you're not the most important thing on her agenda today."

Cain gritted his teeth. Damn, but he'd like to punch Luke Jansen in the face and knock him on his ass. "Look, have you seen her or no?"

Luke shrugged, took his time before answering. "I haven't seen her, but I think she's got company."

"What makes you say that?"

"There was car in her driveway, behind your truck."

Raine was at Cain's side now with Jake and Mac.

"An expensive, sporty thing. Had Georgia plates, so I'm assuming family."

"Oh God," Raine whispered. "She was so afraid after the pictures came out."

Cain looked down into her pale face and his fear tripled. "What the hell is going on, Raine?"

"It's Michael's father, it has to be. She has no other

family in Savannah except her father, and I don't think she's talked to him in years. Maggie's ex must have found them."

Everything inside Cain stopped. Hell, his heart and lungs nearly exploded. It all made sense now. Why she'd pulled away from him and why she'd been so upset about the photos in *Hollywood Scene*. It hadn't just been about Cain and their personal shit. She'd been scared out of her tree.

Maybe for her life.

And he'd left her all alone.

"How can you be sure?" Jake looked at the both of them. "Maybe Jansen's right. It could be family."

"No." Cain shook his head. "No way. This game meant a lot to Michael. She wouldn't let him miss it. Even if she didn't want to see me, she wouldn't." He exhaled. "That's the kind of woman she is.

"Give me your keys," Cain barked to Luke.

"What? Why the hell would I—"

Cain's bared his teeth like an animal, and he was barely able to get his words out. His chest filled with a rage that was hard to contain. If anything happened to the woman he loved, he'd fucking kill her ex.

"I don't have wheels, and if what Raine said is true, Maggie and Michael are in danger. So give me your keys. I'm going to get them."

Luke hesitated, obviously confused, though his fingers went to his front pocket. "I'm going too."

Jake glanced at Mac. "You coming?"

"Hell, yeah, I coming."

"Wait for me." Raine took a step forward.

"No way. There's no room." Jake scowled.

Raine scowled. "That's all you got?" She shoved her hands on her hips. "Why don't you just say what you really mean, Jake."

"Okay, get the fuck out of my face."

Shocked didn't come close to describing Raine's expression, but Cain had no time to coddle or bitch or do anything except get his ass to Maggie's as fast as he could.

Raine tore her gaze from Jake's and whispered, "You guys, be careful. And don't be stupid." Raine ignored Jake and directed her plea to Cain.

"Don't worry about us, but if we're late, go ahead and start the game, 'cause guaranteed, we'll be here to finish."

Luke turned and started toward his car. "I'll drive. The last time one of you got behind my wheel, you damn near totaled the thing."

Mac laughed as he jogged to catch up. "Hell, I forgot about that until now. A 1980 Plymouth Horizon, if I remember correctly. Shit brown. My old man whupped my ass good over that, just so you know."

It took longer than normal to navigate the crowded streets, and some of them were still closed because of the parade. By the time they reached Linden, Maggie's street, Cain was so tense, it felt like his muscles had locked up.

Luke pulled into his driveway, and Cain was out before the car had rolled to a stop. A slick black BMW was parked behind his truck in Maggie's driveway. It was high-end and easily worth as much as Maggie's little bungalow.

He jumped onto the porch, paused for a second, and then tried the door. It was locked, and Maggie had not one but three dead bolts in place.

Fuck.

Cain moved to the window and glanced inside.

Maggie's purse was on the floor, the contents scattered everywhere. His gut tightened. His anger—his rage—toward this faceless bastard who'd brutalized Maggie and her son was all consuming. Everything inside him quieted, and a cold calm overtook Cain.

Just then he heard a noise and stiffened. He moved toward the door, hands clenched and ready. When it opened, his world tipped a little off center. Michael stood there, small chest heaving, cheeks stained with tears. "He found us," was all the boy could say.

Cain scooped the child into his arms and gave him a quick, fierce hug. "Where are they?" Michael burrowed against his body, his small face flush to his neck. "In Mommy's bedroom."

He gave Michael one more quick hug. "Go with Luke. I'm going to get her."

Michael slid to the floor, his voice tremulous. "He's going to hurt her."

Cain shook his head. "No. He won't." He charged inside, followed closely by Jake and Mackenzie.

He saw a tall man just inside Maggie's bedroom. His back was to Cain. The man bent over, and Cain saw Maggie on the floor, her long red hair splayed out and the tulips he'd bought scattered beside her.

He would rip the son of a bitch to pieces.

Everything after that happened in slow motion. Just like in movies when the shoot-'em-up scene occurs.

Cain reached the bastard just as Maggie lunged forward and grabbed hold of the vase that lay on the floor next to the bed.

Cain's fist shot out, and he nailed him with a hard blow to the head.

"What the—" The man fell to his knee and cursed a blue streak as he struggled to gain his feet again, his arm swinging wildly as he tried to aim for Maggie.

Cain grabbed him by the scruff of his neck and whirled him around, his fists flying as he pummeled the man with several hard shots to the chest, shoulders, and face. His rage was such that for a moment he couldn't focus on anything other than handing out a major beating.

But then Maggie was there, her soft touch on his arm, her voice urgent in his ear. "He's not worth it, Cain. Please stop, you'll kill him."

The red haze inside his brain cracked a bit, and he stepped back, watching dispassionately as the man who'd touched his woman spat blood onto the floor.

"He's not worth it," she whispered again.

Cain stepped back, and it took a few moments for him to calm down. He glanced at Maggie and swore when he saw the swelling on the side of her face.

"I'll kill him."

"No, you won't." Jake's rough voice was at his back. "Take Maggie and get her out of here. Mac and I will watch this asshole until Taggart arrives. Luke called the police, so he should be here soon." Jake glanced to Maggie. "I'm assuming you're going to want to press charges against this piece of shit."

"I did nothing to you, bitch." Dante leaned on the bed, his eye already swelling, with blood still dripping from his mouth. He pointed to Cain. "He attacked me."

Mac piped up. "You're in Crystal Lake, dickhead, and we don't take kindly to men beating up our women."

Mackenzie leaned down. "It's the holiday

weekend too. I'm guessing your ass will be in lockup until Tuesday." He shrugged. "Could be Wednesday."

"You can't do that..."

"I suggest you shut your hole, or Mac and I will finish what Cain started." Jake glared at Dante and squared his shoulders. "Go on...give us a reason."

Cain folded Maggie into his arms and led her back toward her living room.

"Oh God." Maggie's voice quivered.

He grabbed her close once more, held her until the trembles lessened and then eventually went away. The absolute heaviness of what had just transpired hit him, and Cain gently lifted Maggie's chin.

"Are you..." He swallowed, so filled with emotion and the need to protect that he couldn't speak. "I'm so sorry I left you alone to deal with him." His fingers grazed the bruised flesh on her cheek. "Maggie, I..."

"It's over." She rested her head on his chest, and a long, shuddering breath escaped. "Oh my God! Michael." She pushed against him. "Where's Michael?"

"Shh, it's okay. He's with Luke, next door."

"Thank you," she said haltingly, "for..."

"For loving your son?" Cain murmured.

"For loving us both enough to come back." Maggie squirmed until she was able to look up at him. Her hands reached for him, and Cain's insides liquefied, then ran hot, at the look in her eyes. She stood up on her toes, and when her lips were inches from his, she whispered, "You asked me last night to think about us and where I stand."

This was it. The moment that would change his life. He knew this as surely as he knew her soon-to-be ex-husband would most likely rot in a Crystal Lake jail cell until Thursday. At the earliest.

"And?" he asked.

She swept her lips across his. "I love you."

He groaned and claimed her mouth in a kiss that had his senses reeling. It was both gentle, and urgent and caressing and sexy. She tasted like everything he'd ever wanted, and as he stood with Maggie in his arms, with the absolute knowledge that she belonged to him on every level that existed, he was grateful.

And for the first time since arriving back in Crystal Lake, he felt like he'd truly come home.

Chapter 36

Later that night…

THE SUN HAD DISAPPEARED OVER AN HOUR AGO, leaving behind the moon and stars. Overhead they shone like a blanket of crystals strewn across the velvet sky. The air was still warm, and anticipation ran rampant.

Maggie hugged Michael as they stood in front of the stage and watched one of the technicians—or road crew, as Cain called them—fiddle with some of the wires. Cain would be on in a few minutes, and she was nervous, which was silly.

The day had been wonderful and awful and amazing and terrifying. Dante was sitting in a jail cell, locked up, and from what she'd been told, his arraignment would be several days away. It had been his bad luck to come after her on a long weekend.

They were pressing charges, and Cain was determined to see him punished. She'd spent a fair bit of time at the station house—there'd been interviews and pictures taken for evidence. They'd missed the football game, but none of that mattered now.

Michael had been spared most of the violence, and though he'd been rather quiet since the morning, he'd slowly come around. Cain had done his best to make her son feel safe, and with his father in jail, there was no immediate threat. They'd promised Michael that his father would never hurt them again.

For the first time in years, Maggie felt free of a past that had brought her nothing but pain. Her chin rested on top of Michael's head, and she hugged him until he squirmed.

"Mom, you're hurting me."

"Sorry," she murmured.

Someone bumped her from behind, and Maggie stumbled. She glanced to the left and tried not to laugh. Mrs. Lancaster and her husband, Pastor Frank, were unfolding chairs, and everyone gave them a wide berth. No one wanted to be responsible for trampling the head of their church.

It was a strange thing to see at a rock show, but this was Crystal Lake after all. Maggie watched as Pastor Frank settled into his seat and his wife joined him. They whipped out popcorn, drew a blanket across their legs, and then Mrs. Lancaster pulled out two sets of the biggest, baddest headphones Maggie had ever seen. They were bright orange—neon orange, really—and she couldn't be sure, but it looked like they glowed in the dark.

"You've got to be kidding." Raine slid in beside Maggie, her eyes on the Lancasters.

"What are they exactly?" Maggie asked.

"They're heavy-duty earplugs, is what they are."

"Oh. Why bother coming to a show like this, then?"

Raine shrugged. "Cain's one of this town's favorite sons. No one is going to miss this concert."

"I've never heard him sing," Maggie confessed.

"What?" Raine was shocked. "He's never picked up a guitar and sung for you?"

"No." She shook her head. "We've been busy..."

"Uh-huh, I know. You've been busy getting to know each other. Busy doing other things."

Maggie blushed and nodded. "I guess so."

"Mom." Michael tugged on her arm and pointed a few feet away. "Tommy's over there. Can I stand with him?"

Sharon and Roger waved. "Sure, babe, but stay in front, all right?"

"He seems to have shaken off what happened with his dad," Raine said quietly as they watched Michael jog over to his friend.

"I hope so. Cain's been wonderful."

"So what are your plans?"

Maggie warmed at the thought. "Michael and I are going to spend the rest of the summer at the cottage with Cain, and then I'm not sure. We haven't really had a chance to talk about it." She paused and then asked a question that she'd been wondering about since she arrived at the football field with Cain.

"Raine, where did Jake go? He came to say good-bye, and I got the feeling it was a long good-bye. Cain was more than a little upset."

The brunette's face fell, and she glanced away for several moments. "Last night...stuff happened, things were said that can't be taken back, and I think Jake pretty much hates me."

"Oh Raine, that's ridiculous. And so far from the truth."

"Really?" she said bitterly. "What does 'I can't stand to fucking be around you' mean exactly?"

Maggie bit her lip. It wasn't her place to speak for Jake. The two of them would work things out eventually. At least she hoped so.

Lauren Black appeared from the dark and immediately enveloped Maggie in a hug. "I'm so happy for you." The woman's eyes twinkled, and her face was lit with a grin that went from ear to ear. "Wonderful news."

Maggie smiled in return, but was a little confused by the woman's words. "I'm not sure what you mean."

At that moment the lights went dark. A single spotlight cut through the night and followed a man as he walked to the microphone setup center stage. Cain had changed into jeans, boots, and simple black T-shirt. His hair was longer than when he'd first arrived, but it suited him, and his smile as he gazed out at the crowd was a thousand watts of beauty.

The crowd was going wild, hooting and hollering for one of their favorite sons to play some music.

He strummed a few chords and let the crowd's excitement build. The entertainment had been ongoing all afternoon, with seven bands performing, and now the crowd was at fever pitch. Nearly five minutes later, he finally had to hold his hands up, and the crowd eventually quieted.

Watching him up there made her heart beat and her stomach roll. He glanced down at her, and Maggie blushed like a schoolgirl.

He had easily slipped out of the skin she'd come to love and stepped back into the part of him she hadn't experienced yet. It was still the Cain she knew, but up there on the stage with the lights he existed on an entirely different plane. His charisma was unmistakable, and it rushed over the crowd as if following an invisible conduit that originated from inside him.

He started to play a melody, a haunting, evocative piece. His fingers flew along the frets, and he pulled such beauty from it that tears stung the corners of her eyes. Something inside her burst, and Maggie's throat constricted, full of emotion. She recognized the piece. It was something he hummed to himself when they were alone together.

"It feel's good to be back home." Cain's spoke into the microphone and smiled as the crowd erupted once more. He gazed out at the crowd. "It's been way too long."

He continued to play the melody, and behind him the lights slowly came up. Maggie saw Dax off to the side, a huge grin on his face. Gone were the glasses. He looked intense. He winked at her and saluted.

"I hope you've all had a great day. I know you've heard a lot of great music, and maybe you guys are getting a little tired, but if it's all right, I just may play all night." Cain grinned and the roar was deafening. "But before I start, I've got something really important to do."

The crowd fell silent, as if sensing something out of the ordinary was about to occur. Cain looked down at her, and Maggie's heart swelled to the point that her chest felt too tight. It was almost painful.

"You see, I left home ten years ago to find my future. I thought it was out there somewhere, far away from here." He shook his head and shrugged. "I thought that Crystal Lake had taught me everything it could, and if I was gonna make something out of my life, I needed to leave." He took a step back and cleared his throat.

"Turns out I was wrong."

He looked down at Maggie, and her toes curled at the heat and intensity in his eyes. "I came home for Jesse Edwards's funeral and ended up finding something I didn't even know I was missing."

Cain continued to play for several moments as the crowd cheered and clapped. "I guess you've all heard by now that Blake Hartley has left the band." Cain glanced at Dax, who shrugged and kept moving to the hypnotic beat that fell from his bass guitar. "We wrote a lot of songs together, he and I, shared a lot of things"—Cain snorted—"including my wife. I'd write the melody, and Blake worked his magic with the words. For a while now I've been afraid that I couldn't write the words like Blake did and that maybe BlackRock was over."

He paused—all music stopped—and the entire football field quieted. "But then I met this girl, and she rocked my world in ways I'd never experienced before, and I realized something." He chuckled and looked out at the crowd as his fingers drew the melody from his guitar once more. "I realized that BlackRock wasn't over. I realized I had all this emotion in me, and last night I wrote some words down. If it's all right, I'd like to sing them for you."

The crowd was now in a frenzy.

"The song's called 'Never Say Good-bye,' and I'll sing it, but first..." His eyes never left hers, and he stopped playing his guitar. "I can't, uh, play another note until Maggie O'Rourke agrees to marry me."

"Holy crap, get up there!" Raine tugged on her arm.

The crowd went silent, eerily so, and for a second Maggie was frozen. Her feet felt like they were encased in cement.

"Mom! You have to answer him!" Laughter greeted Michael's shout, and it rippled through the crowd until the silence was replaced with cheering—loud, animated cheering.

Cain looked down at her. "So what's it going to be, Maggie?"

Raine tugged on her arm. "You need to go to him."

The crowd stood back and watched as Maggie moved to the side of the stage, where a roadie helped her up.

And then she was there with him in the spotlight, and his arms were around her, his hands in her hair, his mouth on hers. The crowd went wild, and when she pulled away, she mouthed the word *yes*. It was all she could do. Maggie didn't think she could speak.

Cain laughed. "I think you're going to have to do better than that, babe."

Maggie glanced out at the crowd, looked down into Michael's shining face, and cleared her throat.

She angled closer to the mike, closed her eyes, and shouted, "Hell, yes, so now sing the damn song!"

The band kicked in, members of Shady Aces and Dax building the rhythm behind Cain's melody and words. Maggie stood beside him as he sang, and the words that fell from his lips were indeed magical.

They spoke of longing, of love and fate.

Crystal Lake was blessed with a concert like none it had ever seen before. Cain Black kept his promise. He played until his fingers couldn't move anymore, and not one person left.

Not until long after the last note was played.

READ ON FOR AN EARLY LOOK AT

The Christmas He Loved Her

Coming October 2013 from Sourcebooks

Chapter 1

THE CEMETERY WHERE HIS BROTHER RESTED WAS A desolate place in late November. It sat upon a drab green hill, surrounded by a forest of pine and birch. In the distance, Crystal Lake shimmered through skeletal tree limbs like wisps of blue silk as a cold wind swept inward and drew white caps on top of the water.

Jake Edwards pulled his jeep over to the shoulder, cut the engine and slowly exhaled. His fingers gripped the steering wheel so tightly they cramped, and though he stretched them out and tried to relax, it was no use. He was wound tighter than a junkie in rehab, and he drummed a methodical tune along the dashboard as he gazed out the window. This particular cemetery was the oldest in town and many of Crystal Lake's founding families were buried within its borders. Grand mausoleums and tombstones rose against the dull gray sky, painted dark, like a macabre, city skyline. He stared at them for several long minutes, eyes hard, mouth tight, as a light rain began to fall. It was nothing more than a drizzle really and created a mist that hung over the cemetery, though he only had eyes for the row just beyond the large oak tree.

Row number thirty-six. His brother, Jesse's, row.

The darkness in him stirred leaving the taste of bitterness on his tongue. He let it settle. He let it burn. Hell, these days it was the only thing that told him he was still alive.

A crow flew lazily in the sky, slicing through the haze until it swooped low and settled on top of a large, stone angel not far from him. The bird ruffled its feathers in slow controlled movements. It cocked its head, then turned and stared at Jake—small beady eyes steady, as it slowly blinked.

Abruptly, Jake turned the key and put his jeep in gear. He continued down Lakeshore Road because he sure as hell wasn't ready to deal with the cemetery yet.

His parents were expecting him, but first he had one more stop—a certain someone he needed to see. A certain someone he was damn sure had no desire to see him, and he didn't blame her one bit. Not after the way he'd left things.

Jake Edwards had screwed up and it was time to set things right.

Five minutes later he stepped out of his truck and slung a worn leather bag over his shoulder as he glanced up at a small cottage set back a few hundred feet from the road. At one time it had been a carriage house and was a solid structure built entirely of large blocks of gray, weathered, limestone. A simple white spindled porch ran the length of it, with empty baskets hung at each corner, their usual treasure of poppy-red geraniums long dead.

An old, rickety rocking chair moved gently on its own there, the legs squeaking as it moved back and forth, pushed by either the crisp breeze that rolled in off the lake, or the ghost of Josiah Edwards, an ancestor said to haunt the woods.

Jake pulled the collar of his leather jacket up to his chin and shuddered as a strong gust of wind whipped across the still green lawn. He glanced up at the sky once more. Clouds gathered, a bulbous display over the lake, their slate gray color barely discernible amongst the gloom.

They were definitely snow clouds.

Jake took a step forward, eyes narrowed as his gaze took in an expensive Mercedes parked near the house next to a rusting and faded-yellow Volkswagen. He wasn't sure who owned the Mercedes but the rust bucket he knew well. The ancient beetle had seen better days that's for sure, but then it had been a broken down mess when she had first bought it.

The car belonged to his sister-in-law, Raine, and in a world gone to shit, was something that hadn't changed.

Jake slowly perused the property. He spied a weather beaten bench near the tree line and knew that if he took the path that led through the woods to his right, he'd end up at his parent's home—eventually. It was still a hike, several miles to be exact, but this parcel of land, boasting an acre and a half of prime waterfront, had been a wedding present to his brother and his then-new bride, Raine.

A familiar ache crept across his chest and for a moment he faltered, his eyes squeezed shut. He pictured the three of them, Jake, his brother Jesse, and Raine decked out in their wedding finery. It had rained that day, a good omen according to some, and Raine's dress was tattered along the hem from dancing outdoors in the mud while his brother's tuxedo had remained crisp and clean. Jake's tux, however, was as ruined as the bride's dress. They'd posed for a picture, the three of them, there beneath the ancient Oak, near the bench.

Jake sighed and opened his eyes, resting once more

on the empty bench. It needed a fresh coat of paint. He shook the melancholy from his mind and strode toward the house, his long jean-clad legs eating up the distance in no time, each step placed in front of the other with an assuredness that belied the turmoil he felt.

Jake Edwards had left Crystal Lake nearly a year and a half ago and damned if he'd not been heading home ever since. He'd just not known it until now. And even though he was pretty sure Raine Edwards wanted nothing to do with him, he was going to try his best to make amends. It was the least he could do. For Raine. For Jesse.

And maybe, for himself.

He stepped up onto the porch and heard voices inside. His gut rolled nervously. She had company. Maybe now wasn't a good time.

His dark eyes drifted toward his jeep. Ten seconds and he could be outta here before anyone knew better. He took a step backward, weighing his options, his jaw clenched tightly as the all too familiar wave of guilt, anger, and loathing washed through him. *Coward*.

Jake ran his fingers through the thick mess of hair atop his head and tried to ease the tension that settled along his shoulders. He'd not seen Raine since the fourth of July, and they'd not parted on good terms. They'd both said some things…hurtful things, but he'd made everything worse by taking off for what had only meant to be a few weeks to clear his head. The few weeks had turned into months and those months had bled into nearly a year and a half.

Jake blew out a hot breath and reached for the door when it was suddenly wrenched open and a bundle of gold streaked past his feet and barked madly as it did so. It was a ball of fur that ran crazily down the steps, with a chubby baby frame barely able to manage them. He stepped back and then the puppy was forgotten as he stared down into the face that had haunted him his entire life it seemed.

Huge round eyes the color of Crystal Lake on a stormy day, widened, while the small bow mouth fell open in shock. Her skin was pale, the kiss of summer long faded and the angles were sharper, more defined. She looked fragile. And beautiful. And delicate. And…

"You cut your hair," was all he managed to say—barely.

Her fingers twisted in the uneven, ebony ends that fell a few inches past her jaw but didn't quite touch her shoulders. It was a reflex action and damn, if it didn't tug on the cold strings still attached to his heart. She pulled on a long, curling piece, tucked it behind her ear and her hand settled against her chest, tightened into a fist.

She wore a pink T-shirt, *Salem's Lot* etched across her breasts in bold, black font. The old, worn jeans that hugged her hips looked dog eared and done for, the ends rolled up past delicate ankles, leaving her feet bare, her toenails painted in chipped, blue polish.

For a moment there was nothing but silence and then she moistened her lips, and exhaled slowly. "Your hair is longer than it's ever been."

The sound of her voice was like a returning memory, one that filled the emptiness inside and stretched thin over his heart.

He nodded, not quite knowing what to say. He'd officially left the military six months ago and hair had been the last thing on his mind. The closely cropped style he'd sported his entire adult life was no more. Now it curled past his ears, the dark brown locks looking more like his buddy Cain's, than what Jake was used to.

"It's been…a long time." Her words were halting, as if she wasn't sure she wanted to speak.

He held her gaze for a moment and then glanced away. The old wicker chair still rocked gently in the breeze and the golden bundle of fur that had shot out of Raine's house was sniffing the ground near his jeep.

"Yeah," was all he managed and even that was hard.

"Nice that you made time for your father." A touch of frost was in her voice now and he glanced back sharply.

Awkward silence fell between the two of them as he stared down into eyes that were hard. Had he expected anything less?

"He's been sick for a while now." Her chin jutted out. "You know that right?" Accusation rang in her words.

A spark of anger lit inside him. So this was how it was going to be. "Yeah, Raine. I know."

Her mouth thinned and a flush crept into her pale cheeks. "Well why the hell did you wait so long to come home to us?"

"I couldn't get away," he said flatly.

She arched a brow and shivered. "Couldn't? Or wouldn't."

He took a step closer and reiterated. *"Couldn't."*

He knew part of it was bullshit. If he'd really wanted to come home earlier he could have. The guys would have understood. But he'd never admit that it was only his father's health taking a wrong turn that had finally brought him back. Because that would mean admitting the reason he'd stayed away for so long was right in front of him.

All five feet four inches of her.

Her toe tapped against the shiny, wooden planks at her feet and her eyes narrowed into a glare that told him everything. Raine Edwards was pissed.

She cleared her throat and raised her chin.

She was more than pissed.

Jake squared his shoulders. This was good. He'd rather her mad as hell then weepy and soft. Mad he could handle. Soft and needy, not so much. Not from her anyway.

"You going to invite me in or are we going to have it out, here on the porch?" Jake arched a brow and waited. Nothing was ever "easy" and "gentle" between himself and Raine. There had always been that friction.

She and his brother Jesse had been like yin and yang, while Jake and Raine were like oil and water.

From the time they were kids—how many nights had Jesse given up and gone to bed long after the two of them argued over the most minute detail, of whatever the hell it was they happened to be discussing? From Scrabble to politics to music and everything in between.

Raine's mouth thinned and she stepped past him, clapped her hands, and yelled "Gibson" as she did so. The puppy's head shot up, its round body quivering as it answered her call. The dog ran toward the house, chasing a leaf as it did so, weaving an intricate path until it climbed the stairs and barked at her feet.

She scooped the puppy into her arms and laughed as it struggled to lick her face. Something inside him thawed in that moment. Something that he'd encased in a wall of ice. It was painful and the dread in his gut doubled. He'd known this was a bad idea, but it was a bad idea he needed to see through. He owed it to Jesse even if he was a year and a half late.

And he owed it to Raine after the way he'd left things.

She stepped back and arched a brow. "You planning on spending the night?"

"Excuse me?" Jake answered carefully, not understanding her angle.

Raine licked her lips, the heightened color in her cheeks a healthy pink in an otherwise pale face. She pointed toward his bag. "Did you pack extra boxers and your toothbrush?"

"No." Jake shook his head. "This is just..."

She turned before he could finish and indicated that he follow her inside as she strolled down the hall, the puppy still in her arms, hips swaying gently. He couldn't help himself. His eyes roved her figure hungrily, taking in every inch from the top of her head to the bottom of her bare feet. His mouth tightened, a frown settling across his brow because he sure as hell didn't like what he saw. She was too thin. Too pale.

Too much like the ghosts he saw wandering the base in Fort Hood. War widows and widowers, distraught families, and friends. All of them had that look. Christ he saw it every day he looked in the mirror, but Raine... damn, he wanted more for her.

Then maybe I should have done something about it. He winced at the thought, mostly because it was the truth.

The house was brightly lit, the sun that shone in through the windows creating warmth against the rich, oak floors. For a second Jake faltered as the heaviness of the moment slipped over him. So many memories he'd tried to forget. He'd helped his brother restore the entire main floor the last time they'd been home on leave nearly two years ago. It was the last time all three of them had been together.

A male voice interrupted his train of thought and for a moment the hot flush of something fierce washed through him. He jerked his head, hackles up and stared at her in silence, hands fisted tightly at his sides.

Raine paused in the doorway that led to the living room/dining area and glanced over her shoulder—eyes still questioning, mouth still tight.

"Look what I found on the porch," she announced and walked into the living room. Jake took a moment and then followed suit, halting just inside the room.

"Son of a bitch!" Mackenzie Draper, one of his oldest buddies, set his beer onto the low slung table in front of the sofa and rose, a smile splitting his face wide open. "You didn't say anything about coming home for the holidays."

Jake grinned. "It wasn't in the plans last time I saw you."

"Wait a minute," Raine interrupted. "When did you see Jake?" Her gaze focused on Mac, who shifted uncomfortably.

"I had business in Texas a few months back and we got together for a drink."

"Texas," Raine muttered. "Right."

She turned stormy eyes his way and Jake flinched at the hurt and accusation that colored them a darker hue. He felt even more like a shit.

"Nice that you have time for *some* of your friends, Jake."

"It wasn't," Mackenzie began, "planned really. I had a couple of extra days and we got together."

Raine set the puppy down. "That's a hell of a lot more than I ever got." She didn't bother to hide the bitterness in her words.

Jake ignored the taunt and remained silent, his eyes locked onto Mackenzie's. His friend was dressed in an expensive suit, tailored to fit his tall frame, the charcoal gray a nice choice against the plum shirt. Though his collar was loose and a thin black tie lay on the table in front of him, Mac always looked *GQ* ready. With his thick, dirty blond hair and vibrant green eyes, he'd been labeled a pretty boy his entire life.

It was good to see him. "You home for the holidays too?" Jake asked.

Mackenzie shook his head. "Nah, I don't think Ben would appreciate it if I crashed his long weekend. I had business in Detroit and thought I'd squeeze in a visit with my mother."

He glanced at his watch. "I gotta hit the road." He arched a brow. "It's a good ten hours until I hit New York."

Mackenzie paused a few inches from Jake, his eyes intense as he studied Jake in silence. "You look like shit, soldier."

"I'm not a soldier anymore."

"No, I suppose you're not." The two men stared at each other for several moments and then Mackenzie lowered his voice. "I miss him too."

The band of pain that sat around Jake's chest

tightened and he nodded, a lump in his throat. "Yeah," he muttered.

They shook hands, but when Jake would have pulled away Mackenzie held on for a quick hug. "Don't be such a douche bag and stay in touch." Mackenzie stepped back and cocked his head to the side. "Give your Dad my best. He's a tough son of a bitch, so I wouldn't worry too much."

Jake nodded. "Will do."

"It's good you're back."

Jake nodded but remained silent.

Mackenzie smiled a million watts at Raine, green eyes crinkled with warmth. "Take care gorgeous and I'll think about Christmas."

The door closed behind Mackenzie, leaving silence in his wake and the oppressive weight of two, ice-blue eyes, shooting daggers at Jake. Now that Mac was gone she didn't make any effort to hide her anger.

Jake turned to her, set his leather bag onto the coffee table, and waited for the hammer to fall.

"I should kick your ass all over Crystal Lake, you know that right?"

Raine didn't know if she wanted to strangle the man in front of her, slap him across the face, order him out of her house or hug him. And by the looks of it, Jake Edwards needed more than just a hug. Judging from the bleak, haunted look in his eyes he hadn't fared well over the last year and a half. But then again, had any of them?

She tore her gaze from his, her heart pounding, her cheeks heated. God, she was so angry with him.

He stood in front of her, hurting so badly it fell off him in waves and yet all she could think about was the fact that he'd been in touch with every single person they shared a bond with, except her.

She'd received exactly six emails from him since he'd left Crystal Lake over a year ago. *Six*. And one drunken message on her voice mail, which, she'd never erased, and sadly, would listen to from time to time when she was feeling more down in the dumps than she usually did. How sad was that?

Raine exhaled sharply, gave herself a mental shake and took a step back, eyes critical as she took him in once more. He was dressed in faded jeans and black leather, a deep blue turtleneck offering some bit of warmth against the late November chill. His hair, so much longer than when she'd seen him last, was wavy, the thick espresso curls now touching his collar. The coffee colored eyes that stared back at her glittered with a hardness in their depths she didn't like. His strong jaw, slightly crooked nose—broke when they he'd been twelve and his brother had dared him to jump off the bridge near the dam—and full wide mouth hadn't changed.

He was still as handsome as ever and she supposed some women would find the hard edge he'd picked up even more attractive. He looked dangerous, very much a bad boy—as if Jake Edwards needed any more weapons in his arsenal. Women had always flocked to his side like bees to honey. Heck, he'd been as much a horn-dog as Cain Black back in the day.

He's so different from Jesse.

They were fraternal twins, so while physically they looked different—her husband had been lighter in coloring, with blue eyes instead of brown and dark blond hair—there'd still been enough of a resemblance between them to know they were brothers. The Edwards twins. The bad boys.

She closed her eyes as a familiar wave of pain rolled through her. It stuck in her chest, tightening like iron claws and she took a step back, hating the sensation more than ever.

She much preferred the numb cocoon she usually existed in. It was just easier to deal when everything was coated in ice and frozen over, smooth as the lake in mid-December.

"Why are you here, Jake?"

Acknowledgments

This book has a special place in my heart, and I never would have written it without a lot of hands in the pot, some stirring, some tasting, and some just inspiring. I need to thank a few of you individually. First off, much thanks to Jon Bon Jovi and Nikki Sixx for inspiring me with your music, your attitude, and—let's be honest—your looks. My hero, Cain Black is very much a blend of the both of you, and I love him to pieces.

Leah Hultenschmidt, you took a chance on a book with a hero who is a rocker. I had a lot of people tell me musicians were a hard sell; thanks for helping me prove them wrong. Elyssa Papa and Tracy Stefureak, thanks for reading my words; your insights and thoughts were much appreciated.

My writer buddies—The Sirens and Scribes, Elisabeth Naughton, Amanda Vyne, TRW—you guys all rock. A heartfelt thanks also to my girlfriends, and Shelli, well, you're sorta famous now, eh? The Mudslides, my family, my kids, and I can't forget my lovely Shelby and Gibson.

To all my readers, thanks so much for loving my books and taking the time out of your day to let me know. I hope you all enjoy Crystal Lake and my bad boys.

The Christmas He Loved Her

by Juliana Stone

His best gift this Christmas is her.

In the small town of Crystal Lake, Christmas is a time for sledding, hot chocolate, and cozying up to the fire. For Jake Edwards, it shouldn't be a time to give in to the feelings he's always had for Raine—especially since she's his brother's widow.

No one annoys Raine quite like her brother-in-law does. But when Jake brings home a tall blond thing from the city who's bad news, Raine needs to stop him from making the biggest mistake of his life. Does Raine want this woman to leave Crystal Lake because she's all wrong for Jake? Or is it because she wants him for herself…?

Praise for The Summer He Came Home:

"Everything I love in a book: a hot and tender romance and a bad-boy hero to die for!"—Molly O'Keefe, author of *Can't Buy Me Love*

For more Juliana Stone, visit:

www.sourcebooks.com

The Day He Kissed Her

by Juliana Stone

Coming home is the only way to heal his heart.

Mackenzie Draper thought he had everything he ever wanted when hired by a hotshot Manhattan architectural firm. But he still needed one last visit back home to Crystal Lake to face the demons of his past. For Lily St. Clare, the charming small town she just moved to was a haven. Big cities only wanted to eat you up and spit you out.

Neither was expecting to stay very long…until the day they found each other, and one amazingly red-hot night followed. But old wounds almost always leave a mark, and Mac's scars run deeper than most. With her flirty charm, Lily could be exactly what he needs—if he's willing give love one more chance.

A Shot of Sultry

by Macy Beckett

Welcome to Sultry Springs, Texas: where home can be the perfect place for a fresh start.

For West Coast filmmaker Bobbi Gallagher, going back to Sultry Springs is a last resort. But with her career in tatters, a documentary set in her hometown might be just what she needs to salvage her reputation. She just can't let anything distract her again. Not even the gorgeous contractor her brother asked to watch over her. As if she can't handle filming a few rowdy Texans.

Golden boy Trey Lewis, with his blond hair and Technicolor-blue eyes, is a leading man if Bobbi ever saw one. He's strong and confident and—much to her delight—usually shirtless. He thinks keeping his best friend's baby sister out of trouble will be easy. But he has no idea of the trouble in store for *him*…

"A heartwarming, humorous story of second chances…sweet at its core. A strong continuation of this promising series."—*Publishers Weekly*

"Brimming with rapier wit and heartwarming moments… Packed with humor and heart."—*Fresh Fiction*

For more Macy Beckett, visit:

www.sourcebooks.com

Juliana Stone's love of the written word and '80s rock have inspired her in more ways than one. She writes dark paranormal romance as well as contemporary romance and spends her days navigating a busy life that includes a husband, kids, and rock 'n' roll! You can find more info at www.julianastone.com.